PRAISE FOR THE SUMERIANS TRILOGY

T0182499

GILGAMESH

Also by Emily H. Wilson
and available from Titan Books

Inanna

GILGAMESH

A Novel

EMILY H. WILSON

TITAN BOOKS

Gilgamesh
Print edition ISBN: 9781803364421
E-book edition ISBN: 9781803364438

Published by Titan Books
A division of Titan Publishing Group Ltd
144 Southwark Street, London SE1 0UP
www.titanbooks.com

First edition: August 2024
10 9 8 7 6 5 4 3 2 1

A CIP catalogue record for this title is available from
the British Library.

Printed and bound by CPI (UK) Ltd, Croydon, CR0 4YY.

For Chloë

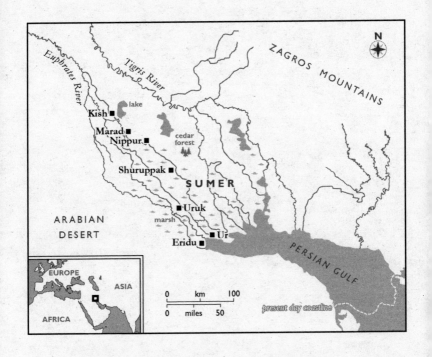

Ancient Sumer in 4000 BC

DRAMATIS PERSONAE

THE ANUNNAKI, HIGH GODS OF SUMER

An | king of the gods
Nammu | queen of the gods
Enki | lord of wisdom and water, son of An
Enlil | lord of the sky, son of An
Ninlil | child bride of Enlil
Ninhursag | former wife of Enki
Nanna | father of Inanna, god of the moon
Ningal | mother of Inanna, goddess of the moon
Ereshkigal | queen of the night, Inanna's sister
Utu | god of the sun, Inanna's brother
Lugalbanda | Gilgamesh's father, and *sukkal* (chief minister) to An
Ninsun | Gilgamesh's mother, the Wild Cow of Heaven
Inanna | goddess of love and war

THE HALF GODS
(Immortal children of the Anunnaki and humans)

Dumuzi | god of sheep, son of Enki, estranged husband of Inanna
Geshtinanna | daughter of Enki, lover (and sister) of Dumuzi
Isimud | Enki's *sukkal*

The Humans

Gilgamesh | mortal son of Lugalbanda and Ninsun

Harga | servant of Gilgamesh and Enlil

Akka | king of Kish

Inush | Akka's nephew

Hedda | Akka's sister

Biluda | royal steward at Kish

Enkidu | the wild man

Amnut | Inanna's childhood friend

Della | mortal daughter of Enlil, wife of Gilgamesh

Shara | son of Gilgamesh and Della

Lilith | priestess in Uruk

Khufu | Egyptian trader

Dulma | priestess at the Temple of the Waves

Lamma | chief priest at Susa

Marduk | boy from the far north

Demons and Other Creatures

Ninshubar | a new god, *sukkal* to Inanna

Erra | the dark stranger

Galatur | the black fly

Kurgurrah | the blue fly

Namtar | priest-demon of Ereshkigal

The *gallas* | demon warriors of the underworld

Neti | gatekeeper of the underworld

Tiamat | lady of Creation

Qingu | a prince of Creation

PROLOGUE

MARDUK

In Kish, capital city of Akkadia

I was mopping up after an elderly dog when the news swept through the court.

The great Sumerian hero, Gilgamesh, had been captured in battle.

Taken prisoner by King Akka himself, on the banks of the River Tigris, and brought to Kish with his hands and feet bound, slung over the back of a mule.

The Lion of Uruk was here, a prisoner in this very palace!

For some long minutes, I leaned on my mopstick, ears straining for every detail of the hero's capture. Only when I felt royal eyes falling on me did I return, most reluctantly, to my mopping.

The dog had done its sloppy business on a mosaic of some ancient goddess. In truth, I was doing more to spread the muck over this holy scene than to in any way clean it. But I had no ambition to be good at mopping.

Two blue slippers appeared in the path of my mopstick. The king's sister, Hedda, stood with her hands on her hips. She was a small creature, lightly made, and handsome in her blue velvet.

"I have a job for you, slave-boy," she said. "Go find out what you can about the prisoner Gilgamesh. And then come straight back and tell us everything."

I began to mop with some vigour around her feet. It was my firm policy never to do anything for anyone unless either threatened or bribed. "I must clean up after your dog," I said.

Hedda stepped back to protect her slippers. "At least find out if he is going to live." She gave me her most playful smile. "Marduk, I will pay you in figs."

"Oh, very well," I said.

Mopstick in one hand, sloshing bucket in the other, I made my way, circuitously, to the palace kitchens. It was my intention to slip through the bakery and out into the palace gardens, where I was sure to run into friends.

But as I stepped into the gloom of the bread-proving room, Biluda, the king's ancient steward, loomed up before me in his kingfisher-blue robes.

"Where in all of Akkadia have you been, Marduk? I have sent out three messages for you."

I held out my filthy mopstick and quarter-filled bucket. "I was clearing up dog mess in the ladies' quarters, sir. As you ordered me to."

Biluda dismissed my story with a wave of one crooked hand. "You have heard the news, I presume?"

"I have been working."

"Of that I am fairly doubtful. However. We have a Sumerian prince here as our prisoner and I would like you to take him some necessaries."

I set down my bucket. "I did hear he was dying."

"Not presently," he said. "Although he is somewhat dented."

Biluda pointed one long, bony finger at a glass and a large clay jug. "You will take these to the captive."

I leaned on my mopstick. "Why?"

"Marduk, you are a slave, not a prince of this household. I have told you to take these two things to the captive, so take these two things to the captive."

"You are a slave, I am a slave. Why not go yourself?"

Biluda smoothed down his long, grey beard, and lowered his voice. "He likes pretty boys, that is what they say. Perhaps he will say something interesting to you if you take him his water."

"And what sort of interesting thing might he say?"

Biluda clawed out his fingers, as if about to strangle me. "Men forget themselves when someone takes their fancy. You would not know that, being so high-minded."

"All right, I will take the water," I said. "I would like to see this great hero of Sumer."

I put my head around the door. The Lion of Uruk was lying on his back in a narrow bed, with a sheet pulled up over his hips.

Black hair and a close-cut beard; tortoiseshell eyes. I had not expected him to be so young. He could not have been more than two or three years older than me; twenty perhaps.

His chest was the colour of dark honey; his arms and face a rich, mahogany brown. His throat looked badly bruised and he had a belly wound that ought to have been bandaged.

All the same he looked very powerful and gleaming, against the linen bedding. A lion of a man, indeed.

"My lord, may I check on you?"

"Certainly." A deep voice; a searing smile. Such very bright eyes.

I made my way into the room, the glass and jug held out before me. It occurred to me then, for the first time, that the Lion of Uruk might be dangerous.

Of course I did not have a weapon, but I could cut his throat with the glass, if I could find a way to smash it first. Or I could hit him with the jug.

"Do you know how I got here?" Gilgamesh said. Again, the dazzling smile.

I paused, glass and jug held out before me. "You passed out entirely, my lord. They had to carry you from your mule."

I could see, from the way he was holding himself, that he was thinking about getting out of bed. I took two steps backwards. "They thought you would be thirsty, my lord, after having slept so long, and I am to bring you a robe after this, and to tell you that as soon as you are recovered, the king hopes to see you at dinner."

All the tension seemed to drain out of him.

"What does that mean, at dinner?"

"The king eats with all the court in the evenings, and you will join him there, sir."

"Does he eat well, King Akka?"

"Yes, my lord. They eat a lot. There is always meat."

"You can put the jug down," he said. "I will not hurt you."

"Very good, my lord." I put the glass and jug down next to him, and poured him some water, careful to keep one eye on him.

"Where am I?" he said, reaching with a grimace for the glass.

"Kish, my lord." I glanced back at the door, knowing that Biluda would have his ear pressed to it. "You are in the palace of King Akka, first amongst the Akkadians, and sworn enemy of your people."

"And do you know where my man is? Harga?"

"He has ridden south, sir, with the news of your capture and the details of the ransom they are asking for you. They told your man to take the tablet to your father."

"Ah, but of course," he said. "My father."

When I had safely delivered the water to the hero Gilgamesh, I went back out into the corridor. Biluda sprang up from the bench there, one finger to his lips.

"What did he say?" he whispered.

"He was interested in dinner. I told him what to expect. I think he's hungry."

"Keep your voice down! And what else?"

I leaned in close to whisper. "He asked after his man Harga."

"That's all?"

"Perhaps he finds me less pretty than you do."

Biluda, looking hugely irritated, handed me a linen robe. "Go back in and give him this. And this time ask him about the war, that kind of thing."

"I think that would be very odd. He will guess I have been told to do it."

"And yet you are a slave, and just this once you will do as you are asked, Marduk."

"I will take him the robe. But I'm not going to ask about the war."

Gilgamesh was lying with his eyes shut, as if asleep, as I opened the door. That line in the old temple poem came to me: *the sleeping and the dead, how alike they are.*

I was about to back out, but he said: "No, come, come." He turned his head to smile at me. "I am only resting." He had one hand on his belly.

I put the linen robe down at the foot of his bed. "For you to wear at dinner."

"What are you?" he said, lifting his chin at me. "A prince? A spy?"

"A slave."

"Ah! How do they treat their slaves, in Kish?"

"Better than the slave trader who brought me here."

"There are no good slave traders," Gilgamesh said. "That's what my father says. It brutalises your spirit, to buy and sell men like animals."

"I've been told your father is a god. Perhaps he could stop men from selling each other."

Another flash of the hero's smile. "The gods are not as powerful as people think. But you are quite right, they should do more." He patted the bed next to him. "Come, sit down a moment. Where are you from? I've never seen anyone so pale before, or with such red hair."

After a moment's hesitation, I sat down at the very end of the hero's bed, careful not to sit on his feet. "Do you know it is rude to ask a slave where he is from?"

Gilgamesh laughed, and then grimaced again, breathing in slowly, one hand stretched out over his belly wound. "I think I have been told that and forgotten it."

"I remember snow along a shoreline. And perhaps my mother's face. But I was taken from my family very young." I lifted my hands and let them fall again. "I've been told there are people who look like me in the far north."

"And who took you from your family?"

"I don't remember. I have travelled all over the world since then, passed from this person to that. Most recently I was in Egypt." I pulled up my left sleeve and showed him the tattoo of the lion-headed eagle on my shoulder. "This is the sign of the god they worship in Abydos. Have you heard of Abydos?"

"Only that it's a holy place."

"It's an evil place."

He lifted his eyebrows at that. "You talk a lot, for a slave."

"I am not a good slave. I have disappointed all my owners." I paused a moment. Well, what harm would it do to speak it? "My plan is to escape," I said.

"And head north?"

"No, I must find my adopted mother. The woman who raised me. I last saw her somewhere south of Egypt."

Gilgamesh moved as if to sit up, but lay flat again, frowning. "I would like to eat at the king's table tonight, but I am not sure I can dress myself with my shoulder as it is. Will you help me with that robe there?"

"Dress yourself," I said, and threw the linen robe over to him.

"You are a terrible slave!" he said.

"It is not my intention to become a good one."

"Hah! Tell me your name, terrible slave boy."

"Marduk. That's what they called me in Egypt."

"A strange name."

"It means 'calf of the evening sun', something like that."

"Because of your red hair?"

"You are a thinker then, not only a soldier."

He laughed. "Do you remember your real name?"

"My adopted mother called me the Potta. That is how I think of myself."

We smiled at each other.

For just those few heartbeats we were only two men on a bed together, rather close, and with him naked under his sheet.

I stood to go, but at the door, I turned to look back at the Lion of Uruk. I had a foolish rush of sympathy for him, for how battered he was, for how low he had been brought. Also, sadness, because our paths, having crossed this once, were so unlikely to ever cross again.

"Good hunting to you, Gilgamesh," I said. "Hero turned captive, who was once the Lion of Uruk."

"I hope to see you again," he said.

I was already half out of the door.

"Good hunting to you too, Marduk," Gilgamesh called after me. "Marduk the terrible slave boy, who was once called the Potta!"

PART I

"Fate is a dog,
Well able to bite."

Ancient Sumerian proverb

CHAPTER ONE

GILGAMESH

In the wilds of northern Sumer
(One full year after his meeting with
Marduk in Akkadia)

We rode north through ice-clad forest, our hoods pulled low against the driving hail.

My man Harga rode out in front, his cloak crusted over white. I followed close behind him, breathing in the frost, the scent of juniper, and the stable smell of my father's fine Asian horses. Harga and I each rode one of these velvet-skinned creatures, shipped in at who knows what cost, and I worried they were not at all suited to such vile and freezing conditions.

Behind us, in one long, straggling line, came fifty soldiers on local-bred mules. The men, and the mules too, all looked very sorry indeed to be out in such bone-clawing weather.

Harga dropped back to ride alongside me. He lifted his black curls to the battering hail, and the dark trees crowding in on us, and leaned in close to speak.

"I do not like it," he said.

"Oh, Harga, you never like it."

"But this I like less than normal. First the earthquakes, then last night the red moon, and now solid hail in early autumn." He leaned in closer. "My lord, these are omens of chaos."

"These things aren't omens, Harga. I have known earthquakes before, and red moons too, and I have known a great deal of bad weather. Why must everything foreshadow something?"

"You are very grand and modern now, my lord Gilgamesh. Yet I saw you only yesterday making the secret signs against bad luck when the red moon rose. The same secret signs the men make."

"That is an outrageous lie, Harga. A total nonsense!"

But he had already squeezed his horse on, and I do not think he heard me.

I huddled down in my cloak and stewed for a while over Harga's rudeness to me, and the unfairness of it.

Harga was a man of dubious birth. A foreigner and a runaway. He was neither a serving officer nor an official servant of my household. He had spied on me time and time again.

Also, I had very recently saved his life: that should not be forgotten. When Harga told stories, they were always of him rescuing me. Of Harga the all-competent hero, and Gilgamesh the drunken fool. But who broke into a prison cell at Uruk to save Harga's useless life? Me!

Harga was an annoying old man. He was probably thirty at least, or older even.

Well, he would be dead soon, but not soon enough.

I tucked my reins under one armpit, so that I could rub some life into my frozen hands. I realised the hail had stopped; the sky seemed for a moment brighter.

Ahead, Harga lifted one closed fist; the signal for a meal stop.

As the men climbed stiffly down from their mounts, I caught

movement above us: a lone vulture circling. A moment later, there was another, and then another, their black feathers stretched out against the cold grey.

"Vultures," I said. "Six of them. Oh no, eight."

"Twenty at least," Harga said, his face tipped to the sky. "No, many more." All the men saw them then and tipped their heads back also to watch the birds wheeling as one above us.

"I'm not sure I've ever seen so many," I said. "Not all at once, at least."

Harga raised one eyebrow at me. "I think you were speaking of omens, my lord. Of how they are only a nonsense."

"I'm sure this is something quite normal and natural," I said, a little louder so that all the men could hear. "A normal gathering of vultures. Just one we've never seen before. Indeed we should think ourselves lucky to see such a display."

A few more moments, and the birds had circled so high that they completely disappeared into the grey.

Harga heaved himself off his horse and down onto the rocky path. "Cold rations only, boys."

When the last of the bread and cheese had been passed out between the damp company, I sat down next to Harga on the wet moss beneath an oak. I set aside my annoyance with him since we were breaking bread together. "I am looking forward to a fire now," I said. "A good fire and a glass of wine. And some dry clothes."

"We won't make the palace before dark," he said. Perhaps his bones were aching, him being so old, so I ignored his disagreeable tone.

"It's better we finish the journey in darkness," I said, "than spend another night camped out in this."

The men who were close enough to hear us, all nodded at that.

Harga shook his curls at me. "Gilgamesh, this is not the weather for night riding."

Even by Harga's standards, this was unusually rude; for him to contradict me so flatly in front of the men. He had been out of sorts for days.

I leaned in close to him, my voice low. "Harga, if you would address me as 'my lord' when we are out on manoeuvres, I think that would be rather more ordinary. And perhaps you might consider my suggestions, before summarily dismissing them."

"A thousand apologies, my lord," he said, not sounding very sorry at all.

"Well, thank you."

Harga chewed on his bread, one thoughtful eyebrow raised. "Are you also looking forward to seeing your wife, my lord?'

After a very short pause, I said: "As it happens, I am very much looking forward to seeing Della." After another pause, I added: "And also my son Shara."

"Well remembered, my lord," said Harga, with a rather vicious grin.

As we climbed, cold, wet, and weary, back onto our animals, it began to hail again. Sharp needles, this time. I rode on rather glum, my head low and my hands freezing, and my wife now very vivid in my thoughts.

Della.

That first glimpse of her right cheek, and her bare right shoulder, and her long hair tumbling so soft and black down her back. I knew at once that everything I had heard about her was true: here was the most beautiful woman in Sumer.

Just her supple, shining skin, so good you wanted to sink your teeth into it. The extraordinary curve of that bare shoulder.

I resolved at once to have nothing to do with her.

Della was a mortal child of the gods, just as I was. More to the point, she was a daughter of Enlil, lord of the sky gods, and my protector and master. I knew that Enlil would torture me just for looking at her. Of course I would have nothing to do with her.

That was Gilgamesh sober.

Gilgamesh drunk had other ideas.

If only I could go back to that ill-fated night and do things differently. But it was far too late for regrets of that kind. I had been obliged to marry Della, and Della had been obliged to give birth to my son and heir. Now I must collect her, as promised, and take her home with me to the great city of Uruk, to be crowned my rightful queen.

Now was the time for sober Gilgamesh. For Gilgamesh the family man. For Gilgamesh the king.

Ahead, Harga rolled his shoulders, and half-turned his head to me.

"This is not the first time I have seen you reform yourself," he said.

The man had such a devious way of working out my secret thoughts.

"I do not know what you mean by that."

He brought his shivering horse back alongside mine. "Remember the summer in Sippur, when you went to temple every day, determined to become some great priest?"

"I might have done it, had I not been called away to war."

"You lay with every priestess. You made terrible sport of them. There was nothing holy about it."

I sat up straighter in my saddle. "There is no need to drag up the ancient past, Harga. I was only a boy."

"Gilgamesh, it was two years ago."

I was about to reply when he froze in his saddle.

A moment later, he raised one hand to the hail, all five fingers spread wide.

At once we all dismounted, in absolute silence, and led our horses and mules into the trees to the left of the path.

Harga and I stood apart from the men, in private council.

"I am sure I heard raised voices," he said. "Just for a moment."

"Pilgrims, maybe."

"Maybe."

"But it doesn't feel right."

"No."

I glanced around at the dark forest, and the frozen sky.

"Surely it cannot be Akkadians," I said. "Not so far south of the border. They have never been so bold. It would signal outright war."

"It cannot be Akkadians. And yet the hairs on my arms are standing on end."

"All right," I said. "We split into two groups. Half stay here, hidden, to be sure of the animals and supplies. The other half of us creep forward on foot. Let us put eyes upon these supposed pilgrims before they put eyes on us."

Harga squinted up into the hail. "At least no one can hear us coming in this."

"Let us hope so indeed," I said. "I'll lead."

I picked my way through the trees to the left of the path, over mossy tussocks and twisted roots, breathing in wet loam and pine resin.

For a moment I thought I could hear voices ahead, but it was hard to tell with the ice beating down upon the rocks and branches. Then it could not be doubted: people shouting, somewhere close by.

I gripped the moss-clad trunk of a juniper and pulled myself up half a cord.

There they were.

It was a melee of some sort on the narrow path through the forest. Shouting and pushing. Men in dark tunics and bright copper armour, hail bouncing from their helmets. The flash of swords raised.

Twenty men perhaps, and they had someone surrounded.

A woman's voice. Bright orange flames; a pulsing light.

The men in armour hurled themselves away from the flames, knocking into trees, one of them falling on his back.

The distinctive orange fire: it could only be my mother, the goddess Ninsun.

Yes, there she was at the centre of the melee, with her bronze helmet pulled down low over her short black hair, and her orange godlight spilling out from the dark bracelets on her wrists. Behind her, a dark-haired woman.

I dropped down from the tree and put my mouth to Harga's ear. "My blessed mother. Surrounded by Akkadian soldiers. Maybe Della and the baby too."

"How many Akkadians?"

"Enough. Twenty maybe. You all spread out along this side of the path. When you hear me make the signal, I will charge them. You pick them off while they are all looking at me. Make your shots good."

"What's the signal?"

"The signal I always give."

"Yes?"

"Harga, how can you not know my signal?"

"You mean that owl noise?"

"It carries well."

"If you say so." He arched one eyebrow as he counted out three stones from his pebble pouch. "Let's do it then."

While the men crept into position, I climbed the tree again, shimmying higher this time for a better view.

My mother stood there amidst the enemy like some hero from the fables: black-browed and straight-spined, ablaze with holy orange flames. My wife was indeed with her. Della's hair hung long and wet around her face, and she held a velvet-wrapped bundle to her chest.

How glorious my mother looked, and yet the soldiers of Akkadia did not seem overly awed by the searing godlight that spilt from her bracelets. They stood well back from the flames, but they looked careful, not frightened.

A soldier in a pointed copper cap called out: "We will not harm you, goddess. We just want you to come with us."

I wished I had a bow with me, to put an arrow into his smirking face.

Ah well, my axes would have to do.

I dropped back down to the forest floor and drew out my bronze axes from the leather straps I wore over my cloak.

I swung them in two careful circles, to be sure I had the feel of them.

The moment before you commit is always the hardest. Best to get it over with then.

I made my owl noise.

Then I ran hard out of the woods, my right axe raised.

I charged straight at the soldier in the pointed cap. He had his head turned away from me; he was looking at my mother. I sank my right axe hard into the back of his neck, in the gap between his copper cap and his leather jerkin. That satisfying wet crunch, as the axe bit deep and true into his spine.

The trick is to get the axe out again before they fall, and that I managed to do, my weight hard on my right foot. I swung around with my left axe raised and sank it deep into the shocked face of a young man who had turned round to look at me.

By then all faces were turned to me. No one was looking at the woods behind.

The second man went down so fast, with my axe in his destroyed face, that I ended up on my knees over him. I had the horrible thought, as I struggled to wrench the axe out, that Harga and the men had not heard my owl noise.

One breath later the air was alive with arrows and Harga's deadly stones, and our men were piling out of the forest and into the glare of my mother's godlight. They hacked and stabbed at the Akkadians in a very lively manner. My mother hauled herself backwards out of the melee, with Della held close to her.

A man was coming at me, sword raised. I leaped up with my right axe lifted; he moved to protect his sword arm. Then I sank my left axe into his right hip. The man went down heavy and I leaped aside to avoid his body.

Both my axes were slick with blood, but they still felt good in my hands.

A young boy was lying on his back just behind me. He had an arrow in his throat, but he still had his knives out. I put my right axe down hard in his neck.

An older man with a spear ran at me from my right. Always

tricky, the reach of a long spear, when you are relying on your axes. But I have always been comfortable throwing them.

I cast my right axe hard at him and he went down with it set into his left eye, the blood spraying out in a wheeling arc around him.

Only moments later, it was all over.

The men of Akkadia were all dead or down. Our men were cutting the necks of the last of them. There was only the noise of the ice falling on the forest, and our heaving breaths.

My mother let her godlight fade, and the men parted to let me get to her.

She looked exhausted, her hands heavy by her sides.

"Are you not mounted?" she said to me.

"We have horses and mules here." I was still getting my breath back. I wiped blood from my eyes; not mine, I hoped.

Harga came to join us, tucking his slingshot into his belt.

"We should get off the path," he said to me, as if I was loitering there, and had not just one second before been hacking men to death upon that exact spot.

"Yes we should get off the path," my mother said, in the same censorious tone. "Hello, Harga," she added. "Are there no horses?"

"I'll take you to them," he said, as if he alone had had the good sense to bring mounts.

My mother turned to follow him, and as she did, I saw that her hands were shaking.

A voice behind me: "No greeting for your wife then?"

I turned to find myself face to face with Della. I caught a glimpse of my son's small red face amidst its velvet wrappings. Della looked frightened and miserable. Her lips were pale with cold.

"Hello, Della," I said. "Are you well? Is the boy well?"

"Of course I am not well, Gilgamesh. Look where we are. Look what is happening. And no, the boy is not well."

"Let me take him," I said.

"You are covered with blood!" She took a step back from me.

I had known she would still be angry with me, for having got her with child, and then having left her for so long. But I had hoped she might have softened just a little.

If anything, she seemed even more furious.

I slid my axes back over my shoulders, slotting them into their leather hoops.

"All right, follow me," I said.

In the glade where we had left the animals, my mother was checking over Harga's ice-covered horse.

"The summer palace has been overrun," she said to me, as she pulled at the animal's girth. "They came in the night and overwhelmed us. They were setting light to the palace as we fled."

"They've never been so far south before."

"Something has changed."

"Do you know where the others are?"

She stopped what she was doing a moment, to look me in the face. "The goddess Ninlil has been snatched. She was gone before the attack happened."

I paused, absorbing.

"I'm sorry," she said. "I know you love her just as I do. Odd as she is."

"She is only a child."

My mother tipped her bronze cap from one side to the other. "You know that's not true."

"I mean she is like a child. She is an innocent. She should not be out in the world on her own."

"I know."

"Enlil will go mad," I said. "He will murder every last Akkadian. He will burn Kish to the ground."

"Or he will die trying," my mother said.

"And the others?"

"I don't know. We were all split up. Now listen, you take Della and the boy to safety. I will go back for the others."

"We'll head home to Uruk," I said. "Nowhere in the north can be safe now."

My mother took off her helmet to adjust the chin strap; her short black hair lay plastered to her skull. For the first time in my life I had a sense of her as a creature that might be vulnerable to harm.

"You saw the red moon?" she said, pulling her helmet back on.

"I have seen red moons before."

"Perhaps, but something bad is happening, Gilgamesh. Something I do not understand yet."

She swung up onto the horse in one easy movement.

"Chaos is coming, Gilgamesh. That is the one thing I am certain of."

She kicked on the horse before I could answer, and was gone into the swirling ice.

CHAPTER TWO

INANNA

On the Euphrates, somewhere
to the south of Uruk

I was standing on the edge of a luminous, blue lake. The shores were crowded with wild animals. All of them were looking at me.

What would happen if I dived into the water?

I woke, gasping, to Ninshubar's steady face, dark against the pale of the sky.

"Another nightmare?" she said.

"No, not exactly."

I sat myself up, holding on tight to Ninshubar with one hand, and to the side of the oak-planked boat with the other.

I breathed in deep on the cool river air.

We were right out in the middle of the Euphrates, our white sails billowing before us. The banks to either side of us were lined by reeds, but here or there they thinned out, offering glimpses of green farmland beyond, and sometimes a reed hut, and a farmer turning to watch us pass.

I realised that Ninshubar and the boat boys were all looking at me. I lifted my chin and smiled very warmly at each of them, to show that I was well and not at all afraid.

"Thank all the stars the hail seems to have passed," I said. "I thought we might sink under all that ice."

"Was the dark stranger in your dream?" said Ninshubar.

"No, no," I said, smiling. "Those dreams are much less frequent now."

There were six of us in the boat, as we sailed south to wage war upon my grandfather.

First there was me, Inanna. The Goddess of Love and War, and the only Anunnaki born on Earth.

I had on my new purple dress and a soft wool cloak, and upon my head I wore a thin band of gold. Experience had taught me that my official temple crown, the famous *shugurra* of the high steppes, was too heavy for an expedition of this sort. Upon my left wrist I wore a narrow band of dark grey metal. It did not look like much, but this narrow band of grey was a weapon of the Anunnaki, brought down by them from Heaven. It was very nasty weapon, and we called it the master *mee*.

Next to me in our small sailing boat sat Ninshubar, my holy *sukkal*, a goddess now in her own right, and sworn to serve me until the ending of the world.

Ninshubar was strikingly tall, with strong, long limbs, very pleasingly proportioned. She wore her hair cropped close to her skull. The whites of her eyes, her teeth, and the eight-pointed ivory star that hung around her neck, all shone bright as the moon against the midnight black of her skin.

She was dressed in an outfit that a city man might wear out hunting: a hip-length leather jerkin, leather trousers, laced-up boots. But over this simple outfit she wore a sheath of copper-mesh armour, and over and under this armour, she had secreted, tucked, tied and hung a shocking number of axes, knives and other weapons. In addition to this large but commonplace arsenal, she also wore, upon her well-muscled arms, eight holy *mees* that had once belonged to my husband.

"You are going to need more hands," I said to her, "if you are to use even a small portion of those weapons."

Ninshubar turned to me with an air of gracious patience. "Inanna, I have never once regretted bringing a weapon with me. More times than you can imagine, I have ended up thinking to myself, *I wish I had my bow.* Never have I thought, *oh why am I carrying this bow?* It is my great promise to myself, for the years I have before me, to always be heavily armed."

"All the same, I am surprised that you will need so many small cutting things, and throwing pebbles even, when you have my husband's holy weapons upon you."

"We will see," she said, very knowing.

She returned to her study of the workings of the boat.

Ninshubar had taken it upon herself to observe, closely, every action of the four young boys tasked with sailing our boat south.

The skiffs that served the White Temple of Uruk were crewed by the very best and the boys were wonderful sailors. Yet they wilted beneath Ninshubar's close observation, much as baby gazelles might wilt beneath the glare of a crouching cheetah.

"I wonder if you are putting them off," I said, as gently as I could. "Perhaps they are making mistakes because they are nervous?"

"I should know how to sail," Ninshubar said, watching intently as a boy tried to tie a knot. "It is good to know how to do things." She turned to address the boys directly: "But you do not need to feel nervous."

The boys all turned wide eyes to her.

"I am only trying to learn from you all," she said to them. "I respect you as master sailors."

The boys all nodded but said nothing.

I leaned over to squeeze Ninshubar's forearm.

"You will soon be a wonderful sailor, Ninshubar."

I lay back down on the damp little bed I had fashioned for myself from a barley sack, and I looked up at the pale blue arch of the sky above me, and the clouds of starlings that danced there. The birds brought back to me the memory of swifts in the sky above Uruk, on the day that I climbed up onto the siege walls with Gilgamesh beside me. I remembered the white of his smile and how strong his hand was, as he helped me up the steps. The warm, cedar-wood smell of him. The thrill that passed through my body when he touched the small of my back.

I shut my eyes, to hide my foolish tears.

What was the point of thinking of him, when he did not think of me in the same way?

Better to think only of my duty. We were sailing south to humble my grandfather Enki, lord of wisdom, and a torturer, a rapist, and a murderer. That is what I had to focus on.

I could not protect the people I loved unless Enki was brought to his knees, and for this brief moment in time, I had an advantage over him. He did not know that my humble looking *mee* was in fact something of great power, if I could only get close enough to use it on him. So, we must go south quickly to take on this great warlord, a man five hundred years older than me, and vastly powerful. I must put aside childish thoughts of Gilgamesh and how he made me feel.

I breathed in deeply and set myself to practising my use of the master *mee*, since our fates now depended on it.

My *mee*, properly used, could allow me to take control of another Anunnaki. I had already used it to overcome my brother, the sun god. The *mee* also allowed me to see, in my mind's eye, a map of where all the high gods were. With practise I could now see not only the Anunnaki, but also their half-god offspring and even their mortal children. With my eyes shut, could I sense Gilgamesh somewhere to the north? He had gone to fetch his wife back to Uruk. I had a flash of him, on foot, on a path. He was looking up at someone on horseback. Had something gone wrong?

I must not think of Gilgamesh.

I dragged my attention around to the south, to the city of my grandfather Enki.

There, a clot of lights: the ancient city was home to many gods.

At the heart of the city, the light that was my grandfather Enki. The king of the water gods, in the Temple of the Aquifer; the man I intended to bring to his knees.

Enki was only a pattern in the blue, but for a moment I could see him so clearly. He was leaning back in a chair, one hand outstretched. Was he stroking one of my lions? He had kept them with him when he sent me north to Uruk.

Yes, he was stroking a lion, and speaking to her.

And now he was looking straight at me.

I withdrew as fast as I could, opening my eyes, pulling myself upright, lurching back into the world of light.

He could not possibly have seen me. Could he?

My heart beat hard and ragged.

"So many hippos," Ninshubar was saying, waving a hand to the west bank. She had not noticed my upset.

Hippos, small and large, were standing half in and half out of the water, all their eyes upon our small vessel as we passed. I breathed in and out, steadying myself.

"It is strange this attraction you hold for wild creatures," Ninshubar said. "I wonder what it is they want from you."

"I cannot say," I said. There were often animals in my dreams, always looking at me, always expectant. But I did not know what they expected from me.

There was then some flapping of a rope, and confusion. A sail blew into my face; a boy scrambled to right things.

When all was shipshape again, Ninshubar turned to me and said: "Let us go over your plan."

"Very well," I said, straightening the gold band on my head. "We will enter the city and ask to see my grandfather. We will claim to come in peace. And then I will overcome him with the master *mee*."

"Which he cannot know you have."

"I don't think he can possibly know about my *mee*. It is probable he knows that I have sent his son down to the underworld. So many people are talking about that. Word is sure to have gone south ahead of us. But I do not think he can yet know about the *mee*."

"And when you succeed in overpowering him, what then?"

"Then we will empty his treasury of all his Anunnaki weapons, and bring them home with us to Uruk. You will have your pick of all these weapons, should they try to stop us leaving."

Ninshubar was nodding, thinking. "And Enki. What of him?"

"I don't know yet," I said.

"If we leave him alive, he will always be a threat."

"I'm not sure I'm a killer," I said.

She nodded, her mouth flat.

"Ninshubar, I know it is not much of a plan," I said.

"No, no," she said. "It is a good plan. It is also the only plan we have."

"But we are throwing ourselves south with nothing but these few *mees* we have, when my grandfather Enki has an army and an arsenal of *mees*. So if I cannot overcome him, or if I cannot even get close enough to try, then we are in trouble."

"It is true that more weapons would be welcome," she said, frowning down at her *mees*.

I lifted my eyebrows at her.

"Weapons of the gods, I mean," she said.

"I will get you more *mees*. You will barely be able to walk, for all the *mees* you will be wearing. Just as I promised you, when you became my *sukkal*."

Ninshubar stretched out her long legs. "You also promised me palaces," she said, with a smile. "And silver. And vast lands."

"All of that will come to you, Ninshubar, whether you want those things or not."

"Inanna, a simple plan is not a bad plan. You will overcome your grandfather with the master *mee* and force him to give us all his weapons. Then we will make our escape. And I will be at your side for all of it."

She leaned over and dropped one warm kiss on the top of my head.

"One step and then the next, Inanna."

CHAPTER THREE

ERESHKIGAL

In the underworld

I was working very hard on my history of the Anunnaki. After I pressed each mark into the clay, I would hold the tablet up to the candlelight, to make sure I had it exactly right.

> *We have many names for the underworld. Sometimes we call it Ganzir, or the Dark City, and sometimes the Great Below. Of course, its real name is the Kur.*

"My queen?"

It was my lovely Namtar, first amongst my black-cloaked priest-demons. He had a lovely furry face, big fox ears, and yellow eyes like a lizard.

Namtar bowed low to the floor.

"My lady, everyone is ready for you in the Black Temple."

"Oh," I said, frowning. Time played tricks on me when I was writing my history. "Namtar, let me just follow this thought through."

I picked up my bone stylus again and bent back over my tablet.

The Kur is simple in structure, although I have made it more complicated with my clever adjustments.

To enter the Kur from the outside, you must pass through seven gates. These gates are designed to keep the elements out. After the seventh gate, there is the special room where my Dark City now stands. At the heart of this room, there stands the gate that leads to Heaven and perhaps many other realms.

Now there must always be an Anunnaki in the underworld, to make sure the gates between the realms stay shut. Or that is what my grandfather Enki told me, when he dragged me down here kicking and screaming.

I became aware of Namtar once more, although I had not heard him make a noise.

"Is there something else, Namtar?"

He lifted a fur-covered hand to his snout and coughed politely. "My lady, they have all gathered just as you requested, for the rites, and they have been waiting there for three bells."

"Three bells!" I was astonished.

"All of the temple candles are alight. Just as you requested."

Namtar was being clever with me. He knew how much I worried about the candles.

All the same: what a waste!

"Send in the dressers then. I will work on my history tonight."

Namtar stood up straight, turned to the door, and with an authoritative flick of one hand, brought in all my dresser-demons, a great troupe of them. They were like mice, but with clever little hands for sewing and each about the size of a cat. They came scuttling in, with my black temple robes stretched out between them, and then dashed back out for my crown and other marks of office.

"My darling little creatures," I said, beaming after them. I was so lonely, in the underworld, until I worked out how to make my demons.

Namtar took one step back to let the dressers pass back and forth. "We long for you to read us the new parts of your history, my queen."

"I am not sure the visitors have been appreciating it," I said, frowning down at my tablet. "I have seen them roll their eyes when I read."

"My queen, I am quite sure they are very interested." He kept his lizard eyes turned from mine, as he always did when he lied.

"I am writing the true history of the Anunnaki. You would think everyone would be interested in that."

"Well quite, my lady."

"We have transformed the Earth since we descended from Heaven. Our history is the history of all the civilised world. How could they not be interested?'

"Exactly, my lady."

"And everything I have done to the Kur, to make it just like the underworld in the stories. Is that of interest to no one?"

"My lady, my thoughts exactly."

The dressers returned with my crown, orb, and jewellery, and these were laid out next to my robes on my bedspread.

"Help me stand, will you?" I said to Namtar.

He put two practised hands out to me, so that I could pull on him while I stood up from my desk. Together we walked over to my bed, and he helped me sit down.

"How is your back today, your excellence?"

"It is not unbearable." I put my arms out, so that he could get my cloak and my bed robes off me. I winced as he pulled off my under-tunic.

"My lady, the holy rites will help you with your pain."

A pulse of delicious anticipation ran through me, at the thought of what was about to happen in temple.

"They do say the plants grow stronger in the fields," I said, "when the ground has been ploughed."

Namtar and I smiled at each other.

"Exactly, my lady," he said.

We walked down twisting corridors to the doors of the Black Temple. Namtar led the way with his oil lantern held high. It threw some small light upon the narrow hallway ahead and upon the dust that swirled around us and gathered in drifts along the walls.

I walked behind the priest-demon, heavy in my temple robes, and with the high crown of the underworld, carved in obsidian, pressing into my curls. My black slippers left crisp footprints in the dust that lay thick over the flagstones.

Behind me came the dressers, ringing the wooden bells that they were only allowed to use in ceremony.

Last came my two silver *gallas*, first amongst the monsters that dwelt in the Dark City. One had the look of a priest, but he was not a priest. The other had the look of a warrior, but he was not a warrior. Both, though, were killers.

All the other demons of the underworld, I had created. These two, though, were a different sort of monster, built by creatures long dead, and mysterious even to me.

At the entrance to the temple, what a pretty scene awaited us!

I had built the Black Temple as the inverse of the White Temple at Uruk; that was the secret of it. What was black in the temple above was white down here, and vice versa. And instead of the bright jewels set into the columns of the White Temple, here the great pillars were studded with obsidian and sea coal.

Now a thousand candles threw their caressing light upon the black and sparkling columns that lined the central aisle. They lit up, too, the dark paintings of the Anunnaki on the walls all around. As the candlelight flickered, the holy figures of my family seemed to move a little, turning their hard faces to look over at me.

The fluttering candlelight also fell upon my beloved demons, sitting so neat and good in the pews, their eyes all wide and turned to me, all in their very best temple clothes and with their fur brushed to a high sheen. Oh, my precious friends!

It also lit up my two visitors.

I had been smiling; now my face fell hard and heavy as I took in the sight of the two of them.

First there was Dumuzi, son of my grandfather Enki, and estranged husband of my sister Inanna. He had been given to me by my sister as payment for her freedom from the underworld, and he was mine now to do as I pleased with.

Dumuzi was standing, hands on hips, beside the sacred bed that had been set up by the altar. He was in temple robes that could be pulled off quickly for the ceremony. He would have looked very fine to me, in his slim elegance, if it were not for the scowl upon his face.

It was not such a great dishonour to serve me in temple. Did he need to look so unhappy?

And then there was the dark stranger, who called himself Erra, sat at the back of the congregation.

The dark stranger leaned back in his seat, in his black-scaled armour and long, black cape, with his legs crossed before him.

He had one hand stretched out along the back of the pew, while the other shielded his eyes from the candlelight.

The dark stranger was tall, thick-set, and snub-nosed. Even here, in temple, he liked to keep his hood pulled over his face so that it was always in shadow. He said he was a visitor from Heaven. He said he had come to us through the eighth gate, which was never meant to open. He said he only sought passage through to the realm of light. But how could I be sure of his name, or where he had really come from, or what he wanted with the world above?

"Are you ready, my lady?" Namtar whispered to me.

I smoothed out my frown. "I am ready." I turned my attention to the sacred bed.

The dressers came to untie the knots in my robe, pulling my dress from me, so that I stood naked before the sacred bed. They hurried over to Dumuzi next and stripped him down too.

I stood there for a few moments, naked, my chin lifted, then with the help of my priest-demon Namtar, I got down on the velvet-covered bed and crawled into the centre of it. With some pain, I turned myself over and lay down on my back, my breasts cradled in my hands, my knees raised, ready for the rites.

As the demons began to sing and beat their sticks on the back of the pews, Dumuzi kneeled on the bed, shuffled over to me on his knees, and put his hands on my thighs.

He still looked sullen, but I could not deny that he was beautiful. He had his father's colouring: the same dark-brown hair, the bronze sheen to his skin, the carved nose. That little black beauty spot near the curve of his upper lip.

Well anyway what did it matter, how unhappy he looked to be there, looking down upon me? This was a duty he was raised to, and he would serve me well.

As Dumuzi lay down to begin his work, I turned, before I shut my eyes, and looked over at the dark stranger. He had not seen us do the rites before, and I saw something in his face that I could not read. Was it disgust, or lust, or both?

In my bedchamber after, when my demons had wiped me down and wrapped me in an old fur, I sat back down at my desk and took up my bone stylus. I blew the dust from my clay tablet and made sure it was still damp enough to press my marks into.

I was very happy in Heaven, which we also call the Great Above. But then my grandfather Enlil did the thing he did to the little girl.

He did not deny raping Ninlil. She was pregnant with his child. But he said he could not remember attacking her.

She remembered though.

The girl was from Creation, the most powerful city state in all of Heaven. The attack upon this girl put everything we had at risk.

They should have sent the girl back to her family.

They should have given Enlil up.

Instead, they dithered. The girl's belly grew. And then the queen of Creation declared war upon us. She swore she would have her vengeance however far we ran.

Yes, it had always been about Ninlil.

A crime committed four hundred years ago, in a faraway realm, and still my whole family was paying for it.

Now this dark stranger had emerged from the eighth gate. He brought with him the threat of terrible chaos, and I could not work out how to stop it.

CHAPTER FOUR

NINSHUBAR

On the Euphrates, heading south to Eridu, Enki's city

The moon rose so red and wide over the river that it might have been the setting sun.

I raised my stone axe to it, in greeting.

"You Sumerians do not like these red moons," I said to Inanna and the boat boys, "but I was born under one." I smiled up at it, as it floated clear of the reedbeds. "It is the totem of my spirit clan. It brings great luck with it in my country."

I returned to the polishing of my new flint axe. I had set the flint into a piece of hard oak and glued it into place with a special resin recipe known only to my people. After that I had bound it all together with dried fish gut. Only the cutting edge of the axe was left bare of resin, and that edge would need to be ground until it was extremely, dangerously sharp.

"Ninshubar?"

I looked up from my axe to find Inanna looking at me most intently. Behind her, the four boat boys sat with their eyes politely turned from us.

"Perhaps we should stop for the night now," Inanna said. "It is not only the red moon that sets our Sumerian nerves on edge. It is also that it comes so soon after the other red moon, and the earthquakes, and all the hail. We would all feel better to have dry land beneath us."

The boat boys all nodded at this.

Who was I to argue with what was bad luck, and what was good, in this strange land I found myself living in? So be it.

"Yes, we should stop for the night," I said. "It would be good to get those ducks over a fire."

By the red light of the moon, we dragged our sailing boat up onto a small, sandy beach.

Along the course of our journey, I had done what I could to bring down game and gather fuel, so it was not long before I had a good fire going with four fat ducks sat over it.

Two of the boys worked to stow everything away properly on the boat. The other two went off, in the red moonlight, to forage for more fuel.

Inanna was about to follow them out of the camp, but I did not want her creeping around in the half-light unprotected, and I called her to sit down with me by the fire. "You can help me turn the ducks."

She sat down, very obedient. "They smell good."

I watched her as she warmed her hands on the fire. She looked otherworldly in the red moonlight: her thin face washed pink, her black hair falling straight as water, and her strangely dark eyes, that seemed to have no whites in them.

She was a young woman, of fourteen or fifteen, perhaps, well-fed, well-watered. Yet a breeze might knock her into pieces. And why did she sleep so much, even in the day?

Our plan depended on her witchery with the master *mee*, but I had come to believe that the witchery was killing her. Indeed I had not liked the look of her since the underworld. She did not come back the same: that was the truth of it.

All these worries, though, must be kept from her. She was worried enough without me adding to it.

So I showed her how to turn the ducks over and sprinkle just a little salt upon their breasts, and then I said: "Inanna, tell me about Enki, and why he has fallen out with his brother Enlil in the north."

"It happened a long time ago," she said, her eyes on the fire.

"You told me your family were divided, those in the north, against those in the south."

She sat back from the flames, frowning. "I think it is all about Ninlil, my step-grandmother. It is said that Enlil raped and kidnapped her when she was only a small girl. That is why my family had to flee Heaven. Afterwards the two brothers fell out over what had happened, and what ought to have happened."

"But Enlil and Ninlil are happily married now. That is what is said in temple."

"I don't know about that," she said. "Perhaps it's true. I would like to meet them both, Enlil and Ninlil, and understand it all better."

"You know, Inanna," I said, "I have met them both. When I was trying to find someone to help you escape the underworld, I met them both in their home city."

"Hah!" she said, clapping her hands together. For a moment she looked like her old self, with her lovely smile and her black eyes dancing. "I did not know that."

"I only met them briefly. Enlil seemed a very serious man. A man carved from granite. He was out in a field, with his sleeves rolled up. And Ninlil, well, I thought she was just a little girl at first. I was waiting for Harga in a courtyard and she came to have a look at me. She was tiny and quite strange."

"My mother says she has kept herself child-sized. That it is a sort of magic, that she has done to herself, although no one can understand why."

"What kind of magic?"

"That I don't know," she said. "My mother never wanted to talk about Heaven. I know so little of her life there."

As she spoke, the boat boys came to join us around the fire. All four put their callused hands out to the flames and their eyes, very firmly, on the ducks.

When we had eaten, and Inanna and the boys had settled down for the night, I got up and paced along the beach.

I was worried about Inanna. But there was something else gnawing at me.

I had *mees* on my arms; four on the right, pushed up over the elbow, and four on the left. I had snatched these eight *mees* up from the mud when the half-god Dumuzi, son of Enki, husband of Inanna, was dragged off to the underworld. They were now rightfully mine.

Two of these *mees* were heavy and golden in appearance; weapons of combat. The others were narrow and cast from a dark grey metal, and they were meant to protect the wearer from attack.

I had done everything I could to make these *mees* work. I had consulted with Inanna's mother. I had practised and practised. But the *mees* of protection would not protect me from a kitten, and the *mees* of combat were equally useless.

I was holy *sukkal* to the goddess Inanna. Sworn to fight for her until the end of the world. Yet I was armed with the weapons of a hunter and gatherer, in a land where the gods could wield magic.

I could not conquer Enki with an arrow, or even my beautiful flint axe.

I remembered the blood gushing from Dumuzi's wounds as he was carried off to the underworld. These *mees* had done nothing to protect him against the *gallas* and their slashing, metal arms.

Of course there was no point worrying Inanna with all this.

We had committed, and if we did not go south for Enki, then he would come north for us. That part I was sure of.

"Ninshubar?" Inanna, lying in her cloak beside the campfire, had opened her eyes. "Ninshubar, you look worried."

"Yes, I am very worried." I sat down cross-legged next to her, and put my hand out to her soft, black hair. "I do not know what I am going to feed you all for breakfast."

"We will forage for something," she said, her eyes bright on me.

I was quite sure that in her whole life, Inanna had never foraged for anything beyond some insect or interesting flower, but I smiled at her encouragingly.

"You are quite right, goddess," I said. "Now sleep, dear friend, and guard your strength."

After a while, she shut her eyes, and her breathing changed.

I felt quite alone then. I wished, just for a few heartbeats, that Harga, Gilgamesh's man, was there with me. Harga did not love me. Why should he? He hardly knew me. But it would have been good to have him there. He would not have known how to bring down Enki. All the same, we could have talked.

I wiped a tear from the side of my nose, and breathed in deep, to stop more from falling.

CHAPTER FIVE

GILGAMESH

The path through the marshes to Uruk

Harga and I stood in conclave, in the hard hail, as the men mounted up.

"We could go through the marshes," I said.

"The paths are treacherous," he said. "Only smugglers ever use them."

"Have you crossed these marshes?"

"I know men who have and all of them warned me never to go into them. You get lost, you get bogged down, you end up swimming. You can never see anyone coming over the reeds. The insects and snakes are deadly. There are crocodiles everywhere. Above all else, it is no place for a baby."

"Do you have a better suggestion, Harga?"

"I do not," he said, sighing out.

"Well, find someone who knows the way then."

"All right," he said, rolling his shoulders.

I went back into the muddle of soldiers and animals to find my wife. She was standing, blank-faced, next to my horse, holding the baby tight to her chest. Her shoulders were white with ice.

"Della, let me take him, while you get up," I said. "I have cleaned my hands." I held them out to her.

"You don't know how to hold him properly."

I could not see how holding a baby could be difficult; my son looked light enough in her arms.

"I have carried babies," I said. "Many babies. At least let me hold him while you mount."

"Your cloak is covered with blood," she said, holding the baby tighter.

Harga appeared as if from nowhere and put out hands of such obvious competence towards Della that she at once handed him the child.

"Thank you, Harga," I said. "Della, do you want help getting up?"

"No," she said to me.

I then watched as Harga helped her up, effortlessly holding the baby in his left arm, while he lifted her up into her stirrup with his right.

"I'll carry the baby awhile," he said to her. "I will find something more weatherly to wrap him in."

"Thank you, Harga," she said.

"Thank you, Harga," I echoed, rather cuttingly, but my tone seemed lost on him. For a moment I thought him upset, as he drew his cloak around the baby, but perhaps I imagined it.

We plunged down through the wet forest and into scrubby bush, on a path that was barely a path. Three leagues on, in the near dusk, the land levelled out and turned to bog. Soon enough it was an effort to lift each foot.

The hail had turned to thin, freezing rain.

Harga and I were at the rear of our very sorry caravan; he had my son upon his front, wrapped in a leather jerkin.

"What a family I have," I said, watching how Harga held my son's head.

"Your family is not so bad. You love your father." He kissed my son's head. "If you knew my father, you would not complain about your family."

"Yes, my father is a good man and I am very grateful for his love. My mother, and you cannot deny it, Harga, is a strong cup of wine indeed. Always at the heart of every battle, every drama. Always the bravest. Yet with not much love for those around her."

"There are some who think, quite wrongly, that you and she are very alike. That you look alike, that you fight alike."

"We are nothing alike."

"Well, I know that," said Harga. "For a start, she doesn't complain about everything."

I wondered for a moment who was the more annoying: Della, my mother, or Harga?

But I saw Harga had dropped his teasing; he was frowning out at the interminable reedbeds. "I hate to think that the Akkadians have Ninlil."

"She's always been so kind to me," I said. "When Enlil first took me in, she made me feel part of the household."

Harga waved a hand out to the marsh and the sky. "What is your opinion of it?"

"Of the marshes?"

"Of what is happening."

"My view is that our spies have failed us. Anything could be happening. We need to get to Uruk and regroup."

He tucked his hair behind his ears. "We should stop soon though. We'll start losing people to the mud if we go on."

"All right," I said. Indeed, I could barely see my own feet in the gloom.

The rain dried up at last as we made a mean little camp amongst the reeds. We ate the very last of our dry food, without lighting any fires. We were all still wet to the skin.

I made sure Della had a thick blanket to sit on, and there she sat in the last of the light, closed-faced and silent, our son on one small breast.

"It will only be three or four days, maybe five, and we will be in Uruk," I said, very friendly and encouraging. "You can have a big bath and everything you want to eat."

She gave no sign that she could hear me, although I was squatting down right in front of her.

"I hope you sleep," I said. "I will be just over there if you need me in the night. You only need whisper and I will hear."

At that she turned cold eyes upon me. "I need water," she said.

My plan had been to make Della fall in love with me. I in turn would learn to love my son, and we would be a strong and upright family. As head of the household, I would be a serious and constant man, much in the mould of my own father.

Della would need to be won over. I knew it would take work. Families were not meant to be easy. Look at what my father had had to put up with, with my mother always in love with some new woman. But I was committed to making it work. It would be the new me, and a new life.

It was hard to hold on to those redeeming thoughts as we made our way into the heart of the marshes the next day. It began to rain again, this time hard and persistent. The boggy path was at times no path at all, and even in the rain, we were beset by huge and evil biting things.

Setting aside the red welts that instantly sprang up all over me, and how very wet I was, there was the matter of Della's cold fury towards me. It already had something of a settled quality to it, even so soon after our reunion.

Indeed, it was hard to feel any optimism at all in the face of the disgust, implacable dislike, anger, hatred, and disdain that seemed to take turns to set up camp upon her finely carved features. It became difficult to imagine her ever smiling at me again, let alone taking me to her bed.

"Why so pensive?" said Harga, as we brought up the rear on foot. He had my son in his arms again, and now and again he beamed a smile down at him.

"Do you think I will be a good family man?" Even before the words were out of my mouth, I had lifted a hand to stop him answering. "What I mean to say is, I feel myself maturing with every day that goes by."

Harga raised one eyebrow but said nothing.

"I used to grab at every pleasure I caught a glimpse of, regardless of what it might cost me, or might cost others. I longed for war and excitement. Now I yearn for some sort of normality. For quiet times."

"There are no quiet times, for men like you," he said, slapping at a mosquito. "That is the truth of it."

"Men like me? I do not see how you are so different from me, Harga. You love to be always at the heart of things. You like to amaze everyone around you, with how you always know everything, and how you are always the man to turn to."

"Maybe," he said. He looked over at my wife, who was riding just a few cords ahead of us, and smiled to himself.

"What now?" I said.

"I am thinking about your wife and the goddess Inanna, living side by side in Uruk, and how they will get on."

"They will get on very well. I am taking Della to Uruk because I have Inanna's word that all will be proper there, and that Della will be honoured. We will have our own palace. Della will live as the queen, just as my mother did, and Inanna will be the goddess of the city."

"And what if Inanna calls you to temple to lie with her in the rites? Surely it would be very usual for the king to serve the goddess when she called?"

"Quite usual and quite proper. Everything in temple is sacred and above the flow of mundane life. What happened in private between Inanna and me, it only happened once, and that is all over now. All done and forgotten."

"Ah well then, it sounds as if they will get on very well. You seem to have it all thought through. Of course, lesser women might be jealous of each other, but these two women, each so mild and sweet hearted, are sure to behave very, very well. Perhaps they will become great friends."

"I do believe they will." At that I cast a very dubious look over at Della, who even at a distance, seemed to be sending out shards of hatred towards me.

The baby stirred in Harga's arms and I drew closer to look at him. He had a very tiny face, red and puffy. I could not claim him as a handsome child.

"He's not a mongoose," Harga said. "You don't need to look at him so suspiciously. He's not going to bite you. He doesn't even have teeth."

"Let me carry him for a while, then."

"Della won't like it."

"A bit of mud and old blood won't do him any harm."

"All the same."

"Why is it that you are happy to do as everyone else bids and yet you will never do anything for me?"

"Yes, I do see it now," he said.

"What?"

"Your new maturity. How much you have grown as a man."

"I do hope you don't choke on one of your pebbles, Harga," I said. "I hope some terrible accident does not befall you."

Then I tried to stalk off in a dignified manner, while being careful not to cross paths with my wife.

CHAPTER SIX

INANNA

*At Eridu, Sumer's oldest city, and
home of the great god Enki*

The sailor boys were the first to spot it: a bruise of smoke upon the horizon.

We caught sight of the towers next, faint at first, then bright and true. Seabirds began to appear above us, and the river was now so wide we could no longer see the eastern bank.

The city was built upon a low, natural hill, and ringed with clay walls that glowed golden against the marshlands and the cobalt of the sea beyond. The glorious square ziggurat of the Temple of the Aquifer stood at the highest point of the hill, and Enki's fabulous palace was set below that, throwing up elegant towers to the pale Autumn sky.

Around these two sacred buildings were clustered the fine, clay-brick city houses that I had so often looked down on when I lived in Enki's palace.

"It is very handsome," Ninshubar said.

"It is strange to me to think that you lived here when I did,"

I said. "That we lived our lives so close together and yet did not know each other."

"I knew you. I was amazed by your black eyes. And although you do not remember me, you did once look at me."

"I was focused on my grandfather," I said.

We passed a sandstone island on our right, and I caught a glimpse of the golden prow of the Barge of Heaven. A moment later it was hidden from view. "Those are the royal docks," I said to Ninshubar.

We were heading for the city docks, where the ordinary traders came in and out, and fishermen brought in their catch.

The wind was against us though, and so we sat with our eyes upon the bustling quay for what felt like an age before our crew could bring us in.

"This is where the slave traders brought me," said Ninshubar. "It looked so different to me then, when I had never seen a city before."

Meanwhile the sight of our white-sailed skiff, known everywhere as a holy vessel of the White Temple, was bringing a crowd down onto the docks.

By the time we finally climbed ashore from our small boat, we did so before an audience of sailors, merchants, and city guards.

They all recognised me, their little goddess of love. But Ninshubar was also something to look at, her outfit now topped by a shining cap of copper, like the men of Kish wear to war.

Our sailor boys looked so very anxious as they let the ropes slip.

"Will you be safe?" one called to me.

"No one is safe," I called out to him. "Not even the dead." I had meant to sound light-hearted, but I saw from his face that I had misjudged it.

Moments later the boys were pulling away fast, the boat leaning over in the wind, all their eyes on me still.

"Praise be to you, Inanna!" the smallest of them shouted.

So, it was time to face Enki.

My hands were shaking.

I clasped them tightly together, before turning to the crowd.

"I am here to see my grandfather," I said.

We were left to wait for Enki in the blue-doored garden that had once been my sanctuary.

The sweet scent of the jasmine; the doves watching us from the edge of the marble pond; the fish that rolled their great eyes up at us: all of it was so familiar to me.

Ninshubar and I sat together on the marble bench where I had so often sat with Enki.

"Can you tell where he is?" she said. They had let her keep her weapons; it seemed they did not think her much of a threat.

"He's close."

I tried to breath evenly and long, to calm my fast-beating heart.

A servant woman, dimly familiar to me, brought a tray of beer and cakes, and put them on a small table in the shade. When the woman had gone, keeping her eyes turned from us, Ninshubar poured us both a cup of beer and then, me having refused even a crumb, ate all the butter cakes.

"No doubt Enki can call for more, if he wants one." She carefully licked the last of the crumbs from her fingers.

"I used to spend almost all my time in this place, when I lived here," I said. "I know all the plants and which insects live where and which birds come to feed."

"It is a strange thing, to think that all this beauty has been arranged for us," Ninshubar said. "Arranged just so, to be seen just so, from this carefully placed bench."

"I had not thought of it like that. Perhaps one day I will show you the gardens I grew up in at Ur, which are even more beautiful than this." I breathed in deep.

Ninshubar put a hand onto my right knee. "I am here with you, Inanna."

"But I don't want you endangered, by what I have decided to do."

"You need not fear for me, Inanna. You do what needs doing, without looking to keep me safe."

She stood, casting a professional eye upon the pond fish. "Can you eat these?"

"I would be sad to, Ninshubar. I am most fond of them."

She sat down again. "When I lived here, I would visit the slave market every day, looking for my Potta. I told myself that I was doing everything I could."

"I don't know what more you could have done."

"I once told your mother that I had never done anything wrong. But on this I can never be sure."

"Ninshubar, my mother has sent spies out across Sumer looking for him. If he has passed through Sumer, we will hear of it. No creature so strange-looking would go unremarked."

"If he ever came to Sumer."

"If he didn't, we can send the spies further. What is the point of us being goddesses, and queens too, if we cannot find one boy?"

And then the old and familiar pull: Enki was coming.

First though came my lions, streaking ahead of him.

"Oh!" I shouted as the hot and writhing weight of them hit me hard.

They were all over me, knocking me from the bench and onto the paving stones, growling deeply and loudly. My thin gold crown fell from my head, ringing out on the stone.

Ninshubar was on her feet, a knife in each hand, but hovering, weapons raised, unsure how to intervene when I was making kissing noises, and laughing, even while under attack.

"You have grown far too big to batter me so," I said to my lions.

They were wearing their beautiful carnelian and gold-link collars.

I managed to sit up, my sweet lions thrusting their faces into mine for kisses. Oh, the good, hot, clean smell of them, and their warm satin fur, although my right hip was now rather bruised.

"This is Crocus," I said to Ninshubar, kissing Crocus's head, "and this is Saffron." I rubbed my face into their necks.

"Soft names for dangerous creatures." She took a firm step back but made no move to sheath her knives.

"They have good hearts." I rubbed them in front of their ears and made them purr with pleasure.

"Lions killed my father and my brothers," she said.

And then my grandfather was there.

He was as tall and powerful as ever, and so handsome, his skin the colour of burnished bronze. His blood-red robes were heavy with carnelians.

He paused beneath the jasmine bower that led through to the pond.

Just a little too far from me.

His strong arms were wreathed in *mees*, of gold, silver, and the same darker grey metal that my master *mee* was cast from.

"Inanna," he said, looking at me without expression.

He turned to Ninshubar and lifted his beard a fraction. "You again."

Was he not going to come closer?

"What happened to all your scars?" he said to Ninshubar.

I forced myself to stand up, my hands on my lions' heads.

"I have come to make peace, grandfather."

"Have you?" he said. No smile, no warmth.

He was still just a little too far away from me.

"I'm told my son is in the underworld, dragged down there by the *gallas*, who ought not be walking this realm. That is a strange way to make peace, Inanna. Especially when I helped you escape death."

He took a step closer to me, his hands upon his gem-studded belt. "I helped you when I had no need to. No need at all, other than duty to family."

"I have your box for you, my lord," Ninshubar put in. "We thank you for your help." She sheathed her knives and pulled out a grey-metal box from her leather jerkin. The box contained two small lumps of obsidian that sometimes turned into flies, and sometimes turned into shadowmen. She held it out to Enki.

My grandfather looked from one to the other of us but did not come forward to take back the box. "I should kill both of you."

I kneeled between my lions.

"Grandfather, your son will come to no harm with Ereshkigal. She only wanted a companion in the underworld, to serve her in the rites."

He was still too far away from me.

Enki nodded, his leopard eyes on my face. "You did not have to send my son to her. Anyone might have done."

"I was angry with him. For the way he treated me. For loving his sister more than he loved me. For threatening to chop off my arm when he wanted to take my *mee* from me."

Enki shrugged at that. "I still don't see why you are here."

I bent my head over my hands. "I need peace, my lord. I cannot live in fear any longer. I cannot live in a world where at any moment you might come for me or for my mother."

I suppose most of it was true.

I looked up at him, and almost without thinking, perhaps, he took a step towards us.

"Whose *mees* are you wearing?" he said to Ninshubar. "Are those my son's *mees*?"

And I had him.

Although he did not know it yet.

I traced one thin, invisible line of blue fire around the so-called lord of wisdom and pulled it soft against him.

Enki shuddered. Just very faintly.

He had his hand out to Ninshubar, but he dropped it and took a step back. He looked at me as if he had forgotten what he was going to say.

I climbed to my feet, my hands in prayer to him. "Let us stay here in Eridu and make our case to you, grandfather."

He frowned. Fearing that I had gone too far, I let my invisible blue rope run just a little looser.

At once he seemed to relax. He came over to us; he took the box with the flies inside from Ninshubar.

"The lions are certainly happy to see you," he said to me. I caught the familiar scent of him. Olive soap, and sun-warmed skin.

He paused a moment, standing between us, a faint frown upon his brow. "Perhaps I have missed you also, Inanna. Very well, stay a while, and we will talk."

He looked over at Ninshubar and her assemblage of weapons. "You may not need all of those knives here."

"We will see," she said to him.

They gave us my old rooms. My bed along one wall in the sleeping chamber; a cot made up for Ninshubar along the other. The familiar paintings of pomegranates and peacocks on the walls.

In the bathroom, Ninshubar stared open-mouthed at the huge copper tub. "I have never had a bath," she said.

"Just ask them for hot water."

I lay down on my bed, stretched out on my back, and shut my eyes. I must have plunged straight into sleep because I woke to Ninshubar's face, and her hand on my shoulder.

"They have come to say that Enki wants you to come to lunch with him."

I shut my eyes again.

"Are you tired?" she asked.

"I am unnaturally weary."

"Is it the *mee*?"

I nodded, my eyes still closed. "I am trying to trap a soul and his is not a simple soul to trap. And I am a beginner, wrestling with a weapon forged in Heaven, and with no instructions on how to do it."

She put her hands on my shoulders. "Please be careful, Inanna. This is dark magic."

"I will be as careful as I can be," I said.

CHAPTER SEVEN

ERESHKIGAL

In the underworld

For my first one hundred years in the underworld, I ate my dinner in bed.

Then my sister Inanna sent her husband Dumuzi to me, in payment for her freedom, and the dark stranger, who said his name was Erra, appeared with no warning.

Now meals were very formal in the Dark Palace.

The walls of the dining room were lined with black velvet and the long ebony table was covered in candles and good glass. I sat at the head of the table in my best black dress and I looked down with great complacency upon my embroidered sleeves. My dressers had stitched little skulls into them, and how pretty they looked in the candlelight!

Dumuzi sat to my right. His purple robes were much hacked about when he was first delivered to me in the underworld; my *gallas* had slashed at him very cruelly. But it was only a matter of darning and the careful washing out of blood, and now his robes looked very fine indeed, even in this bright candlelight. Oh, and how handsome he did look with his long dark lashes and his high-cut cheeks.

The dark stranger sat to my left, opposite Dumuzi. You could not call him handsome, but he had a presence to him that could not be denied. He wore the same black armour that he always wore, but he looked very grand in it.

So formal! The candles, the lids upon the dishes, and all my dresser-demons wearing their aprons; no would guess they were not born to wait at table.

We might have been in the dining room at Ur, my beloved home city, if it was not for the dust of the dead, falling so constantly. The dust coated your food, if you did not eat it quick enough, and it fell as a heavy film upon our wine.

My two *gallas* stood either side of the doorway, their silver faces turned to the floor, and next to them stood my priest-demon Namtar. He cast stern looks at the dresser-demons as they passed in and out with the trays of food, and he scowled and wrung his hands at every plate dropped, or glass overfilled.

Dumuzi put up some fuss about the food and the wine when he was new to the underworld. Now he attacked his plate and glugged at his wine in a steady and uncomplaining manner.

The dark stranger, still new to our table, picked at the food before him, frowning most suspiciously at each new offering. Occasionally he would put something to his flat nose and sniff at it.

I watched the dark scales of his armour flutter as he shifted in his seat.

My demons and I itched to get our hands upon this armour. At night Erra slept beneath some sort of protective shield, and we could not get close enough to fiddle with the black-scaled outfit. All we could do was watch how the scales of his armour moved around as he himself moved, exposing his face or hands as needed.

"Ereshkigal," he said, feeling my eyes upon him. "How much longer must this go on?"

"It must go on until we have finished eating and drinking," I said. "As it does every night, my lord."

The dark stranger nodded grimly and put down his fork. "I mean, how much longer do you intend to hold me prisoner here?"

"You are not a prisoner." I too put down my fork.

He pushed away his plate and leaned back in his chair. "You say I am not a prisoner here. And yet you will not let me leave."

"I did not invite you here," I said. "You have found your way into the Dark City, from where I do not know, with no help or encouragement from me." The upset came bubbling up. I tried to steady my breathing. "It has made me feel unsafe here. As if anyone might come bursting in on us, at any time. And yet I have made you very welcome because you claim to be an Anunnaki. So do not be complaining to me, about how you are treated!"

The dust began to fall so thickly that Dumuzi was obliged to stop eating.

My priest-demon, Namtar, came to my elbow. With a soft nod and a smile, he took away my befouled wine and poured me some fresh in a new glass. "Shall I bring in the cheese, my queen?"

"Yes, I would like some cheese." The dust thinned; the air slowly cleared.

The dark stranger clenched his armour-coated fists, and then laid his hands out flat on the black tablecloth before him. "Ereshkigal, I am not here to cause you distress. I am come from the Great Above, as I have said many times. I seek safe passage through the Kur and out into the realm beyond. I come with a peace treaty for the Anunnaki. It will do no one any harm to let me through. In fact it may do you and all our family a great deal of good."

"I do not believe in this peace treaty," said Dumuzi. He helped himself to a generous portion of the black cheese. "And I am not at all sure that you are family to us."

"Anyway, I have no power to let you through into the world of light," I said to the dark stranger. I cast a benevolent smile at Dumuzi, who looked beautiful even with cheese smeared on his teeth.

The dark stranger looked from one to the other of us, and then, after a heavy sigh, said: "It has been four hundred years since the Anunnaki fled Heaven. The lords of Creation have allowed me to build up the house of the Anunnaki once more and I have permission to bring you all home now. The Anunnaki's crimes are long forgotten."

"I did not commit any crimes!" I said. "It was my grandfather Enlil who did it, no one else, so do not talk of Anunnaki crimes!"

"No one blames you, Ereshkigal," said the dark stranger.

"I really don't see what's in it for you," Dumuzi said to him. "What do you care about these stray Anunnaki, grubbing about here in another realm?"

"You are all my family," said the dark stranger. "Even you, Dumuzi." He turned to me. "You were only a baby when I met you, Ereshkigal, but I remember you. You must remember me being spoken of."

"No," I said. "I have never heard the name Erra before."

Of course, I did remember an Erra being spoken of, although I could not be sure that this was him. All of that side of the family were left behind in the terrible scramble to escape from Heaven.

"And we will all be forgiven now for what Enlil did?" said Dumuzi. "For the rape and kidnap of a young girl. Not only a young girl, but the daughter of a citizen of Creation. It was a crime that would never be forgiven. Yet now it is forgotten?"

"There will be a price, for the peace," said the dark stranger. "But yes, if the price is paid all will be forgiven and the exile of the Anunnaki will be at an end."

"What is the price?" Dumuzi asked.

The dark stranger shook his head at him. "The message I bring is for An and Nammu, who are the heads of our family here on Earth."

"Hmm," said Dumuzi. "I do not believe any of it."

I gave Erra my widest smile. "It is all very interesting to me, but as I have said, I have no power to let you out." I cut myself some cheese.

The dark stranger put his forehead down upon the table and took a deep breath. Then he looked back up at me. "Madam, I know full well that you can let me out, should you choose to."

Dumuzi gave the dark stranger one of his most supercilious smiles. "It is her policy to lie about everything. Or almost everything. It took a while for me to work it out."

"Dumuzi, surely you also want to leave?" the dark stranger said to him.

"She's not going to let me out." He shrugged and kept on eating. "Anyway, you found your way in here, you find your own way out."

I nodded at that. "You should go back to Heaven, my lord Erra, if you are so unhappy."

"What's interesting to me," said Dumuzi, pointing a fork at me, "is why you don't leave the Kur, now that your watch here is long over, and you are perfectly free to leave. You keep on pretending to be a prisoner here, but you have full control over all the gates."

"I control none of them!" I said.

The dark stranger brought both his hands down onto the table, with a great thud. A cloud of dust rose into the air.

"Ereshkigal, you complain of me being here and yet your demons stop me returning the way I came. They have locked the gate to Heaven. On your orders. They have also locked the seven gates that lead through to the Earth. On your orders. So, what am I to do now, if I cannot go back to Heaven and I cannot pass through to the realm of light?"

"Oh, I didn't know she'd barred you from going back," Dumuzi said. "So, you're trapped then, are you? I hadn't understood that." He laughed most jovially.

"I am trapped and yet she keeps on lying about it," the dark stranger said. "Lies after lies."

This was too much for me. I burst into tears. "I do not tell lies! And I am truly a prisoner here! I have been locked in the underworld for one hundred years! My family said they would come back for me, but they never came!"

The dark stranger listened to this speech most intently, but Dumuzi went back to his food.

"The family have come here and tried to get her to come out," Dumuzi said, as he loaded a blackened biscuit with more cheese. "Nammu, queen of the Anunnaki, was here perhaps twenty years ago, begging to talk to her. But Ereshkigal wouldn't let her in."

"Stop it!" I said. "Stop talking nonsense!"

The dust fell thick and heavy on us all.

My priest-demon was at my elbow again, with more wine and a small plate of black berries. "My lady, these are the last of the berries we found upon that little bush."

"Yes," I said to my Namtar, "I would like some berries." While I nibbled upon one, I held up my face to Namtar so that he could wipe the tears from my cheeks.

"She tells the truth to her demons," Dumuzi said, waving his cheese-knife at my priest-demon. "I've worked that bit out too."

The dark stranger watched Dumuzi eating his dust-covered cheese, and then looked over at me as I drained my wine glass. "And what is going on with this sex in public? What game were you playing today in temple?"

I pulled myself up in my chair. "It is the rites that keep the world turning. It's no game."

The dark stranger shook his head. "You make no sense. I cannot work out if this place is real, or if is this somehow the inside of your head. I was told it would only be a room."

I am a munificent hostess, but there must be limits.

"From now on you will eat in your bedchamber," I said to the dark stranger. "You will be let out when you have decided to be good again."

My two *gallas* stepped forward.

After dinner, in my bedchamber, my dressers helped me into a soft nightdress that did not annoy the sores on my belly, and draped my black fur cloak over my shoulders.

I sat back down at my writing desk.

The clay tablet was still damp enough to press my marks into, beneath its furring of fresh grey dust, and after I had done my best to blow it clean, I picked up my stylus again.

Ninlil was too young to be pregnant.

I sucked the clay off my stylus, remembering Ninlil's small face when I first saw her, and her huge eyes, too big for her head. How she shook with fear as they unclasped her cloak in the doorway, and the strangeness of a swollen belly, on a girl too young to bear a child.

The baby was snatched from its cot before we had a chance to flee.

What did they name the baby?

I could not remember what name they gave him.

I blinked my eyes to clear my head and breathed out heavily.

I had not thought of the baby for many, many years. It made me think of my own babies.

I wiped away my tears and went back to my writing.

Enlil stole Ninlil away from her family. He also stole the master mee, although he said he did not know how he came to have it.

It was me who worked out how to open the gate with it, and it was me who worked out how to get the Kur down to Earth, when we found ourselves stuck up in the sky. I have always been the cleverest of all of us, at making things, at moving things, at opening doors, and at making sure that sometime doors stay shut. They have never given me any praise for it.

"My queen?" Namtar was at the door, his ears pricked. "It is time you slept, my most glorious one."

I did feel weary and achy, after all my work in temple, and upon my history, and the terrible rudeness at dinner. I let him help me up and steer me to my bed. He eased me onto my soft mattress and arranged my blankets and furs over me.

"My empress, would you like me to sit with you a while, until you sleep? Perhaps sing to you a little?"

"I would like that."

He put out a furry hand and brushed my hair from my forehead. "They tire you, these visitors."

"Yes."

"And we should not trust this new one," Namtar said, in a strangely urgent voice. "How long before more strangers come through the eighth gate?"

"Do not frighten me, my priest, when I am meant to be going to sleep!"

"We will all protect you from him, my queen. I did not mean to worry you. Whatever it is he does, this man who calls himself Erra, we will be here to protect you."

"I know that," I said. "You protected me when my sister came."

"Yes we did," my priest-demon said. "We savaged her. And we will do the same to this one if you only give us the word."

"Thank you, dear, dear Namtar," I said. "Leave the candle burning please."

After he had gone, I got up again and blew the new dust from my clay tablet. I still had words in me that needed to be set down.

In Heaven, the light is different. Dimmer, more subtle.

    It is a huge, curling world, that loops around its sun. So much bigger than the Earth.

    The lords of Creation rule over it.

    We do not often speak of them here.

    But they call themselves the Anzu.

CHAPTER EIGHT

MARDUK

*In Kish, capital city
of Akkadia*

After Gilgamesh brought disgrace on my lovely Hedda, and her terrible death at the siege of Marad, there was a great reordering of the palace at Kish. It was decided that the royal women would henceforth only be attended by slave women or by male slaves so ancient or maimed by war that they were barely able to walk.

Eventually that reordering worked its way down to me.

One warm morning, I was told to leave the washing that I was meant to be spreading out in the sun, and report to Biluda, the head of the king's household.

In his cramped lair beside the palace kitchens, Biluda eased himself down into his old, leather chair.

"You can sit down, Marduk," he said, pointing to a wooden stool.

I sat, although reluctantly. I knew my days serving the royal ladies were bound to soon be over, but I did not know which part of the palace compounds I might be assigned to next. I hoped above all it was not the kitchens, which on the coolest day were hot enough to suffocate a man.

"I have not finished with the washing," I said.

"Marduk, I know you still dream of escape, but I also know that you have made this place a home and found friends here."

He pressed his forefingers into his brows, which he only did when he was upset.

"We have all got used to you, Marduk," he said.

I sat up straight on my stool. "Do say it, Biluda."

"You are being moved over to the compound of Prince Inush, the king's nephew."

I kept my face plain. "I'm to leave the palace?"

Biluda sat back in his chair. "You will not be going far. It is only the other side of the royal precinct. A short walk."

"But I will live there, in Inush's household?"

"Not specifically in his household. As you are no doubt aware, Inush is master of the king's dogs and the kennels are within Inush's compound. You have been assigned to the kennels and you will live there with the other kennel boys."

"Am I being moved because I am good with dogs?"

Biluda frowned down at his lap.

"I believe that Inush asked the king for you. As a gift."

I nodded, but for a moment could not say more. I remembered Inush's eyes, heavy on me, when I first served the king at supper. How my hands shook under the weight of that stare. I had felt in me the old dread that I felt in Abydos, when the god picked me out from the other slaves in the temple.

"So, I am a gift from the king to his nephew?"

"They say Inush is not unkind."

What more was there to say? So I said nothing.

"Marduk, if I could have stopped this, of course I would have." He was looking full at me, beseeching.

"I know. I've been lucky so far here. I should not have got so used to it."

"I'm very sorry, Marduk."

"I do like dogs."

"You must be careful of these new dogs. You cannot make pets of them." Biluda pushed himself up to his feet with a groan. "Do you have some things to gather up?"

"I have only what I stand in. Except for my blanket, which is in the slave quarters."

"They will have a blanket for you there."

Kish, the capital of King Akka's empire, was built on a hill and Akka's palace stood at the peak of it. The palace's ornate mud-brick arches and turrets were visible from every point in the city. All around it, amidst fine gardens, were arranged the palaces and compounds of Akka's family and most favoured generals.

Biluda led me along the palm-lined avenue that linked the palaces of the royal precinct. We walked with the stables and barracks to our right and the maze of temple buildings to our left.

"It will not be so bad," Biluda said. "Inush knows you are a master tracker; that you grew up as a hunter. Perhaps he will take you out hunting, just as the king did. And as you say, you like dogs."

"I should have tried harder to escape."

"You tried hard, Marduk. And each time the king forgave you because I begged him to. Or because Hedda begged him to. But they will not be so soft in Inush's household."

Inush's palace complex was surrounded by high, clay-brick walls. The gate was carved from solid oak, with guards at it, and even from the avenue outside, we could already hear the dogs.

"I do not know how they can bear that noise," said Biluda, as we waited for the gate to be pulled open for us. He then remembered who he was speaking to. "But I am sure you will get used to it very quickly."

The gates opened. Two small boys peered out at us and then stepped back to let us through.

Ahead of us stood a large house: square, substantial, three storeys high, and with a flight of steps up to the main door. To our right lay a stable yard and beyond it, the outer walls of a compound within the compound. This compound could only be the kennels from the terrible noise that emanated from it. To our left stood a long, low building, built of straw and mud. "You will bunk in there," Biluda said, nodding to it.

Inside, by the very dim light from the doorway, I could make out a long line of sleeping mats. I sat down on the mat that Biluda pointed me to.

"I will come to check up on you," he said. "To make sure you are causing no bother here."

"Thank you, Biluda."

"You wait here now for the kennel boys to get you."

When he had gone, I sat there a while on my thin mat, as low as I had felt in a long time. My one goal was to escape and find my adopted mother, Ninshubar. In that I had been failing very badly; every escape attempt thwarted. Most recently I had hidden myself in a cart of dirty washing, destined to be taken out to the launder women in the outer city. I had succeeded in reaching the outer city, but there the launder women did not take pity on me, as might have been hoped. Instead I was returned with little delay to Biluda and then put down in the punishment cells for one full moon.

I had felt safe in the king's palace, though, after feeling very unsafe for a long time before. It had made me complacent. Now I must redouble my efforts to escape. I had been a slave long enough.

That afternoon, though, I was still a slave. I was taken to the kennel compound. It had a solid-looking set of gates of its own, and even there at the gates, the noise of the dogs was so loud it was hard to hear myself think.

I was handed over to a man with no smile on him. He took me into the cobbled yard and pointed over a low wall. On the other side of the wall: there were the dogs. Not normal dogs, but dogs with wreaths of fur around their necks and jaws as wide as my skull. Many of them seemed to be trying to kill each other.

The man handed me a wooden bucket. "You fill up the bucket," he said. He pointed over to a water trough. "You climb over the wall with it and you sluice the dog pit down. And you keep doing that until the pit is clean."

"What about the dogs?" I said. I did not take the bucket from him.

"Stay away from the dogs," he said.

I frowned into the pit. There was a dead dog along the back wall; it looked to have been freshly killed, its throat bitten out.

"What if I say no?"

"You'll be flogged."

I took the bucket from him. "Very well."

As I made my way over to the trough, I noticed that a fair number of the kennel men were out in the yard, all apparently busy with one thing or that. They kept their eyes turned from me, but a nasty thought occurred to me: *have they come to see me go over the wall?*

I paused, holding the half-filled bucket to my chest, and then I thought over what a man's back looked like after he had been flogged.

My head held high, I balanced the bucket on the wall and swung my legs over.

I was immediately bitten.

A deep bite, pain flaring; the dog was still attached to me.

On instinct I brought the bucket of water down hard on the dog's head and it let go. I sprang back over the wall, screaming with the pain.

As I lay on the ground, holding my leg, the men in the yard doubled over with laughter.

It was a horrible injury. It throbbed all night. I turned my back on the men and boys who shared my sleeping space and I tried to lift myself away from the pain and the sadness of where I now found myself.

The next morning, I limped about without my usual smiles. When I was told to clean out the dog pit again, I limped between the trough and the pit, throwing buckets of water over. I was not going back over the wall.

The other kennel men seemed to walk amongst the dogs without fear. They carried heavy clubs, and dealt out awful blows to the dogs, apparently at whim.

I was not going to risk another bite. My calf had blown up and turned a foul purple overnight; if anything it hurt more, not less.

When the pit was wetted, if not very pristine, I was set to cleaning out the dogs' feeding bowls. I sat down on the cobbles to do the job, scratching away at them in a half-hearted manner while trying to keep my bitten leg out of the filth. I was working out a very clever manner of escape when a man in riding leathers came to stand over me, a whip in his left hand.

It was Inush, my new master. He was a slim man and handsome in a fine-cut way, with black hair falling soft as feathers around his cheeks.

"You will get used to it here," he said, smiling down at me. He had the same clipped accent as all the other high-born men of the court.

"I can't see how," I said, looking up at him.

Inush looked around the yard. He cannot have failed to take in the ghastly din, the stench, and the general violence of the place.

"They're not animals, they're weapons," he said. "We can't keep them like the dogs up in the palace. We need them to bite men's throats out."

"And the legs of kennel boys, apparently."

Inush delved into his leather jerkin and brought out a palm-sized wooden pot. "Use this," he said. "It will help."

I caught the smell of him: perfumed, clean, everything fresh laundered, everything expensive.

"What is it?" I said, but I reached out and took the pot from him.

"You put it on. Dab it on your wrists, and neck, and ankles."

"Why?"

"All the men wear it. It's the kennel scent. The dogs will mostly leave you alone if you smell of it."

"How can that be?"

"By the gods," he said, "don't put it on then." He tapped his boot with his riding whip as he walked off.

It was a strange sort of clear-coloured grease in the pot, a medicinal smell when I put my nose close. I did daub some of it on. I did not go back over the wall, but in the jobs I did as I went about my day, the dogs were different to me; none of them growled or snapped at me through the fences.

I found out later that this was the scent that every soldier would daub themselves in before battle, to prevent mistakes when the killing started.

I thought, at the time, that that was kind of Inush. A day or two later, though, the kennel master called me to the nook he ate his meals in. He was a big man, with a huge snake tattooed all the way up his chest and around his neck; its jaws opened onto his left cheek.

"You're to go over to the big house," he said. "You're being moved in with the household slaves."

"Why?"

"You'll know why."

"What does that mean?"

"It means whatever Lord Inush wants it to mean," he said, without expression.

I did not want to show emotion before this man, but I felt I might burst into tears at any moment. "I will not go."

"You'll do as I tell you or you'll be flogged."

The memory of the god in Abydos, pointing his finger at me, came back to me so very clearly then. The heavy honey smell of him and the jingle of the silver bells stitched into his skirts as I followed him to his rooms.

"I will take the flogging," I said to the kennel master.

Biluda came to watch them whip me.

They took off my shirt and tied me by my hands to a post in the dog yard.

It was ten strikes only, but I knew from seeing it done so often that only one strike, done hard enough, could strip a man to the bone.

The kennel master took up the leather whip and I turned to face the post. I did not hear him moving and so the first strike seemed to come from nowhere. The pain was so terrible, so shocking, that I could not help but cry out. After that I kept on breathing, as steady as I could, as the man went about his savage work.

Afterwards Biluda came to the small storeroom they had locked me up in and put salve onto my wounds.

"Your back is a mess."

"I could feel him leaning into it."

"Why not just do as they asked?"

"I cannot."

"Marduk, you must."

"I doubt Inush will want me now, with my bad leg and ripped-up back."

"Marduk, they say you will be flogged every day until you agree to do as you are told."

"I cannot do it."

"You are being childish. Even a king must do things he dreads."

"I'm sorry, Biluda, but I cannot. I had it all in Abydos. I would rather die than go through it again."

"It will not be so bad," he said. "If he were cruel, I would know about it."

"And yet he has had me flogged for not going to his bed."

Biluda looked about the storeroom; at the piles of dog harnesses, leashes, and spiked collars. He lifted his hands at me, despairing.

"Marduk, you are going to die in this room. And there is nothing I can do to stop it."

CHAPTER NINE

GILGAMESH

On the road home to Uruk

On our second night in the marshes, the men built a simple reed shelter for Della and the baby, so that they would at least be out of the rain. I worried that a crocodile or leopard might make short work of the baby in the darkness, so the rest of us slept out in the wet, in a wide, protective circle around the shelter. I was so bitten and itchy that it took a while to fall asleep, but as I was finally drifting off, Harga prodded me hard in the ribs.

"Gilgamesh, you are snoring," he whispered.

I opened my eyes to a star-studded sky, the great arch of Heaven wheeling over me. The rain clouds had cleared, at least.

"How can I be snoring," I whispered, "when I am wide awake?"

"Well, you are making an awful noise. A sort of wheezing, clicking noise, like a dolphin dying on deck."

"I am doing no such thing."

"You will wake the baby."

"All right, all right." I turned onto my side, my back to Harga.

I found myself too annoyed to sleep.

"I must say, Harga," I said, turning over again to whisper at him, "you are never exactly cheerful, but you have been particularly foul this whole trip."

"During this trip beset by bad omens and Akkadian invaders, and now through deadly marshland?"

"You were foul even before the bad omens and the Akkadians and the marshes."

I turned back away from him, and tried to find my sleep again, although a mosquito was buzzing at me.

And then a thought occurred to me. I turned back to him.

"Is this about Ninshubar?"

"Be quiet," he hissed.

I had struck a nerve.

"I know you had moon eyes for her, Harga."

"Just leave it."

"I know you liked her."

Harga turned over to face me. "I told you to leave it."

"Old and ugly as you are, did you have hopes of her?"

He turned away from me and was silent.

My thoughts turned, gloomily, to Della, and her fury with me. I needed to find out what she liked, what her interests were. I need to charm her. It must be possible. After all, had I not charmed my fair share of women?

Then, unexpectedly, Harga turned back over beneath his cloak.

"I might have said something to her."

"What?" I said. "To Ninshubar?"

"If we'd had longer together, just as a plain man and a plain woman, before she took the *melam* and became a goddess, I might have spoken to her."

"What would you have said?"

"I don't know. But I might have said something. It had crossed my mind, more than once."

"I'm truly sorry for your disappointment, Harga. Although I cannot think she would ever have accepted you even when she was only a mortal woman and much criss-crossed with scars."

"True enough."

"I do not say it to hurt you. But everyone has their level. And you are very old and very ugly and also without any charm."

"Yes, thank you, Gilgamesh."

After a pause so long, I thought he had gone to sleep, he said: "She did speak to me though."

"What?"

"She spoke to me, of the two of us."

I sat up.

"In invitation?"

"Whisper!"

"Did she speak to you in invitation?"

"Yes, I think so."

"And what did you say?"

"That the divide between us was too great. She a goddess, me a mortal. Too wide a river separated us."

If it had not been night-time, with everyone asleep around us, I would have punched him.

"Then you are a fool, Harga," I hissed at him. "A stupid old fool. If you, a single man, with no ties and no prospects, are asked to go to bed with a woman like Ninshubar, you go to her bed. Divides! Oh, the divide is too great! The river is too wide! What nonsense! You have had your chance with her and thrown it away. All of my sympathy for you has evaporated.

You are a fool far worse than I have ever been."

I lay down, on my back, too genuinely outraged to feel anywhere close to sleep.

After a few long minutes, Harga whispered: "Gilgamesh?"

"What?"

"Please turn onto your side."

The next day I tried again with Della. I insisted on leading her horse, even if she wouldn't let me hold the boy. She had the baby on her breast as she rode, and now and again would look down at him and for a moment look more sad than angry.

It had stopped raining: that was something to celebrate. The frogs had started up their singing; another sign of better weather, according to the native marshmen in our squad.

"Is the baby dry at least?" I said, my head tipped up to Della.

"Yes." She didn't look down at me.

"Have you been to Uruk before?" I said, smiling up at her.

She seemed to consider not replying, but then, without turning to look down at me, said: "No."

"It's a wonderful city, the largest in the whole world. Fifty thousand people living in it and then there are farming villages for leagues around. And it's beautiful! The White Temple is like nothing you have ever seen. And there is an enormous canal that leads straight into the city from the Warka. That's what we call the river there, although really it's just a branch of the Euphrates. Anyway, it's the most beautiful stretch of river in the world."

"It is of no interest at all to me."

Harga, walking just ahead of us through the reeds, turned round to throw me a grin.

I ignored Harga and tried again. "They are getting my parents' palace ready for us. It's small, but very comfortable. There are fine views of the river from the upper apartments."

"I did not agree to this," Della said, looking straight ahead of her. "If we had not met as we did, under attack from Akkadia, I would not be here with you. It is my intention to return north to my father as soon as it is possible. And I will be taking my son with me."

"Oh," I said. The truth is that it had not occurred to me that Della might refuse to come to Uruk.

"Did you think all would be well between us?" She was looking at me now, a tight, false smile on her face.

"I suppose I thought we would try."

She made a sort of scoffing sound and then leaned down low in her saddle, to speak to me in something like privacy. "Gilgamesh, I am revolted by you. I will never touch a man who has lain with another man. I am disgusted by it."

I kept on walking, quiet while her words sunk in. "Perhaps we should talk when you've had time to rest."

"Do you deny it?" she said.

With some effort, I lifted my eyes to her. "No, I do not deny it. I have lain with a man. A woman too, since we were married."

"You say a woman, but I know it was the goddess Inanna you lay with. Whose city you are now taking me to. How do you think that is going to work, husband?"

I said nothing. What was there to say? I did not blame her for her anger. I did not blame her for any of her conduct. I had told her no harm would come to her, when I was whispering drunk into her ear, when I persuaded her to lie with me. But harm did come to her, or at least a baby she did not ask for, and a husband she could not bear to look at.

I turned from her and kept on walking, the reins tight gripped in my right hand, my eyes on the mules ahead of us.

I remembered Enkidu riding ahead of me, on our way to the village where he died. His sea-green eyes, as he turned round in his saddle to smile at me.

CHAPTER TEN

INANNA

In Eridu, Enki's city

E nki and I ate alone in his private rooms and the lunch
stretched into the evening. My lions lay so flat before the fire,
they might have been shot down by arrows.

My robe of pure azure was very thin against my skin and
Ninshubar had brushed my hair until it lay flat and glossy upon
my back.

"You look different," Enki said. "Older, I suppose. Is that cloth
from Kish?"

I only shrugged.

Slaves covered the table between us with plates of my favourite
foods. I ate steadily: salt-baked fish, fried okra, boiled greens,
spiced beans mashed with butter. I felt half-dead of hunger.

Enki looked closely at his food but did not put it to his mouth.

"I am glad you are here," he said.

I sipped at my glass of date wine.

Enki frowned into his own glass. "Does the wine not taste off
to you?" He was already not quite himself.

"Drink your wine." I smiled at him, to soften my words; I did not want him suspicious.

"If you say so," he said.

He drank his wine down, and I at once poured him more; he drank that down too.

"I like having you back," he said.

"I am glad to see the lions."

"Are you glad to see me?" He was looking hard at me, most intense.

"I was very frightened of you, when I lived here," I said, again with a soft smile, my dove face.

He nodded at that, frowning, and as he frowned, I pulled the line of invisible blue fire a little tighter and threw a second hoop around him.

He sat up straighter.

"I did miss you after you left," he said. "I wondered if it was right to give you to Dumuzi."

I nodded and kept eating.

"Was Dumuzi unkind to you?"

"Not especially."

"But you are angry with him?"

"I was angry with him. But now he is vanquished." Again, my dove face, lifted to him.

Enki sighed out. "Dumuzi did nothing I did not ask him to do. I should make sure he is freed from the underworld."

I helped myself to more of the bean mash.

"In temple they say the underworld is full up with the dead," I said.

"Ah, but you know better now." He gave me a catlike grin. "Now that you have seen the underworld, you understand that it is only a portal."

"Do I?"

"Yes. It is a pathway through to other realms. It's how we got here." He grinned again. "Neti is the only ghost down there."

"Why tell such lies, grandfather?"

He pushed away his plate. "Inanna, stories are all we have to protect ourselves with. And you know I did not just make everything up. I took what the people already believed in, and made it work for us."

"They say in temple that the Kur was a thunderbird. That you flew down from the sky upon its back."

"That story is ours." He laughed. "It's also true. Everyone saw the so-called thunderbird coming down. We had to work it into the stories."

I sipped just a little from my glass and watched Enki down his. I reached over to pour him more.

"Why was the Kur in the sky?" I said.

He drank down a full glass of wine. "When we left the Great Above, we were heading for a gate here on Earth. But we ended up on the Kur. A wrong turn. So then we were floating out there amidst the stars."

"But why was the Kur amidst the stars?"

He waved a lazy hand at that. "You will have to ask the creatures who built it."

"Who built it?" I realised I was leaning in to hear his story; I had forgotten for a moment why I was there. I sat back and put my hands in my lap.

"They say the Kur was built by the old gods, but what does that mean?" he said. "Everyone claims to have old gods. Inanna, your mother should have talked to you about all this."

"And yet she did not."

He laughed again. "She's a squeamish one, your mother. She's ashamed of her part in what happened here in the first days. It was the stories that established us as gods here, but I can tell you that brute force was also necessary."

He helped himself to more wine. "You know I have never felt at home here. I love it, but after all this time, it still does not feel real to me. You will never have that problem. This will always be your home. At least your mother has given you that. You will not be like me, a creature whose heart is split between realms."

"I heard the Great Above whispering to me, when I was in the underworld." I breathed in deep, as the memory of it shivered through me. "I saw something glistening in the darkness."

He looked up at me, thoughtful. "My mother believes they will come for us."

"Who will come?"

"Old friends, you could call them. The Anzu. Once our friends, now our enemies, after what my perfect brother did." He was shaking his head. "You know, I'm feeling strangely tired, Inanna. I think I need to lie down."

"Very well," I said. "I'm taking the lions to my bed tonight. From now on they stay with me."

I thought he might say something, but instead he only looked sad and strangely aged.

"Rest well, Inanna."

Isimud, Enki's *sukkal*, looked more like a wraith than a man as he walked ahead of me down the dark corridors. He was holding up a lantern for the both of us, and he turned every few steps to look at me.

"What are you doing?" he said.

"I am walking behind you."

"You know what I mean."

"I cannot be at war with my grandfather. I want a life of peace."

"I do wonder that you sent Dumuzi to the underworld, if it was peace you were looking for."

"I regret that."

"I am not at all sure that you do."

I returned to my bedchamber to find Ninshubar wrapped in a piece of white cloth; she smelt of roses and bathwater.

She scowled at the sight of my lions. "It is a small room to keep lions in."

"Ninshubar, they grew up in this room."

The lions at once leaped onto my narrow bed and stretched themselves out there.

Ninshubar stripped me of my azure dress and dumped it on the floor next to her cot, with no thought at all for the cloth.

"Is it done?" she said.

I sat down on the bed, naked, heavy with my strange exhaustion.

"He is open to suggestion," I said. "But it is not yet done."

I dreamed that I stood on the shore of a brilliant blue lake. The shores were lined with animals; hippos, lion, flamingos, gazelle, all stood together. All of them looking at me.

The water glowed with a strange and powerful energy. Blue light swirled and pulsed in its depths.

What would happen if I threw myself in?

∽

The next morning, as we were breakfasting upon the terraces below my rooms, Enki abruptly appeared. He looked strangely grey-skinned in the full light of the morning sun.

He stood silent for a while, watching me feed raw venison to the lions.

"Will you walk with me, Inanna?" he said at last.

"Yes," I said, standing at once, my lions rising to follow me. As I walked towards Enki, smiling, warm, I threw a third loop around him, but he seemed not to feel it.

At the door to our garden, he turned to me, putting out a hand to me, but then withdrawing it. He started to cry. "You will never forgive me."

"There is nothing to forgive." My dove face.

"What I mean is, you will never love me." His leopard eyes were very close to mine. "Did you always hate it, when I took you to bed?"

"I was terrified," I said. "How could I have enjoyed it?"

A muscle twitched in his jaw, as I held his eye.

"You might have enjoyed it," he said. "People enjoy different things."

For a moment, my anger overwhelmed me. "You are hateful," I said.

He lifted his hands to me in apology. "I did not think then of whether you liked it."

"I did not," I said. "No one could have. You are a monster."

He was about to answer me, but I stopped him. "The garden, Enki. We are going to the garden."

He at once dropped his hands, turned, and went to open the blue door for us. I sent a fourth loop of blue fire out as we walked through into the garden. He shivered just a little as I pulled it tight.

CHAPTER ELEVEN

MARDUK

In Kish, capital of Akkadia

I sat on the floor of the storeroom in the royal kennels. A tiny room with one small window, too high to get to; a heavy door that bolted from the outside. The walls were lined by large baskets stuffed with leashes, muzzles, and heavy collars.

My freshly flogged back was a wall of molten agony.

The time crawled past and all I could do was scold myself. I should have escaped from Kish long ago. I should have found my mother Ninshubar by now.

At last, with no warning, the door was flung open.

Prince Inuch, my new master, stood looking down at me, his mouth a flat line.

He wore a blue velvet robe and slippers with long, pointed toes, as if on his way to dinner.

"All this rather than come to my house?" he said.

"Yes," I said, looking up at him.

He glanced out into the corridor and then looked back down at me. "You don't have to come to the house. You can stay here in the kennels, I don't care. They were wrong to flog you without asking me first."

"Thank you, my lord."

"All this fuss because you thought I wanted you in my bedchamber. A man might be insulted."

We regarded each other for some moments in silence.

I said: "This man prefers to choose."

A little pink seeped into his cheeks. "I had only been thinking of you as a slave." He smiled. "Well, you have me there, Marduk."

He turned and left, but the door stayed open behind him.

I limped back out through the kennels, my back very sore indeed, my bitten leg more swollen than ever.

"So, you are staying," the kennel master said, looking up at me from his chair. I realised that his arms were spotted with dried blood.

My blood.

"You don't look good for much," he said.

"I would be happy to take the afternoon off, sir."

"If I'm stuck with you, I'm working you. That old dog whose pups died. Do you know the one I mean?"

They did not name the dogs at the kennels; they did not want us getting attached.

"I know which dog you mean."

He drew a heavy finger across the snake that wound up his neck.

"Go up and do the right thing for her. Then put her in with the meat for the morning feed."

"I heard she bit your leg," I said.

He put his left hand to his thigh. "Not badly, but she's no good for anything now. Too old to breed from, too old for war. Now get on with it, before I have to flog you for a second time in one day."

I made my way, very slowly, to the sheds to where they kept the dams with pups and those about to welp.

The last stall on the left looked empty at first, but then I saw her in the shadows at the back of the pen. She was crouched over, her head down, shaking. No straw in her stall; no water. No food. Just the earth, and puddles of her filth.

It was hard to see in the shadows, but she looked to have been beaten; her thick, brown fur was matted with blood.

She was grey around her snout.

"Hello, old girl," I said.

The dog turned her head, just a little, and rolled one almond eye at me.

When I was very young, I was sentenced to death, but Ninshubar stood up for me. She stepped out in front of the elders of her clan and said that she was adopting me. She risked everything she had for me. I looked down at the old dog and I remembered how I felt when Ninshubar saved my life that day.

"I won't hurt you," I said.

They don't let the dogs keep their tails in the kennels of King Akka; she had only a stump. But when I spoke to her, her stump thumped against the floor.

At first I moved as if in a dream. I fetched her a bowl of water and went straight into her stall with it, never considering she might hurt me. I went to the kitchen and took chunks of good red meat, diced for a stew, from beneath the fly nets in the cool room. I fed the meat, morsel by morsel, to the dog.

The old dog made no move to bite or growl at me. She nibbled each piece of meat from my hand as delicately as any royal lapdog.

I ran my fingers over her battered head and with each rub I gave her, her shaking eased.

"I will call you Moshkhussu," I said. "Like the monster. Because you are so frightening."

My mother taught me that if you are going to do something, it is better to do it quick.

As soon as Moshkhussu had finished her meat, I walked straight through the sheds to the storeroom where I had so recently been a prisoner. I took up a studded collar and short leash from the baskets there, and I walked straight back through the maze-like kennels to Moshkhussu. There I opened her stall, kneeled, and put the collar on her as if I done it a thousand times before. She gave me one warm lick as I tightened it around her throat.

Then I walked out of the kennels with her, my head high, as if I had been asked to take her somewhere; perhaps even to do the kind thing that I had been asked to do.

She was limping heavily, just as I was. She did not look fit to go far. But I said to her: "Moshkhussu, we are going. We are going to go out into the world and make our way together there." I said it quietly, and smiled at those I passed, just as I normally would have. The men we passed scowled at me, but no one tried to stop me.

It was dusk outside, and the air was thick with the smell of the stew that would soon be served for our dinner. By chance, the gates to the dog compound stood open, and with everyone looking another way, we went straight out through them and headed on to the main gates out of Inush's palace.

Those second gates also stood open; carts, stacked high with supplies, were about to come through. Moshkhussu and I squeezed ourselves past the carts, with a soldier only glancing at me and the dog. It was not so unusual, a slave being sent out between the various palaces and temple compounds.

And then we walked along the main road towards the gates that led out into the city.

Oh, what a very, very good girl Moshkhussu was. Walking along, on a tight leash, next to a stranger. Walking to a destination unknown. Yet she did everything she could to keep up with me.

The gates to the outer city were large, of aged oak, studded with bronze. There was a small wooden shelter off to the right of them. There two soldiers sat, both with bowls of food in hand.

"What's this?" one said.

"I'm taking out this dog. On the orders of Prince Inush."

The man put down his bowl. His friend did the same.

"Why would the prince want this dog taken out into the city?" the man said.

"She's a gift for a friend of his," I said. "They are going to fight her against a bear."

"A bear?" said the second soldier.

The first man stood up. "I don't think so."

He stepped out of his shelter with an arm out to me; I took a step back, pulling Moshkhussu with me.

Someone grabbed me by my arms from behind. I must have dropped Moshkhussu's leash; the next moment she had the first soldier's arm full in her mouth and was savaging him.

Then someone had a spear in her and I was down on the ground, a man on top of me.

⚭

This time I was put into a real prison cell, in the royal precinct's central barracks. In addition to my ripped-up back and damaged leg, I could now boast of a number of painful swellings and gashes.

"Where is the dog, please?" I called, time and time again.

No one answered.

Biluda came; I heard him begging for me. He was turned away.

And then Inush came.

He leaned against the doorway and frowned down at me on the floor of my dark and nasty cell.

"Twice in one day," he said. "First you refuse to obey a simple order and you are flogged. I choose to show you mercy. Half a day later and you are trying to break out of the city with a stolen dog at your heels. What a creature you are, Marduk."

"Is she dead?"

"The dog?"

"Yes, the dog."

"No. Missing. She bit several soldiers and ran off. I'm sure it won't take long to find her."

I pushed myself into a kneeling position, my hands held out before me. "My lord, I beg you not to kill her. She is a good dog. She has years of life in her."

Inush tapped at his left boot with his whip. "The king's men want you killed, never mind the dog. That is the matter at hand. This is not your first escape attempt."

"Please, my lord, I will do anything." I bent my head over my hands.

Inush shifted against the doorframe. "Marduk, she is old and unpredictable. She bit the kennel master. Now she has attacked a group of soldiers, thanks to you. And I am also told that you have no connection with this dog. That this was the first time you were asked to look after her. This is all a nonsense."

I put out my hands in supplication, my head still bowed. "I will do anything you ask, my lord, if you help me save her."

I lifted my eyes to him then, to make it clear what I meant.

"That's a bit dramatic." He sighed, tapping at his boot. "All so dramatic." He sighed again. "Biluda warned me that you were dramatic."

"Yes, my lord."

"What a gift you have, for behaving appallingly and then making everyone else believe that they are in the wrong. And all this now over some ancient dog."

"Moshkhussu, my lord."

"Are you telling me that because it is the dog's name?"

"Yes, my lord."

"The kennel men also want you strung up this time. They are done with you. So, what am I to do?"

"You could take me into your household staff, my lord. I am an excellent slave, my lord, ask anyone. I was wrong to make a fuss before. Also, I am a superb huntsman and tracker, as the king himself could tell you."

He laughed. "You made Biluda your servant. You twisted my aunt Hedda round your little finger. And now you attempt to negotiate with me!"

I stood up, careful not to cry out with the pain of it. I was a great deal taller than Inush. "I will come over to your household staff," I said, looking down on him, "but only if the dog comes too."

Inush laughed again. "Marduk, you are not in a position to bargain. I have not even agreed to you yourself coming over. Anyway, I doubt anyone can catch her. They have gone after her with spears."

A smile burst from me. "*I* can catch her!"

He tapped at his boot. "You really are impossible."

"Yes, my lord," I said, bowing my head again.

Inush gave out a great sigh. "It seems there is only one fool here today, Marduk, and that fool is me."

CHAPTER TWELVE

NINSHUBAR

In Eridu, Enki's city

I paced back and forth in Inanna's small set of rooms. I could see nothing from the shuttered window in the bedchamber except some clay-tile roofs and some sort of defensive wall. In the distance, the shimmer of marshland.

For some time I examined the painted birds on the walls. They had blue chests and enormous green tails, the feathers spread out like fans. I would ask Inanna about the birds if she ever returned from her lunch.

But then Inanna might be with Enki far into the night. Would it be such a bad thing to walk out a little in my old city and put my nose up to the wind?

I had a yearning to visit Dulma, the priestess who took me from the slave market and gave me safety when I was first brought to Eridu. It was in her temple, the Temple of the Waves, that I learned Sumerian and the ways of the Anunnaki. The temple was dedicated to the queen of the gods, Nammu, and since my time there, the golden-haired goddess had returned to Sumer as mysteriously as she had once disappeared from it, many generations before. I wanted to know what Dulma made of these great events. And I wanted to be sure she was safe, after my fall from favour with Enki and his henchman.

Also I needed to practise with my *mees*, weak and inadequate as they were. That I could not do in the cramped confines of Inanna's chambers.

The corridor in either direction was empty.

I turned right, that being the direction we had arrived from.

The walls of the corridor were covered with elaborate woollen hangings. The polished tile floor seemed to undulate beneath my feet.

At the end of the long corridor, Isimud, Enki's *sukkal*, stepped out to block my way.

He wore a bronze chest-plate and stood with his legs apart, his hands behind his back.

"You can stay there in your room, slave-girl," he said.

"Can I?"

Corridors led off to my left and right; both empty. He seemed to be alone.

I had my new stone axe slung over my back and I wondered what it might do if I swung it hard into his chest plate. It might knock the breath out of him. Or I could just aim for flesh and have the whole thing over quicker. But then I had no idea what the *mees* on his arms might to do to me.

I took a step closer to him.

I was taller and heavier than him, and perhaps he thought my own *mees* were worth something.

"I am going to visit my old temple. You are welcome to walk the way with me."

Close up, the whites of his eyes were yellow and his skin was dry and thin as ancient leather.

"You are not a real *sukkal*," he said. "You don't have the blood of the gods in you."

"A very short time ago, I had never heard of *sukkals*. So, it does not make much difference to me, whether or not I am a real one."

"I don't like this," he said. "I don't like any of it. He should not have let you in."

"Now I am going out." I made my way past him, each hand on a knife. I did not look back for his reaction.

I found my way out to the wooden gates of the palace, and then stood there looking up at the men in the watch tower, while they looked down at me.

"I am very happy to climb up and hurt you," I said, "if you are not happy to open the gate for me."

I pulled my stone axe from its sling and passed it from hand to hand.

They were all looking past me. Isimud had come out of the palace behind me and was standing at the top of the steps, frowning.

In the end he shrugged at the men and they opened the gates for me.

The smell of lamb grilling; the hubbub of carts and donkeys; women hanging out washing between the houses: the city felt like home to me.

I made my way, from old habit, to the slave market. The nasty sharp smell of it was so familiar; the smell of fear and unwashed skin.

I sat up on my wall there and looked at the face of each poor slave and then every slave trader, as I always used to. Had it been two years now, since I last saw my son?

Of course, my Potta was not there and I did not recognise the traders.

As I was about to climb down from my vantage point, I caught a glimpse of Isimud, watching me from the shadows of the archway that led into the market. I waved one hand at him, cheery, and he stepped back from sight.

Did it matter if he was following me? I decided not, since I had already told him where I was going.

I threaded my way through crowded streets to the Temple of the Waves. When I was a slave in Eridu, I was often stared at, being taller and darker skinned than most people in Sumer.

Now the people in the streets shrank back from me, their eyes turned away. I wondered if it was the *mees* on my arms that made them shy away or whether Isimud had spies tracking me through the crowds, and setting all nerves on edge.

At the edge of the city, near the ancient seawall, stood my old temple, its walls pressed with zigzag marks, its roof drooping with age. This was the Temple of the Waves, a humble-looking place, but dedicated to Nammu, the queen of the Anunnaki.

I had last glimpsed the temple when I lay on its steps, bleeding to death, in the days before I drank the *melam*, that gives the gods their long life.

I was simply standing there, smiling up at the clay-brick building, when Dulma came out of the doorway. She was unchanged, in her long black robes and headdress, and she lifted her hands to me as if we had seen each other only moments before.

"You look better than last time I saw you," she said.

"Thank you," I said, grinning up at her.

"You missed the goddess being here," she said. "Everything has happened, and you were not here to see it."

"Can I come in?"

"Yes, yes," she said. "The water is almost boiling."

I followed her through the clean-swept temple, past the gorgeous statue of the goddess Nammu, with her golden skin and aquamarine eyes, and out through the holy of holies, to the humble yard beyond.

There I got out all the tea things, while Dulma fussed over the fire and the water pot, and then we sat down together on our cushions beneath the trellis.

"I have had no one to protect me here," she said, "with you suddenly disappearing. I thought at first you had just run away, until I heard that Enki had taken you."

"I am sorry I was not here to protect you."

She leaned forward, her voice low. "We have gold now. Everything is different. We get crowds now, for the rites. A temple with a live goddess always does better."

I looked about at the dirt yard, the humble sleeping cells, the crumbling outer walls, and the temple's rolling roof, and saw no evidence of new income.

"I am saving up to have the roof fixed," Dulma said, following my eyes. She was not a woman for questions, but then she said: "They gave you the *melam*?"

"They saved my life with it."

She nodded, her mouth turned down. "How does it feel?"

"I'm stronger. I heal better."

"I'm glad for it, Ninshubar."

"So," I said. "What was it like? To wait all your life to see the goddess, with no real hope of her ever returning here, and then suddenly she walks out of the sea and is returned!"

Dulma poured out two cups of mountain tea.

"The goddess gave a lot of orders."

"Ah," I said, blowing on my tea.

"She was not here long. But we are still getting the crowds."

"Where is Nammu now?"

Dulma shook her head at that, frowning. "She left not long after you were here. She did not say where she was going."

I could see she had more to say.

"Where do you think she went?" I said.

Dulma swayed her head from side to side. "There are things I cannot tell you, Ninshubar. Even now that you have the *melam* in your veins. Temple secrets, that I am sworn to keep." She put one hand out and touched the Anunnaki weapons on my arms, very cautious.

"I always knew you were someone," she said. "Even standing there in the market, with your hands behind you. Even with those bad men pushing you forward. I saw you were someone."

"Thank you, Dulma. For rescuing me and for all your patience with me when I was new here."

She was still sucking over something.

"Ninshubar, I cannot tell you what Nammu is doing. But I can talk to you of something else."

I put my cup out for more tea.

"The Anunnaki are not the only gods," she said. "First there were the old gods. Everyone knows about them. But they are all dead now. Now we have the Anunnaki, here on Earth. But in other realms, there are other kinds of gods."

"We had the old gods, in my home country."

She tipped her head from one side to the other, in polite disagreement. "Have you heard of the Anzu?"

I shook my head.

"Perhaps you have seen their totem? A lion-headed eagle. You see it in some of the old temples. There are things the Anzu want from this world and one of them is that goddess you follow."

"Inanna?"

She nodded, solemn. "Do not leave her side, Ninshubar."

I put down my cup. "You think she is in danger? And not only from Enki?"

"I do."

"Dulma, I will take your warning seriously and go straight back to the palace."

She began to clear away the cups. "You know Isimud is taking things from the treasury?" she said. She lifted her nose to the wall that protected the temple from the sea. "Look for yourself."

I sprung to my feet and crossed to the seawall. I climbed up carefully, placing my hands with thought on each crumbling brick. I kept my head low as I looked over.

A gust of salt air; the glittering sea. On the narrow beach, a boat was pulled up and men were loading metal crates into it.

I dropped down and turned back to Dulma. "He looks to be taking something out of the city."

"He doesn't trust Inanna," she said. "They say he is stealing valuable weapons from the treasury, but he does not want Enki to know."

I stooped to catch up one of her thin hands in mine; and kissed it. "Thank you."

"Do not forget what I said to you. Keep your eye on the small goddess."

"Dulma, do not fear on that account." I smiled at what I was about to say. "You have my sacred promise as a goddess. I will never leave Inanna's side."

"The promise of a goddess," she echoed. "I hope you can keep it."

CHAPTER THIRTEEN

ERESHKIGAL

In the underworld

A*ll my babies*

Tears rolled down my cheeks and onto my clay tablet.

I had been thinking about Ninlil's lost baby, the one that got left behind in Heaven. It had brought back all the memories of my own.

I think the last one would have lived if

My tears were puddling upon my ebony desk.

Namtar was at my elbow and he coughed gently. "You should not..." he said. "You do not have to..."

"Yes?"

"My queen, this is your history to tell. It is your choice what to put in and what may be left out."

I wiped my eyes. "Someone must tell their story. They only live in my mind now and when I am gone, they will be lost."

He squeezed my arm, his fox ears twitching. "You are the Queen of the Night. You will live on through the ages. Of that I am certain, my lady." He looked me in the eye as he said it.

"I am not going to fall into my pit again. That is all in my past. I am only wanting to write down what is true, so that it is not forgotten. I will not go back to the dark dreams. You do not need to fret over me."

"I know you will not sink again," he said, his yellow eyes turned from mine.

There was something on my lap. Was it bread? No, it was something like plaster. I frowned up at the ceiling and then down at the stone floor. Huge patches of the ceiling had fallen down. I had ceiling plaster on my lap.

Namtar was still standing over me.

"What is it, Namtar?"

"I'm very sorry to bring this news to you," he said. "But we have another visitor."

"No!"

"I'm afraid so, my queen."

"Through the eighth gate?"

"No, my lady, a visitor from the realm of light. She is trying to get into the Kur."

"Just tell me, Namtar."

He bent very low to deliver the news. "My queen, it is Nammu, your great-grandmother, queen of all the Anunnaki."

I stood up, slowly, the dust of the dead falling hard and heavy about me. "She was here before, a long time ago."

"She wanted you to leave the underworld," he said. "But this time she is here for the dark stranger and she is trying to blast her way in through the first gate. Have you noticed the earthquakes this past hour?"

I looked down at the crumbled plaster on my skirts. "I did not notice them."

Namtar slowly stood up. "Also the gatekeeper, Neti, demands to see you most urgently. He says Nammu is going to damage the Kur irreparably if nothing is done. He was very angry indeed that I would not fetch you at once, but I knew you were deep in your history."

"I don't like it when things are urgent." I said, my eyes full of tears. "I don't like talk of being 'fetched'."

"You have always hated to have things thrust upon you. The gatekeeper knows that."

"I don't want to see him."

"My lady, of course."

However, he continued to hover before me.

I looked about me in the gloom; at the piles of rubble that lay even upon my bed. I wiped my tears onto my sleeves. "There is always so much to do! How can I write my history and look after my guests, if I am always having to worry about damage and more guests and messages from the gatekeeper?"

Yet Namtar continued to stand before me, his ears back against his scalp.

"Also, my lady," he said, bowing again, "the dark stranger, who calls himself Erra, is asking every day to make his case, since you sent him to his rooms."

"He should not have been so rude to me."

"Indeed, my queen."

For so many years I had been left alone with my demons, with no demands on my time except my own. Now I was being hit from this side and that by all the problems that were being thrown at me!

A decision came to me; a bright light in the gloom of my mind. "Namtar, I will sit in audience. I will hear all these messages and applications. I will do it all at once. I will put on my good furs. Let the little ones know."

"A full audience?"

"Yes, a full audience."

"May I tell the demon suppliants, my lady, that will you see them too?"

"I will see them too. Yes, it is too long since I have sat in state."

"My lady, we do not deserve you," Namtar said. He had a tear in the corner of each lizard eye. I stood, and kissed him on each ear, the fur warm against my mouth.

"I will not let anything bad happen to you," I said. "That is the promise of a goddess." I kissed him again, this time on his soft snout.

The Black Temple had never looked more glorious. It was not a day to worry about candles and everything was brightly lit.

When I had settled myself on my blackthorn throne, Neti, the ancient gatekeeper, appeared abruptly, from empty air, at the far end of the temple. He came forward along the great colonnade with his hands behind his back. He wore the plain blue suit that he always wore inside the Kur and the dust fell straight through it as he walked.

At the steps to my throne, Neti bowed his head very slightly to me, but then looked around him at my demons and my two visitors in a rather superior manner.

"Lady Ereshkigal," the gatekeeper said. "You are looking better. Sleeker. Transformed, really."

"Take a seat, gatekeeper. You are not the only suppliant here today."

Neti paused a moment, looking up at me hard from beneath

his neat eyebrows, but then he went meekly enough to take a seat in the pews.

Namtar came up the steps to my throne. Together we looked over the clay tablet that he held before him, and then, when we were satisfied with our decision, he called out: "The thing about the mittens."

A young demoness approached my throne, bowing almost double as she walked. She had ears like a cat, but the body of an otter and neat little human hands.

"Great queen," she said, her voice soft and timid. "Someone has stolen my woollen mittens and I know who has done it, but she will not give them back."

At this Neti crossed his legs, and then recrossed them. My two visitors rolled their eyes at each other.

"Let us hear the evidence," I said, casting a dark look upon my visitors, and a very kind look upon the mitten demon. "Leave out no detail," I said to her. "There is nothing worse than thievery."

The young demoness cast a nervous glance at Neti.

"Do not look at the gatekeeper," I said. "You need not fear his temper here." I scowled most viciously at Neti. "I am sure he would also like to know who has stolen your mittens. Start right at the beginning."

After the case about the mittens, there came a young demon who had lost the chance to work in my kitchens because of a curse put on him by another demon. The young demon had the long and awkward legs of a fawn; how my heart went out to him! This case too we heard in detail, while the dark stranger pressed his forefingers to his temples, and Neti crossed his legs, and sighed, and then crossed his legs back again. Dumuzi took something from his jacket and began nibbling at it.

"Why do this just to enrage me?" Neti called out. "Why be so difficult, Ereshkigal?"

"You may call me Queen Ereshkigal," I said to Neti, and for the impudence of him calling out, I then called up a young dresser demon. "I'm told you would like to report the wasting of candles?"

"Yes, my queen," she said, round eyed. "A terrible wasting!"

Finally, after two more cases, and further whispering with Namtar, I said: "Gatekeeper, you may approach."

Neti leaped up and came forward to the steps of my throne. "Ereshkigal, I have been trying to warn you, for some time now, that you have another Anunnaki banging on your gates."

"Do I?"

"Nammu, queen of the Anunnaki, is damaging the Kur in her efforts to get in. And you, Madam," he added with real venom, "have endangered the Kur, by refusing to see me without delay."

"How very rudely you speak to me, Neti."

"Madam, I guard the gates and the gates are under attack. I am impelled to inform you of it. And so here I am. I am not impelled to guard my tone with you when you ignore requests for an immediate audience and damage the Kur as a result. My duty in the end, Madam, is to the Kur and not to you."

I tipped my nose into the air. "I would watch my tone, Neti, with a person who knows so much about you."

Neti paused for a few moments, as if frozen. "I do not mean to be disrespectful, my queen, but Nammu is causing damage."

Dumuzi gave out an elaborate sigh. "Neti, she knows full well that Nammu is outside the gates. And we all know the damage Nammu is doing. The whole of this city shakes as she batters at the gates. What is the point of telling Ereshkigal what she already knows?"

I scowled at Dumuzi, and then turned back to the gatekeeper: "Neti, you may consider me warned. Now sit down."

The gatekeeper, his mouth tight, returned to his pew.

"So, who is next?" I said to Namtar.

My priest-demon made some show of running a finger down the clay tablet, his ears twitching at each new name. "My lady, it is the dark stranger, who says his name is Erra."

"Very well, I said. "You may come forward, you who call yourself Erra."

Erra stood and slowly approached, looking me in the eye. He was a big man, and his eyes were almost on a level with mine, even with me sat up on my throne. I watched how the black scales of his armour seemed to slide around as he moved, moulding to his movement; how sometimes they seemed to open, and briefly flutter, especially around his neck.

Erra got down upon his knees in a slow and steady manner, all the while keeping my eye.

"Speak then," I said. "You who say you are Erra."

"Why not just call me Erra?" he said. "Since it is my name."

"How do I know it is your name?" I said. "How can we be sure that anything you say is true? You wear our marks upon your cloak, but what does that mean?" I breathed in deeply to calm myself. "I do not remember meeting any Erra when I lived in Heaven. I cannot know who you really are."

"But you have heard of me," the dark stranger said, from his place at the foot of the steps. "You know I am family."

"Make your case," I said to him.

He bowed his head. "Madam, as you know, I claim you as a cousin."

"And what of it? I have many cousins. Dumuzi is my cousin."

"Madam, when the Anunnaki fled to this realm, we who were

left behind were forced to spend centuries in hiding. But now I have begun to rebuild our house and I bring with me a peace treaty that could allow you all to return with me. I only ask that you let me pass through onto the Earth, so that I may be able to deliver my message to your family."

"And the lords of Creation have allowed you to pass through to this realm?"

He sighed heavily. "They have."

"And why is Nammu here?"

"She is the one who helped guide me to this realm."

I looked over at the gatekeeper. "What do you think, Neti? Should I let this stranger out into the world?"

The gatekeeper shrugged. "It makes no difference to the Kur whether this stranger is here or in the world of light. But he must not be allowed to reopen the gate to Heaven with the Kur where it is. The Kur has already been badly damaged. That is the thing that matters."

I looked back at the dark stranger. "Well anyway I have no power over any of the gates," I said, lifting my hands to him.

Neti crossed his legs again and the dark stranger looked down at the steps of the throne, his face set hard.

I rubbed at the plaster dust on my skirts. "I don't know what to think any more, when anyone can just walk into the underworld and no one can be safe here and even my gatekeeper cannot be relied upon."

Neti leaped back onto his feet. "Ereshkigal, I have barred your family from this place for a hundred years, on your exact orders. I even kept Nammu out when your time here was over, and still you refused to leave. Dumuzi, I let in at your specific request, and this other creature came in through a different gate, that I have no control over, as I think you well know."

"And you let my sister in!" I screamed out. "And then you let Enki's flies in! And Namtar says they fiddled with things!" My whole body was shaking. "I don't know what to think about all this, but I am still very, very angry with you, Neti!"

Neti sat back down. "Madam, Nammu is going to keep on knocking."

"I am beset on all sides," I said.

"She would leave you alone if you let Erra out," Dumuzi said, from his pew. "She is only here for him."

"What are your instructions, Ereshkigal?" Neti said. "Am I to keep on ignoring Nammu?"

"Yes! What else would you have me do?"

"Very well," he said, and disappeared.

"How rude he is to me!" I burst out.

Namtar climbed up the steps to me. "He only cares about the Kur," he said. "He does not care about us."

"I have had enough!" I said, half sobbing, half shouting, the noise bursting out of me, and scaring the little demons in the front. "Enough of everyone bullying me!"

Dumuzi came and sat by my bed while I sobbed. He had never been in my bedchamber before. He looked about him with interest at my writing desk, and all the little beds for my dresser demons, lined up along the walls, and at all the treasures from the Kur that I had arranged on shelves behind my bed.

"What are all these things?" he said. "Are some of them *mees*?"

"They are none of your business."

"Oh, Ereshkigal," he said, stretching out his legs. "I don't see what you're so upset about. Why do you always get so upset?"

"I am not upset," I said, into my wet pillow.

"You knew perfectly well that Nammu was outside the gates. You know perfectly well that she is here to make sure Erra is released. You know they are conspirators. You always know everything and pretend to know nothing. Presumably that amuses you. But I do not see why it makes you cry. I find all the crying very tiring and it makes the dust fall so heavily. I cannot see why you go on with it."

I pulled myself up in bed and wiped my hair back from my face. "I very rarely cry."

He rolled his eyes. "I do wonder what your real view on this is."

I ignored that. "What does he say to you, the dark stranger?"

"Only what he says to you. He knows I can't help him. He's not interested in me."

"Do you believe it? That the lords of Creation have agreed to a peace treaty?"

"Of course not."

"I believe him exactly," I said.

Dumuzi sat forward in his chair. "Ereshkigal, have you ever said one single thing to me that was not a lie?"

"I never lie."

"Ah," he said, and sat back in the chair, his hands raised.

I looked over at him. He did look quite delicious to me.

"You could get into bed with me," I said. "You do it to me in temple. Why not do it to me here, while we talk?"

"Ereshkigal, I mind you a great deal less than I thought I would, but there is a difference between temple and lying together in private."

"I'm not sure there is," I said. A dresser demon jumped onto the bed next to me and began rubbing her cheek, very comforting, against my right hand.

"You are going to weep again, I can tell," said Dumuzi.

"I never weep." I wiped at my face.

"I will lie with you here in private, if you agree to let my sister Geshtinanna in. She is sat out there in Neti's hut. What harm can it do to let her in?"

I stopped crying. "Everyone always wants something from me. I am sick of everyone wanting something from me."

"Oh, never mind," he said, and got up and left.

When he had gone, my back and my hips began hurting again, but I got myself out of bed, and let my demons wrap me in my furs. I sat back down at my desk.

Ninlil's baby was snatched away from its cradle in the chaos of our departure, and afterwards the loss of this baby drove the little girl Ninlil mad.

Ninlil's parents were servants. At some farm in Creation, the heartlands of the Anzu empire. What were the names of Ninlil's parents? I could not remember.

Namtar appeared at the doorway, a mug of warm demon milk in his hands.

"Why do you look so thoughtful, beautiful queen?" He put the warm milk down next to my clay tablet.

"I was thinking of Ninlil's baby." I began to cry again.

"And it made you think of your own babies."

I nodded and mopped at my tears. "Perhaps Erra's story is true. Perhaps he really has rebuilt our house on the other side. I do remember my parents talking of him."

"But the whispers, my lady."

"What whispers?"

"The whispers in the darkness, that I think you hear too, my lady."

I turned my head to him. "I only heard the voices when I was very ill," I said. "The voices were not real, and I do not want you talking of them."

"My beloved queen, you must forgive me for pressing this, but the voices whisper of a lord of chaos. What if Erra is that creature?"

"Oh, I know," I said. "I know." I put my hands over my eyes.

"Now come, my lady, it is time you slept."

As he helped me stand, the floor beneath us began to shake and I found myself clinging on to him.

"It is getting worse, my queen," he said. "The city is becoming unstable."

"She is very wrong to damage the city so."

"I will get the cleaners in here," he said. "There is rubble upon your bed."

In the morning I woke to find my bed shaking again and the air thick with plaster dust.

Namtar came rushing in.

"Are you well, my queen?"

"Let her in," I said. "Let Nammu in."

CHAPTER FOURTEEN

INANNA

In Eridu, Enki's city

E nki and I spent all day together, often not speaking. We petted my lions and we drank wine, beer, and a fiery aniseed spirit. I found that with just a little effort my master *mee* kept my head very clear.

In the evening, Isimud, uninvited, came to look at us. Enki and I were sitting together in front of the fire in the main audience chamber. We each had a glass of beer in hand, and our feet on a sleeping lion.

Isimud looked very unhappy. "My lord, is all well?"

"All is well," Enki said.

Isimud put his right hand to his sword. "You do not seem yourself, my lord."

"I thank you for your attention," said Enki, "but you can leave us now."

Isimud stood there for a moment, looking at Enki and me, and the jug of beer on the table between us. Finally, he bowed and left.

"Prove your love to me," I said, turning back to Enki. "Give me one of your *mees*."

"Which one?"

"This one." I pointed at a golden cuff on one of his wrists. "And this one," I said, pointing at its twin.

He took the *mees* off and put them on my right arm, pushing each up above my elbow. "They kill, this pair. Be careful with them."

A surge of energy travelled up my right arm. It was immediately obvious to me what these weapons could do and how I might work them by force of will alone.

"I still don't love you," I said. "But I will think about what you have said. Now I'm going to bed."

Isimud looked at me with deep suspicion as he walked me back to my rooms.

"What are you doing with those *mees*?"

"My grandfather gave them to me. Perhaps he feels guilty for what you and he have done to me."

"He's Anunnaki. He can do just as he chooses."

"Am I not Anunnaki, too?"

"It's not the same."

"No?"

"He is an ancient warlord of great power and huge intellect."

"And I am nothing."

"That's exactly right."

Ninshubar was dressed and fully armed when I arrived back at our rooms.

"Isimud is moving things," she said, as soon as the door was closed behind me. "If we delay, there may be nothing left to take from the treasury."

I sat on the bed, my limbs limp. "I have these for you," I said, passing my new golden *mees* to her.

She pushed one up onto each of her wrists. They looked very fine, shining out against her skin. "What do they do?" A moment later, she said: "Oh."

"What?"

"I feel the difference. I feel the power. I think they are weapons of combat."

"They are."

I lay down on my bed.

"They kill mortals," I said. "I don't know what they do to gods."

"They feel so much stronger than Dumuzi's *mees*." She was frowning down at them. "There is life surging through them. But I must practise. I will stay up all night and practise."

"Good," I said.

"What if the treasury is empty when we get to it?"

"Then it's empty," I said. "And we will have to come up with a new plan."

In the morning, as Ninshubar and I were dressing, there was a knock at the door and in came Enki, without explanation.

He sat down, uninvited, upon my unmade bed.

Isimud appeared in the doorway behind him, his sword in his hand.

"My lord, she is bewitching you," he said. "This is not right."

Enki waved a hand at him. "Leave me here."

Isimud looked from me to Ninshubar, and back again.

"Run along, Isimud," I said. "Your master does not want you here."

Isimud at once turned and went, and Ninshubar shut the door behind him.

"We need to hurry," she said.

Enki lay down, pressing his face into my pillow. He no longer seemed concerned by what was happening around him.

My lions moved to lie either side of him, nudging at his face, smelling at his ears.

"I am dying of love," he whispered to them.

I sat down next to his feet and looked up at Ninshubar.

"The master *mee* gives me control of all his *mees*, but I need to do more than that. I need to capture his *melam* too. It is not quite done."

"Time is not with us," she said. "I'll pack."

I moved up to sit by Enki's head.

He opened his eyes and smiled up me. "So that's the master *mee* you are wearing."

"Yes."

"He's a tricky one, my father. He convinced us all the master *mee* was lost on the way down here."

"It is a lot of power for one person," I said. "It might have tipped the balance against him if someone like you got hold of it."

"It's very old, you know. An ancient artefact. Much older than the other *mees*."

"I feel how old it is."

"Enlil stole it, you know, when he stole the little girl. He took both and ran."

"I did not know that."

"We could never understand how he came to have the *mee*." He shut his eyes. "Anyway, my father said it was lost, and I believed it would never be found, but my mother never gave up looking for it. She always knew it would be important. That in any final battle, we must be the ones to have it."

"Well, here it us upon my wrist, quite safe."

"I did not recognise it before. It used to have a gold casing and red letters painted on it. But that's the master *mee*."

"An pushed it onto my wrist when I was still in my cradle."

Enki opened his leopard eyes. "It's the strangest thing, to no longer have control of one's feelings."

Ninshubar, axe in hand, was hovering over us.

"I love you, Inanna," Enki said. He seemed only half conscious and I shut my eyes, for a moment, and looped more blue fire round him, round and round, trussing him from head to foot. A final strand of tension within him was abruptly gone.

"It's done," I said, standing up.

"Just like that?" said Ninshubar.

"Yes."

"Then let's go," Ninshubar said, shouldering her pack. She came over to pull Enki off my bed.

I put on my slippers and my cloak, but everything else seemed to have been packed away. "I am ready, Ninshubar."

Enki allowed Ninshubar to pull him up.

"I'm worried Inanna will not forgive me," he said to her. "She's never going to love me." He put his head against Ninshubar's shoulder. "I will do anything to make her love me."

I came to stand beside them, a hand on Enki's arm.

"Grandfather, give me everything and I will forgive you. We will live in peace. That is my sacred promise to you."

"Do you mean it?" he said. Tears rolled down his face. "I will gladly give you everything."

I made him start with the *mees* he had on his arms. Ninshubar stripped herself of Dumuzi's old *mees*, throwing them down on my bed, and pushed on all of Enki's.

"This is power," she said. "These are strong."

We set out to the palace treasury, Enki leaning heavily on Ninshubar, the lions roving ahead of us. We glimpsed servants disappearing into rooms, but no one came to challenge us. Every few steps, a bright purple shimmer appeared around Ninshubar and then instantly snapped away again. "I am practising," she said. "It is a protective shield."

Enki led us up four flights of stairs to the top floor of the palace and then along a corridor to two great cedar doors. A pack of soldiers, all looking nervous, came forward to block our path.

Enki put a hand out to the first of the men. "I need all of you to help me," he said. He smiled around at them. "Open the doors."

One of them was going to say something. But he looked hard at us and then drew the bronze bolts.

Inside lay a warren of rooms, piled high with treasures from across the world. Enki led us past the gold and jewels into a room stacked with grey metal chests.

"I think Isimud has been taking things," Enki said, looking about at the dusty spaces between the crates.

I sat down heavily upon a metal chest. "We must make do with what is left."

The soldiers clustered in the doorway, looking on nervously.

Enki sat down next to me on my box. "Inanna, you should stay close to me. Isimud might try to hurt you. He has taken all the big weapons."

Ninshubar waved the soldiers forward. "We're going to take everything in this room and put it on the Barge of Heaven. That is what our lord god Enki is asking of you."

"Yes," Enki said, lifting his head. "We'll need rowers, too, for the barge. We must gather men to us as we go. We'll need sixty men at least, to move the barge. A hundred would be better."

As the men set to with the stripping of the treasury, Enki reached out for my left hand. "Are you well, Inanna?"

I could have fallen asleep where I sat. "The master *mee* is draining me."

"You should be careful of this weapon." He pressed his mouth to my *mee*. "It was not designed for the likes of us. They say you never really recover from it."

"How do you mean?"

"It's bad for the victim, but also for the one who wields it. The effects wear off quickly. But we may both be left with scars. I think you can already feel what I mean."

"I cannot," I said, shifting away from him. But of course, I did feel it. A pull towards him, that should not have been there.

"Not long now," Ninshubar called over. "Stay strong, Inanna."

We made our way to the docks through an empty city. A strange procession of gods, lions, and soldiers, each man carrying a crate from the treasury.

The streets were empty, the windows above dark and silent. I found I could barely lift my feet. I walked with my right hand upon Enki's arm and my left upon Ninshubar's.

Ninshubar's purple shield burned bright around the three of us.

"As soon as we are gone, he will come to himself," I said to Ninshubar. "Then they will come after us."

"I am coming with you, Inanna," Enki put in. "I will not leave your side now."

Ninshubar dipped her head to me. "Inanna, while he lives, he is a threat."

"I know," I said. "But what we are doing is enough."

Enki laughed. "Inanna won't kill me now."

Ninshubar frowned over at him, and then lowered her voice to me. "Let's take him with us then. They cannot attack us with him on the ship."

Enki's arm was so hot beneath my hand. His leopard eyes glittered down at me.

"He stays," I said, taking my hand from him. "He lives. I'm sorry, Ninshubar, but that's what it must be."

The royal docks lay in the lee of a sandstone island, protected from the estuary and its weather. The Barge of Heaven, with its three huge masts, cedar decks and gold-foiled rails, sat in solitary splendour there, tied up to the long, marble wharf.

"It was my idea to build it," Enki said, as we climbed down the steps to the quay. "A ship worthy of the gods."

Only when we were right down on the wharf did we see the squad of soldiers waiting for us with their swords drawn.

Enki was very helpful; he did not need to be told what to do. "All of you men are with us now," he said. "Help load the ship and then you will all be rowers."

The men looked at Enki, standing in the bubble of Ninshubar's shield, and at once went to work for us, carrying the chests full of *mees* onto the ship.

I sank down onto the hot marble of the wharf. My lions and Enki sat down with me, and then Enki lay down with his heavy head in my lap.

"I will never be happier," Enki said, turning his face up to mine.

"Promise me again you will forgive me."

"I've made my promise."

He looked very beautiful to me, although I knew it was the *mee* meddling with my mind.

"I always wondered if my brother was really to blame for what happened to Ninlil, or if one of the Anzu arranged it for reasons of their own," he said. "They stood to gain a great deal from us fleeing our kingdom."

I shut my eyes, and for a moment had the clearest vision possible of Nammu, queen of the gods, standing before the Kur.

"Is your mother at the Kur?" I said to Enki.

He gave a shrug against my legs, his leopard eyes on mine. "She is obsessed by the Anzu and trying to make a peace with them. She wants us all to go back home to Heaven."

"Is that what you want too?"

"For a long time, yes, I wanted to go home. But I know now it was a foolish dream. There can never be a place for us there. This is my home now."

I felt the draw of Isimud, above us. I looked up and caught sight of him on the top of the cliffs behind the docks. He had his personal guard ranged out behind him.

"Inanna, enough," he called down to me.

"Come closer," I shouted back.

He took a step backwards.

"I would like Isimud's *mees* too," I said to Enki, my hands in his thick bronze hair.

"Oh yes," said Enki, "of course you must have them." But he took time to get to his feet, disorientated, and by the time he was up, Isimud and the soldiers had disappeared.

"Inanna, we need to go," Ninshubar said. "Quickly."

Enki helped pull me up off the marble wharf.

"I am coming with you," he said.

"No," I said. "I want you to stay here for me. That is what you must do for me."

"I will do it then," he said, "although it breaks my heart." He leaned over and kissed the lions. "I will miss you both," he said to them, his eyes full of tears.

We were quickly underway, very quiet, just the dip and drips of the oars and the grunts of Enki's soldiers, rowing in armour that was not meant to be rowed in. I threw a thin line of invisible blue around them and watched as they began to row a little harder.

Enki stood on the wharf with one hand raised to me.

"I will be back," I called to him.

"I will stand here until you return!" he called back. "I will not move from this exact place!"

He was still standing there as we pulled out into the main body of the river.

I let my blue ropes slip from him. Ninshubar let her shield fade and disappear.

"Best we go fast," I said to her, "before his eternal love begins to fade."

PART 2

"Enlil said to her:
'I want to kiss you.'
Ninlil said to Enlil:
'But my lips are too young.
They do not yet know kissing.'"

From the ancient Sumerian poem
known as "Enlil and Ninlil"

CHAPTER ONE

NINLIL

In the wilds of northern Sumer

I am painted on the walls in every Anunnaki temple. I am there in all their stories.

What everyone forgets, is that I am not an Anunnaki.

My family have a different name.

We call ourselves the Anzu.

My kidnappers took turns to carry me over their saddles. Copper armour and black curling beards: Akkadians. A squad of eight soldiers, all seasoned men, all stinking of sour sweat.

Having snatched me from my bed in the dead of night, they were now trying to be kind to me. They wrapped blankets around me before lifting me up onto their mules and put a leather coat over me when it hailed. They untied me when I needed to relieve myself. They offered me food and water at every stop.

But I could not stop making the noise.

Since the moment of my capture, I had been letting out a scream like a pig makes at slaughter.

Carried through corridors, bundled on to a mule, and now, day after day, I kept on making the noise. I did not choose to start doing it and now it seemed it would never stop.

Day and night, the terrible scream, surging out of me. You would have thought my throat would be torn apart by the effort of it, but I found the more I screamed, the better I was able to do it.

Once we took shelter from heavy hail beneath a giant ash tree. The captain of my kidnappers kneeled in front of me on the damp forest floor. He took off his copper helmet.

"Lady Ninlil, you have to stop it," he said, his voice raised over my screaming. "Please. You are driving all of us mad."

But I could not stop the noise.

Until the moment of my kidnap, I had been at anchor. Unhappy, warped, but chained safe. Now my anchor was dragging along the sea floor, and I could not control what was coming out of me.

"Madam, you do not need to be scared of us," the captain said. "We will not hurt you."

But I could not stop the scream.

The captain looked up at his comrades. "Let's gag her then. It might help a bit."

That night, lying trussed hand and foot, screaming into my gag, I thought: *I cannot survive this.*

That was when I stopped breathing.

My breath, my heart, my blood: everything stilled. Had I made it happen?

At last the scream stopped coming out of me.

The rain fell onto my skin and the balls of my eyes, and I lay completely motionless, looking up into the darkness.

My husband Enlil had said to me that nothing bad would ever happen to me again. He said I would always be safe. But it was all happening again.

Now ancient memories nudged at the edges of my mind.

I had thought I could not remember what happened to me on the day that Enlil attacked me. I had thought I could only remember the journey, afterwards, to the lands of the Anunnaki.

Now I could see that the memories were there, somewhere deep inside me. The screaming came straight from them.

Lying there so very still, I tried to imagine the memories locked up in a small, wooden box deep inside me. Locked up, safe, where they could not again hurt me.

A warm stream of relief seeped into me. When I felt strong enough, I could choose whether to look into the box, but until then, the memories would be locked away and I would be safe from them. There was no need to scream.

When the soldiers of Akkadia woke up that morning, the captain, while he was still in his bedroll, said: "By all the gods, she's finally stopped!"

They came to stand over me. They looked younger with their armour off.

"She's not breathing," the captain said.

He snatched me up, wrenched off my gag, and slapped my cheeks.

Then all of them were pawing at me, blowing into my mouth, beating at my chest. They broke two of my ribs. They pinched me and slapped me, over and over.

When they had done all they thought could be done, I lay, lifeless, in the captain's arms. No breath, no heartbeat, my eyes open, unblinking, looking straight at him.

"We are all going to get it for this," the captain said.

"Did she choke on the gag?" one of the men said.

And then I breathed in, a great and gorgeous gasp, and let my heart start again.

The captain, slowly, put me down onto the mossy ground.

I smiled up at his pale face, and then at the other soldiers.

All of them took a step back from me.

It was good to breathe again. It was good to no longer be screaming.

A strange craving swept over me.

"I'm hungry," I whispered.

My wrists were bound, but I reached my hands over to my left side, twisting my body, and I managed to grab some moss and leaves. I stuffed it all into my mouth. How sweet it tasted. Loamy, moist, nourishing.

After that they untied my hands and fed me dried meat and green onions. But it was not enough. All day I asked for more and they gave me what they had. Some dried-out flat bread, some old white cheese.

When they stopped to make camp that evening, they propped me up against a tree, my hands and ankles bound in front of me. While they were busy making their fire, I levered myself onto my knees and tipped myself onto my front. Face down on the wet and muddy ground, I ate like a dog, chewing down twigs, small stones, pieces of grass.

"Stop that," the captain said, moving over to me. "What are you doing?"

I swallowed down a pebble. "I am famished."

"We're preparing food." He looked up to his comrades. "Someone come and stop her doing this."

I quickly crammed more moss into my mouth.

"What is wrong with her?" one of the men said.

The captain, lifting me, shook his head. "They say she was kidnapped as a child. Perhaps this is just too much for her, it happening again."

"Or she's simply mad."

"Or that," the captain said.

I ate everything they gave me and when I could snatch it up, I ate grass and handfuls of earth. Whatever I could get at.

When I was bound up too tight to be able to get at the ground, I found myself making a growling noise, like an angry cat.

They all looked at me differently. They cast lots over who had to touch me.

Once, when my hands were untied, I swiped an unplucked duck from one of their saddle bags and crammed it all into my mouth; feathers, raw flesh and bones too, crunching it all down. It tasted sweet to me.

They all looked on aghast.

"I'm still hungry," I said.

I could only think about food and my raging hunger, but I knew that the memories were there now, tucked away safely inside me.

CHAPTER TWO

NINSHUBAR

Heading back up the Euphrates to Uruk

The Barge of Heaven was a handsome ship, but it was too slow.

Even with one hundred men at the oars, the barge seemed to barely creep forward against the flow of the surging Euphrates. For a while the wind turned in our favour, but our crew was made up of soldiers, not sailors. They looked at me as if they did not understand me when I called for them to raise the sails. By the time I had dragged the blood-red sail cloth from the cabin on the rear deck, the wind had already turned.

And so we crept along the western flank of the great river, beneath a pale sky, and there was nothing I could do to speed us along.

Inanna stood at the rails to the left of the vessel, looking out over the lush farmland to the west. She had her purple travel dress on, but her head and feet were bare, and had she not had two full-grown lions at her side, you might have thought her some merchant's daughter.

"Can you sense them?" I said.

She blinked and turned to me. "They're catching up with us."

"Enki?"

"Enki. Isimud. And lots of soldiers."

Her eyes were even blacker than they usually were, and she had dark shadows beneath them.

"I'll keep practising," I said.

I had pushed as many *mees* onto my arms as there was room for and, slowly and deliberately, I was testing out each one of them. These were not at all like the *mees* I had taken from Dumuzi. These were powerful, humming with life. Some of them hurled out blasts of invisible energy and with these I took pot shots at logs and other detritus floating by. Some of the *mees* threw out lines of blazing purple fire, and I had to be careful to keep the flames away from the barge. The other *mees* were designed only for protection, and these I worried and worried at. If I could make all my protective *mees* work in concert, perhaps I could protect us from whatever Enki might throw at us.

I stopped my practising to have another look through a chest of Enki's *mees*, to see if I could find anything better than the weapons already on my arms. As I did so I cast a glance over at Inanna and realised she was too tired to be standing up.

"Take a break," I said, going over to her. "I have some dried figs in my bag."

I put out two leather-backed chairs for us at the very front of the ship. There were dents in the deck for them to be set into.

"I sat here once with Enki," Inanna said, as she took her seat. "When he brought me to Eridu." She looked up at the main mast. "There was a shade set up over us. And I think we ate figs then too."

"Perhaps these will taste better," I said, passing her two good ones.

Inanna took the fruit, but then shut her eyes. "They're on horseback," she said. "Chariots. They're dragging sleds behind them."

She opened her jet-black eyes again. "I was too slow to capture Enki."

"You did everything you could," I said. "What's on the sleds?"

"Anunnaki weaponry. Things I've never seen before. But my *mee* knows them."

"Eat," I said. "We're going to need our strength."

There were elephants on the west bank, a strange sight in the midst of farmland. They were standing with their front legs in the Euphrates and their eyes on our boat. On Inanna.

Inanna raised one palm to them.

"Are they our old friends?" I said. "The ones who helped us on our journey to the underworld?"

She shook her head.

"So, I have a plan," I said, leaning forward in my chair. "I'm going to try to stretch out my protective shield around the barge."

"The whole ship?"

"I think so."

"Perhaps I can help you," she said.

"Have you used *mees* like this before?"

"No," she said. "But I want to help you."

"Stay here and eat while I keep working on it," I said. "It's my job to protect you now."

I went forward to the very front of the boat again, put my hands on the shining rails, and rested my attention, very gently, on the eight *mees* of protection I now had stacked up on my arms. I had already learned how to activate them all separately, by directing my thoughts firmly at them. Now I pulled hard at all eight of them, while also pushing quickly outwards.

A heartbeat later I was lying flat on my back on the deck, looking up at a bubble of purple light.

I had landed hard and awkward on my stone axe and my arrow quiver, but the shield was holding. "Do you see it?" I shouted out.

I turned my head, and only then did I realise that Inanna had somehow fallen from her chair; that all the men seemed to have been thrown from their rowing benches. Only the lions were still on their feet, although they were baring their fangs at me.

I looked back up at the sky. The entire barge was surrounded by a shield of brilliant purple fire.

I felt I could hold it forever!

"This is wonderful," I called over to Inanna. I would have gone to help her up, but I was not yet sure if I could get up and walk around, as well as hold up the shield at such a distance from the barge.

"I wonder what it will protect us from," I said. "I wonder how we can test it. I do hope you are not hurt, Inanna?"

"I am quite well," she said, pulling her dress straight.

"I can maintain this very easily," I said. I was flooded with delight, lying there on the deck with my axe digging into my spine, and the light playing above me.

Very slowly and deliberately, I relaxed my mental grip on the *mees*. At once the purple fire was gone.

I leaped up to my feet. "Yes, that is excellent. But I need to keep practising."

⸏

The river was narrowing; we could now see reeds in the distance to the east. I practised over and over again with my shield, shouting out a warning each time so that everyone had time to brace themselves.

In the late afternoon, a heavy, unseasonable heat settled over the river. Inanna's lions slumped as if lifeless on top of the sail cloth in the rear cabin.

The men stripped to the waist and came forward now and then to the water barrel, but they kept rowing.

Inanna, very solemn, made a little speech for them. "All of you will be freed when we reach Uruk," she said, lifting her voice to be heard by all. "This is the promise of a goddess. I will give you each a compound of your own within the city walls. And if you have family anywhere in the river lands, I will have them safely brought to you. Take us safely north and you will all be men of Uruk."

"You are using your *mee* on them," I said. "I can tell by how dreamy they seem."

"I am grateful to them nonetheless," she said.

Later she stood with her eyes shut and her hands on the gold-leafed rails at the front of the barge. When I came to stand next to her, she said: "They are coming on mules, from the west. Ninshubar, they're going to catch us up very soon."

Still the Barge of Heaven crept up the river so very slowly that at times I felt we were only holding our place against the current.

Inanna tied up her lions to the middle mast, each on a short leash.

"Some men are on the east bank, too," she said to me. "Isimud is with them. They must have crossed by boat. Those men are on foot now, but they also have heavy weapons with them."

I climbed up onto the left-hand railings, one hand wrapped around a rope, and looked out over the reeds and date palms. "I still can't see anything."

"They are bringing weapons that each take four men to assemble," Inanna said. "The heavy *mees* contain demons. Like the *gallas*, but smaller."

As I dropped back down from the rails, Inanna caught at my arm, her eyes wide.

"Ninshubar. They will come at us from the sky and from the water. Many demons. You need to destroy all of them."

"I'm ready," I said, squeezing her by the shoulders.

"I see Isimud," she said, pointing east.

Enki's *sukkal*, a blade of darkness against the green, was standing on the eastern bank, his helmet visor raised.

Behind him, amongst date palms, there was movement, but it was hard to make out what.

"Inanna!" Isimud shouted out to us. "Give me the boat, and you can go on. Enki says he will not harm you if you give the boat and the *mees* back."

"My lord, I cannot," Inanna called back.

We both moved over to the right-hand side of the boat.

"The barge is mine and the *mees* are mine, given to me in front of many witnesses," Inanna called out. "No god goes back on their word! The *mees* are mine now. Tell Enki that I thank him, and I will honour my promises to him."

Isimud came forward to the river's edge as we passed; so close I could have almost got an arrow into him. I slid my bow into one hand and pulled an arrow from the quiver on my back.

"Enki has ordered you to give up the boat," Isimud shouted. "These are words of state, Inanna. It is time to give up. Enki was not in his right mind when he gave you the *mees*, as many witnesses can attest. Time to give up, Inanna, before things go very wrong for you."

His words were eerily clear across the water. Behind him, his soldiers were busy with something low to the ground.

"I do not believe it," Inanna shouted out, across the earth-brown river. "My grandfather Enki would not break his word like this. He gave me his solemn pledge, in front of witnesses, that I would be his great queen. All this is mine. I order you to stand down!"

She looked up at me and winked.

The rowers, their faces turning from Inanna to Isimud and back again, all looked horrified.

"Stand down, Isimud!" Inanna shouted.

But we had edged back into the middle of the river by then, and he was out of earshot. I slid my arrow back into its quiver.

"I almost had him," Inanna said, her eyes on the riverbank. "If he had come one step closer."

She put her hand out to me, a hard grip on my arm.

"They are coming now, Ninshubar."

CHAPTER THREE

NINLIL

In Kish, capital of Akkadia

The forest gave way to low scrub and then the scrub gave way to farmland. My kidnappers followed the most heavily used paths between the fields and palm groves. They had no fear of being seen now; they lifted hands most cheerfully to all we passed.

I was tied up over the captain's mule, and he was sat astride just behind me. "This is Akkadia now," he said to me. "Have you been here before?"

"I'm hungry," I said, turning my face to him. "I need food now."

"Well you will have to wait."

The rain had stopped, but the paths were still heavy with mud. For all the rest of the ride that day, I thought how good the mud would be if I could only get it into my mouth.

When the captain lifted me down from his saddle that night, he said: "You seem bigger. Heavier." He looked round at his men. "Does she seem taller to you?"

"I need more food," I said.

When they had fed me, for a short time I was free of hunger. I lay down on the wet grass that they had sat me on, and for the first time in almost four hundred years, I thought about my family.

Not the Anunnaki, but my true family. Who I never, ever thought about.

A clear image came to me: my mother standing over me in darkness.

Something glistening.

The scream almost came out of me again, but I sat myself up, breathing hard, and the noise faded away inside me.

"Hungry again?" said the captain, looking over at me from his place beside the fire.

"Yes," I said. "The answer is always yes."

On the fourth evening, at dusk, a city appeared in the distance. It was built on a hill with a palace at its highest point and a turquoise lake stretching out below it.

I twisted around to try to get a better view of the city. "Where are we?" I said to the captain.

"We're home," he said. He grinned about at his men. "And not a moment too soon."

When we reached the city walls, ancient oak gates opened before us with only nods exchanged between my kidnappers and the city guards. We rode on at a trot into narrow streets; I caught glimpses of faces in doorways and windows.

More wooden gates and we were inside what looked like a palace compound. We came to a halt at last beside a block of brick-built stables.

∞

I didn't notice him at first.

I was being lifted down from the captain's mule and untied. There were men everywhere, exchanging news, handing over their animals to stable boys. I realised, once I was stood on my feet, that we were at what looked like the back entrance to a palace. It was a fine building, with arched doors and windows.

And then I saw him.

His bald head and round face, his yellow robes. The heavy gold chains around his neck; the chunky rings on every finger. The wide gold *mees* on each of his thickset wrists. The copper sheen he had to him.

It was Utu.

God of the Sun, child of the moon gods, brother of Inanna and Ereshkigal. My step-grandson. One of the original twelve.

I had known Utu since I was a young girl. He had been a guest in my home countless times.

It made no sense him being here, in the stronghold of our enemies.

"Hello, Ninlil," he called over. "They say you are eating mud."

Utu turned to the old man beside him; a man with a long grey beard, dressed in bright blue robes. "Put her somewhere very safe, will you? She is worth more than the whole of Akkadia."

The old man nodded, looking over at me very sombrely.

"Utu," I called out. "What are you doing here?"

He left the old man and made his way over to me, through the crowd of Akkadians.

"There's no need to look at me like that," he said, his voice low. "There is nothing personal about this."

"Utu, these men have kidnapped me. They took me from my bed in the summer palace."

He waved a hand at me, as if irritated. "We'll have time to talk later," he said.

The old man led me through dim-lit palace corridors to a small bedchamber with long brass bolts on the outside of the door.

Inside: a narrow cot along one wall, a wooden bathtub along the other. Beneath the small, high window, a meal of cheese and fruit had been laid out on a wooden table.

"You can leave us now," the old man said to the soldiers clustered behind us at the door.

When the soldiers had gone, the old man said to me: "Will this be suitable for you?"

I went over to the table, sat down, and began to eat the food set out for me.

"There will be some soldiers out in the corridor, to make sure you are safe," he said.

"Do you think I am safe here?" I said, but without looking up from my food.

"My lady, I don't know what to think." He came over to stand close to me, his eyes on my plate.

"I will need more food than this," I said.

"I will send for more food. Something hot. And I will have them pour you a bath."

I looked down at myself and realised that I was still in my night dress and it was covered in filth.

"Yes, a bath," I said. "And something hot to eat. But also more of these cheeses, and more of these pears."

I luxuriated in the warm, oily water, and then I dressed myself in the new velvet robe that the old man had brought me, admiring the gorgeous blue of it. It was the same blue he wore, and with the same kingfishers embroidered on it in a slightly darker blue.

And I ate. Roast duck, roast swan, slivers of venison, braised lettuce, buttered lentils, boiled greens, crisp lamb chops, lemons to squeeze over it all, and a bronze bowl and bronze spoon to eat it with.

"You are a good eater," the old man said, as he put down a new plate of venison for me.

"I am still hungry."

"They are baking some breads for you. I have woken all the cooks up. And they are churning you some fresh butter. They will send out for some soft cheeses. They are stewing some apricots in cinnamon and honey."

"Good," I said, my mouth full of venison.

The old man kneeled next to my chair.

"Goddess, I recognise you," he said, his hands in prayer before him. "They said I should expect a prisoner. But they did not say it would be you. I recognise you from the temple here, the temple dedicated to Enlil. You are the goddess Ninlil."

"I am."

"In the temples here, they say the Anunnaki are false gods. That the true Anunnaki died a long time ago."

"How long will the cheeses be?"

"Now Utu, the God of the Sun, is here. And now you."

"Yes."

"You both seem very real to me." The old man wrung his hands together. "Oh, my lady, this feels very wrong. That you should be here like this, a prisoner."

I looked up from my food. "Where is this?"

"You are in Kish, my lady, in the palace of King Akka."

For a moment I could see the whole pattern of the thing; I understood what was happening. Then the hunger reared up again, blocking out all other thoughts. "I liked those mashed chickpeas that you brought me."

"I can bring you more of those immediately," he said.

When he had come back with the chickpeas and another platter of lamb, I said: "What is going to happen to me?"

"My lady, I think the god Utu is going to take you to the city of Susa. Why I do not know."

"You can sit down on the bed," I said. "Where is Susa?"

The old man sat down, as instructed, and folded his bony hands in his lap.

"Susa is a long way away, my lady, in the Zagros mountains. At least half a moon's ride away."

I kept eating. "Can you help me get away from Utu?"

"I do not think I can, my lady."

"You could advise me though. I have a question I would like answered."

"I would be honoured to advise you."

I stopped eating and drew myself up. "What is your name?'

"Biluda, my lady."

"Biluda, I have a memory that I have pushed away inside me. Very deep. For a long time, I thought it lost for ever. But now I can feel it lying there. I imagine it tucked out of sight in a wooden box. My question is: should I face the truth, or should I leave it well alone?"

He was frowning at me; I could see his mind working. "Is this the memory of something very terrible?"

"Terrible enough," I said.

He stretched his face into something like a smile.

"My lady, in my experience, you cannot hide from the hard things in life."

I nodded. "Thank you." I nodded again. "Perhaps I have been hiding. Perhaps there is truth in that."

He watched me eat my cutlets, meat, and bone too. "I do not mean to pry, but are you ill, my lady? I have never seen someone eat so much."

"I am making myself stronger and bigger," I said. "I am preparing myself for what is to come."

When Biluda had gone to fetch more food, I lay down on the bed on my back and shut my eyes, breathing slow and steady. I drifted slowly downwards until I had a perfect view of my wooden box. The lid was tight shut. I was safe from the memory. It was my choice whether to open it or not.

The other memories though. Not the memories of the attack, but the memories of my life before. Those memories now drifted around me, hard to chase away.

Then my hunger had me again, impossible to ignore.

Oh, the raging, tearing hunger!

I leaned out of bed and reached for the spoon that the old man had brought for me.

I crammed the bronze into my mouth, and chewed it slowly down.

CHAPTER FOUR

NINSHUBAR

On the Barge of Heaven

Inanna put her hand out to me, a hard grip on my arm.

"They are coming now, Ninshubar."

I was about to answer, when I sensed something odd, as if the barge was slowing. For one heartbeat, there was only that. Me completely still; listening with my whole body; that slight sensation of the ship dragging.

And then the air and the water exploded into movement.

Monstrous wild-haired insects came surging up out of the river and over the sides of the barge.

A heartbeat.

I could not make my *mees* work.

An oarsman screamed. There was blood in the air.

A heartbeat.

And then the barge was surrounded by crackling, purple light.

Demon creatures fell hard and heavy to the deck. More surged out of the river at us, but exploded against the great shield around the boat.

Inanna's lions slashed at the air and roared in their frenzy to get at the creatures.

For a heartbeat, everything was still again.

Inanna went to the oarsman, but he was already dead. There was blood all over the deck and all over the man's shocked comrades.

I went over to one of the creatures, now lying motionless on the cedar planking. It was like a spider, with the main part of its body about a hand's width across. Countless long, thin arms extending from the main section; so many that in motion, they had given the appearance of wild-flowing hair. Both the body and the arms were made of some strange dark substance that I had never seen before, and each limb ended in a long, black blade. I took a knife up, hooked it under the creature's body, and heaved the thing out into the river.

"Put them all over the side," I called out to the rowers. "Be careful not to touch the arms."

Inanna returned to her post at the railings. "There are more coming," she said. "Many more."

I looked up at my purple shield.

"I'm ready."

A heartbeat.

A wave of creatures came at us from the sky. Bigger demons this time, each the size of an adult leopard. Together they blocked out the sun as they fell.

A heartbeat.

When the demons touched my cracking shield, they simply hung there in the air, large and heavy as they were.

"I am holding them," I said to Inanna, my cheeks hot with relief.

I shut my eyes, and I could sense each of the monstrous creatures caught up in my web. I went to push them away and a heartbeat later the giant demons fell into the river and were gone to the depths.

A heartbeat.

A third wave came, surging through the water towards us.

Again, they reached my shield and stopped.

I waved one hand and flung them far out into the river. I was about to turn to Inanna in triumph, when I saw that the creatures were still alive. They surged towards the east bank; towards Isimud, who now stood, legs apart, watching us.

In the long, shocked silence after those first three attacks, I said: "Keep rowing." The oars began again.

A fourth wave came. Falling on us from the sky with an ear-piercing, whistling scream.

I looked over at Inanna, and saw she had blood running from her ears.

A heartbeat later I hurled all the creatures away. Perhaps I was only imagining it, but the weapons on my arms no longer seemed as powerful as they had.

A fifth wave, this time of tiny flying insects with nasty, flashing wings. It was an effort by then to keep the shield ablaze. It seemed to press down on me, squashing the air out of my lungs.

But each time I kept us safe.

∽

For a long time, as the day began to fade, nothing happened. I let the shield fall and sat down in my chair next to Inanna.

"Are you able to go on?" she said.

"Perfectly able. I just need to catch my breath."

"You look very tired."

"So do you, Inanna."

In the true dusk, Enki appeared on the western bank.

He jumped lightly down from a chariot and raised one hand to us as we heaved by in the gloom. He moved with purpose, no longer the love-stricken man who had waved us off at the docks. Then he was gone into the palms.

The darkness soon came down on us, but the river ahead glinted in the light of a very thin moon and the men kept rowing.

I sat in my chair, next to Inanna, listening to the night and the sounds of the river. She had the unfocussed look on her that she always had when she was communing with her *mee*.

"More are coming," she said. "You need to raise your shield again."

In the darkness, new monsters came slithering out from the riverbanks and slammed into my shield.

More fell from the sky.

Once, my shield failed, and in less than a heartbeat, six of our men were dead, sliced open, blood everywhere. But with a huge heave I lifted the purple fire again and we were safe.

The next time I went back to sit with Inanna, my whole body was shaking with the effort of keeping the shield alight.

"I could try to use the weapons," she said.

I leaned over to speak quietly to her. "The weapons are fading faster than I am."

"Could there be more like them in the boxes?"

"I've looked through everything."

"Could the *mees* of combat help us?"

"Not with so many different creatures coming at us, and when one could kill us all."

"There must be a way to get more power into the ones you have," she said.

"No doubt there is. But I cannot think how we can do it now."

After a long moment of silence, she said: "I dream sometimes of a blue lake, down at the heart of the Earth."

I did not understand the import of the blue lake, but then I never understood her dreams.

"One step and then the next," I said to her.

Twice more they came, but I kept the shield ablaze. I was sitting on the deck by then, with no strength in me to stand.

The third time, the shield died.

And would not work again.

The mayhem was instant.

A demon creature knocked me flat as it bowled past. Agony in my left side, blood surging. I could not sit up for the pain.

Melam helps you heal, but it does not protect you from the agony.

I did not know where Inanna was; I could see nothing except movement around me in the dark. I could only hear screaming.

"Oh, Inanna," I said, into the whirling, thrashing darkness. "I am so sorry."

I had both hands to the wet agony that was my side. I could not tell how bad it was.

Something landed heavy on my left leg; a many-armed demon, black, hard, slicing at me. I sat up to try to fight the thing off me, just as a man fell on top of me. I could not tell which of us was screaming.

Then Inanna was there, looking down at me. She seemed to glow with a pale blue light, very soft. She looked so small, so neat, so untouched, even in the mayhem.

"Please stay alive, Ninshubar," she said.

Her soft blue light grew brighter. It began spilling out of her, lighting up all the air around her and the scene of carnage on the ship.

The demon creatures fell limp as the blue light washed over them. The oarsmen who were still alive turned to stare at the goddess.

Inanna's blue light billowed out over the river and lit up the banks on either side of the Barge of Heaven.

It lit up Enki, who was standing watching us on the left bank with his soldiers ranged out behind him.

For a heartbeat, all eyes were on Inanna.

And then a blast wave of burning, raging power swept out from her.

The whole night sky lit up as if it was day.

The demon insects were swept violently out of the barge and into the river in the first blast. A wave of blue flame surged out behind that blast, boiling up the river and setting fire to the riverbanks. In the distance, men were screaming.

Another burst of brilliant blue and the entire world shook.

The sky seemed to bend in to the small dark figure standing over me.

Inanna turned her black eyes down to me. In that moment, there was nothing human in her.

"I will not let them hurt you," she said.

CHAPTER FIVE

INANNA

Home to Uruk

I dreamed that I was lying on a beach with my left cheek pressed into the wet sand. The warm surf flowed up and over my body and washed back down again.

A man in bronze armour stood over me. He leaned down and whispered to me.

"Aphrodite, wake up."

I awoke, gasping, in darkness.

I was not on sand.

I was face down on the deck of the Barge of Heaven.

I pushed myself up; it was almost dawn. Ninshubar was propped up against the railings next to me with her left hand pressed to her blood-drenched side. She turned her head and gave me a smile that was half grimace.

"They have stopped coming," she said. "If any of them still live, they are running back to Eridu."

"You are alive," I said. "That's all that matters." I shut my eyes just for a moment, and there, in the blue lightscape, I saw Enki riding away from us.

"What did you do, Inanna?" Ninshubar said. "The whole world shook. How did you do it? Was it your *mee*?"

I reached out a hand to her and felt the warmth of her left arm. "I jumped into a lake," I said.

"What lake?"

I shook my head. "You are alive," I said.

I sank back down into my dreams.

I woke again to the mewling of a buzzard high over the river.

A lilac sky, gold edged. The loamy smell of marshland.

Ninshubar was asleep on the deck, her face turned to me. Her side was a mess of wet blood, but I put my face close to hers and she was breathing.

Only then did I realise that the boat was no longer moving.

I stood, to a scene of quiet horror.

The Barge of Heaven lay askew, its prow embedded in the reeds, its stern sticking out into the river. My lions were alive, tight leashed against a mast. But all about me lay the bodies of our oarsmen.

For a few terrible moments, I thought all of them were dead, but when I approached the closest of them, I found that he was still warm. Much bloodied, his hair stuck to his skull, but breathing.

I went round to each man, to be certain if they were alive or dead, and whether I might be able to help them. One man seemed caught halfway between life and death. I took a knife from my belt, hacked at my wrist, and fed him a few drops of my *melam*-rich blood. A great shudder and he was breathing.

I released my lions, and then I went and sat back down on the wooden deck next to Ninshubar. My lions came at once to sit either side of me.

I put one hand out to Ninshubar. She was warm.

She was alive.

I smiled up at the lilac sky and breathed in the sacred river.

After a long while, I lay down again and slept.

She was alive.

When I awoke, the barge was moving. The oarsmen, their ranks heavily thinned, were back on their oars. The lions were drinking from a large, clay bowl. We were passing between the two stone watch towers that guard the entrance to the Warka; we were not far south from Uruk.

The men in the watch towers leaned out to see us better as we slid past on Enki's famous ship.

Ninshubar crouched down next to me with a waterskin.

"You look better," she said.

"I'm quite well," I said. "How is your wound?"

She sat herself down and stretched out her legs on the cedar. "Still sore. But the *melam* saved me." She pulled up her leather jerkin to show me her crusting wound. "I'm healing fast." She passed me the waterskin. "Half the men are dead."

"I am very sorry for that."

"Inanna, I do not mean to press you, but how did you do it? Was it the master *mee*?"

I drank down the whole of the waterskin. "No," I said at last. "It wasn't the *mee*."

I looked over at the rowers; all of them had their heads down, none of them looking over at us.

"They are all terrified of you now," Ninshubar said. "Power was pouring from you. The river boiled. The reeds were set on fire for leagues and leagues around."

"Yes." I raised my eyebrows at her and smiled. "You always said I was a witch."

"I knew you were a witch. Now I know you are a great witch." She leaned over and squeezed my hands in her hands, and I caught her citrus scent.

"You are alive," I said, smiling at her.

And I looked around me at this scene that might be now, or might be a warning from the future, or might only be a memory of my very ancient past.

We came in sight of Uruk on the evening of the fourth day. Its vast ramparts gleamed gold against the green of the farmland all around.

The wind was behind us, and we hoisted the ship's three great sails on the approach. What a sight we must have been as we sailed the Barge of Heaven straight for the Nigulla gate that led, via a wide canal, directly into the city.

Children ran along the riverbank ahead of us, clapping and singing.

"What are they singing?" I said.

Ninshubar smiled. "That you are as wide as the Earth and as tall as the sky."

I laughed. "If only."

My mother was stood out to greet us on the White Quay. She wore her full temple regalia, wings, and crescent crown too.

She got down onto her knees and kissed the marble quay as Ninshubar lifted me off the ship.

"Welcome home, great goddess," she said.

Later I sat with my mother in her private garden, each of us on a soft leather chair, and my lions on the flagstones beside me. My mother kissed my hands and pressed her tears into them.

"I thought it was another earthquake, but they say it was you who made the world shake." She kissed my hands again. "I am so glad to find you well."

I looked down at her beautiful curls, as she leaned over my hands. Just for half a moment, I saw her lying dead.

We were in Babylon. A city I did not yet know.

She was lying dead in a bed with black sheets, her mouth, and eyes open.

"Inanna?"

My mother's lovely face turned up to me.

"My love, what is it?" she said.

I shook my head, clearing it. We were not in Babylon. We were in Uruk. And my mother was here with me, and alive.

She knelt on the flagstones before me, holding my hands between hers. "They say great power poured out of you."

I could not yet speak; I could not quite free myself of the image of her lying dead.

"Inanna, was it the *mee*?"

I shook my head again.

"The ground shook, Inanna. Even here."

I gave a great breath out. She was alive. For now, she was alive.

I pulled my face into a smile. I picked up her hands and kissed them in return.

"Mother, you ate up all the *melam* in the world when I was growing in your belly and I am the strange creature born of that. Is it so odd that I have strange powers?"

She was frowning; such small, delicate creases in the soft skin between her brows. "I can help you now, Inanna, if you will let me."

"I'm something new," I said, forcing cheer into my voice. "Now we must get dressed for the feast."

The small creases in her brow took a while to fade.

She sat back up on her chair, and put on her formal, temple face. "I should tell you that your father has written to us, inviting us both to Ur."

"Oh, yes?" I sat up straight. I had heard nothing from my father since the day of my wedding to Dumuzi. Since the day my father sailed away to Ur, leaving my mother in one of Enki's prison cells.

"Your father says he is ready to forgive me for stealing his *melam*," my mother said. "And he wants to see you."

"I will put it on my list," I said, "of things to be considered later."

I paused a moment, looking into her bright eyes. "Mother, have you ever been to Babylon?'

"I've never heard of it," she said, shaking her gleaming curls. "Is it near Uruk?"

"No," I said. "Never mind."

There was a great feast that night in the precincts of the White Temple. All across the city, the people roasted goats and danced and sang into the night.

My mother watched me eat. "You need rest. You have been through too much, in too short a time."

"I'm quite well," I said.

My mother and Ninshubar exchanged glances.

It was at that moment that my chief priestess, Lilith, came to stand beside my chair.

"We had word of that missing boy," she said to me.

"Which boy?" I said, blank for a moment.

Lilith looked to Ninshubar. "The one you call the Potta."

All expression fell from Ninshubar's face. "Go on."

"There is a man here who says he has seen him," Lilith said.

The man who claimed to have seen the Potta was brought to us in the White Temple and made to kneel before us.

He was a round-bellied northern man, from the high mountains that give birth to the Euphrates. "I saw the one you are looking for," he said. "White skin, red hair, blue eyes. It was two years ago, in a village market. My friend bought him."

"And where is the boy now?" said Ninshubar.

The man shook his head. "I don't know. But I was in Eridu one moon ago and I saw my friend again. The one who bought the boy."

"And did he have the boy with him?" said Ninshubar.

"No, no," said the man. "But he's the one who bought him."

"Did you ask about the boy?"

The man shrugged. "I did not think to ask about a slave, even one so strange-looking. But my friend is headed west, and I know where he's going. You can go after him and ask him yourself."

There was then some heated discussion.

Finally, Lilith stepped forward. "The man who bought the Potta cannot have gone far from Eridu. If it is true that he is heading west along the coast path, then you can catch him, Ninshubar, if you take a boat and go fast."

"I wonder if it is the Potta that you really saw," I said to the pot-bellied man.

"I don't know," he said. "But I do remember him. He held his chin up, you know?" He lifted his chin, just so, looking at Ninshubar.

"I do know," said Ninshubar. She turned to me. "It was the Potta."

We sat with my mother, and Lilith, in my mother's bedchamber.

"If I go south at once, in a fast boat, I could be in Eridu in two or three days," Ninshubar said. "The trail west runs close to the coast, almost upon the shore once the marshes end, so I could follow the trail by boat, and very quickly catch him. I could be there and back half a moon, maybe less."

"I will come with you," I said.

"There is no need at all," she said.

"I made a sacred promise to you. That as soon Uruk was safe from Enki, I would go out in the world with you to find the Potta."

Ninshubar shook her head. "Your promise was to help me when you became Queen of Earth and Heaven."

"Do you doubt that I already am?"

No one said anything to that.

My mother shook her head at me. "Inanna, you made a promise to help find the Potta. But we do not yet know where he is or if he is alive. When we know more, then you can go with Ninshubar. You should stay here now and settle yourself in the city."

"I will go alone," Ninshubar said.

"And you should be here when Gilgamesh and his wife arrive," my mother said. "You should be here to see them crowned."

I looked down at my hands. I had a strong flash of Gilgamesh, etched out in blue. He was walking beside a horse. He was not far away now. He looked up, as I watched, and for the first time I saw

Della. Only the blue outline of her, sketched in light, but even so, how beautiful she was. The shape of her, the way she moved.

It was as if I had been struck in the gut.

I simply could not bear it, to see him with her.

It took a few moments for my upset and confusion to dim. Then I put on my dove face and looked back up at those assembled.

"I am coming with you," I said to Ninshubar. "I promised that I would go with you. And if we do not go quickly, we may never hear of your Potta again."

I turned to my mother. "Will you look after the city for me?"

"Please, Inanna," she said. "No."

"I have decided," I said.

We took a small boat, smaller even than our temple skiff, and we went just the two of us, unless you count my lions of course, in which case we were four. Ninshubar wore Enki's *mees* up and down each arm, her flint axe across her back, her bow and quiver over one shoulder, and at her waist, a bronze sword.

"No knife?" I said.

She lifted her left trouser leg to show me her knife.

"Of course," I said.

"Are you sorry to be missing Gilgamesh?" Ninshubar said.

"Very sorry," I said. "And I would have liked to welcome his wife." It was an outright lie, but better that than admit to the truth.

Ninshubar leaned over and dropped a firm kiss upon my head.

"One step and then the next, Inanna."

CHAPTER SIX

GILGAMESH

In Uruk

Beneath a brilliant pink sunset, we passed the Uruk city marker; a huge block of almond stone, sunk into the earth and emblazoned with a curse against enemy soldiers. Giant bats were coming down to drink from the Warka, each creature sending out ripples across the river as it skimmed over the surface.

Ahead of us, the White Temple gleamed pink above the vast siege walls of Uruk.

Harga and I approached the elephant gates on foot, at the head of our party. Behind us came our fifty heavily armed men on their mules, and in their midst, my lovely wife on one of my father's high-stepping horses.

Harga and I both lifted a hand at the boys on the walls and the gates were promptly lifted.

"They're awake anyway," Harga said.

"But no men on the road, no men at the marker, no one on patrol all the way in."

"Your father took the good men north," he said.

The city was alive with the smell of cooking fires, barley stew, and lamb searing, and the cheerful noise, coming down to us from the rooftops, of families setting out their carpets and cushions to eat upon. You would not have thought there were men of Kish raging through Sumer and burning palaces, from this happy hubbub all about us.

As we drew up at the royal precinct, the holy gates sprang open before us.

Inanna's mother, the moon goddess Ningal, was standing on the lowest of the steps that led up to the ziggurat, her hands upon her hips, her dark curls floating soft upon her shoulders. She was dressed only in a simple white shift, but her arms were covered in unfamiliar *mees*, of all shapes and sizes.

"Ningal!" I paced up ahead of the others and kissed her on each soft cheek. "Where is Inanna? We have a lot to tell you, and she should hear it."

"Inanna is gone," Ningal said. "Gone south to find Ninshubar's lost son." She widened out her hands to me. "They left only yesterday."

"We need to get them back," I said. "The Akkadians have come south of the border. It may be a full-scale invasion."

"They are on the river, in a small sailing boat."

"Send out a temple skiff after it," I said. "Send out riders. Whatever it takes. We will need all the help we can get if Akka arrives at our gates."

"I'll do it now," she said, her forehead creased with upset. "How I wish I had stopped them going. I knew it was wrong for them to rush off so quickly."

"Get them back," I said.

When all the news was exchanged, or the largest parts of it at least, I took Della and the baby to the royal palace I had grown up in. With my parents gone north with An, it had been set aside for us.

The ancient palace was built of clay-brick, but every wall was covered in beautiful paintings or fine-woven rugs. Every corridor, every tile, every carpet and chest, was so beloved to me. I found myself beaming at it all as I showed Della around.

"It's so small," she said, holding our son up high up on her shoulder, as if keeping him clear of some poisonous ground-fog. "It's like a termite's nest. Why are the ceilings so low?"

I looked about my old home with new eyes. It did seem rather cramped and maze-like with Della's stern frown upon it.

"It was only me and my parents here," I said. "And we ate all our meals with An in the temple precinct. I suppose we did not need more than this."

The bedrooms were not yet ready, but the household servants brought us some of my mother's favourite mountain tea. Della sat down, looking pained, on an old patchworked couch. She uncovered a breast for the baby and sat looking upset as he fed. "It smells strange," she said.

"Perhaps it is just unfamiliar. It smells clean and good to me."

"I will not share a room with you," she said.

After a pause, I said: "No one has suggested that you share a room with me. You will have my mother's rooms, as I think I have already said. There is a lovely courtyard leading off the bedroom with a pool in it that the boy will like when he is a little older. I will only be just over the corridor, in my father's old rooms. But Della, I must leave you now, just for a while, to make some plans with Ningal and Harga. The servants will bring you food in here."

"You are leaving us here alone?"

"Alone with all the men and women of the house, who I have known since birth, who can be trusted above all others."

"Go then," she said. "Hold your talks. What does it matter what I might think?"

"It matters to me what you think," I said, not altogether truthfully. "I'll be back soon."

On my way to the holy palace, on a dark corner outside the barracks, the high priestess Lilith stepped out in front of me.

As she stood on her tiptoes to kiss me on each cheek, I caught her lovely jasmine scent.

"Where is she?" Lilith said. I knew of course who she meant by that.

"My mother is being the hero," I said. "Akkadians have attacked the summer palace. She got Della and the baby out, handed them to me, and now she's gone back for the others." I kissed her forehead. "There is no need to worry about Ninsun."

"But I do worry."

"Lilith, nothing can kill Ninsun. You and I both know that, more than anyone. Now there is something you can do for me. My wife and son are here. Will you go to them and try to make them feel welcome?"

"If it will help."

"I'm not sure what will help, but Della is very alone."

Lilith nodded, frowning.

"Della," I reminded her.

"Yes, yes." She squeezed my arm. "Ninsun said nothing? No word for me?"

"There are men of Kish ransacking Sumer. There was no time for the passing of kind words."

"Of course not," she said. And then she went off into the night, towards the royal palace.

Watching her dark shape slipping down the street, I felt pity for her. But there are fools everywhere and chief amongst them are the fools that love my mother.

Ningal and Harga were already together when I arrived in what had once been An's private apartments.

The two of them sat as friends might, on the terrace that looked out over the temple. The sky above was bright with stars; the terrace was golden with the light of candles and oil lanterns.

Two smooth-coated black dogs, powerful creatures with ears like daggers, came over to greet me or possibly to savage me. Their fur gleamed like sea coal in the candlelight.

"Are these Dumuzi's dogs?" I called over to the moon goddess.

"They are Inanna's dogs now," Ningal said. "Although they squabble with the lions."

I reached out to touch the dogs' heads and found them friendly.

"Come, sit with us," said Ningal, pushing out a chair for me. "Drink some wine. Warm yourself."

I pulled a leather-backed chair up to the fire bowl and kicked off my mud-caked boots.

"Is Della settled?" Ningal said. She held a cup of date wine out to me.

"I've asked Lilith to visit her," I said, by way of answer.

I took my cup of wine, and for a moment I simply luxuriated. It was a long time since I had sat in front of a fire, on a chair, with wine in my hand. "The wine is good," I said. "Thank you."

Harga leaned forward to me. "We have guards posted everywhere, every gate locked down, even the secret ones. Patrols are on their way out. And I've sent spies north, to see what King Akka is up to."

"And what about the canal into the city?"

"The metal bars are being lowered at both ends."

A servant came onto the terrace with more wine for us all. Others came with plates of food and small tables to set the food on, and we were quiet until they had finished plying to and fro. I helped myself to some venison and leek stew.

"Our spies have reported nothing unusual from Kish," said Ningal. "What we know for sure is that eight days ago, the main army was still in Kish. So that is something."

I looked up from my very good, very hot stew. "If Akka was planning to attack Uruk, how long would it take for him to get here?"

"He moves slow," Harga said. "One moon perhaps. Maybe longer."

I helped myself to a bowl of spiced lentils and topped it with seared lamb and fried green onions. "There are ways in and out of this city that you two don't know about. I will see them all plugged up."

"Water is a problem," said Harga. "If they poison the canal, then we are left with only four working wells. I'll get more dug tomorrow."

"The water is not far down," I said. "We should also be bringing food from the farms, grain reserves, animals, whatever can be moved."

"Perhaps we should block up the city canal entirely," Harga said. "It seems like madness to me to have these great holes in the walls."

I shrugged, not liking to hear that, when the canal flowing directly into the city had been my father's idea.

I would have stayed longer and done more planning, but the thought of Della on that old couch was scratching at me. I pulled my boots back on. "I'm sorry I missed Inanna's triumph," I said. "How I would have liked to see her sail in on the Barge of Heaven."

"She is first amongst us all now," Ningal said. "More powerful than any other Anunnaki."

"And it was not her *mee* that gave her the power?" I said. "It was something else?"

"Something happened that I didn't think could happen here," said Ningal. "Not in this realm."

"All the more reason to have her back here," I said.

I stood to go. "In the morning, we will ready the city," I said. "Everything that can be done to prepare, we will do. We will turn Uruk into a city ready for war."

"Good night, Gilgamesh," Ningal said. "I hope Della likes the palace."

"Who would not?" I said, avoiding Harga's eye.

I stopped at Della's door that night, a candle in one hand, and almost went to enter. Instead I put my ear to the cedar door, and listened. The noise of the baby crying, a strange woman's voice. No doubt the night nurse.

Della had said she would never lie with me again, because I had lain with a man. My heart sank within me.

I let my hand, poised to knock, fall to my side.

I had all the years ahead to make it right with Della, if it could ever be right.

Why press now when she was resolutely against me?

∽

They had made up the bed for me in my father's rooms, which lay just across from Della's chambers. It looked strange and unwelcoming in there, even with the candles lit.

I found myself making my way to my old childhood rooms at the far end of the palace. Not so long ago I had shared these rooms with Enkidu.

I stood for a moment in my old room, only breathing, and then I went into the small side room that Enkidu had slept in. I looked about at the simple leaf-pattern painted on the walls, then I sat down on the small, cedar-frame bed and set down my candle. I blew out the flame and laid down there on the bare mattress with my cloak over me.

It no longer smelt of him.

"Goodnight, Enkidu," I said, to the dark room.

Just to hear his name said.

CHAPTER SEVEN

ERESHKIGAL

*Rising up into the
realm of light*

The Anzu can do things that the rest of us cannot.

I sucked upon my stylus, forgetting that I would get clay in my mouth.

We call the little girl an Anunnaki. They speak about her in temple as one of the Twelve.

Yet of course she is not Anunnaki. She was never one of us.

"Nammu is here," Namtar said, interrupting me without warning or apology. "She is on her way through the Dark City and will soon be at the temple."

Was he shaking?

I put down my stylus. "Do I have clay on my face?"

"Only a little, my queen. Let me clean it off for you."

I looked up into his eyes as he wiped at my mouth with his black handkerchief. "She will not hurt you," I said. "That is the sacred promise of a goddess. Do you know what that is?"

"A promise for all time," he said, and bowed low, but he kept his eyes from me.

"For all time, yes."

"I do not worry for myself." He lowered his voice. "I worry for the little demons. And also I worry for you."

"I will not let her harm us," I repeated, gripping his furry hands tight between mine.

As I pushed myself to my feet, my back cramped in sudden agony.

After a moment, I said: "Namtar, send in my dresser-demons."

Nammu, queen of the Anunnaki, was a bolt of gold and emerald green against the darkness of the city. As she drew close a verdant light began to flood from her, cascading out across the dark ruins. She bounded effortlessly up the huge steps to the Black Temple.

We were a welcoming party of four: me, Dumuzi, the dark stranger, and my priest-demon Namtar. But of course, hidden in the shadows, all my darling creatures stood to watch her.

I had forgotten how beautiful Nammu was.

As a girl, how I worshipped her! The golden skin, the shining curls piled up upon her head, the astonishing, hibiscus-red of her lips. The way she moved: such grace.

At the top of the temple steps, Nammu cast her glittering gaze upon me and frowned. She turned, very serious, to the dark stranger. Slowly and deliberately, holding his eye, she kneeled before him.

"My lord," she said. How deep and regal her voice was; how imperious. How it carried! I had forgotten.

I did not like to see her kneel.

The dark stranger did not seem to think it wrong. He put out one armour-covered hand to her, and she took it in both her hands, and kissed its strange scales.

Dumuzi and I turned to each other, eyebrows raised.

I called out: "You should kneel for me, great-grandmother, if you are going to kneel for anyone. It is my city, after all."

Nammu stood, her face hard. "What have you done here, Ereshkigal?"

"Why did you kneel to him?" I said.

"Erra is the head of our house now. All of us are subject to him."

Nammu looked out at the dark streets that wriggled with my demons, and then turned back to me. "What are all these creatures?"

"What creatures?"

"And what is all of this?" she said, opening her hands to the city.

"It is the Dark City," I said. "It is the city from the temple stories!"

Nammu took a deep breath in. "I had not realised how bad things were."

So, there were four gods at the table for dinner that night.

Nammu was stern but beautiful in the candlelight, her sapphire eyes flashing. She directed all her questions towards Erra. She wanted to know all about the new House of the Anunnaki, and all the up-to-date politics of Heaven.

"Have you two met before?" Dumuzi said to them.

"We have not met until now," Nammu said. Every word she

spoke was delivered as if part of some great pronouncement. "Although we have found ways to communicate," she added, slow and solemn.

"You did not meet in Heaven?" I said.

"I was away when Erra visited us as a boy," Nammu said. "But of course, I know his father very well, and I was sad to hear that he did not survive the fall of our house."

"If any of this man's story is true," I said, frowning down at my plate. We were eating eel heads and I was worried they were rather tough.

"Tomorrow we will travel out into the realm of light," Nammu said. "We will find my husband An and work out what to do next."

I shared a look with Dumuzi.

"You left your husband An two centuries ago," I said to Nammu. "What loyalty can you possibly have for him?"

"I left him only to walk the world. To try to find more *melam*. To try to find the master *mee*. To try to find a way home for our family. There is no bad blood between us."

"Now that is certainly untrue," Dumuzi said.

"Which bit?" I said.

"What is this dust?" Nammu said, lifting her hands to it, and grimacing. "It is getting in my food." For a moment, she was no longer her solemn and careful self.

Dumuzi waved a hand at the dust. "It's worse if you upset her." Then he leaned forward to the queen of the gods. "Will I be coming out with you?"

"No," Nammu said.

"I will be here with you," I said to Dumuzi. "You will be quite safe."

Nammu lifted her delicate chin at me. "Ereshkigal, you are

coming out with me. You have been in here too long. It is time
to return to the realm of light."

"What does it matter to you," I said, "whether I come with you
or not?"

Nammu pursed her beautiful lips. "I don't understand what you
have done in here, Ereshkigal, or how you have done it, but you
have made a terrible mess of the Kur. And of yourself. You have
become a grotesquery. As soon as we have done what we need to
do in the world of light, we are going to come back here and clean
this place out."

I tried to keep my face plain, but the dust began to fall so heavily
that it threatened to put out the candles. I turned my head just
a little and caught the terrified eye of my priest-demon. I looked
quickly away again. Tears were tumbling down my cheeks and into
my lap.

"More tears," Dumuzi said, but only quietly, and through a
mouthful of eel.

"Tell me what this dust is!" Nammu said. She put down her
spoon and shook out her hair.

"I did warn you not to upset her," Dumuzi said to Nammu. "She
likes all these little demons that you are threatening."

"I cannot come with you," I said. "There must be an Anunnaki
here. Dumuzi is not that."

"He is half an Anunnaki," Nammu said. "Neti says it will do.
Now enough of your cowardliness, Ereshkigal. It's time for you to
leave the underworld."

As I walked back to my chambers that night, with my beloved
priest-demon by my side, my back was worse than it had been for
many moons.

"Will you do your history tonight, my queen?"

"I do not think I have quite the strength for it."

"What did she mean, that she would clean this place out?" Namtar said. "Does she not like how I keep the palace?"

"She meant nothing by it, and anyway, I will not let her change anything."

Namtar tucked me in to bed, as he always did, and bowed to me. "Goodnight, our beloved queen," he said.

In the night I got up and, with some difficulty, set about my writing again.

> *I do not think I can have another baby. I think the loss of one more will kill me. I will never be a mother.*

I sat looking at the door for a while, my lovely Namtar bright in my mind.

> *When we first came down from Heaven I lived in Ur with my parents the moon gods, and my brother Utu, God of the Sun. It was only a village when we got there but*

I woke with a start, my left cheek upon my clay tablet, and Nammu standing furious at the door to my bedchamber.

"Ereshkigal!"

She was dressed as if to travel, her green cloak fastened at her throat.

I lifted my head from my desk and picked a piece of plaster off my forehead.

My dresser-demons leaped from their beds and Namtar came rushing in from the corridor beyond.

"Ereshkigal, what are you doing?" Nammu said.

"I am doing my work."

She did not stamp her foot, but she looked as if she wanted to. "For the love of all the realms, Ereshkigal, we are leaving this very moment. Erra and I have been waiting for you and you are not even dressed. Enough of this stupidity."

"I need to pack."

"Ereshkigal, put on a dress and some sandals, find yourself a cloak, and come. You do not need to bring anything."

"I am bringing my demons."

She gave out a heavy sigh. "You cannot take these demons with you through the gates. They cannot survive outside the Kur. Just come."

I tipped my chin up at her. "My *gallas* can survive outside the Kur."

"The *gallas* are not your *gallas*, Ereshkigal. They are part of the Kur and they belong to us all. They will stay here to make sure Dumuzi stays inside the Kur and that everything keeps running smoothly. From now on the gates to the underworld will stand open to all our kind. We will not go back to the madness of you locked inside here, refusing to let anyone else in, and yet refusing to be let out. Stand up, get dressed and let's go. It will take us time to get Erra through the gates. He will need time to adapt. We are going now."

When she had gone, my demons dressed me for my journey, all of them weeping. Namtar mopped at his tears with his handkerchief.

"It is very selfish of us to be sad," he said. "For so long you have dreamed of this day, of your captivity ending."

I was weeping too. "I do not know why they insist on me going."

He said: "They think that if they leave you here, you will lock the gates against both of them, and they will never get back in."

"Yes, I think that is what I would certainly do. But then what if she batters the gates again and makes everything crumble!"

"My queen, stay!" Namtar burst out. "Stay!"

I took his velvety hands in mine. "I feel I should do as they tell me. I fear that Nammu is right and I have been lost in madness here. She is the adult."

"Are you not also an adult?" he said. "When you are more than four hundred years old?"

"I don't know," I said, mopping at my tears with my dress. "I feel no different now from how I felt as a young girl." I sobbed harder. "I do not want to be a grotesquery. I do not want to be a coward. I was not a coward, in the first days."

Namtar stood up straight. "My queen, if you have decided to rise up into the world of light then you must follow your heart. When you return we will be here waiting for you."

I nodded, my face crumpled. "Do not let Dumuzi waste the candles."

Namtar dried his eyes. "We will keep it almost pitch black here, except to give him a little light to eat his food by."

"Thank you. And you will guard my history tablets?"

"With my life, great queen," Namtar said, and bowed low to me.

I thought then of taking some of my secret things with me; treasures I had found hidden inside the Kur. But I did not want Erra and Nammu finding out about my precious finds and possibly stealing them from me.

"Will you hide all my very secret things?" I said to Namtar. "I do not want Dumuzi creeping about in here."

"I will hide them all immediately," he said.

"I do not mean the things on the shelves, but the other things," I said.

"My lady, I know which things you speak of. We will keep them safe for you."

Dumuzi came out onto the steps of the Black Temple to watch us leave.

"To think I thought it could get no worse here," he said.

"Someone must man the Kur, unless we want to lose all control of it," Nammu said. "For now, that's you, Dumuzi. Do your duty, and I may look on you with favour later."

"I'm not sure I care much for your favour," he said.

I went and took his hands in mine. "Please be kind to my demons," I said.

He took his hands from me, but then reached out and patted my left shoulder. "I will be kind to the demons," he said.

Along the streets of the Dark City, my demons peeked at us from doorways and corners.

"Hundreds of them, thousands!" Nammu said. "Ugh!'

We climbed the long, thin bridge up into the starry sky of the underworld. Erra cast nervous glances at the abyss beneath us. "Is it real?" he said to Nammu.

"How can it be?" she said.

As we drew closer and closer to the first of the seven gates, my back began to hurt so terribly, and my hips too, and my feet, which were not used to walking.

Erra and Nammu drew far ahead of me, time and time again,

each time eventually standing to wait, Nammu with her hands upon her hips.

As I limped up to them for perhaps the tenth time, I heard them discussing me. Nammu was saying: "Do not underestimate her, and what she might know."

Erra said: "There's no more time for her nonsense."

"You seem in a such a hurry," Nammu said to him. "Is there a time limit upon this peace treaty you have negotiated for us?"

They realised I had caught up with them.

"I can still stop you leaving this world!" I shouted at them. "Only I decide who leaves! I am not a nonsense!"

"Ereshkigal, no more," Nammu said. "It is time to grow up."

She turned to lead the way, and after I had stood and cried a while, I followed on behind them.

CHAPTER EIGHT

NINLIL

In Kish, capital of
Akkadia

The old man knocked politely before drawing the bolts and entering, almost as if I was not a prisoner. As he made his way into my small chamber, carrying a heap of leather bags in his arms, I realised that I was as tall as him.

"You are growing so fast,' he said.

"Is it time to go?"

"Yes, they're getting the mules ready," he said. "I have brought you a cloak and some shoes, and also plenty of food."

"That is good of you, Biluda."

He sat watching me as I put on the soft leather shoes, and the magnificent blue cloak.

"You are a vision in blue," he said.

"I must try to stop growing any bigger, because I love this dress."

"May I ask you something, my lady?"

I looked up at him. "Go on."

"They teach us in temple that Enlil came upon you on the banks of a river and was consumed with passion. That he raped you and then kidnapped you."

"Yes."

"My lady, is that the memory you have buried away?"

"They teach the story in temple, but I do not myself remember it happening."

"Did you bury the memory so that you could forgive him?"

I sat and looked at him, my hands in my lap. "I don't know yet. I am not quite ready to face it all."

Biluda kept turning to look at me, as he led me out of the palace. "My lady, where are your parents now? Where is your family?"

I frowned before answering, because it was so long since I had spoken of them. "I think my mother is still in Heaven," I said. "I think my father is dead."

Biluda put a hand out to help me down the steps to the stable yard. "My lady, is Utu taking you to your mother?"

I found I did not want to answer him.

There were two mules standing saddled in the stable yard in the cold morning light. As Biluda tied my packs of food to one of the animals, Utu appeared, wearing a tufted sheepskin coat over his yellow robes.

He looked at me without expression and then used a mounting block to heave himself up onto his mule.

On impulse, I reached down and scooped some pebbles up into my hand. I slid them into the pocket inside my cloak.

"Do you need help mounting up, my lady?" said Biluda.

"I can get up myself," I said. Indeed, I found I could swing onto my mule very easily.

"I hope to see you again, Biluda," I said.

Utu snorted. "Ninlil, you will not be in Kish again."

The old man put up a hand to me as we rode out through the gates of palace, and I sent him back a smile.

"Is this Anzu nonsense?" Utu said, as we set off eastwards through a land of lakes and willows. "The eating and the growing. Is it Anzu business?"

"I am very hungry." It was hard to think of anything else. I liked having my own mule, though, and I put my hand to his warm neck as he moved beneath me. And I liked how gorgeous my cloak and dress were, so blue against my leather saddle.

But I was hungry.

"I must eat soon," I said.

Utu let out an angry sigh. "The old man packed you enough food to feed us for half a moon, and you have gobbled it while we are still in sight of Kish. You cannot possibly be hungry."

"Where are all your men?" I said. "You never go anywhere without a fleet or an army at your back. Why are you out here all on your own?"

"Some things one doesn't need witnessed," he said, looking away from me.

"I wonder if I could overpower you, even with those *mees* on your wrists."

"Nonsense," he said.

"I wonder."

I realised I still had my pebbles in my pocket. I crammed them all into my mouth and crunched on them until they were slurry and could easily be swallowed down.

Utu spun his mule around. He rode up close to me and grabbed my reins from me.

"Stop it," he said.

"What?"

"You will break your teeth. And I will be blamed for the damage."

I stretched out my lips, to show him my teeth. "I am not damaged."

He let go of my reins, still scowling at me. "Madness," he said.

"My husband Enlil showed such kindness to you," I said as he rode away from me. "He included you in everything, even though he knew you carried tales to his brother Enki. He supported you when you started taking men into your temple rites. And now you have turned on him. You are a man of no worth at all, Utu."

Utu turned to wag a finger at me. "I know what *you* are worth, Ninlil. And that is why I am forced to listen to you moaning like this."

All afternoon, as we made our way across grassed river plains, Utu kept turning around in his saddle, apparently only to frown at me.

"You seem to have doubled in size," he said at last. "Grow any bigger and you will be a giantess."

"I am not yet as big as you. But perhaps I soon will be."

He shook his head at me. "The sooner I hand you over, the better."

"And who are you handing me over to?"

"Your rightful owners," he said.

For a while he rode on in silence, and as I watched a herd of elk, grazing in the distance, I began to feel disconnected from everything around me. I felt a moment of danger, as if my wooden box of memories might pop open accidentally before I was ready for its contents.

But then Utu was talking to me, drawing me back into the world. "You had a different name when you first came to us as a little girl. What was it?"

"My name was Sud." I had not remembered it until that very moment.

"But Enlil changed your name to Ninlil. To an Anunnaki name."

"I suppose so."

"To hide you."

"Perhaps."

"Who were your parents?" he said. "I was told they were high-born citizens of Creation."

I turned my face to him. "Why were you in Kish?"

"Oh that." He waved a dismissive hand at me. "A simple trade."

"What kind of trade?"

"They gave me you. And I gave them information. About how to beat the Anunnaki. Nothing a schoolboy couldn't have worked out for himself."

"What did you tell them?"

"That the powers of the Anunnaki are spectacular, but they burn themselves out quickly. That they are few in number and can be easily overrun. That the secret to doing it is to make the people of Akkadia unafraid. It is only fear that has been holding them back."

"And how do you undo the fear?"

"You tell them that we are not the real Anunnaki, but only fake gods, who need not be feared. On my advice, they have been preaching the new stories and it is already making a difference."

"Will you not be sorry when the Akkadians wipe out your family?"

"Ninlil, it is my family who have forced me to make some very unpleasant choices." He seemed lost in thought for a while. "How did you have a baby so young? Was that this same Anzu magic that is making you grow now?"

I said nothing to that, only riding on past him, looking straight ahead.

After a while though, I turned to smile back at him. "If I was a giantess, I could crush you."

Utu grimaced. "You really are an awful creature, Ninlil. I will not be sad to be rid of you."

CHAPTER NINE

MARDUK

In Kish, capital of
Akkadia

Biluda, the head of the king's household, was standing in my doorway, his arms raised in almost comic fury. "Marduk!"

"Hello, Biluda," I said from my bed.

"Marduk, she is a dog of war, not a pet. Get her out of here!"

Moshkhussu lifted her heavy snout and drew back her lips at the steward with a low but serious growl. I kissed her wide, velvety head and she dropped her nose back onto our pillow.

"This is her room too," I said. "Inush insisted on it."

"Inush said you could keep her," Biluda said. "There was no suggestion of her living in your room. How you twist at the truth, Marduk! It was agreed that she would live in the stables."

"I'll put her back," I said, dropping another kiss on her head.

"It is enough that he has given you a room of your own here and made a pet of you, without you abusing his hospitality further."

I sat myself up. "It is always good to see you, Biluda, but is there a reason you are here?"

He pulled at his beard. "Is your back recovered? And your leg?"

"Well enough," I said, suspicious.

"He is planning to take you out hunting," he said. "Although I cannot see how you deserve it." He paused a moment before going on. "Marduk, there are things happening."

"What kind of things?"

He stretched his face into a smile, but he looked very sad. "Bad things, I think. Promise me you will be careful?"

"I am carefulness itself!" I said, grinning at him.

"If only that were true," he said.

Out in the stable yard, I found Inush already in his long leather riding coat, tapping his whip against one boot. A young boy stood nearby with two mules in his care and his eyes averted.

"You cannot have that dog in the palace," Inush said. "She is not a pet. She will kill someone. You are making everyone unhappy."

I looked down at Moshkhussu and she turned her almond eyes up at me, sitting very sweet and good at my heel. The effect was somewhat dampened by her huge jaws and savage-looking teeth. "I will find somewhere else for her to sleep."

Inush tapped again at his boot. "I'm told you're a useful tracker." He pointed over at the smallest of the mules. "You can take that one."

We rode out through the king's hunting woods, veering east through land I had never ridden across before.

I watched Moshkhussu zigzagging across the path in front of

us, nose down. I thought, *if I were her, I'd just run off, and keep running. What stops her?*

Inush rode alongside me, our mules showing their teeth to each other.

He was watching Moshkhussu too, and as if reading my mind, he said: "What would you do if you were free?"

"I would go to find my mother. My adopted mother. The one I told you about."

"Where was she when you saw her last?"

"Somewhere south of Egypt. But I believe she was taken away in a boat, so she could be anywhere."

As we spoke, the woods began to thin and we emerged onto the edge of a massif. Below us lay the river plains and a sweeping turn in the great Euphrates.

In the curve of the river, there were hundreds of men working. It took me a few heartbeats to absorb what I was seeing.

Scores of huge, circular coracles were under construction. Alongside them lay dozens of long, wooden barges, most already completed.

Amidst the outlines of this new armada, hundreds of workers roved to and fro with planks, ropes and buckets. The smoke from countless fires rose into the autumn sky.

"This is what I wanted to show you," said Inush.

"A fleet," I said, rather stupidly.

"The greatest fleet ever constructed."

"To attack Sumer?"

"Yes. We are going south against the Sumerians. We're going to put an end to all the years of war."

We dismounted and stood together, looking down on the fleet.

"You know it was Gilgamesh who gave me the idea for this," Inush said. "He made jokes, when he was a hostage here, about how slow King Akka was to go to war. How the spies of Sumer die of boredom, waiting for the army of King Akka to arrive. So then I thought, what if, just for once, the army of Akkadia moved like the wind? Or at least as fast as the great river."

"So, the whole army goes south on these boats?"

"Not only the whole army. Also the mules, the chariots, the supplies. We have already begun to distract the Sumerians with other attacks. By the time they think to look harder at what we are doing here, we will already be upon the river."

"And where will you head?"

"You mean, where will *we* head? I'm taking my household with me, and you will be part of it."

My mind turned to new thoughts, of chaos, of slaves left unattended and what that might mean for me, and I looked around for Moshkhussu.

Inush was still looking down to the river and the huge fleet under construction.

"This will be the war that will end the war," he said. "This time, we will crush the Anunnaki."

CHAPTER TEN

NINSHUBAR

Heading south to find the Potta

I was confident that I would quickly learn to sail.

After all, I had arrived in Sumer in a sailing boat and I had watched my captors sail the vessel. And then in the temple skiff, on our journey south to Enki's city, I had paid close attention to everything the boat boys did. I believed I had a grasp of all the first principles of the thing.

And yet on that first evening of our journey south, and all the next day, we made pitiful progress. There were some things set against me, in my defence. The wind, first off. It blew up the river, making sailing south more complicated. Second, our boat was rather smaller than the temple skiff, which perhaps put my eye out a little. Last of all, I came to believe that the boat had been put together wrongly.

However hard I worked to set the sails and steer us well, we only went from one bank to the other. Each time we neared a bank I would be obliged to strip down, climb out into high water or heavy mud, and heave our small boat around myself.

Each time I was forced to repeat this procedure I was also obliged to bear the sight of Inanna widening her eyes very slightly, and casually looking away. And by the end of the first full day of our journey, we could easily have walked back to Uruk for our dinner.

"Would it not be better to sail down the middle of the river," Inanna said at last, "more in a straight line, following the main direction of the flow? Much as the boys in the temple skiff did?"

"There is no need to be satirical," I said. I softened my tone. "Yes, it is my intention to follow the line of the river, as much as is possible in a boat driven by the twistings of the wind. But this is a very different boat from the temple skiff and the river is dangerously high now after all the bad weather. Also I think perhaps this boat has been assembled incorrectly, with the ropes and other pieces put on wrongly."

"But surely," she said, "if we just sat in the middle of the river with the sails down, and let the current take us, and perhaps used an oar to steer, we would make better progress than this?"

"No doubt we would," I said, "but I must learn to sail this boat before we reach the open sea, and so that is what I am doing. Now perhaps you could keep your lions out of the way when I am trying to deal with the sails."

Again, the very slightly widened eyes, and the casual turning away.

Late that afternoon we made camp on a gravel beach. As Inanna ate her flat bread with green onions and white cheese, I removed all the ropes and sails from the boat, and also everything else that proved removable, including all our supplies.

I frowned down at everything as it lay before me on the gravel. "I will put it all back together again now. So that I really understand how it all works."

For a long time, in the fading light, I held up pieces of rigging and sail cloth piece by piece, and moved them around on the sand, going back and forth between them.

"I wonder if there is someone we could ask for help," Inanna said.

I tipped my head to one shoulder and then the other, before turning to her.

"Why don't you find out where your lions are? It would be sad if they were out there eating children." I did not mean to sound as sharp as I did.

"Certainly I will go to find them," she said, looking a little affronted. She lifted her skirts and followed the lion tracks up into the dunes.

When I had reassembled the boat and all its contents, I was left with one piece of rope and one small piece of wood that I could not on any account find a home for.

As I was stuffing these stray items beneath our sacks of food, I realised Inanna had been gone too long and that it was getting dark.

I snatched up my flint axe and paced up the dunes after her.

She had not gone far. She was lying on her back on a stretch of flat sand, with her lions either side of her. It was the first time I had ever seen any good in them.

She was breathing but only barely.

I sat down and moved her head carefully into my lap. She had a flush on her and her forehead was damp. I had seen animals like it, after a terrible shock.

When she opened her eyes, I said: "How do you feel, Inanna?"

"I don't know yet."

I helped her sit and for a moment she rested her forehead against me.

"You smell of fresh-cut lime," she said. "Did you always smell so delicious?'

"I am famous in my country for my fine natural scent."

She pushed her hair back from her face. "I think I fainted."

"Are you ill?" I said.

She stood up. "No, not ill. It is just my head swirling around with all that has happened."

I stood also and put my hands on my hips. "From what happened to you in the underworld? Or what happened to you on the Barge of Heaven?"

She pulled her face into a smile, her chin raised. "It's all one piece."

"Inanna, we should not be going south if you are unwell."

"I am quite well." She began to walk back to the beach, each step careful and slow. Her lions, their faces on hers, prowled along on either side of her.

"I'm going to take you back to Uruk," I said. "You do not need to come south with me."

She turned back to me, her hands out to me, warm and earnest. "Ninshubar! I am fulfilling a promise. I am coming with you. I was torn apart by demons, resurrected, and then I exploded with blue flames! Of course I am beset by nightmares and now I seem to have fainted. But there is nowhere I would rather be than here on this journey with you."

I stood and looked at her a while. "Let's stay here tonight and rest up, and we will set off in the full light tomorrow."

"That sounds good," she said.

We were climbing back down to our scrap of beach, in the very last of the light, when I caught sight of white sails out on the river.

It was a skiff from the White Temple, sailing arrow-quick down the centre of the river. They were heading south, just as we were, but rather faster. A crew of boys, all busy on their ropes.

I realised they were the same boys who had taken us south! Their serious faces were so familiar to me. I watched them, for some heartbeats, in renewed awe of their fine sailing skills.

Inanna came to stand next to me. "Is that the same skiff we sailed in?"

"I think so."

We each raised a hand to the fast-moving boat, but the boys showed no sign of seeing us.

"I wonder where they are going," Inanna said, "and what message they are carrying. I wonder if it is my mother sending out word to my father."

"Could the message be for us?" I said.

She shut her eyes for a moment. "I can sense my mother," she said. Her face broke into a smile. "I think she is sitting with Harga!"

"But she seems well?"

"Perfectly well. If the message is for us, it cannot be urgent."

"Well, we cannot catch them now," I said, as the skiff slipped out of sight.

CHAPTER ELEVEN

MARDUK

Heading south towards Sumer

Biluda came to tell me the news: we would be leaving at dawn. Twenty of us from Inush's household servants and all the kennel boys, and of course the dogs of war.

"And will you come?" I said to him.

"I'm too old for war," he said. "Someone must look after things here."

"I will miss you," I said, rather awkward.

"And I you, Marduk. You are a very strange boy. But I wish you all the good in the world."

I was woken well before dawn the next day. By the light of my candle, I dressed in the riding leathers that Inush had given me, and put a heavy collar onto Moshkhussu. I looked around the room once, but there was nothing to take with me, so then we walked straight out into the yard to join the others.

We were near the front of the household as we trooped through the dark woods to the ships. Inush rode past and cast a scowl at me when he saw that Moshkhussu was with me, but nothing was said.

I suppose I had thought, after being woken so early, that the fleet would soon be loaded and on the river.

In that I was sadly mistaken. The loading of the army and all its supplies took all day and half the night. I was ostensibly in charge of Inush's tents and those did not take much time to stow aboard a large coracle, a vessel perhaps six cables across. However, the loading of hundreds of mules and onagers was a delicate business when one panicking animal could upset an entire boat, and all were required to help with it.

By the time we were out on the water, there was only a waning moon to see by.

The fleet was led by six barges loaded with troops. Next came the king's barge, with a tent set up for him on deck, and then came thirty giant coracles, with barges hemming them in on either side to stop them drifting into the banks. On these coracles were put the tents and slaves, and also the dogs, mules, and onagers. Also live birds, goats and sheep, and sacks of dried foods, for an army that might be away many moons. Behind came sixty more barges, also thick with soldiers and with chariots set out on their decks.

Moshkhussu and I were assigned to the very last of the giant coracles and we travelled on top of Inush's tent bags.

As we set off down the great, dark river, the fleet was silent. That was the most astonishing thing of all.

It took us three days and three nights to make our way down the Euphrates. We slept and ate on our boats; the animals stood or lay in their own dung.

The men kept up their astonishing silence, with only the odd shout of warning as boats came too close or drifted too far towards the banks. The dogs, mules and livestock were not always so quiet, but for most of the journey we slipped downstream in a cocoon of river noise and the sweet smell of the reed beds.

Inush came to inspect his tents on the second day. His barge touched to, and he quickly jumped on board to look around. He paused a moment before me and Moshkhussu, as we sat bundled up together on top of the tent bags.

"It will not be long now," he said. "Are you nervous?"

"Should I be?"

He laughed, and then, looking around first, sat down next to us. "I hope you will be safe enough at the supply camp."

"Are you yourself nervous?" I said to him.

He smiled. "I have spent half my life riding out against Sumer."

"I wonder why you follow King Akka. What more can you need than the things you have already?"

"Did you know I was orphaned very young, just like you?" he said. "King Akka has been a father to me, just as your mother from the far south was a mother to you."

"Ninshubar," I said.

"Who is Ninshubar?"

"It's my mother. My adopted mother. Her name is Ninshubar."

"I didn't know that was her name." He nodded to himself, frowning. "I've heard it before though. Is it a Sumerian name?"

"I only know she's from the south, from a land with no cities and no farmers. Where people sleep in caves or beneath the stars and worship the old gods."

"*Nin-shooo-barr*," he said, worrying at it. "The name is familiar to me. I cannot think why."

At last, we were there. A bend in the river, and the word was passed back at a whisper that we must start poling ourselves towards the western shore.

The unloading, onto a wide sandy beach, took half a night. We sweated and swallowed curses and everyone was at least wet up to the waist. Even I was forced to wade in and out of the river with heavy tent bags, in the general panic to get everything and everyone on shore before we were discovered.

Well before dawn, however, a camp had been marked out, the boats were all beached, every hoof was muffled, every dog muzzled, and the wheels of the chariots were all covered with fleece.

The army moved off then, fast but quiet, heading for the city that lay just a league downriver. Inush lifted his chin to me as he rode past. "Stay out of trouble, Marduk."

We household slaves and one banner of soldiers were left to stand guard around the heaped-up mounds of supplies and drawn-up boats.

I sat with every nerve in my body alive for a sudden noise or some unexpected movement. Moshkhussu sat under one of my arms, her ears twitching this way and that, her body quivering with the drama and excitement of this strange night.

I think, to be truthful, I did fall asleep for a while, with my head on my knee. I only woke, guiltily, because Moshkhussu was licking my cheek. But I missed nothing and nothing happened for a long time after, although we strained our ears for distant shouts and flinched at every bird noise.

And then a flicker of energy ran through the camp.

One by one we all stood, soldiers and slaves alike. All of us looked south.

The horizon was lighting up a dull orange, although it was too early for dawn.

The light crept higher into the sky and I thought I could smell smoke. Was it fields burning? Farms? Villages? Could it be the city? Could I hear screams, very distant, over the song of the river?

I wondered if they were awake yet, inside the city walls.

I looked up: something was falling from the sky, soft and white. It began to settle on my jacket.

Ash.

I thought of Gilgamesh when he was a hostage in Kish, and how he had smiled at me, his extraordinary smile. How the charisma came in waves off him.

The Lion of Uruk.

I said to a boy standing near me: "Will Gilgamesh be here, do you think?"

The boy shrugged. "It's his city, is it not? But perhaps he is already dead."

CHAPTER TWELVE

ERESHKIGAL

Rising up into the realm of light

I had been queen of the Dark City for a hundred years. At first I fought to leave. Then I refused to be ordered out.

Now I felt quite muddled.

I did not want to leave my lovely demons. I had made a home for myself in the darkness. But part of me craved the things I had lost, even my foul and untrustworthy family.

In this muddled state, I now passed through the first of the seven gates that led out into the realm of light, with Nammu and Erra walking ahead of me. For a while we all stood in the small metal space together, blinking in the blue light, with the sixth gate directly ahead of us.

The seventh gate slid shut behind us.

"We must pass through one at a time now," Nammu said to Erra. "It is the protocol on the Kur. Ereshkigal, you will go first."

"Why me first?"

"Because if you stay behind you are likely to lock the gates against us and refuse to follow us out."

I could not argue with that.

"Will he suffer?" I said. "We all suffered."

Nammu looked up at Erra, with what I think she meant to be a reassuring smile. "It hurts at first. The air and the Earthlight. We will build you up slowly."

"My suit will protect me from all that," he said. Even before he had finished speaking, the black scales had flowed up over his head, hiding his face. I could still see the wet of his eyes though. Were there transparent scales over them?

"The air here will not hurt me," he said. "I will not need to get used to it."

I peered closer at him, observing how the scales seemed to flutter around his mouth when he spoke. How I lusted after that armour!

"You will wear that the whole time you are here?" Nammu said.

He let the scales fall from his face. "Why not?"

She shrugged and then turned to me. "Go on then, Ereshkigal."

I then made my way through the system of gates, until finally I stood alone, except for Neti, in the blue light between the first and second gates.

"You need only put your hand to it, and it will open," he said.

"Do not hurry me, Neti."

Brave and bold as I was, I found myself very frightened.

"Will it hurt?" I said.

"Not as much as the first time," said Neti, his face expressionless.

At last I put my hand out to the door, and it snapped open.

The Earthlight blinded me.

Oh, and the cold, clean, cutting air!

Painful, yes. But good!

"I had forgotten," I said, with my hands over my eyes.

One hundred years it had been, with no sunlight upon me! With only ancient, stale air in my lungs!

I stepped out onto the mossy ground and sank slowly down onto my knees.

The air was hard on my lungs at first. But not poisonous, as it was the first time I stepped onto the Earth. Very soon my *melam* was helping me and I could see again, although my head hurt.

Oh, the beauty! I had forgotten.

Even glimpsed through fingers, the glory of the high mountain lake and the walls of the crater beyond: it was overwhelmingly beautiful. Oh, and the deep blue brightness of the early morning sky!

I sat down on a mossy tussock, and rested my eyes in my hands, and breathed in the mountain air.

As the sun rose high into the sky behind me, I began to see much better.

The first thing that surprised me was that my best dress, so velvety black inside the underworld, no longer looked very splendid. In fact it now looked very soiled; it seemed to be caked in grey gunk. And my ankles were so dirty. I pulled my dress up. My legs were filthy. How had I not realised?

It was true that I had not had a bath for a long time, but I sometimes let my demons flannel me. Was this all the dust of the dead, fallen upon me, and clogging up my creases? Could I even smell myself, upon the clean morning air... a sharp smell, like stale urine?

As I buried my face in my skirts, in order to get a proper smell of myself, Neti appeared before me in a sheepskin robe of the sort a shepherd might wear.

"Erra is struggling," he said. "You need to help him out of the Kur, so I can get Nammu out. He is blocking the last gate."

I made no move to quit my mossy tussock. "What about his fabulous, black-scaled suit?"

"The suit appears to have malfunctioned and will not come up over his face."

"That is unfortunate. It is going to be very hard on him, the Earth air, and the Earthlight." I put my face up to the warming sun. "He will surely be in agony. But I do not see why I should help him."

"I do not have the strength to help him myself, even in my most solid form. And I need him out now. It is my job to keep the gates clear. And if you will not help me," Neti said, pausing rather menacingly, "then I do not see why I should honour our agreements. You are not the only one of us with information that might be precious to an enemy. Perhaps you forget, Ereshkigal, that although you know my secrets, I also know yours."

We frowned at each other for a moment. "I will try to help you," I said.

As I stood, I realised that the crater in which the Kur had landed was not as I had left it. There were huge tumbles of rock everywhere that had not been there before.

"What are all these rock falls?" I said.

"When the gate to Heaven opened, to allow the dark stranger through, the whole world shook," said Neti. "It was not only the Kur that was damaged."

I made my way back to the Kur. Its rocky exterior, so natural looking, gleamed a brilliant red in the morning light. I marvelled now, having spent so long inside, how much smaller the Kur was from the outside. How clever I had been!

The first gate stood open, a round, blank circle in the rough-hewn side of the Kur. I put my head in through the open door but I could see nothing inside except darkness.

"Erra?"

A groan from within.

Neti appeared at my elbow. "He is half in and half out of the second gate. That is his head there." He pointed into the gloom.

"Nammu should have come out ahead of him," I said. "Or passed through at the same time. This is not a time for sticking to protocols."

"Wise words, Madam," said Neti, "and yet of absolutely no use to us now."

As my eyes readjusted to the gloom inside the Kur, I thought I could see something that might be a head, jammed up against a wall inside the first gate.

"You must help him," Neti said. "He is past sense."

"I do not think I can," I said.

"Ereshkigal, you certainly cannot help him by standing outside."

Frowning, I put one foot into the Kur and then the other, feeling my way. The blue light came on then and I could see what was going on.

Erra was sprawled unconscious with his head in the outermost chamber, but the rest of him lying awkwardly between gates two and three.

"The doors cannot shut with him lying like that," said Neti.

"Yes, I see that."

Erra had thin lines of blood running from his nose and from both eyes.

Oh, and his head.

His hood had fallen away and for the first time I could see his hair and the top of his skull.

Someone or something had hacked at him. Ghastly stretches of wet bone lay exposed amidst his hair. I caught the horrifying glint of brain matter. Yet they did not look like fresh wounds.

"What is this?" I said, but no one answered me.

I kneeled next to Erra on the hard metal floor of the outer chamber, very awkward. On a whim I put a hand out onto his head, to feel at one of the gashes in his scalp, and I was surprised, I do not know why, by how soft his hair felt.

On another impulse, I leaned over and smelled him. First his hair and then the warmth of his neck. He smelled good and clean, of fresh sweat. Why did he smell so good when I smelt so sour?

His head was cruelly damaged though. How was he walking around with wounds so terrible?

I leaned over and smelled him again. I had a strong desire to bite him. I had not been able to smell him in the Great Below. But now I was very drawn to his good and animal scent. I rubbed my nose into his neck.

"What are you doing?" His voice was not much above a whisper, his breath upon my neck.

I sat back up. "You need to move your legs so that we can shut the second gate. Nammu is trapped on the other side."

"My lungs…" he said. "And my eyes. I cannot make my helmet work."

"I am good at fixing things," I said.

"I'd have to take it all off," he said. "I can't do that now."

My mind was whirring with the thought of getting hold of the armour.

"Nammu will be able to help you, if we can get you out of here," I said. "If you can just bring your knees up to your chest."

He reached out to me, and to my surprise, took hold of one of my hands. Not for help, it seemed, but just to hold it. For some moments, we stayed like that. Something very odd happened then, in that small handful of time. A powerful charge rushed through me. A charge of feeling both physical and mental. Erra was looking at me; we were looking straight at each other. I knew in that moment that he felt it too.

Then with a grunt, holding on tighter to my hand, Erra pulled his legs over the threshold and the second gate snapped shut.

Moments later Nammu was standing over us in the tiny compartment. "What are you doing, Ereshkigal? Move out of the way. Get out of the Kur."

I felt rather aggrieved as I climbed back out into the sunlight. Had I not been most helpful? Had it not been me, yet again, who had been the saviour of the moment?

It was then that I had the idea of cleaning myself. I was not sure, after what had just happened, that I wanted the dark stranger to see me with grey gunk on me, or smell my stink.

I did not like the look of the lake. It looked very deep and black. But I had a memory of having crossed a stream, somewhere on our way out of the crater, in the days after the Kur first landed. I set off very boldly to look for it, picking my way around the huge piles of fresh rockfall.

At first I could not see the water but could hear the rush of it. Twice I had to clamber up onto a rock, to try to work out where it was. But at last I found it. A tumbling froth of white, falling from the edge of the crater. I kneeled and scooped the icy liquid straight into my mouth. Then I took off my sandals and my clothes and sat down on the wet rocks beside the stream so that I could splash at myself. The shock of it!

I saw that there was a little pool further down towards the base of the crater, and after a while I went and sat in that, all the way up to my breasts. I no longer felt the cold so badly, but instead felt a burst of warmth and good cheer running through me.

"Ereshkigal!"

It was Nammu, looking very angry. She was standing on a boulder just above me, her hands on her hips.

"What are you doing?"

That I chose not to answer, since she could see for herself what I was doing.

"Erra is in trouble," she said.

"So I have seen. But you told me to go away."

"I did not mean for you to wander off and sit in a stream. I need you to help me get him back through the gates into the heart of the Kur. I cannot lift him alone. He can only withstand short periods outside unless we can get his suit working." She paused, and then added: "There's something wrong with his head. Something his *melam* should have fixed."

"Why not just give him more *melam*?" I said. "It will speed it all up."

"I have no *melam*, foolish girl."

"But he does," I said.

She tipped her head to one side. "How do you know that?"

"It's hidden in his belt," I said. "I know things."

"How do you know things?"

"I'm not telling you because you are so horrible to me."

I thought then that Nammu might come down from her rock to kick me, so I said: "Why don't you ask the girl to help you?"

"What girl?"

"Dumuzi's sister. She is in Neti's hut. Just over the horizon. Did you not know that? Did you not see her there when you were battering at my gates?"

"Geshtinanna is here?"

"She is always making Neti bring me messages. Always begging to take Dumuzi's place."

"No, I did not know she was here," Nammu said.

She prowled off in the direction of the gatekeeper's hut.

I was going to stay in the water longer, but Nammu and her foul temper had ruined my mood.

Well, I had soaked; I might as well now get on with the business of properly cleaning myself.

I first washed at myself with the grit from the bottom of the stream, then I got out onto the edge of the stream and gave my dress and cloak a good soaking.

By then I was very cold, but I only had my very wet dress and cloak to dry myself on. I was also further downcast to find that my clothes-washing upon the banks of the stream had left me with streaks of dark red mud upon my newly washed limbs.

As I did my best with this, all the while feeling very cold, I realised the gatekeeper was watching me.

"Perhaps you would like to wait in my hut, Madam, while the others look to Lord Erra. There are things you can dry yourself on in there."

"Yes, I could wait in your hut. Thank you, Neti." I felt very grateful to him in that moment. "Do you still have those honey cakes?"

"I do, Madam."

Soon enough I was dry and wrapped up in warm blankets on Neti's narrow bed. I looked about the neat little hut, and said: "I wonder, Neti, if you have something that I could write on. I am writing a history of Sumer, from the very first days. Perhaps you have heard of it."

"Of course I have heard of your history. Let me see what I can find you in the way of some very good clay."

"You are being very nice to me now."

"You are my guest now," he said. "I must be nice to the guests."

That evening I sat before the fire in the little cottage with a fresh clay tablet on my lap and in my hand, the small stylus that Neti had fashioned for me from an eagle's leg bone.

I did not want to go down into the underworld.

I paused a moment. Would my last baby have died, had Enki not forced me into the Kur?

I loved each of my babies so much

I looked up and saw Neti watching me, standing pale and expressionless beside the door. He had the look that he had when he spoke not only for himself but also for the Kur.

He said: "I hope you have not risked everything, by letting this man Erra out into the world."

A bolt of anger shot through me, at how unfair his words were.

"Neti, I expressly asked you for your opinion on it and you said it made no difference to you whether he was in or out."

"Nammu was damaging the Kur. That took precedence."

I put down my stylus. "I consulted with you."

"This man who calls himself Erra intends to return the same way he came. Out through the eighth gate. The Kur will not survive it."

"You just keep on worrying about the Kur, then," I said. "And I will worry about the stranger and the fate of this entire realm."

CHAPTER THIRTEEN

INANNA

Heading south to find the Potta

I lay back on the sacks of provisions, my lions stretched out alongside me, and I watched Ninshubar sail the boat.

I had become frightened of falling asleep; terrified of what might be waiting for me when I slipped down into the dark. Sometimes I was in the underworld again, with giant worms eating at my insides. Sometimes I was on the sand dunes outside Ur with my friend Amnut, who had died so long ago now, and I would wake up awash with grief. Sometimes I was back beside the luminous blue lake of power and I would feel myself about to topple into it.

Once I found myself in a room and I did not know where I was or who I was. There was a shape at the doorway; a woman covered with golden scales.

"It would be better if you spoke to me," Ninshubar said, her hands busy with the ropes.

"I am not sure it would."

"I cannot make my calculations, Inanna, if I do not have all the facts."

"My words will not help you."

"Try me," she said. "Please, Inanna."

I sat up, careful not to disturb my lions. "Ever since the underworld, I have found myself confused about *when* this is." I lifted my eyebrows and made my face cheerful and light.

"What do you mean, when?"

I lifted my hands to the skies. "Is this now? Has this already happened? Or is this something that will one day happen to me?"

She frowned at me. "Inanna, this is now."

"So you say. But sometimes I think that this all happened a very long time ago. That this is just a memory of my happy past." I blinked back tears. "I am going mad, Ninshubar."

Careful not to tip the boat, she moved closer and put a hand onto my shoulder.

"Inanna, this is now. I promise you. This is where we are. You and me together."

I did not tell her that the dark stranger still walked through my dreams, or of the other presence, stronger every day, of a woman who might be a monster. The memory of her feathers, glistening in the darkness.

"This is now," Ninshubar repeated. "You and me, here."

I pulled the master *mee* from my wrist. "I need to be ordinary for a while. Or as ordinary as is possible."

She leaned over and took it from me. "I'll keep it safe," she said.

We passed out of the river delta into open sea and the sun began to beat down strongly on us. Piece by piece, we abandoned our carefully chosen travel outfits. In the end I wore only my linen nightshirt. Ninshubar stripped down to a short linen tunic, although she kept her axe and knife strapped to her.

I licked salt from my lips and rubbed it from my lions' whiskers.

We stayed well out towards the horizon as we made our way past Eridu, but tucked in close to the shore as we headed west. We watched the towers of Eridu growing small upon the horizon, and when they were gone, there was only the sea, the sky, and the white line of the shore.

"This is the second great sea journey of my life," Ninshubar said. "It is strange to reflect upon all that has happened since I was brought as a slave to Eridu."

"Do you feel very different?"

She gave me her warmest smile. "I know more than I did. But the *melam* has not changed the essence of me."

"We just need to find your Potta." I lay back then, but kept looking at her, smiling.

"The thing about time," Ninshubar said. "About when this is. Does it still weigh on you?"

"No, no," I said. "It was a brief madness. Please do not worry."

She smiled and then looked up at the sails. As she tipped her head, I remembered her sitting on a huge, unfamiliar creature with two lumps on its back. Was it a memory or a premonition? I breathed in deep to clear my swirling thoughts.

When the wind blew steady and there was no need for Ninshubar to be pulling on her ropes, we often talked about the Potta. The same conversation over and over, worrying over the little that we could be sure of.

"He could still be dead," Ninshubar said, always with one stern eye upon the shape of the main sail. "But the trader says he was sold for slavery. So that means he did not die in the gully where I last saw him. That is a definite thing."

"I think he is still alive," I said. Sometimes in my dreams I saw the Potta, or at least someone I thought was him, but I did not want to tell Ninshubar that. How could I be sure if it was real?

"I trust in your instinct then," she said.

The main thoroughfare from Eridu to the outer reaches of Sumer ran so close to the beach that at times we could see men and animals walking along in silhouette. Two or three times we put to shore and quickly learned from those we stopped to ask that the man we sought was ahead of us still, but not by much. He had eight wagons with him pulled by oxen, was the thing that all agreed on.

At every bay after that we would pull in and Ninshubar would walk up to the road to check for signs that the eight wagons had passed. Each time she came back and said: "He has already passed."

But at least he had passed and we were still on his trail.

Sometimes, when the wind died, Ninshubar would swim around the boat, powerful and solid as a dolphin as she cut through the water. When she had swum long enough she would pull herself into the boat. She did it so lightly and elegantly, despite her size, that she barely rocked the boat.

"You know I dream sometimes of waking on a beach," I said, as she sat, dripping, beside me. "I have dreamed it so many times that I feel it to be a prophecy. And the dream has come back to me whole now, watching you in the sea."

She dried her face on her shift. "What exactly is the dream?"

"I wake up with my face down upon the sand and with warm surf washing over me. I sit up and the sky is very blue. I can see a rock cutting up through the water, just off the beach. I think..."

"What?"

"I think I should learn to swim. That it is important that I can swim through the water and that I am strong."

"I could teach you. Stranger things have been done."

I looked over the side of the boat, at the dark blue water, light spiralling up from its depths. "I am not afraid. I think that if I sink my *melam* would not let me drown."

"Well, no doubt," she said, "but wouldn't it be more pleasant to move over the top of the water and not sink?"

"Much more pleasant!"

"I will teach you then. You will learn. I have every confidence in you."

All the same, she tied a rope around me before she let me go over the side and even then, she insisted on coming in with me. She kept one hand beneath my belly, and the other on the side of the boat, as I tried to paddle with my hands and feet, and not let my mouth go under.

"I am doing it!" I gasped. "I think I am doing it!'

A moment later a dolphin leaped from the sea and landed only a cord ahead of us. At once the sea around us was alive with its brethren, all rolling bright eyes at me.

"They come to wonder at you," Ninshubar said, pulling me in closer to the boat.

She was smiling out at the dolphins.

"I would like to get back in now," I said.

The eyes of the animals upon me were no longer a wonder to me. Instead they filled me with a dread that I could not bear to examine. What was it they expected of me?

The dolphins followed us all day after that and I tried to smile and focus only on their beauty.

"You are a wonder to wild creatures," Ninshubar said. "This witchery of yours is very strange."

"I know they want me alive," I said. "I cannot yet be sure why."

Then one morning, upon the shore, the dark shapes of what might be wagons. Yes: eight wagons, drawn by oxen. We sailed straight for the beach.

I sat in the boat without getting in the way, with my lions close to me, as I had been trained to, as Ninshubar leaped out into the surf and waded the boat up onto the sand.

She handed me the master *mee* before lifting me out of the boat. "Just in case," she said. It shrunk around my wrist as I pushed it on; the familiar blue network spun out around me.

"Now let us hurry," she said.

The rough sand beach was backed by an escarpment. I scrambled as fast as I could up the rise, with Ninshubar holding my hand tight and my lions close behind me.

We headed west along the sandy road and soon outpaced the wagons.

The man we sought was sitting with a whip in hand on the front of the lead wagon. He turned his black beard to us and, after a moment's thought, pulled up his oxen.

"Goddesses," he said. He slowly climbed down and kneeled to us both, his eyes on my lions.

Ninshubar waved at him to stand up.

"We are looking for a tall boy with pale skin, red hair and blue eyes, who you bought at market perhaps two years ago," she said.

The man climbed slowly to his feet. I saw that he was thinking of lying and I threw out one fine blue strand around him to be sure that he did not.

Another moment and he said: "I did buy a boy, with pale skin and red hair. Maybe one or two years ago. But he got sick before I had a chance to take him. He had some kind of head wound. So I made the villagers give me my money back and I left him there with them."

I threw another loop of blue around him. "And what next?"

"I took my money and left. I never saw or heard of the boy again. If I could tell you more I would, but I have nothing to tell."

"He's telling the truth," I said to Ninshubar.

I saw that she was sunk into such severe disappointment that she could not speak.

"Describe the village to us," I said to the man. "Tell us exactly where it was, and how to find it."

The lions leaped onboard first. Ninshubar lifted me back into the boat before pushing us off the beach.

"We should go back," she said, as we were heading out to open sea. "This is not a fresh trail. The Potta will be long gone if he even survived his head wound. You are more and more unwell, less and less yourself. We must go back."

"It is only a few days on to the village," I said. "Let us just do it, while we are here. If it leads nowhere, we will go straight back to Uruk. We may never get a chance like this."

"No." She shook her head.

"Ninshubar, I am quite well. I am improving every day. The sea air is washing all the darkness and confusion out of me. And look how I am loving my swimming!"

She shook her head again.

"I know he's alive," I said to her at last. "I am sure of it."

She turned to me, very serious. "Have you seen him? In your dreams?"

"I think so," I said.

"Why not say before?"

"Because my dreams confuse me." I drew myself up. "We are going on, Ninshubar. I command it."

"All right," she said. "If you have seen him, I know that must mean something. We will go on."

We went quickly along the coast, stopping only twice for fresh water. I could see from the way the boat ate up the sea now that Ninshubar was becoming a master sailor. I knew she would have taken pleasure in it had she not been so low about her Potta.

I was content to stay out of her way, feeding dry meat and water to my lions, never touching anything that I had not been expressly asked to touch. I only spoke of joy and small things now. After all, it did not matter when this was. Only that she and I were here together.

Ninshubar sailed with her face upon the shore, trying to remember something she recognised. Sometimes she would shout out and we would ply inland. She would walk about on a beach, but it would be somewhere she had been with the slavers, not with him, her Potta.

One morning the land to our right seemed to disappear towards the north, but ahead we could see more land. "Are we crossing between islands?" I said.

"I don't know," she said. "But I think I remember this. I think we must continue west." On we went, cutting through the blue sea as a sharp blade cuts through stretched linen.

When we were going as fast as we could, the dolphins returned, twisting in our wake, leaping with the thrill of it. My lions leaned as far as they dared from the edge of the boat, hoping to get a claw into one of them.

On most days there would be a lull and I would be allowed to overboard, always with a rope around my waist. Ninshubar and the lions would watch me from the boat. My challenge would be to swim back to them without having to be hauled up from the depths by the rope.

I was paddling towards the boat, thrashing and gasping somewhat, when Ninshubar's gaze was caught by something on the horizon.

"I am getting better," I said, holding on at last to the side of the sailing boat, my ribs heaving, my hand almost too weak with exhaustion to hold my weight. "I am becoming quite the dolphin."

But Ninshubar was not listening.

Her eyes were hard upon the land.

"This is it," she said. "This is where it happened. I recognise the hills behind."

"Are you certain?" I was suddenly chilled, although the water was warm.

I looked up at her face, dark against the vastness of the sky. I had a flash, of two lions tied up in a fire pit, burning alive.

"I am certain this is it," Ninshubar said. "This is where I lost him. This is where I was captured."

She pulled me out of the water by my wrists, in one easy motion.

"The village will not be far from here," she said.

CHAPTER FOURTEEN

NINLIL

On the road to Susa

We soon ran out of food and Utu was an indifferent huntsman. He let me ride out in front of him while he tried to bring down rabbits or game birds with the gold *mees* he wore around his wrists. It meant I could get down from my mule whenever I liked, to eat grass, earth or stones.

"You are growing too fast," Utu said, watching me as I stuffed my mouth with leaves. "It cannot be safe."

I swallowed my leaves. "What have you been promised, in return for my kidnap?"

"*Melam*, of course," he said. "A few extra hundred years of life. My father promised to share his cache of it with me, but then I learned that my mother ate every last scrap of it so that she could give birth to my sister Inanna."

"My husband said Enki had *melam*."

"Ah, yes he did, but my mother also ate that. I am sure she is now in perfect health and looks not a day over twenty. So that is wonderful for my mother. And wonderful for my sister Inanna, who is apparently quite the prodigy with the *melam* running so thick in her veins. But sadly, I now have bones that are starting to ache and I feel the inevitable coming fast at me. So, I have taken things into my own hands."

"What will life be like for you when the Akkadians have killed all your family?'

"I will bear it well enough, thank you Ninlil."

Utu was little more than a distraction to me by then. My mind was firmly on my wooden box. When we lay down to sleep in the shelter of a palm grove that night, I turned my thoughts inwards. I focused on the wooden box in which lay the memories and secrets of the time before I forgot.

I would take just one small peek.

I had a flash, so strong, so real, of my brother sitting beside me, his face closed to me, his right hand upon my wrist. We were on our way to the river gardens. I had been excited when he said he would take me. Why wasn't Bizilla with us?

Bizilla, who was sworn to protect me always. Who was never allowed to leave my side.

It was just me and my brother, and I felt more and more nervous. Why wasn't Bizilla with us?

I sat up in the dark, breathing deeply, my heart hammering.

Utu sat up also, on the far side of the campfire.

"What is it?"

I swallowed. "Do you have food?"

He leaned over to feel around his bag, then heaved himself upright, and came over to me with a piece of dried venison.

As I chewed it down, I said: "My brother was there on the morning that it happened."

"Do you mean on the day Enlil attacked you?" He was standing over me still.

"My brother took me there. I remember him taking me there, to where it happened."

Utu was silent a while. "You did not remember that before?"

"No." I lay back down. "Thank you for the venison."

Utu picked his way back to his blanket.

"Who was your brother? Is he someone I might have heard of?"

I didn't answer.

"Do you think your brother engineered what happened?"

But I turned my back on him and did not answer.

The lid was back on the wooden box, but I could not now unforget the peeking I had done.

Why was my brother there on the day I was attacked?

All the next day, through endless farmland, I thought about my brother for the first time in four hundred years. My brother was already an adult when I was born; already a general. He was used to wielding power. But in Creation power passes down the female line. From the day I was born, he knew that one day everything would pass to me.

I remembered his heavy hand on my wrist that day as we walked through the gardens to the riverbank where my happiness and health would be taken from me.

∞

Utu watched my face as we rode. "What would your brother gain, from what happened that day?"

I pulled my mule up short. "Would a brother sacrifice a sister in return only for power?"

Utu gave a short, dry laugh. "With power comes glory, and riches. He might do it for any one of those things."

"I had forgotten my brother's name," I said. "But I've remembered it now."

There was no need to tell Utu.

But my brother's name was Qingu.

We began our climb into the Zagros mountains. Rocky crags, evergreen trees, and cedar-scented air. Everywhere, water cascading down.

Utu rode ahead, rarely turning to check on me.

I thought about escaping, but very idly. I was not so very unhappy about the path I now found myself on. My body felt large and strong. My beautiful blue dress was already too small for me; I had had to cast off my shoes.

I thought about the idea Utu had given me, of becoming a giant and crushing him. I thought about what it would feel like to do it and drew pleasure from it. But already, he did not seem very significant to me. Except of course as the guide to my future.

So I kept on riding behind him.

I did not return to my memory box straight away. For two nights I only ate and then made myself go to sleep. It was too much to even think of opening it again.

But on the third night, in a camp in a small stand of acacia, I pulled up my cloak over me and I turned my mind back to the box. One more small peek and then I would draw back, as I had before.

∞

We were walking through my brother's beautiful gardens. We were following the course of a gorgeous stream as it cascaded through rocks and flowering bushes.

I glanced up my brother's dark and unsmiling face.

"You just be good," he said to me.

In the distance, a tall man stood on a grass-covered bridge over the stream.

"Who is that?" I said.

Qingu let go of my wrist and began digging in his pocket. He drew out a gold bracelet with tiny red marks painted around the edge of it and pushed it up onto his left wrist.

"What is that?" I said to him.

"Just a toy," he said. "Now let's go meet my friend."

I walked on beside him. I knew it was not right that Bizilla was not with me. It should not have only been me here, with my brother and now this strange man.

The man turned to look at us. He was very old and powerfully built, with a dark beard and serious eyes.

"Sud, this is Enlil," my brother said. "Enlil, this is my little sister." He gave Enlil a strange smile. "Doesn't she look beautiful to you?"

I had meant only to peek, but then it all crashed down upon me.

All night, I wept.

I had not wept since it happened. Since I woke up with Enlil sitting next to me, both of us covered in mud.

Now I wept and wept. For myself. For the pain. For my lost

childhood. For my brother's betrayal. For being taken. For how terribly, terribly frightened I was.

"You must stop crying," Utu said. He was standing over me in the darkness. "Ninlil, I cannot sleep with you blubbing like this."

In the end he moved his sleeping blanket halfway down the hill to get away from me.

I must have fallen asleep at last, but when I opened my eyes, I remembered it all, and began to cry again. I ate my breakfast crying and I cried as I climbed onto my mule and set off along a path into thickening bushland. By mid-morning my cloak and dress were wet with tears. My mule was wet with tears. He kept flicking his long ears back at me, upset by my distress.

Utu rode further and further ahead of me to get away from the sound of me sobbing. When he stopped to make me my lunch, on a stretch of open grassland, he was quivering with tension.

I climbed off my mule, sat down on a rock, and kept on crying.

"What is this?" Utu said, his hands lifted in rage at me. "Is it self-pity? Sadness? Grief? What is it? It is too much! Plenty of women have been through far worse than you and they do not make such a fuss of it."

I looked up at him through a heavy veil of tears. "I am also crying for the other girls."

"Oh, for all the stars, what nonsense," he said.

He gave me some cold duck to eat and then went to sit away from me to eat his own lunch.

I ate my duck, jamming it into my mouth, downing it in four or five great chunks, bones and all. Then I scavenged through Utu's bags and found some old cheese and some nuts, and a skin of water, and I got that all down too.

I went and sat near my mule, and watched it graze.

I remembered the journey from my brother's estate to Anunnaki lands after Enlil attacked me. The vast curve of the realm below us. Enlil's face, hard and closed.

He sat well away from me, looking all the time at the golden bracelet he had on his right wrist. He told me that he did not remember what had happened, although it had only been an hour or two before. He said he could not understand why he was wearing the bracelet. He said he could not remember my brother being there.

Last of all, he said: "Sud, did I hurt you?"

It was then that I began to grow the baby.

Why did I do that? Why did I choose to bear his baby?

By the time we landed on Anunnaki soil, I was already beginning to swell with it.

Did my brother use the weapon on me too?

"I don't care any more," Utu said, when we were on our way again. "Either you stop crying or I am going to force you to stop."

I did just for one moment, stop crying. I turned upon my mule to face Utu. "You cannot make me do anything," I said.

After that he followed me quietly.

CHAPTER FIFTEEN

GILGAMESH

At Uruk

"Gilgamesh?"

There was a man at the door, holding up a lantern, and for a moment I thought it was Enkidu.

Harga.

Always Harga.

He had his battered old breastplate on and a sword in his right hand.

"Uruk is under attack," he said. "The city is surrounded."

I got out of bed and found myself still dressed.

I picked up my sword belt from the floor and retrieved my knives.

"King Akka?"

"Yes."

"Are they in? Inside the walls?"

The briefest pause.

He said: "Everyone has been looking for you, and not able to find you, because you were not in your father's rooms."

"And?"

"Your wife and son are missing. I have people searching. But the night nurse who was with them is dead on the floor of their bedchamber."

We stood in silence for half a moment.

"What has been done?" I said.

"I have people looking everywhere. Inside the palace and out."

I nodded, my right hand on my sword, still not moving. I was thinking of standing outside her door; how I decided not to go in. The sound of my son crying.

"Gilgamesh," he said.

"All right, first to the walls. Let me see what's happening."

I followed Harga down half-lit corridors.

We passed servants still in their bed clothes. The chief of the household was there at the main doors out onto the street, his hands clasped before him, his face distraught. He was about to say something, but I cut him off.

"Send my armour after me," I said. "I'll be on the walls."

"Yes, my lord." He stepped back to let us out.

We made our way across the palace yards. There were soldiers everywhere, torches and lanterns held high.

"How did we not know that Akka was coming?" I said to Harga.

"They may have come by river."

"Numbers?"

"Fifty banners at least. It may be the whole army. Too dark to tell yet."

We passed into the city proper and then moved at a jog towards the eastern walls. The streets were crowded with the ordinary people of the city. Many were still in their night robes, makeshift weapons in their hands.

All stepped aside to let us pass.

We took the narrow stairs up onto the city walls, two steps at a time. Even in the dark the ancient steps were so well known to me that I could run up without leaning upon the wall.

The great rampart of Uruk was three cords thick. We paced across it and put our hands on the mud-brick outer wall.

In the distance, villages were burning. The night air was thick with smoke.

Below us, the dark plain pulsated with movement.

A flaming arrow lifted off our walls and for a moment it lit up the ground below us.

There were thousands of them, flashes of copper armour.

They were forming up a front line.

Their voices lifted up to me; a terrible howling noise. I glimpsed huge dogs running between the soldiers. The Akkadians' infamous dogs of war.

"This is bad," I said to Harga.

"Very bad indeed, my lord."

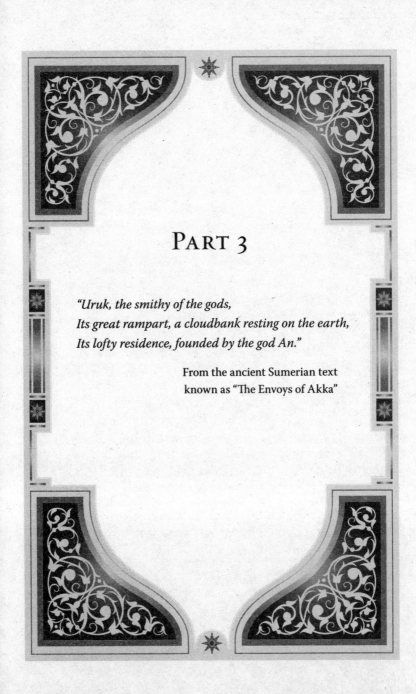

PART 3

"Uruk, the smithy of the gods,
Its great rampart, a cloudbank resting on the earth,
Its lofty residence, founded by the god An."

From the ancient Sumerian text
known as "The Envoys of Akka"

CHAPTER ONE

GILGAMESH

At Uruk

We stood out on the walls, on that first morning of the siege, waiting for the sun to come up. The plains, stretching out into the distance, were dotted with fire, but it was still too dark to see properly.

"Are the canal gates down?" I said to Harga.

"Now they are. But only just. They were open all night. It is my fault. I should have checked that they had done it before I went to bed. They said it was being done, but it was not."

"I also went to bed without checking. We are a pair of fools amongst thousands of fools."

Another burning arrow lit up the Akkadian army below. Their front line was well drawn up now, just out of reach of our archers.

"You think they got in through the canal?" I said. "For Della I mean."

"Or through one of your secret passages."

"I cannot believe I was sleeping through this."

"The guards did think to look into your old rooms, but they missed you there in the servant's bed," Harga said.

There was then a short silence between us.

"We were lucky the alarm was raised as early as it was," Harga went on. "A group of men came in the early hours to the elephant gate, saying they were pilgrims on their way to Nippur. Luckily the boy on the gate did not believe them and raised the alarm."

Another flaming arrow rose off our walls.

"We should stop wasting our arrows," I said. "We will need them when they attack."

"If they attack. Cities tend to surrender when King Akka comes calling. He tends to sit and wait for that to happen."

Two men from my household arrived with my good armour. The bronze chest plate, etched with the wild bull of Heaven, the lion helmet, and my copper-sewn skirt, all smelling strongly of the cedar chest they had been stored in.

As the men strapped me into my chest plate, Harga said: "They say Akka killed all the men and boys when Larak fell. Not just the fighting men."

I nodded but waited for my household men to go before speaking.

"Would Akka have let them live if they'd surrendered quicker?"

"They only waited a day to do it," Harga said. "And still there was no mercy."

I stood quiet a moment, breathing through the rage that threatened to overwhelm me.

"I should have gone north and killed Akka, after he killed Enkidu," I said, nodding. "I should have done it then."

"We should have killed him long before that, at Marad," Harga said. "That day when I snatched his son. We could have killed him then."

"I could have done it. Akka and I sat on our mules just a cable apart. I could easily have done it. I was soft-hearted and short-sighted. I will not be so again."

As the morning mist lifted from the banks of the Warka, the autumn sun picked out for us, field by field, the full truth of our situation.

The glorious city of Uruk, pride of Sumer, was surrounded by perhaps thirty thousand fighting men. They were ranged out around us to the north, south and west. Should there be any thoughts of us swimming to safety, the men of Akkadia were also camped in force upon the east bank of the river.

What had been green fields, cut through with canals, was now a land of mud, men, shelters and campfires.

This army of besiegers looked well-seasoned and well-drilled. There was no royal camp in sight, as there had been at Marad. Had King Akka left his court at home this time?

Every farmstead in sight was burning or blackened.

Inanna's mother, the goddess Ningal, came climbing slowly up onto the walls to join us, her huge white wings scraping the ramparts, her left hand out to the brick wall for balance.

She was in full temple dress, even the crescent-crown of the Goddess of the Moon and the bronze chest plate of Ur. Behind her came a fleet of priestesses in white, purple, and orange.

Ningal came to stand beside Harga, and the three of us looked out over the besieging army. "I believe Della and the baby have been taken out of the city," she said.

"Go on," I said.

"She was taken out through the canal before the fighting began. Six men dressed in black took her in a small boat." She put out a soft hand onto my arm. "I'm sorry, Gilgamesh."

I nodded. "The baby?"

"She had a bundle in her arms."

"You don't think she was with them willingly, do you?" I said.

Harga looked sideways at me. "Can things be so bad between you?"

"She was angry with me, that's all. But you're right. She's no traitor. Do you think Akka will hurt them?"

"No," said Harga. "I think he will keep them alive and well until he can use them against you."

At that moment we caught the flash of azure blue in the seething army below us: the colour that heralded the king and his household.

"I wonder who has taught him not to fear us," Ningal said.

"There is no mystery there," I said. "We did the teaching. Our actions have been his guide. He learned that he could attack us and suffer nothing. Time and time again, they attacked Sumerians and the property of Sumerians upon Sumerian soil and all we did was chase them back to the borders."

Harga was standing with both fists tightly clenched. "Why did Enlil not finish this long ago? That is what I cannot understand, when he is so wise in all things."

"But there are so many of them," Ningal said. "Enlil always knew that if we faced them on an open plain, they might overwhelm us."

"And now we will die because we are so many," I said. "Trapped inside this city, unprepared for siege."

"Very soon, we will go hungry," Ningal said.

"You will go hungry," Harga said. "We humans will starve."

I put out my hand to Ningal. "Let us walk the walls, goddess. Let us give heart to our people and let us give the Akkadians a good, long look at us. Let them wonder if Akka was right when he told them that all the real gods were dead."

And so the Goddess of the Moon and the Lion of Uruk walked the walls together, she in her wings and costume of brilliant white, and me in my gleaming armour.

We said a word to each of the protectors upon the walls. Men, women and children; some soldiers, most not. Ningal dropped the blessing of the moon upon them and told them of the good things that would come to them in the afterlife for the work that they did. I told them what to do if the men of Akkadia put ladders up against the walls or sent burning arrows over. I told them to throw down anything unpleasant they could think of at the Akkadians: excrement, sharp stones, burning fat.

But never to send anything over that you might want back, and only to use an arrow if you were sure on your life that it would hit its target.

I told them about the siege of Marad and how we bested Akka then, with so few men, against his thousands. I left out the part where Harga kidnapped a child and was forced to kill a blameless woman in order for us to triumph.

Afterwards, I said to Ningal: "You and Lilith are in charge of keeping the people of the city fed, watered, and housed. Harga and I will take the walls."

"Very well," she said. "It's work I've done before, in Ur."

"Better to keep the rations small even from the start."

She laughed at that. "Gilgamesh, I am five hundred years older than you. I was in Ur when the barbarians came at us from the sea. I can ration out food."

"Of course you can," I said, and watched her white skirts swirl as she turned to climb back down into the city.

Harga, on his way up onto the walls with two of his boys behind him, stood back to let her pass.

"My mother despises Ningal," I said. "She says the woman has no spine and that she sided with the southern gods, not because she believed in them, but because she was too frightened to do otherwise."

"She sided with her husband and father," Harga said. "It does not seem all that spineless to me."

As the sun rose into the sky above the river, two long lines of refugees began making their way towards Uruk, one towards the north gate and one towards the south. Every farming family for fifty leagues around, being driven forward by mounted Akkadians and packs of howling war dogs.

"King Akka is going to force every refugee on the river plains into the city," I said.

"That's a lot of mouths to be letting in," Harga said. "What are your orders?"

"You know what they are."

"We'll be starving within days."

"Just let them in," I said. "What else can we possibly do?"

CHAPTER TWO

NINSHUBAR

Somewhere to the south of Egypt

I did not recognise the beach, but the hills behind, the grassed steps, the rocky gully cutting through it: this was where I had last seen my Potta.

I drove our sailboat onto sparkling sand and leaped out to pull us all the way up the beach, the lions and Inanna clustered in the prow.

The sand was hot and crisp beneath my bare feet.

The lions leaped out and then I lifted Inanna, wearing only her nightshirt, out onto the beach. She had an odd look to her as I put her down, as if she might faint again.

"Are you all right?"

She looked at me for several heartbeats before answering. "I am well," she said. "It is just I feel as if something is pulling at me."

"Is this the dark stranger, acting upon you?"

"I wish I understood it." She leaned against the boat.

"Should you take the *mee* off again? Is it making things worse?"

"We may need it here," she said.

The beach was backed with granite outcrops and the good shade of full-grown acacia. As we began to walk along it, looking for a path up, the lions found us a small spring at the foot of a cliff, and all four of us drank our fill.

"You are sure this is the place?" Inanna whispered.

I stood up straighter, listening. "Are we being watched?"

"I thought perhaps I sensed someone, but now there is nothing."

As she spoke, the lions lifted their heads from the water and smelled the air. Inanna slipped their gold-link collars on to them and tightened them. But the lions went back to drinking, apparently unperturbed.

I gave a casual glance about me and touched my hands briefly to my *mees*.

"This is definitely the place," I said.

I slung my stone axe over my back and took up a spear from the boat, and then I led us up the thin, sandy path through the acacia.

We soon found ourselves in a narrow gorge, flanked on either side by outcrops of dark, grey granite. The higher we climbed, the more familiar it was to me.

The path beneath my feet was well used.

Then there it was.

A cleft in the side of the gorge.

Where the Potta and I had made camp.

As Inanna and the lions looked on, I made a careful search of the place, moving aside the grass, running my fingers through the sand. No footprints now; no mark of the fire that the Potta and I had made. I could not remember now if we had managed to light it.

Then: something in the grass. A piece of white and orange flint. The distinctive buttery shimmer that means a stone has been worked by hand. I picked it up and felt the weight of it. I paused a moment, before holding it out to Inanna.

"It is… a stone," she said, peering at it.

"Yes, it is a stone. But it is also a knife. I made it for him. Sometimes he wore it around his neck, and sometimes he would tie it to his arm." I held the flint tight in my left hand. "This is where he was taken from."

"What now?" said Inanna. "Should we keep following the path?"

"Can you sense anyone now?"

She shook her head. "Nothing."

I hesitated a moment. I only had my *mees*, my axe and my spear with me. The Potta's knife was for foodstuff, not for killing. Should we go back to the boat, put our boots and shoes on, and fill up some waterskins?

But the merchant had said the village was only a short walk away.

"Come on then," I said, and led the way north up the gorge.

Inanna walked slower and slower behind me.

"I could carry you?"

"I'm so sorry, Ninshubar," she said, very quiet. "I find it hard to get my breath."

I stopped, torn between what might lay ahead of us and my concern for Inanna.

"Walk on!" she said. "I can keep up with you."

At the top of the ravine, the acacia scrub opened onto grassland. About a league away, to our right, beside a stand of plane trees: huts.

"Inanna, that's it," I said, grinning at her. "Come on, let me carry you on my back."

"All right," she said. "Just for a bit."

∽

When we were still a long way out from the village, I began to suspect that something was wrong. The path beneath us faded and there was no movement in the village ahead.

Close to, the truth was obvious. The whole village stood empty. The mud and grass huts were in an advanced state of decay.

I let Inanna down from my back.

The lions ran ahead of us, roving between the deserted huts. We looked around for a while, but they were all empty. The fires were long cold. The people had gone, taking everything with them except the grinding stones that were too big to carry.

"How long has it been empty, do you think?" she said.

"A year maybe."

I felt I might burst into tears.

I had thought we might at last be on his trail.

But the trail had ended.

"We should get back to the boat," I said.

Beside me, Inanna was sitting on the grass.

"I'll carry you again," I said.

The walk back to the beach was much longer than the walk out. Inanna, on my back, seemed heavier and heavier. She seemed to have gone to sleep, her full weight slumped against me. The lions prowled either side of us, casting yellow glances at me.

I walked with my head and heart so heavy. I had failed my Potta so badly. I should have left Eridu as soon as I got there. I should have retraced my steps so long ago.

But then of course I would not have met Inanna.

In the ravine, I stopped one last time at the place where I had found the knife, and let a tear fall down my face, since I did not have a hand free to wipe it away.

At last I walked out, heavy with my load, onto the beach where we had left our boat.

Brilliant white sand. The gorgeous, glittering blue sea. A lovely breeze after the heat onshore. Nothing else.

The beach was empty.

The boat had gone.

"Inanna," I said.

As I tried to put her down, she slumped backwards; she was unconscious. I grappled with her legs to stop her falling but ended up dropping her hard onto the hot sand. I paused for one heartbeat to check she was breathing, and then ran out into the centre of the beach.

Footprints that were not our footprints. Long carved lines where the boat had been dragged up out of the sea, and down again. The prints of perhaps three large animals.

They must have come along from the far end of the beach while we walked the other way.

I spun around and looked out to sea.

Nothing.

Not even a distant sail.

The lions had lain down next to Inanna. I went back to her and listened to her breath again and felt for her pulse. It was faint but she was alive.

Her mouth was moving. I put my ear close.

"Tiamat," she whispered.

"What?"

"I see her."

For one heartbeat her black eyes were open and she was looking at me.

"Who is Tiamat?" I said.

Then she was gone again, her eyes closed, her head slumped over to one side.

I got Inanna back into the shade and laid her out on a clear stretch of sand. Her lions lay down on either side of her. I sat down heavily next to them, my legs straight out in front of me, my back against a tree. She might have been dead, but for the tiny rise and fall of her thin chest.

I looked out at the sparkling sea and the cloudless, azure sky.

And I cursed myself, a hundred times, a thousand times.

From the day I met her, Inanna had been on a spiral down into the dark places where shamans go hunting. I should not have let her go down into the underworld alone. I should not have let her go south against Enki. And I never should have let her come out on this foolish quest that had no chance of succeeding.

I had sworn to protect her, but I had only put her in danger.

I sat there, tears running, my sides heaving, so deeply angry with myself.

Then I nodded, and wiped away my tears, and even put a hand out to one of the lions. They were looking at me almost as if concerned for me.

So.

So.

I must get Inanna back to Uruk. She needed to be in a shaman place. The Sumerians did not use caves, but Inanna's temple at Uruk would do. She needed to be safe and surrounded by her priestesses, while we worked out what her nightmares meant and how to protect her from them.

So.

I had my *mees,* my spear, one flint knife, my flint axe. The tunic I stood in, and the leather strap for my axe.

Inanna had her nightshirt, the master *mee,* and her lions.

The lions had their collars: they could be bartered with. Their leashes were somewhere; perhaps they would be useful.

We had no supplies, no waterskins, no boots, no cloaks. Inanna's gold head band was in my leather backpack on the boat.

Oh, and of course, we had no boat.

We were a long way from Uruk. We had crossed a wide stretch of open sea to get to this beach. Inanna was unconscious.

I must simply make my calculations and act.

"One step and then the next," I said to myself, and to the lions, as I climbed slowly to my feet.

CHAPTER THREE

GILGAMESH

At Uruk

"Now would be a good time for one of your tricks, my lord," said Harga.

We were stood together, in the cool afternoon breeze, at what was now our command post on the ramparts. Harga's boys had brought up some leather and wood campaign chairs, and a small table to set our jug of beer and half day meal on. But for now we were standing, for the best possible view of the besieging army. Every once in a while, the Akkadians would fire an arrow at my distinctive armour. So far, all had fallen short.

"So, you want a trick," I said. "Some great trick that no one has ever thought of before in all the history of sieges."

"Exactly that," said Harga.

As I stood there, thinking over what might possibly save us, there was new activity in the muddy fields to our north. The men of Akkadia were dragging dead bodies towards the canal that flowed directly into Uruk.

"You have someone digging more wells?" I said.

"They may need to dig quicker," said Harga.

We watched as the Akkadians threw the bodies into the water, with a rope tied to each. These ropes were tied to stakes and soon a dam of the dead began to form in the water.

"I think they're stuffing poison into the bodies," Harga said. "Just to be sure."

"Just once I would like to be the one besieging a city," I said. "Rather than standing inside it trying to come up with tricks."

Harga's two new boys appeared, one very tall, one very short, and both were at once sent away with messages about the poisoned water and the need for new wells.

When we were alone again, Harga said: "If Akka didn't bring the royal household, then his son will not be here this time. Otherwise I could have snatched him a second time."

"But if his son is still in Kish, you could go there and snatch him. They would not expect that."

He rubbed a pebble against the palm of his right hand. "I am not unwilling. But it might take a full moon to do it."

As he spoke, there was a flash of crimson in the ranks of Akkadians: an envoy, sat upon a mule.

Could it be?

"It is Inush!" I said, with plain astonishment.

"Are you sure?"

"Yes. But how extraordinary, that Akka would risk sending him as an envoy for a second time, after everything that happened last time."

"They have your wife and son. I suppose they think that makes him safe."

"I suppose so."

The moon goddess, Ningal, appeared beside us on the walls.

She had removed her wings and crown but was still in the white of Ur. "Who will we send out to meet the envoy?" she said.

"Me," I said. "I know this envoy, and I would like to meet him again face to face."

"I expect he will try to kill you," said Harga, with hearty confidence.

"I agree that you will not be safe," Ningal said. "Unless I come with you."

Harga and I turned to look at her, both frowning.

"What do your *mees* do?" I said, trying not to sound doubtful.

"They do enough," she said. "Gilgamesh, I can protect you. These *mees* were Enki's. Some are *mees* of protection. I know how to use them."

"You are not a goddess of war," I said.

"Those are nonsense words," she said. "I will be the goddess I need to be."

"Have you ever been in a fight?" I said.

"I do not have military training, as your mother does. Agreed. But I can use a *mee* of protection."

I looked out, at Inush, and how very relaxed he looked, as he made his way towards the elephant gates.

"All right," I said. "We will make quite the diplomatic delegation, at least. The Goddess of the Moon and the Lion of Uruk setting out as envoys of this city. It will be something for these Akkadians to tell their children about."

Harga tucked his curls behind his ears. "Especially if you are struck down and captured," he said. "That they will remember."

"Thank you, Harga," I said. "Most inspiring."

∽

We stood behind the elephant gates, the goddess and I, staring ahead of us at the ancient wood and brass bolts. There was a hush all around us in the crowded square behind the gate.

I had my helmet down and a bead of sweat ran down my forehead and into my left eye. I glanced round at Ningal through the slit in my helmet. She must have been frightened, but she wore the stern face that the Anunnaki put on in temple.

They brought up my horse, and a mule for Ningal. "He's steady enough," I said to her, as she climbed onto her animal.

Ningal's priestesses stood on wooden boxes to arrange her skirts and wings across the mule's back.

I mounted my horse, and Harga checked over my armour, to make sure everything was fastened properly.

"Ready?" I said to the goddess.

Ningal lifted her chin just a little in answer. Close to, she had a thin veil of sweat upon her forehead and a tightness to her jaw.

"Open the gates," I said.

The grinding noise, as they winched up the gates, echoed through the city.

Harga handed me up a crimson flag, tied to the top of a spear; red being the envoy's colour.

"Don't make a mess of it," he said.

"Thank you, Harga. What a font of wisdom you are today."

It was so quiet as we rode out that all I could hear was my horse huffing beneath me and the cry of an eagle overhead. Then the men of Akka began to shout and bang their weapons. They were stood ten cords back from the ancient gate, a strong line across our horizon, with the sun bouncing bright off their copper helmets.

I pushed up the faceplate of my famous lion helmet, so that they could all be certain it was me.

"Can they not get their arrows into us from there?" Ningal said.

"But I have this small red flag," I said, throwing out my smile at her. "Surely we are perfectly safe?"

It was good to see her smile.

"Be ready with your *mees*," I said.

"I am ready."

We rode towards the Akkadian front line through the detritus of the night's panic and turmoil. Pots of who knows what filth, thrown down. The bodies of two men, thick with arrows; it was hard to say whose men they were. A burned log, still smouldering. The smell of burned flesh, sweat, blood and animal dung lingered in the air.

And before us, the bright eyes, and jeering mouths of the Akkadians.

Their eyes were not for me: they were for the goddess.

Had they ever seen an Anunnaki before?

They did not kneel to her, yet they were not unmoved by the sight of her outstretched wings and crescent crown. Those closest to us dipped their heads a little, although I do not think they meant to.

I breathed in and breathed out.

I could not see Inush over the lines of men with long fighting spears and heavy, copper-covered shields. Then the ranks before us parted and there was my old friend in his crimson envoy costume.

I had not seen him since Marad when he beat Enkidu almost to death as I watched.

I pushed my face into a smile.

Inush looked older, more serious, and yet very much like himself. He rode with his hands crossed over on the pommel of his saddle.

Ningal and I pulled up our animals.

"Well, you are getting good use from that outfit, Inush," I called over to him.

He drew up his own animal, level with the front line of Akkadians.

"It was made especially for me," he said. "Will you come no closer?"

"I am quite happy here. Why not come closer to us?"

"Even with a so-called goddess beside you, you still fear these humble mortals?" He lifted his nose at the soldiers around him.

"Inush, you have my wife and son. I promise on my life, on my honour, on my wife's life, on my son's life, that we will do you no harm here. Come over and let us talk as men. You cannot expect me to ride straight into the open arms of your soldiers."

Inush glanced over his shoulder, to the spot from which, I supposed, Akka was watching. He then glanced up at the walls of Uruk, where, high above, Harga and the others stood watching.

"Oh, very well," he said, and kicked his reluctant mule forward.

He drew up close to us, still leaning on his pommel. I'd forgotten how handsome he was, with his long eyes and sharp-cut features.

"This is Ningal," I said to him. "Queen of Ur. Goddess of the Moon."

He ran his eye over the goddess. "You look about fifteen years old," he said to her. "They should have chosen someone full grown at least, to pull the trick off."

Ningal shifted in her saddle, her dark eyes upon him, her curls moving in the wind.

"Time has been good to me," she said.

Inush turned back to me.

"I hear you are king here now, although not yet crowned."

"We've had little time for ceremony this past day or two."

"Congratulations nonetheless." Inush gave me a thin smile. "Now, Gilgamesh, the terms I am going to offer you will never be improved upon."

"That I believe. What are they?"

Inush sat up straighter in his saddle. "They are the same terms we offer everywhere and choose never to deviate from."

"Get on with it," I said.

"Open the gates. Send out the fighting men. Let them drop their weapons and kneel. You yourself will lead them out and speak the words of surrender. Do all that and no one will be harmed."

"Well, that is tempting." I looked him over. He bore no weapons that I could see, except a long, nasty-looking knife, sheathed upon his right hip. "You will even spare the fighting men?"

"The fighting men will be enslaved, but they will live. Everyone will live. Even you. Even this fake goddess here."

"That's not what happened at Lakar."

Inush was about to answer.

But then I pushed my horse forward hard, straight at him.

For one long moment, I had one arm around his neck and our mouths were so close we might have kissed. How sweet he smelt, of saddle wax and cedar.

I am not sure what our embrace looked like to his men, but for an instant no one reacted.

With one great wrench, I dragged Inush off his mule and onto my lap. Somehow, he had his knife out and stabbed it into my left knee. In the agony of the moment, I brought my own knife down into his right shoulder.

Then I was galloping for the elephant gates with Inush limp across my lap, and his knife still hanging from my left leg.

I think I screamed "With me!" and a moment later Ningal's mule was galloping flat out to my left, with the goddess leaning forward over its neck.

And then the world around us exploded into action.

Perhaps a thousand arrows sprang at us from the ranks of the Akkadian army. I carried a prince of Kish with me and you would have thought them sorry to hit him, but in the moment, it seemed none of them thought of that.

A moment later a thousand more arrows sprang down towards the Akkadians from the walls of Uruk; a fair number of these arrows, too, seemed to be flying directly at me and the goddess.

I had forgotten, in the general excitement, and with my knee in agony, why I had brought the goddess with me. But then the air around us crackled into life and we rode on within a bubble of white fire.

Arrows burst into flames and disappeared as they hit Ningal's shield, and moments later we were back inside the city and the gates were rattling down fast behind us.

The crackling white shield around us instantly collapsed. Ningal leaned back in her saddle and gasped for air. Blood ran down from both of her nostrils onto her beautiful white robe.

A crowd of soldiers and servants ran out to help us.

I threw Inush's near-lifeless body down onto the cobbled street, and then, mouth turned down, I pulled his knife from my leg. It was stuck in at an awkward angle between thigh and knee, and blood sprayed out all around as it came free.

Harga appeared, holding out a cloth to my knee. "That looks nasty, my lord."

"It feels it," I said, trying to breathe through the agony.

He stood back as I dismounted, but stepped forward to hold me as I doubled over with the pain of it.

"Let me bind it," he said.

I nodded, and stood, leaning heavily on him. "Just one moment."

I forced myself to hobble over to the goddess and help her from her mule.

"You did well," I said, lifting her to the ground. I kissed her once, firmly, on the forehead. "Thank you, Ningal."

"You could have told me." She was very pale. "You could have told me what you were going to do."

"I didn't know until I was out there. I couldn't know he would come close."

I turned back to Inush, still lying on the ground as if dead, in his bright-red envoy's costume. "Put him somewhere dark and horrible," I said. "Do not fear too much for his fine robes."

"Let's hope Akka loves his nephew very much indeed," Harga said. "Now come, you need to sit."

He helped me over to a bench, and lowered me down onto it.

"Akka could choose to kill your wife for this," Harga said, as he did his best to stop my knee bleeding. "And if he kills your wife, he will still have your son as a hostage."

I breathed in and breathed out. "You asked for a trick, Harga. There was your trick. Now we all have to live with it."

CHAPTER FOUR

ERESHKIGAL

In the realm of light

I*n the first days, our greatest fear was that the Anzu would follow us down from Heaven. The master* mee, *that had let us pass through: what if it was one of many?*

"Lady Ereshkigal?"

It was the girl Geshtinanna, Dumuzi's sister. She had been living in Neti's hut for some time, hoping that she might gain entrance to the underworld. Upon my arrival she had been forced to give up the one bed and move into a little nest in the roof space. But she claimed she preferred her attic nook and we had learned to get on well. She had become a sort of a maid to me.

"I thought you would like some mountain tea, my lady."

"You are a very clever girl, Geshtinanna." In fact, I did not think her very clever, but there was no point in hurting her feelings.

"Will you come and drink it outside, on your rock, my lady?"

"Yes, I will."

I was wearing a dress that Geshtinanna had given to me from her own chest of belongings. It was cut from a lovely piece of white linen. On Geshtinanna it was a flowing robe. On me, it was tight-fitting, perhaps too tight over my breasts. But I liked the colour hugely after so long dressed in black. Now I put over it my new sheepskin cloak, that Geshtinanna had fashioned me from the sheepskins hanging in Neti's hut, before stepping out into the cool but sweet-smelling mountain morning.

I settled myself on my rock. It was just the right height for me to easily sit down upon and it boasted the most beautiful view of the river plains. Geshtinanna brought me my big clay mug, full up with tea, but not too hot. She squatted down on the grass to watch me drink it in the hope, I knew, that I would talk to her about her brother.

"Are you feeling well, my lady? You look well."

"Not really," I said, but I could not put much energy into my complaint. The Earthlight, the sweet cakes, and the mountain air seemed good for me. I could not remember feeling so well.

Geshtinanna pulled her face into a polite but pleading sort of shape, and said: "Goddess, I was told by your sister Inanna that I could share my brother's punishment with him. That after six moons, I could serve in his place and he would be free. And then after another six moons, we would swap over again. And so on and so forth."

"No one has spoken to me about that," I said. "It sounds very complicated."

Neti appeared beside us, dressed in his shepherd clothes. "I was the witness when you agreed to let Geshtinanna share her brother's punishment. I was the witness to the agreement you made with Ninshubar, holy *sukkal* to the goddess Inanna."

"It is not a punishment," I said, "to serve me in the underworld."

I turned my head from him and tipped up my nose.

"It was a promise made between the Anunnaki," he said, "with me as the go-between and the witness. I am bound to mention it."

"Do go away, Neti," I said. "You are not needed here."

I wondered if it might be interesting to have Geshtinanna in the temple rites. Her skin looked very soft and plump to nibble at. It is sometimes allowed for a woman to stand in if no man is to hand. I had grown very fond of Dumuzi, though, and I was not sure I wanted to be without him for half the year.

"I would not think it a punishment to serve you," Geshtinanna said, as if reading my thoughts.

It was only then that it occurred to me that I might have both of them with me, down in the Dark City. After all, who was there to stop me?

"If anyone had spoken to me about your arrangement," I said, "of course I would have honoured it."

Yes, would it not be possible to have both her and Dumuzi in the Dark City? As I thought this over, Nammu paced past us without stopping to speak to us.

She was going hunting, as she did every morning.

When she was out of sight, I lifted my eyebrows at Geshtinanna, and she at once went to fetch me my basket of honey cakes, with my newest history tablets tied up in cloth beneath them.

With one last glance around to make sure that Nammu had gone, I set off for the crater above us.

"I can come with you!" Geshtinanna said.

I would have liked her to carry the basket for me, but the awkward thing was that she was very pretty, and that did not suit me in these particular circumstances.

"You rest, sweet girl," I said. "I will be back soon."

As soon as I was out of sight of the hut, I dropped my limping and shuffling, and bounded up the rocky path very quickly, enjoying the fine morning air. I wanted the honey cakes to still be warm when I reached the Kur.

As I reached the top of the crater wall, I could see, far below me, what must be Erra, sitting out in the little camp he had made for himself beside the Kur. My face broke out into a wide smile; I could not help it.

By the time I reached him, my sides were heaving from the pace I had kept up, but the honey cakes were still warm.

Erra was sitting on a mossy tussock before a meagre campfire, with his eyes covered over. He had his hood pushed back, and the mess of bandages around his face did nothing to hide the sad state of his skull, so cleaved and hacked about. But he was smiling; he had heard me coming. He had a lovely, warm smile.

"Is Nammu here?" I said. "I have brought her some cakes."

He laughed. "Ereshkigal, I know very well you would walk a league to avoid that woman. However, I am here, as ever, and you know I love your cakes."

"I suppose you can have one of them," I said.

I sat myself down close to him and passed over a cake into his outstretched hands.

"Did you bring some new writing?" He held the cake to his nose, breathing it down deeply, before biting into it with obvious relish.

"I did not," I said. "I have been too busy baking." Of course, Neti made the cakes, but I had asked him never to correct me on the subject.

"Perhaps you have an old tablet with you then," Erra said. He could not see me of course, but he smiled in my direction.

"I suppose I might do," I said.

I unwrapped a clay tablet from the bottom of my basket and began to read it out to him. It was all about the first days in Eridu, before we Anunnaki split off into our clans. Erra loved to hear all the stories of our earliest times on Earth, and I had taken to concentrating my writing on the things he was most interested in.

"Shall I fetch you some water to wash down all those cakes?" I said, after I had read him a third tablet and he had eaten all the honey cakes.

"I would like that very much," he said.

As I stood, a sad sight greeted me. Nammu, a mountain hare in one hand, was climbing back down into the crater after her hunting trip.

"Oh, I must go," I said to Erra, very glum.

He turned his head towards the path. "Is she coming?"

"Goodbye, then," I said, sullen.

I took up my basket and made my way, heavy footed, across the crater towards Nammu. I could not see a way of avoiding her.

As we drew close, she said: "We will be going tomorrow, Ereshkigal."

"What?" I said, stopping. "Erra is still blind."

She narrowed her crystal eyes at me. "We've wasted enough time here, with you two eating cakes and giggling together. Erra is well enough to travel."

"Perhaps it's me who is not well enough," I said, and shuffled off very slowly past her towards Neti's hut.

The next morning I was sitting very happy on my rock, mug of tea in hand, when Nammu appeared before me, leading Erra by one hand.

They made a strange pair.

Nammu was as ever a vision of golden beauty, so fresh to behold, and smelling of rose oil. Erra looked barely able to stand, certainly not well enough for a long journey in search of our lord god An.

I felt pity for him, looking at him standing over me, but then the memory rose up in me, of whispers in the darkness. I put down my mug of tea.

"Lord of War and Chaos," I said. The words came unprompted, but I knew them to be true.

"Why do you say that?" Nammu said. "Where did you hear that, Ereshkigal?"

"I did not speak," I said.

Nammu breathed in and out, slowly and deliberately. "Ereshkigal, are you ready to go? You do not look ready to go."

"Are we going now?"

No one answered. Nammu had tipped her face back to the sky, her eyes shut.

"I need to gather my things," I said.

Geshtinanna followed me into the hut and helped tie up a handkerchief of fresh honey cakes for me.

I was thinking over how rude Nammu had been to me and how nice Geshtinanna was to me.

"There is something I could tell you," I said to the girl, very quiet, to be sure no one else would hear.

"What is it, my lady?"

I looked around to check that no one was at the door. "Your brother has been barred from leaving the underworld, but if you want to go into the underworld, then go."

"I have tried but been barred by the gatekeeper."

"Neti?" I said, looking around for him.

He appeared next to us in the blue suit he wore inside the Kur.

"This one can go in, Neti, when I am gone."

"Very well," he said, and disappeared.

"No one can stop you entering now," I said to Geshtinanna. "Although you would be wise to wait until Nammu is out of sight. Go through all the seven gates and find your way to the Dark City. Neti will help you if you are ever unsure of the way. Once you are there, there should be plenty of room for you if you want to stay with your brother. You say promises were made, of you and he sharing his punishment, half a year for one and then half a year for the other, but never together, but I have no interest in punishing either of you, so just go in. I only ask that you are kind to my demons."

As this great speech progressed, I found myself shedding a tear for my demons. As my import sank in, Geshtinanna also burst into tears. She got down on her knees and kissed both my hands. "Madam, I am yours forever. Thank you."

"My demons have sharp teeth, but big hearts."

Geshtinanna kissed my hands again. "I will look after your demons and be very, very kind to them."

"And be careful of the candles."

"I will keep it very dark."

"That is what Namtar said, but I can never trust anyone with the candles."

And so Nammu, the dark stranger and I set off for Nippur, the holy city. Nammu said she expected to find her husband, An, there.

Geshtinanna had begged me to take a knapsack with food, water and a blanket in it, but I had chosen to leave upon our adventure with nothing except the clothes I stood in, except for my handkerchief of honey cakes. My clay tablets I had secreted in the attic of Neti's hut, in the hope no one would disturb them there.

I walked ahead of the others, breathing in great lungfuls of the good mountain air and enjoying the eagles wheeling overhead and the familiar smell of the damp earth and mountain mosses.

As I walked, I reflected upon my time in the darkness; how lost I had been and how full of anxiety and pain and upset. How clouded my mind had been, for so long.

I reflected too, on what I wanted.

I was out in the world. I could do anything! But what did I want? I thought of my demons and how much I loved them. I thought of Erra, walking very slowly behind me with one hand on Nammu's right shoulder.

"Ereshkigal!"

Nammu had a hand raised to me.

She and Erra had fallen rather far behind me. They were both carrying heavy packs and Erra struggled to keep up any speed at all. Nammu had to be on hand to guide him along the path and help him get past rock falls.

"You could help me with him," Nammu said to me, as they caught up.

I shrugged. "Was it my plan, to escort this stranger to Nippur?"

"Even if it means nothing to you, that I am your grandmother, and have striven for years to save you from yourself, you might help me out of common civility."

"I do not see why," I said, and walked on, smiling to myself at the sight of two harriers on the air.

"When did all this happen, all these rock falls?" Nammu said, when she caught up with me as I was drinking from a stream.

"It was all like this when I went down into the underworld," I said. "A very long time ago."

"The falls look very fresh," she said.

Later, when we stopped to give Erra a rest, Nammu said to me: "Come and help me fetch water for him."

"I don't want to."

"Ereshkigal, come with me. I cannot carry the water alone. We need to clean his wounds."

I went after her, most unhappily, but as soon as we were out of earshot of Erra, Nammu turned on me, the water apparently forgotten.

"Who has been talking to you?" she demanded. "Why did you call him the Lord of War and Chaos?"

"No one has been talking to me." I lifted my chin.

She pressed her hands together before her. "Ereshkigal, I am not your enemy. Who said these words to you?"

"Why should I tell you what I know, when I do not even know what your plan is?"

"That is fair," she said. She sat down on a lichen-covered rock. "Erra has negotiated a peace settlement for us. But there is a price. A terrible price." She smoothed her face and lifted her eyebrows to me. "We must hand over my son Enlil to the Anzu."

"And?"

"If we hand over Enlil to the Anzu, for what he did to Ninlil, we will all be allowed back into Heaven."

I laughed out loud. "You would hand over your son?"

"Yes," she said, her face hardening. "To save An. To save us all. Yes, I will do it. I would have done it before, but An refused. Everyone refused. And the girl made it more complicated, claiming that she loved Enlil."

"So Erra is here to collect Enlil? That is the price?"

"I have been negotiating this for many years."

"And you are sure of who Erra is, and what his reasons are for being here?"

"The Kur is sure he is Anunnaki," she said. "Ereshkigal, some of us do not have much time left. We have run out of *melam*. An is close to death. Others too. This is a chance for us to survive even if there are risks. Now tell me who has been talking to you."

"No one has been talking to me," I said. "No one ever tells me anything. And anyway," I added, "what do you care for An and how much time he has left? Your husband who you abandoned centuries ago?"

I made my way back to Erra, my nose held high.

We were there awhile, while Nammu went out to hunt for us. She used her *mees* of battle to strike down small antelope, or freeze the motion of all about her, so that birds would come tumbling down, insensate, from the sky. These creatures she would then gut and pluck or skin very efficiently, and cook for us upon a fire, having also gathered all the wood together, and got the flames going. "While you do nothing," she said to us that evening.

"That is not fair," Erra said. "As soon as I am strong, I will join you on the hunt."

"I did not mean you," she said, and went off to get more wood.

"So, you are not a hunter?" Erra said to me when it was just the two of us before the campfire.

"I could be a hunter," I said. "I could do it very well, if I chose to."

He lifted his filthy blindfold just a little, to look at me. "How long have you been like this?"

"Like what?"

He opened his palms to me. "Mad, I suppose."

We sat and looked at each other. Me with my mouth flat, him with just that one bright eye showing.

"You are the mad one," I said. "To be here at all. Why are you here? What do you gain? What do you care if your long-lost ancestors are allowed to return to Heaven? It makes no sense."

"You look better out here. Your features were strange before. The proportions were wrong. Your eyes seemed to swim about. But now your face looks quite ordinary."

"That is rude."

"I did not mean it as rudeness. Your body too, seems more ordinary. Before it made no sense."

"I know who you really serve," I said, by way of riposte.

Erra went still. "What are you talking about?"

"About the creature whose bidding you are doing." I gave him a big smile.

"What creature?" he said.

"You know which creature."

"Be very careful, Ereshkigal," he said. "I do not want to hurt you."

"You are the one who should be careful," I said. "Or I wonder what stories I could think of for Nammu?"

"Nammu knows who I serve."

"I do not believe she knows everything." I smiled at him again. "Tell me why your head wounds do not heal."

He pulled down the bandage over his eye and turned his face from me.

"Why not tell me?"

He shook his head. "Talking can't help me," he said.

"I can help you!"

"No," he said. "No one can help me."

I did not know what to say to that, but I unwrapped the last of my honey cakes, and went over to him, and pressed the cake into his hand.

"Thank you, Ereshkigal," he said.

I breathed him in for a moment, before returning to my spot beside the fire.

"Thank you," he said again.

CHAPTER FIVE

MARDUK

At the Akkadian supply camp, near Uruk

From our camp all we could see was the great river to one side of us and then the palm groves all around us on the shore. We were dependent for news on the squads of soldiers who came every hour or so with new batches of captives. They would stop to drink and eat before riding out again. Some presented wounds for stitching or bandaging, but these were not downbeat or battered men. This was an army in the ascendant.

I looked at the captured men, women, and children they brought with them, all reeking of smoke and fear, and thought, *any of these people could be me.*

"What will happen to them?" I said to a soldier friend.

"These are the ones we'll keep," he said. "The others will be driven into the city."

"So Uruk has not yet fallen?"

"It's a siege now," he said. "We could be here many moons."

∽

I wondered what would happen if I simply walked off into the palm groves with my dog. Would we get away?

One small part of me, however foolish, felt that leaving would be a betrayal of Inush and Biluda and all the other Akkadians who had been kind to me. I looked down at Moshkhussu and I could not be sure what was right or wrong.

I was set to moving bags and crates. They wanted me to put all the parts of the royal tents into one large pile and then to double check that no part of the tents was missing. This task I did turn my hand to, albeit very slowly; I was bone tired, after a long night of very little sleep.

In the late afternoon it occurred to me that if I rearranged the sacks of canvas and crates of tent poles and pegs in a more clever fashion, I might create for myself a sleeping place. Once I had fashioned this depression in the tent bags, right at the centre of the heap, I waited until all eyes were turned elsewhere and then climbed into the sleeping place, with Moshkhussu tucked in with me.

I wrapped her leash around my waist, pulled my travel cloak over us both, and looked up at the smoky sky a little, listening to the shouts and bustle of the camp.

And then, very quickly, I passed out.

I woke with a great start, almost choking on smoke.

It was night but the sky was bright with orange fire.

Moshkhussu was panicking, writhing, and straining against me.

I sat up.

A woman was standing over us, her legs apart. She was ablaze with orange fire and yet not herself burning. She was looking straight at me.

This woman was a creature like no other I had ever seen, otherworldly and yet vibrantly human. Beneath her bronze helmet, her black hair was cut short to her scalp, and straight across at the forehead. She wore copper-mesh armour over an orange temple robe.

On her wrists the woman wore heavy metal bracelets and from these bracelets poured the orange fire, in a strange and looping flight. The air of the night seemed to bend in towards her.

All around us, the camp was in uproar with soldiers riding back and forth, and screams ringing out on all sides. A group of men in black, on mules, was clustered around my tent pile.

"What are you?" the woman said to me.

Moshkhussu, beneath this woman's gaze, stopped struggling, and was still.

"What are you?" the woman said again. She seemed upset to be looking at me. She let the orange fire fade and disappear but she was no less terrifying for it.

I shrunk back from her, my arms tight around Moshkhussu. I tried to speak, but no words came.

The woman leaned down to me and grabbed hold of my right wrist with one hard, cold, hand. "Who are you?"

"I don't know what you mean," I said at last. I pulled my arm away from her and stood up, almost tipping over on the heaped-up tents. I held Moshkhussu close to my legs.

"What are you doing here?" the woman said.

"I'm a slave."

She shook her head at me as if she did not believe me. "Are there more of you here?"

"Yes, there are lots of us."

She shook her head again and turned to the men sat on mules behind her.

"We should take this one," she said, pointing one firm forefinger at me. "Free all the slaves and the fresh captives but keep this one." She looked to her right, towards the boats drawn up on the riverbanks. "Kill anyone who is not a captive. Burn everything else. The supplies, the equipment, the boats."

One of her men climbed off his mount to stand beside my heap of tent sacks. "Ninsun, we could try to get some of this food into the city. They will need it."

"There's no time. Burn it all." She moved off into the chaos of a camp in uproar, with two of her men following behind her.

They had not forgotten me. A man dismounted and came clambering over the sacks to get to me. Moshkhussu strained forward at him, her teeth bared.

The man was about to bring an axe down into her head, when an arrow hit him clean through the neck and he fell dead at my feet.

For some heartbeats, no one was looking at me.

My mother used to say: *if you are going to do something, better do it quick.*

I dropped low and clambered to the edge of the heaped-up tents, pulling Moshkhussu with me. Then I simply walked off, holding Moshkhussu very tight on her leash. I did not glance back for the woman who must surely be a goddess.

A moment later, I saw a wooden chest on the ground and picked it up. I had long ago learned that a man carrying something is less likely to be questioned or stopped.

And so, laden down with my heavy box and with Moshkhussu's lead wrapped tight around my left elbow, I picked my way with calm purpose between men rolling and fighting, and screaming mules charging this way and that, and sacks of grain and canvas ablaze. Only when I was clear of the ruckus did I put down the chest and keep on walking.

A little further on, I stopped to stoop over a corpse and got myself a bronze knife. This I tucked it into my belt, and then, when I was truly clear of the camp, I unleashed Moshkhussu. At first fast, and then slow, I dropped into the hunter's run.

Into the night I ran, with Moshkhussu bounding along next to me.

Strong and steady.

One step and then the next.

CHAPTER SIX

GILGAMESH

At Uruk

Upon the small bed that had once been Enkidu's, I let the priestess Lilith sew up my knee.

"It's bad," she said. "Oh, Gilgamesh."

"I just want it to stop bleeding," I said.

"Everything is cut through. Gilgamesh, you will need to go very easy. This is going to take a long time to heal."

"I heal more quickly than most men. I am only mortal, but I have *melam* in me."

"Even so," she said. "The goddesses must give you their blood."

"It's never helped me," I said. "You know that. I'm too much of an in-between-creature."

"You must drink it anyway, just in case."

When she had finished, she kissed my bloodied kneecap. "We cannot be as careless of ourselves as the gods are."

"Of that I am all too aware. But heroes must be heroes."

"This is the first day of the siege and look at you." She had tears in her eyes.

I looked back down at my knee. "How I wish Inanna was here now. Now that would be a good trick. To send her out alone against the Akkadians, looking so small and sweet, and then for her to unleash her fury on them."

"I only saw her return to Uruk, but it was glorious. I did not understand, when I met her, what power she might one day have."

"I always saw the war in her. Everyone else saw love. But I saw war."

"She loved you though," said Lilith.

"Everyone loves me," I said, winking at her. "At first."

On the steps back up onto the walls that evening, I found that if I pushed myself up on my right leg, and then kept my injured left leg completely stiff and straight as I drew it up, then the pain was not too bad.

I looked up to see Harga watching me climb the steps, his curls tucked behind his ears. "I suppose it won't stop you riding," he said. "We can tie you to your horse."

"I have no energy for you, Harga," I said, continuing my slow progress.

Having finally gained the wall, I sat myself down in my camp chair, my left leg stretched out before me. Harga came to sit next to me. The Akkadians were cooking their supper and a thousand campfires twinkled in the fields below us.

"They seem cheerful enough," said Harga, "despite the loss of Inush. Have you interviewed him yet?"

"I'm not really sure what I'd ask him, except where Della is."

"And he would not tell you anyway."

Harga passed me a clay cup and then poured some beer into it from a jug he had beside him.

"What if I challenged King Akka to a duel?" I said.

Harga gave a snort. "He will never accept."

"What if I made him accept? Kings have always fought duels, in Sumer and Akkadia too. He will lose face if he refuses."

"What does he care about his face when he is stood on the brink of conquering Sumer? He will never accept."

"What would make him accept?"

"Gilgamesh, he will not accept."

"He will not want to camp here into winter. He will not want to spend moons and moons here. A duel will be a chance for him to end it quickly."

"You are half his age. A renowned fighter, although why so renowned is hard for me to fathom."

"He might put up a champion."

Harga shook his head. "He will never put up a champion. This is not the plan. This is not how we win. Besides everything else, you can barely stand on that knee. If there was a duel today between you and Akka's infant son, you would lose it."

"What if we killed Inush and threw his body down? That might rile Akka enough to make him fight."

"It will rile him enough to kill your wife and baby. But he will not fight."

"You're not being very helpful, Harga."

"I watched them fashion two battering rams earlier," he said. "They are not going to agree to a duel."

There was then a long pause. I glanced sideways at Harga; even in the dim light, I could see he was not quite himself.

"What?" I said. "What are you sucking at?"

"Would you say you have been in love?" He was not looking at me. "Did you love Enkidu?"

I made a sort of choking noise. "Harga, what has come over you?"

"I cannot see how we win this one," he said. "I cannot see how we survive this."

"Harga, is this you thinking your life over?"

"Perhaps."

"No," I said. "No. Don't be thinking over your life, Harga. Don't be doing that. No good can come of that sort of thinking. Think instead of how to slaughter Akka. That is what our job is. We must murder Akkadians. Not think of chances lost, love not followed, or whatever nonsense is filling your head."

"But for all your faults," he said, "for all your terrible and unforgivable faults, you have taken your chances. You have followed love." He turned to look at me and I saw that he was serious. "In my youth, I lost people, and it made me learn never to hope for anything. So, I live my life alone."

"Harga, I am going to have to move my chair, if you continue to prattle on like some lovestruck shepherd boy, rather than the old and very ugly soldier that you are." I reached down and poured myself more beer. "Focus on the slaughter," I said. "That is where our expertise lies."

My eye was caught by something new: a blaze on the horizon, north of the city.

There was no village there. Only Akka's fleet and his supply camp.

A hard excitement gripped my heart.

"I wonder what this is," I said to Harga, very casual. "Is that not where Akka's boats are laid up?"

Harga stood up, apparently without much interest. "Their supply camp is over there somewhere," he said, very mild. "And the boats too."

"Help me up," I said, and he pulled me up by my left arm, while I held on to my beer with my right.

It was almost too much to hope for, but the distant flames were growing higher and higher.

For a few long minutes it was only us with our eyes upon the horizon, but then as the flames streamed higher into the night sky, shouts began going up. Before long the whole of the army of Akkadia was looking and pointing at the horizon and heaving into motion. Men were on their mules and riding out north in the dark, and the anxious hubbub from their enormous camp rose to us on the cool night air.

"I do hope it isn't their supplies," I said with a grin. "That would be a shame, wouldn't it, when they have done such a thorough job of burning all our farms and will have no food to fall back on."

Harga could not help grinning back at me. "I do think it's their supplies."

"Perhaps it was your misery that brought this good luck upon us," I said. "You should prattle like a shepherd boy more often."

Only then did I see the moving arrow of orange fire, coming hard at us through the ranks of the Akkadians.

It was godlight. A goddess on horseback, spilling out orange godlight, with a crowd of black riders behind her. All coming at us at a full gallop.

"Ah," I said. "My mother."

Of course, my mother.

Harga clapped his hands together. "We should have known that Ninsun would come."

CHAPTER SEVEN

NINLIL

On the road to Susa

As I wept, and wept, with the memory of what had happened to me, thoughts of my mother began to rise up.

Had I locked thoughts of my mother away, along with the thing that happened to me?

In my mind's eye, I now remembered my mother as some kind of demon-creature, with scales, feathers, and claws. Could my mother have really been a demon or was it only my mind playing tricks?

I remembered loving her, my heart almost bursting with the pain of it.

I remembered my mother hurting me.

I remembered my protector Bizilla, in her golden-scaled armour, stepping out to protect me from my mother.

Bizilla, who I had loved so much.

I wondered if Bizilla was still alive and if so where she was.

∞

I opened my eyes.

Trees overhead. Oaks.

Utu was poking me with one foot. His round head was copper-bright against the green.

"You have to get up," he said. "And get on your mule. Enough of this, Ninlil."

I stood, and realised I was taller than him. "Don't touch me with your foot again."

My beautiful dress was soaked with tears, as I climbed back up onto my animal.

We rode through endless forest. Sometimes we would emerge briefly at the edge of an escarpment, and for a moment get a sense of how high we had climbed. But mostly we rode through thick forest with only occasional glimpses of the sky. And I wept, and I wept.

On the third day of weeping, towards dusk, I began to feel better with every tear that fell. I cannot say what changed, but with the wooden box of memories fully open, a restoration had begun inside me. It made me remember what I had once been; the promise that there had been in my Anzu flesh. It made me enjoy the sweet scent of cedar in the air and the bird calls in the forest.

I felt a warm sea building up in me. I felt my hands prickling with what they might one day now achieve.

"Well done for stopping crying," said Utu. "Although you must have set some sort of record, for how long that went on."

"Utu, how can this be the way to Susa? I have been meaning to ask."

"It's the long way round," he said. "Which I've had plenty of time to regret, I can assure you."

I had stopped crying. I had also stopped growing. Now I would be turning my attention and my energy to what I wanted to be next.

"I need more food," I called ahead to Utu, as we picked our way over a wooden bridge. A river rushed white below us.

"There'll be more food when we get to Susa."

"I need some now. I am starving."

Grim-faced, he got himself off his mule, gripping tight to its mane as he did so. He peered down into the river. "Well let's try to do some fishing here."

"I can do the fishing for both of us," I said.

I had seen Utu use his *mees* to stun fish as they leaped up out of the water, although he was an unlucky fisherman and rarely succeeded in catching anything.

Now I climbed down the rocks to the icy water and found that, if I concentrated, I was quick enough to catch the fish with my hands. I snatched one from the air, and threw it onto the bank for Utu, and then I snatched up another huge fat fish and carried it over to a rock.

I ate it alive: mouth, eyes, bones, tail, guts, sweet flesh, all of it.

"It's good,' I said. I was soaked to the skin and covered with fish scales, but I felt supremely alive.

Utu killed the fish I had thrown him, but only set it down beside him, so I went and took that one up and gobbled it down too.

"Who is your mother, Ninlil?" he said, as he watched me eat.

"I think you know. I think you know who your deal is with, even if you went through intermediaries. I think you know the depth of your betrayal."

"And your father?"

"My mother ate him," I said. I felt shocked by the sudden memory of it.

"Well, that I believe," said Utu.

I went back down to the river to wash my hands and face.

"I think it's time I faced my mother," I said, but Utu could not have heard me over the river noise.

We followed that same river downstream for two days. On the third day we rode out of the forest onto open farmland, and there, in the distance, was Susa.

The city sat within huge, rammed-earth walls, with a mud-brick ziggurat at the heart of it. It had been built on a piece of high land between two substantial rivers, on good farmland. So far, so familiar. But the great novelty of the place was that its houses were all made of wood.

I rode into the wooden city well ahead of my kidnapper, smiling at the people as they came out of their houses to look at me.

I had heard of Susa, but I had been expecting a market town. This was indisputably a great and venerable city, its wooden streets lined with ancient fruit trees and palms, its people well dressed and orderly. The sun was bright, and I filled up my lungs with the clean air of a city set with its back to mountains.

The priests and other city elders gathered to meet us at the wooden gates of the temple precinct. As I rode up, one black-bearded priest stood out before them all, his hands folded before him. He wore a tall red hat upon his head, and he had a look of great seriousness to him.

"I am Ninlil," I said to him.

The black-bearded priest kneeled on the sandy street and tipped his tall red hat to me. Behind him the priests and the elders kneeled also, and when Utu rode up to join me, he found me sitting upon my mule, amidst a hushed and reverent crowd.

Utu slowly dismounted, a frown on his face. "There is no need for that, Lamma," he said. "You will take us to our rooms now."

Lamma ignored Utu; he was still looking up at me. "Goddess Ninlil, I would ask you a question."

"Ask it," I said, still sat on my mule.

"I would ask what kind of goddess you are."

Utu took a step towards Lamma. "She's not any kind of goddess. Just do as I ask, Lamma."

I stepped down from my mule and went to stand next to Utu. Lamma was still on his knees.

"If you stand, I will tell you what kind of goddess I am," I said to him.

He stood, looking from me to Utu and back again. I leaned into him and caught the scent of myrrh. I whispered into his ear. "I am a healing goddess."

Until that moment, I had only been thinking it. Now it would be real.

I looked down at my hands, so strong and capable, and I felt the brightness contained within them.

Lamma leaned forward and returned my whisper. "There are no healing goddesses."

"That may have been true yesterday, but it is not true today."

He and I looked at each other, silent and serious.

"Enough," said Utu. "Let's get her inside."

They put me in rooms of my own, high up in the temple buildings with a view out over the city. Already, I felt the tension in those around me, their fear, but also their hope.

Priestesses came to my rooms, their heads bent low. They

brought me bowls of stew, and good wine, and bucket after bucket of hot water for a bath.

My beautiful blue dress from Kish was too tight around my shoulders and hips now but Lamma brought me a new black dress to wear after my bath, while they had my blue dress cleaned and altered. "We can sew in some extra cloth from your cloak," he said.

"Blue is my colour now," I said.

"We will have a new cloak made for you, in a similar blue. And we are making some shoes up for you, now we have your measurements."

"I will need more food," I said to every priest or priestess or bath pourer who came near me, and each of them would go to fetch more.

Lamma, the high priest, came to watch me eat grilled lamb, pomegranates, soft breads, and rosemary-flavoured butter. "We will keep bringing you food," he said. "You will not go hungry here."

"It's all so good," I said. "I will take more of everything."

I could see Lamma's mind was on other things.

"There is an old temple, that was here before the city. A temple of the old gods. The priests there talk of a god who could heal the sick and save the dying. But I never believed the story."

I shrugged at that and kept on eating.

"We knew to expect Utu and a prisoner," Lamma said. "But there was no word of you coming, my goddess."

"You will come to no harm because of this, Lamma," I said. "You did not know what you were agreeing to, when you promised Utu safe harbour."

"It is said in temple that you are a grain goddess."

"I could eat grain," I said. "But I also think I could heal."

There were women in the room fussing with my bath; I sensed them go still.

Lamma was still kneeling in front of me. "If I brought you someone, goddess, would you look at her?"

"A test?"

"Not a test. But before we take you to temple, perhaps it might be good to try here."

"If you bring me more food, I will take any test you like."

"I'll bring the girl then, and some food."

"But not grain," I said. "I would eat grain, raw or cooked, but it would not be my first choice."

"We will bring you the best food in the city," he said.

They did bring me food, but afterwards, Lamma brought in the girl.

"This is my daughter," he said.

She was dark-skinned and dark-haired, very small, and one of her eyes was only a dry, empty socket. Her remaining eye was wet and red-ringed, bulging strangely and seeping pus.

Lamma, holding the girl's shoulders tightly, kneeled next to her. He said: "It was worms that ate her eye. And now they are in her good eye and we can find no medicine that will work."

I sat myself down comfortably in the chair next to my bed.

"I do not think I can help the eye that is gone," I said. "Perhaps I can't help her at all. I have never healed anyone before. But I will try."

I brought the child into my lap, her back against me, and I covered up her eye sockets with my hands. I shut my own eyes and rested my forehead on the girl's oiled hair.

"Ah!" I said. "I can feel you thinking."

"I'm not thinking," said the little girl.

"Be quiet now," I said. "Let your thoughts go. Just feel my warm hands on you and let them do their work."

I relaxed. I let myself feel her warmth, and her breath, and slowly, I crept inside her, feeling, feeling, slowly, slowly. The warm sea that flowed within me found its way into the frightened child.

I felt her fear, her terrible pain, and now, the flicker of hope coming alive in her.

"Hello," I whispered into her hair. "Hello."

I came first to her deadened eye, the empty socket. I felt the dry ache, hard within it. and then I moved, bracing myself, into the piercing well of pain that was her left eye. Yes there, inside it: a creature, wriggling, eating, growing. I pinched the life out of it, and then, carefully, dissolved it. I sat myself inside her eye and let the wild salty waters inside me do their work. I let her, for those moments, be a part of myself, and l let the part of myself that was Creation take control.

The girl let out a low moan as I worked, but it was not pain, it was blissful relief. I had almost finished my work when I felt something tugging at me. I shifted my perspective: in the other eye socket, where there had only been dry ache and darkness; something was happening. Something moist, bright, alive, was budding in the wrinkled tissues.

"Oh!" I said out loud. I had not expected it.

When I had finished, I do not know how long later, the girl had two bright, perfect, brilliant eyes.

Lamma wept. The girl wept, with her good, bright, beautiful eyes, and she kissed my cheeks and nose and lips. The room was by then full of priests and priestesses. They all got onto their knees and pressed their heads to the floor. We all wept together for both Lamma's happiness and the happiness of the little girl.

Lamma's wife came in then and took the girl from me. She kissed her eyes and hugged her, and then passed her to her husband so that she could kneel before me and wash my feet in her tears.

"Anything," Lamma said. "Anything you command, we do. Anything."

"I must sleep," I said. "I thank you for your gratitude, but I cannot stay awake now."

Later, Utu opened my door without knocking and stepped into my room. I was lying on my bed resting, with priestesses sitting quietly around me.

"What is this?" he said.

The priestesses got to their feet, all ranged against Utu.

I sat up. "Utu, you must go to your rooms and stay there," I said, "or I am going to eat you."

He kept on looking at me, his face without expression.

I bared my teeth at him. "Do you not believe me?"

He stepped out of the room and shut the door behind him.

CHAPTER EIGHT

NINSHUBAR

Somewhere south of Egypt

I carried Inanna over my left shoulder, through staggering, unwavering heat.

One step and then the next.

It was hard country, with sharp sand and thorns under foot. The hot, mineral smell of sand dunes filled my lungs.

I had grown soft. Would I have complained of thorns when I lived in my home country and I was the runner at the back of the hunt? Now my feet hurt and I missed my soft Sumerian boots.

I had followed the tracks of the three large animals up from the beach, since I had no better idea of what to do. Now I kept on following their prints along the dusty coast path that led north. The prints were large, rounded and cleft at the front. They must surely be from some beast of burden, but they were unlike anything I had seen before.

I will admit the lions were useful for sniffing out every spring or scrap of a stream as I sweated and huffed along the way. Without anything to carry water in, I drank my fill wherever I could. Each time I drank, I used a shell or leaf to dribble water into Inanna's mouth. I could not make her swallow, but she was still breathing, if only faintly. I could still hear her heart beating if I pressed my ear to her chest.

It was already dusk when I saw three large animals in the distance ahead of us. They were shaggy, long-necked creatures, with two large humps on each of their backs. A man, dressed in black, was sitting between the humps on the lead animal's back. It was a rather awkward-looking arrangement. The remaining two animals followed behind on ropes.

I could not run, with Inanna heavy and awkward on my shoulder, but I walked faster and gained on him. He could have pushed his animals on, but he allowed me to catch up. When it was almost dark, he slowed down to a halt and turned to watch me approach.

"Please, will you help me?" I called ahead of me. "My friend is very sick."

He was frowning; perhaps he did not understand me.

I tried again, in my home tongue. He was still frowning. I switched to a trading language, that I knew the men who sold me as a slave had used.

"I can help you," he called to me, in that same trading language. "Put down your weapons first."

I put Inanna down on the sandy path, her lions milling around her. I put down my axe and spear next to her.

"I think she's dying," I said to the man. I walked towards him with my empty hands held out to him.

His animal was lowering itself down on the ground: an amazing sight. The man then simply stepped off the creature, very elegant.

He was a tall man, in a long black robe and turban, with a face like a hawk. It was hard to tell what weapons he was carrying under his cloak.

"What's wrong with her?" he said.

"What kind of animals are these?" I said.

He looked round at his animals, rather proud. "Camels. Very rare."

"Interesting," I said, raising my left wrist.

I blasted him with one of Enki's *mees* of combat.

The pulse of energy knocked him hard over. He landed on his back, with blood pouring from his nose.

I blasted him again, to be sure of it.

A heartbeat later the camels made their escape. They careered off in a very ugly and chaotic fashion, being all tied together. A heartbeat or two later, they came rushing back towards me, with Inanna's two lions behind them. I leaped towards one of the camels and held on hard to its halter. Its breath stank rather fetid, as I wrangled it, but it was worth the smell and the struggle. These camels were large, strong animals, with numerous saddlebags tied to them.

I did not thank the lions out loud, but I did nod to them.

So. I would tie Inanna over a camel. I would ride another. We could make better time. For now, I held on tight to the lead camel.

There was still the question of this man, lying on his back in the sand and now moaning a little.

I squatted down next to him with the three camels clustered behind me. The man's nose was still bleeding. His eyes were open just a crack.

"I need you to tell me the way to Sumer," I said.

He was looking at me but said nothing.

"Tell me how to get to Sumer, and I will let you live."

He cleared his throat and put one hand up to his nose. "If you had a boat, it would be quickest."

"And if I can't find a boat?"

"You can go overland. You have my camels."

"How long if we go overland?"

"A moon maybe," he said. "Maybe more."

I nodded at that.

"Before I leave you here," I said, "I am going to need your boots and that cloak. And any gold you have about your person."

"Take what you will," he said.

"Also, I am going to need you to tell me where our boat is."

This time he opened his eyes properly.

I said: "I am not normally a killer or even a torturer. But my friend here is dying. So, tell me where our boat is, quickly, or I am going to start to cut things off you."

"It wasn't me that took your boat."

"I can see that," I said. "I can see you do not currently have our boat. But I think you know exactly where it is, since you and your camels were on the beach when it was taken. It is not my first time reading tracks."

"I'm Khufu," he said.

"Hello, Khufu. Will you take us to our boat?"

"Yes," he said. "It would be my pleasure. But I was about to stop for some supper if you are interested in some food."

Khufu made us a fire and produced a pot, onions, and a desert hare from his camels' saddlebags. To my astonishment, he also produced poles and leather sheets, and in a matter of heartbeats had erected a small tent.

"For the girl," he said, lifting his chin at Inanna. She lay, still unconscious, with her head in my lap. "It will keep the night damp off her," he said.

I moved Inanna into the tent and her lions wriggled in alongside her.

For Khufu's final trick, he produced water, dried herbs, and small bronze cups, and made me a cup of tea.

"We saw a boat just sitting on the beach," he said. "We thought it might have been abandoned."

I gave a short laugh. I was settling Inanna into the small tent, with one of Khufu's camel-felt blankets over her.

"It was just sitting there," Khufu went on, "full of treasures. As if the gods themselves had left it there for us."

"We were the gods who left it there," I said. "And sadly, those gods have now found you." I returned to my seat by the fire.

"Is that what you are? Gods?"

"It's what they call us, in Sumer."

"I have heard there are gods like you in the temples along the Nile. Gods who look forward to their food and leave footprints in the sand. It is said that they are the children of the gods of Sumer."

"That does not recommend them to me," I said.

Khufu served me a bowl of hare stew. "My men were going to take your boat around the coast to the port of our hometown. They should be in port by the morning. I will make sure that everything is returned to you."

The stew was very good. "I like these spices," I said. "Thank you."

"Goddess, may I ask what you were doing here, when we took your boat?"

I looked up into his lovely green eyes and gave him a rueful smile. "I was looking for a tall, pale-skinned boy. With red hair and blue eyes. He was sold as a slave here, about two years ago."

"Oh yes, I know the boy," said Khufu as he took a large spoonful of his stew.

I remembered to breathe.

"How do you know the boy?" I said.

Khufu chewed on some hare. "My men took him up to Abydos with a number of other slaves. He was very distinctive looking. We called him Marduk, because of his red hair, like the setting sun. It means 'calf of the evening sun.'"

"Marduk," I said.

"I think he was put for sale in Abydos."

I could only nod.

"You still want to find this boy?" he said.

"I do."

"We could go to Abydos. It means heading inland. But we have three camels. We could do it."

"You are being so helpful, Khufu."

He smiled. "I am thinking there is value to be had, in escorting two goddesses."

I breathed in deep. "I must get my friend here to Sumer as quickly as possible. The boy Marduk must wait."

"All right," he said. "If you are sure."

"It seems there are no good choices."

"Certainly, there are no simple ones," said Khufu.

I lay down with Inanna for a while before we set off again. I rested my nose and mouth against her hair and breathed her in. She smelt of lion.

"Please stay alive," I said to her. "Please stay alive."

CHAPTER NINE

ERESHKIGAL

On the road to Enlil's city

After so long in the underworld, my skin was greedy for Earthshine and very quickly my arms turned a deep and gorgeous brown. They looked very fine in contrast to the white dress that Geshtinanna had given to me, even if the cloth was not as clean as it had once been. I held my arms out in front of me as I walked, in order to better admire them.

"Why are you smiling at your arms?" Erra said.

He was walking just behind me.

His eyes were much improved; he had abandoned his bandages. His head wounds had not improved, but he wore his hood pulled low over this face, to hide them. I liked the look of him now as he stood smiling down at me on our path through a stretch of marshland. But then I had liked the look of him before, even when he had bloodied bandages all over his face.

Nammu walked ahead of us, a shimmer of green against the brown reeds. The frogs were in full cry: an extraordinary cacophony.

"I was wrong to think you less mad," Erra continued. "Now, what is all that noise?"

"What noise?"

He laughed. "The very loudest noise, Ereshkigal. The astonishing animal noise."

"It is deer making that noise." I said the name very clearly for him again: "*Deer.*"

"Oh." He frowned down into the reeds. "*Deer.* Are they in the undergrowth?"

"The reeds are full of tiny deer. They croak all day and night in certain seasons. It can drive you mad after a while."

He was still frowning. "I don't know why but I had it in my mind that deer were something you might hunt."

"Certainly, you can hunt them," I said. "You collect them in nets." I mimed the throwing of a net. "But you need twenty or thirty deer to make any sort of pie."

He was looking at me rather suspiciously, so I added: "We call it *venison* pie."

"I think I've heard of that. In the stories of the old gods."

I smiled up at him. "I too knew of deer, even before I came down from Heaven."

Nammu brought down several ducks along the way that day, and in the early evening I helped Erra hunt for things to make a fire with.

"Ereshkigal, you are meant to be gathering sticks," he said.

"I have this one." I held out a small twig to him.

He had a whole bundle of sticks and dry reeds in his arms. "I would suggest you help Nammu with the ducks, but I cannot see you making a success of it."

"I have plucked many ducks," I said. I leaned over to pick up another small twig.

We arrived back in camp both laughing over my meagre collection of twigs.

Nammu watched us build the fire together with a hard frown on her face. "I cannot stand this constant whispering and giggling. You are like two silly children together."

"I have never giggled in my life," I said.

Erra laughed at that, but then pointed towards the pathway. "A snake!"

"Where?" said Nammu.

A small deer of some sort had inadvertently crept up on us and now stood frozen at the sight of us.

"There!" said Erra, pointing at the deer.

"That is a deer," Nammu said, with a dark look at me. "Not a snake. When will you learn? Everything she says is a lie!"

"What is a snake then?" he said to me, still very good-humoured.

"A serpent," said Nammu, answering for me. "It's the same thing. You have them in Heaven. You know what a serpent is."

A cloud passed across his face. "I know what serpents are."

"I did not mean to upset you," I said to him, because I did not like to see him so sad.

Erra burst out laughing again. "You said a true thing to me."

I put my hands on my hips. "I did not!"

"You said something true."

Nammu stood up, her arms raised. "I cannot stand one more moment of this. I expect it of you, Ereshkigal, but Erra, I thought you a more serious man."

"You hardly know me," he said, his face closed for a moment.

Nammu stalked off into the reeds.

Erra turned to me, grinning again, and wagged one finger at me.

"That was a deer. Yet you told me it was deer making all this noise. There cannot be hundreds of animals that size hiding in the reeds."

"There are big deer, but also very small deer," I said. "Some are no bigger than my thumbnail. Those are the ones that croak."

The next day Nammu walked well ahead of us, apparently to avoid our chatter.

Erra and I were arguing over the fair sharing of the blankets when we saw that Nammu had stopped and was turning back to us.

There was a haze on the horizon beyond her. I smelt smoke.

A moment later, Nammu was jogging back towards us along the sandy path through the reeds. "Something is wrong," she said.

In an instant, Erra grew very distant from me. All the humour dropped from him.

"Let's go," he said.

The sky was a strange grey in front of us. I could smell something else on the smoke; something almost sweet.

"What is the smell?" I said.

"Bodies burning," Erra said.

He pulled something small and black from his belt band, and shook it out into some sort of baton. He walked on with it clenched in his right fist.

"Erra, will you slow down a little?" I said. "Will you tell me what is in your mind?"

He did not turn to answer me.

It was not long before the refugees began to pass us, coming at us down the sandy path with children in their arms and at their heels. Many were wounded.

The adults were all women and they barely looked at us. Their faces spoke of one thing: disaster.

After the women and children came their goats, dogs, and donkeys.

Nammu stepped out to block the path of a woman walking alone. The woman's hands were horribly burned.

Nammu said to her: "What has happened?"

The woman looked from one to the other of us but walked on without speaking.

"I do not understand," I said. "What is it that has happened?"

"Nippur has fallen," Nammu said. "Someone has attacked the holy city. Something has shifted."

We both of us looked at Erra and he glowered back at us.

I saw him then not as my friend and co-conspirator, but as something dark and frightening.

"War and chaos," I said to him.

Erra seemed about to speak, but instead he turned and walked on towards Nippur.

"I should have brought my secret things," I said to Nammu.

"This is no time for your nonsense, Ereshkigal," she said. "Now let us hurry."

I remained still for a moment, planted to the path in protest at her words. "This is all wrong, Nammu. We should not have bought him here."

But she did not turn back to answer.

A feeling of deep dread passed through me.

"I do not think this wise," I said, although she was already too far away to hear me.

I knew Erra had been lying to us. But what was he going to do?

I shouted ahead at both of them to stop and wait for me, but they kept on walking. First Erra, in his long black cape, and then Nammu in her emerald green.

"Nammu, you must stop him!" I shouted.

But it was as if neither of them could hear me shouting.

The city had fallen, but gangs of Akkadians still roved on foot, looting and killing. Here or there, we saw Enlil's men, some confused, some set on the saving of some friend or relative, or intent upon the killing of Akkadians whatever the cost.

The streets were clogged with rubble, burning roof beams, piles of bodies, and the rubbish left by people fleeing for their lives.

The dust fell thick and heavy upon me.

I thought, *oh it is the dust of the dead,* but then I remembered that it was ash that was falling.

That it was all real.

Nammu lit up a shimmering green shield and walked within its shelter, but no one came to interfere with us. All seemed too focused on their day of death and turmoil.

Erra walked out in front, picking his way over charred beams and piles of bricks, his black cape growing grey with ash. Nammu walked almost on his shoulder, turning her golden curls to peer into gaping buildings.

I stumbled along behind them, shouting for Nammu, although she would not turn her head for me. I realised, from the blackened tree trunks that lined the road we turned into, that we were in the central avenue through Nippur. Ahead of us lay a sea of crumbled brick and burning wood.

It was the ruins of the Blue Temple.

When I was not much more than a girl, I stood with Enlil to watch them painting the outer walls of the Blue Temple. They called it the Blue Temple because of the lapis lazuli-studded columns on the top level of the ziggurat. But the building itself they painted white and when it was done, it could be seen for leagues around.

Later I watched the master craftsmen paint images of the Anunnaki, in brilliant colours, upon the inside walls of the temple. I saw the purpose of these paintings, their true function, when the people of the city came in to worship for the first time. The paintings, the shining columns, the wonderful views from the upper sanctuary: all of it spoke of the divine spark.

Now the men of Akkadia had razed it all to the ground.

Erra was making straight for the ruins; Nammu behind him. I broke into a shambling run, trying to catch them both up.

And then there, at the edge of the ruins, I caught sight of my grandfather, Enlil, Lord of the Sky, wearing bronze armour over his black robes. In Nippur, they called him the Great Mountain. Now the mountain was on his knees, trying to get something out from under the wreckage; men of Nippur were trying to help him.

Enlil stood up with a small child in his arms. For a moment he cradled the child, and then he passed it to one of his men.

A soldier said something to him; he turned to face us, his hands on his hips.

Nammu pushed past Erra and was first up the steps of what had once been the glorious ziggurat of Nippur.

I was too far back to hear Enlil's reaction, but I saw him put out his arms to his mother. He pulled off his bronze helmet and the two of them stood for some moments, their faces pressed into each other's necks.

I could not hear what passed between them.

I heaved myself up the steps, staggering, pushing past Erra, gasping for breath.

"This man is here to kill you," I shouted out to Enlil. "He is not who he says he is."

But I was too late.

Tendrils of dense shadow began pouring out of Erra.

I stared at him, trying to understand what he was doing and so it was a moment before I realised that the black tendrils had wrapped themselves around my body. I could not move my arms or turn my head.

I tried to speak but could not.

I thought to myself: *his weapons are better than our weapons.*

The ash was no longer falling; a bird above us appeared frozen against the sky, its wings outstretched. The noise of the city, of the burning, of the men searching for survivors, was muffled and distant.

I thought, turning my eyes to my left, I could see Enlil's booted foot.

Was he on the ground?

I turned my eyes down to the right and I could see Nammu's face, turned up to me as if lifeless. Her eyes were closed. A thin line of blood flowed from her nose and down her golden right cheek.

Erra walked into view, his eyes down towards Enlil.

He compressed his black baton into a small cube, and slid it into his belt. He then brought out a different black cube and gave it one shake. It transformed into a long, black machete, heavy enough to fell a sapling with.

Erra lifted the machete high over his head and brought it down hard on something, although I could not see upon what.

I could not unhear it though. The sound of metal crunching through flesh and bone.

A moment later Erra was holding up Enlil's severed head in his left hand. He held it out from himself, so that the blood gushed down onto the temple rubble as he pushed his machete into his weapons belt.

Then he was coming at me.

He grabbed me by the hair with his right hand and pulled me after him. "You will come with me," he said.

We walked through the streets of Nippur. There was blood all down the front of my white dress. It could only be my grandfather's.

Close behind me came the dark stranger, the Lord of War and Chaos, who had told us his name was Erra.

In his left hand, he held up the head of the god Enlil, pumping blood still, so that all who bore witness would know the Lord of the Sky was truly dead.

We walked surrounded by Erra's black tendrils and in the muffled space within them, all I could hear was my breath.

Now and again I would stumble over something and Erra would poke me in the back with his black baton. "Quicker," he said.

"Nammu will come after you," I said. "She will punish you."

"Do you see her running after us?"

"They will all come down on you. All the Anunnaki."

He jabbed me in the back again. "Keep talking and I will hurt you."

CHAPTER TEN

GILGAMESH

At Uruk

My mother, the goddess Ninsun, rode into Uruk at a dead gallop, the arrows of the Akkadians exploding useless upon her orange shield.

Oh, how the city erupted in joy as the elephant gates rattled down behind her.

My mother had been queen of the city since time out of mind. She had always kept them safe.

I gave out a heavy sigh. "We had better be there to greet her."

I could only move slowly and my mother was already in the White Temple by the time I'd made my way across the city. She was stood beneath the god's throne, unbuckling her bronze helmet. Inanna's mother, the moon goddess, and a fleet of priestesses stood in plain-faced attendance.

My mother lifted her chin at me in curt greeting.

"The holy city has fallen," she said.

"What?" said the moon goddess, stepping forward.

My mother ignored her. "Akkadians have swept through all the northern cities, except Sippur I think."

"Where are all the family?" I said. "And where is the army?"

My mother sat down on what I still thought of as An's throne. She ran her fingers through her short, black hair. "Most of the army was in Nippur when the city was attacked. For all the good it did us. As for the family, Enlil is going mad, looking for Ninlil."

"And my father?" I said.

"I think he has taken An north." She stretched out her legs before her. "So, King Akka has Della and the baby?" she said. "You said you would keep them safe."

"We believe he has them," I said.

"And do you know where he is holding them?"

The pain of standing had become too great and I sat down on one of the wooden pews. "Mother, if I knew where Della and the baby were, of course I would have gone for them."

My mother tipped her nose up at the moon goddess. "What are you doing here?"

"I followed my daughter Inanna here," the moon goddess said. "This is her city now."

"Is it?" said my mother. "Anyway, I have burned the Akkadians' boats, tents, and supplies."

The priestess Lilith, for so long my mother's lover, had come to stand beside me. My mother did not acknowledge her.

"Come to the palace," the moon goddess said. "And we can talk over some food."

My mother tipped her cap of hair sideways. "Oh, it's your palace now, is it?"

Harga smiled to himself as we followed the goddesses across the torch-lit precinct to Inanna's palace.

"What?" I said.

"Your mother makes me smile, that's all."

"Because she is foul to everyone and especially to me. That is what amuses you. There is no great mystery to it."

He rolled his shoulders thoughtfully. "You could be right." He stopped then, to watch me as I tried to walk without wincing or collapsing. "You should have some crutches made for you."

"I can walk," I said, although it was agony.

In more ordinary times, Harga and Lilith would not have dined with the Anunnaki. But that night they sat down with us in the purple-decked dining room of the holy palace. We all made good of our suitably small supper, in keeping with the times.

When the servants had withdrawn, my mother poked a silver knife in my direction. "So, you chopped down my tree?"

I was blank for a moment. I had until that moment entirely forgotten about the huluppu tree.

"Yes, I did chop it down," I said, very solemn.

"What reason could you have to do it? It was the most beautiful tree in this city. Why would anyone chop it down?"

I could not say, "to impress a girl", and so instead I sat up straight and said: "You were not here, mother."

Lilith leaned forward: "Goddess, they were strange times, with Dumuzi running this city."

"It is being burned for firewood now," my mother said. "My sacred tree."

"We are lucky to have so much wood," said the moon goddess, which I did not think very diplomatic.

My mother stabbed at her mutton and said: "We should surrender the city. And in the chaos after, we Anunnaki must slip away."

I put down my knife. "You cannot mean it."

"And yet I do. Even having destroyed Akka's supplies, we cannot win this. Thousands and thousands of innocents will starve or die of thirst if we do not surrender."

"And my wife and child?" I said.

"You have Akka's nephew. A trade can be made."

"And what of all the fighting men? All will be slaughtered. He may also slaughter all the other men and enslave all the women and children. That is what he did at Larak."

"Some of them will live," my mother said. "People will live who might not otherwise. And perhaps if it is over quickly, more will live. Perhaps he will even leave the city standing."

"It is not the clay bricks I am worrying over," I said.

I looked over at the moon goddess. She lifted her soft shoulders at me. "I don't know what to think, Gilgamesh."

"We will not be surrendering," I said.

"That is the wrong decision," my mother said. "And I cannot let you make it."

I leaned over and was about to point a finger at her in hard anger, but instead I sat back. "I am king here," I said, my hands flat upon the tablecloth. "It is my city now. I hold it for Inanna."

"This was my city for two hundred years," my mother said. "And I say we will surrender. That is how we save thousands of lives at the cost of a few hundred. I say this because I love this city and its people. I even love its walls and do not wish to see them torn down."

"No," I said. I stood, and then for a few moments could say nothing at all, because of the pain in my leg.

At last, I said: "Mother, I want you to go through all the *mees* that Inanna brought back from Eridu and work out what they all do, and what we can use now against Akka. That is the task I am setting you."

A laugh burst from my mother. "I do not take orders from you, Gilgamesh."

I raised both my eyebrows at Harga. "Shall we go?"

I must say he got up rather reluctantly, casting sheepish glances at the women.

The two of us were on our way out, me setting a very slow pace indeed, when Lilith also stood. Until then she had not said anything. "I will come with you, Gilgamesh," she said. "I agree that we cannot surrender."

My mother put her fists down upon the table. "Do not make out that I am the coward here," she said. For the first time, she looked full at Lilith. "I am only saying what is true and right."

"And yet I say it to you," Lilith said. "Coward."

There was then a horrible silence as Lilith and my mother glared at each other.

"Come, Lilith," I said.

We left the moon goddess with her eyes wide, and my mother with her mouth hard and her arms crossed over her chest.

Harga stood sentinel on the north wall and I sat in a chair next to him, my bad leg stretched out. The blaze of the supply camp was finally dimming and it was too dark to see the army below. My hands were shaking. How long had we been awake?

Lilith stood alongside us, upset and silent, huddled up in her cloak.

"We could send a messenger to Akka," I said. "Tell him that he must send me my wife and son, or we will push Inush off the walls at dawn."

Harga rubbed a pebble between his right thumb and his right index finger, and frowned, shaking his head. "If he doesn't send them, what then? Then you must either kill your hostage or be proved a liar who need not be feared."

We were silent for a while, listening to the howling of the Akkadian dogs.

"We should have our own fighting dogs," I said. "I cannot think why we do not."

"Horrible creatures," Harga said.

I sighed out. "They are meant to be horrible, Harga. Anyway you've never liked dogs. You were not even keen on my otter hounds and they were beautiful creatures."

"I did not mind them."

"I hope they are being well looked after," I said, ashamed of not having thought of them for so long. "I wonder when we will be in Shuruppak again."

We stood silent then, thinking, thinking.

"Akka does love Inush," I said. "I know he does. We must be able to do something with Inush."

"A nephew is not a son."

"Harga, I am only trying to think of something. Something to change the odds of us in here, with very little food and water, and him out there with unlimited supplies of clean water and able to go hunting whenever he chooses to."

"I will go north and snatch up Akka's son again if that is best. But is it the best use of me?"

"We need a bigger trick," I said.

"It would be better if Inanna and Ninshubar were here," Harga said.

"On that we can agree," I said.

"So how do we use Inush?" Lilith put in.

"Maybe Inush keeps Della and my son alive," I said. "Maybe that's all he does."

"Maybe," Harga said. "Maybe."

"What do you think, Lilith?" I said.

She gave a little shrug. "Your mother has the experience," she said. "She has fought in countless wars."

"And now she wants us to surrender."

"I am just saying, it would be good if we had her on our side. I do not like being at odds with her."

"You get used to it," I said.

Even being very careful of my knee, I ended up wincing out loud as I crept down from the ramparts, an oil lamp in my left hand, my right hand hard against the wall.

I had been punctured and beaten so often, but I could not remember anything so painful as this savaged knee.

Lilith, stood at the top of the wall, watched my slow progress down the steps.

"Be careful, Gilgamesh, of looking too human," she called down. "It was when my knees started hurting in the mornings that your mother lost interest in me."

"Thank you for the warning, Lilith," I said. "But we both know she's never been very interested in me."

I had been focused so tightly on the steps, that I had not noticed my mother, standing waiting at the bottom of the narrow steps.

"Is that what you think, that I've never been interested in you?" she said, her face plain, her dark eyes steady on me. "I have always loved you, Gilgamesh, even when you've been at your most foolish."

"Well, you have hidden it well."

"Perhaps I have held back a little," she said. "Knowing how little…" She swallowed what she was going to say.

I breathed in, breathed out. "The sad tale of my failure to be immortal and the toll it has taken on you and my father is very well known to me. Now stand aside, mother, so I can get past."

She stayed where she was at the bottom of the steps. "I came to Nippur when I heard that Enkidu, this boy you loved, had died. I stood for you at the funeral. Yet you refused to see me after."

"And?"

"And yet I am here. I could be out there searching for your father, but I am here, for you. So do not be moaning to Lilith that I have not been interested in you when I am only here because of you."

"Yes, what about Lilith, who has done nothing but love you and serve you faithfully? Who has been more of a mother to me than you ever have? What do you have to say about your treatment of Lilith?"

My mother was quiet a moment. "Do you reprimand me, Gilgamesh, for how I have treated a woman? Is that not a little much, coming from you?"

I gave her my full smile. "Mother, I do believe you have done your best by me. Does that satisfy you?"

At last she stepped aside, and I limped past her.

"I have done better than you will do with your own son!" she called after me. "I think everyone can agree on that!"

∽

They had stashed Inush in the deepest bowels of Uruk. I should have had him brought up to the walls, but I was already six flights of stairs down when that occurred to me.

At the entrance to the lowest cells, a bowing jailor came out to greet me.

"Get me a chair, would you? And one for the prisoner."

I sat in the small and gloomy waiting room there while they roused Inush out of his cell.

He was produced, his hands bound behind him, looking a little rumpled in his crimson suit, but otherwise more elegant than he had any right to be.

"Bad knee?" he said. No smiles, then.

"Do sit down," I said.

And so Inush and I sat opposite each other, me with my hands on my knee.

"I'm told the tendon is cut through," I said. "It's a mess."

"I hope it was me that did the damage."

I suppose I had not expected him to be so angry. "How's your shoulder?" I said.

"It doesn't matter how it is."

I frowned at that. "I wish you had stayed in Kish, Inush. Not just you. I mean all of you."

"I could do with some water," he said. "To drink I mean. There's plenty on the floor here but I'm not quite thirsty enough to drink it."

"Fetch him some," I said to the jailor.

While the man went off for a jug of water, Inush said: "It was you who brought us down here, Gilgamesh. It is because of you we are here. It was the death of my aunt Hedda that set my uncle on this course. But of course you have ruined so many girls, perhaps you do not even remember her."

"I remember her," I said.

The jailor returned. Inush took the jug from him and drank all of the water before handing it back.

"Your uncle killed my friend, because of what happened to Hedda," I said. "Even though her death was an accident."

"My uncle meant you to die, of course, not your friend. But whether you meant to Hedda to die or not at Marad, you had already dishonoured her, even before that."

That I could not deny.

"Do you know where my wife and child are?" I said.

"I knew where they were yesterday, but he will have moved them the moment I was captured."

"You should not have let me get so close to you," I said.

"I thought you'd be worrying about your son. That you would do nothing to put his life at risk."

I sighed. "I'm new to fatherhood."

"So, what will your next great trick be?" he said. "I'm sad to be missing it, stuck down here."

"Am I famous, for my tricks? Even in Akkadia?"

"What else do you have to boast of, except trickery?"

I nodded. "Inush, I am very sorry indeed for what I did to Hedda when I was a hostage in Kish, and to what happened to her after at Marad. My man did not mean to kill her, but I am thoroughly ashamed of myself for everything that happened nonetheless."

He shrugged. "It is too late for apologies. My uncle is here for Sumer. He wants it all now. And you know, I think he is going to get it."

It was a long way up the stairs from the cells that night, one agonising step at a time.

I was going to let all of them down. That was the truth of it. Because I did not have a trick left in me.

At our outpost upon the wall, I found Harga as I had left him, looking out into the night, a pebble in each hand. "The enemy is still out there," he said. "In case you were wondering."

I breathed in, breathed out. "I think we are all going to die here."

Harga laughed. "Of that I am in little doubt, my lord."

CHAPTER ELEVEN

MARDUK

Somewhere near Uruk

I was a free man for the first time in years. Yet there was no pleasure to be had in freedom, I soon found out, in a land of burning villages.

My intention, when I escaped the Akkadian supply camp, was to head directly to Egypt and from there strike south to find my mother, Ninshubar.

Very quickly, I realised that would be impossible.

On my first dawn as a free man, Moshkhussu and I found ourselves mud-splattered, cold, and lost.

The land to the northwest of Uruk was a patchwork of fields, canals, and open stretches of water. Here or there we would find ourselves on an embankment with a dry path running along the top, but each time we did so, we immediately spotted soldiers coming at us.

How could we cross this land without being seen, but also without drowning in some marshland?

Moreover, I could not be sure which way to head. From Kish,

I think I could have found my way. Perhaps. I had often, casually, probed my fellow slaves about the way to Egypt and generally they would hold out one hand and point west.

But I was not in Kish. I was somewhere to the south of it, but south down a river that had wound this way and that. And here in this land of fields and so much water, I could not simply strike west, unless I was willing to cross a thousand canals in the doing of it.

I leaned down and kissed Moshkhussu's beautiful nose, and she wagged her cropped tail and smelt at my ears. "Which way it is, my lovely girl?"

The first night we slept in a muddy ditch and I lay, with Moshkhussu's warmth against me, listening out to the sounds of the night. I had been a slave; now I was free. One step and then the next.

I went to sleep with a strange feeling nagging at me; that I had forgotten something important.

It came back to me in the night.

The goddess of orange fire, looking down on me. Her shock and confusion, as she struggled to understand what she was looking at. What was so strange about me that a goddess would pause in the midst of battle and ask me what I was?

I had been to temple in Kish. There they taught that the Anunnaki gods of Sumer were imposters. But the goddess in orange flame had seemed very real to me.

On the second day of my freedom, I was very hungry. We drank muddy water from ditches and kept going, but with heavy cloud and smoke in the sky, it was easy to lose our bearings.

At dusk we came to the outer edges of what had once been a reed-hut village but was now not much more than smouldering embers.

There was a boundary stone at the edge of the dwellings, with markings on it that I could not recognise. I sat down, exhausted, on the stone.

"I am a free man again," I said to Moshkhussu. "But I am also a hungry one. Are you hungry?"

What a good girl she was. As soon as I said those words to her, she was off into the remnants of the village, her nose down. Very soon there was a terrible, high-pitched squawking noise and Moshkhussu returned to me with a large bird wedged into her mouth.

"Is it a goose?" It was certainly goose-like, but it was hard to be sure of it when the bird was so muddy and bloody.

"You are very good to me," I said to Moshkhussu. "You are the best of dogs."

By collecting up some flammable things and adding them to the still-glowing remnant of a chair, I got a fire going and began to pluck the goose thing. Meanwhile Moshkhussu went back through the remains of the village, looking for more unfortunate poultry.

Why did the goddess ask me what I was and where I was from?

What did she mean by that?

I could not shake the memory.

That night I made us a shelter from scraps of old planks and reed matting, and the two of us curled up and tried somehow to sleep.

The next day we made another attempt to leave, but again we were turned back by the sight of Akkadians troops.

That night I improved on our shelter, widening it, clearing the rubble away from the floor of it, and finding more matting to soften the ground for us. We tried again the next day to leave, but returning, it came to me that we would be wise to lie low for a while in the village until the land was less full of Akkadians.

That place then, that village that had once been home to people now dead or gone, became the place that Moshkhussu and I lived.

Once, a group of four Akkadian soldiers came through, a dog of war with them. Holding Moshkhussu tight to me, I lay down behind a tumbled wall, rigid with fright.

The soldiers' dog came straight through the ruins to our hiding place and thrust her snout out at us. Of course, she knew us, and Moshkhussu knew her. She wagged her stump at us and licked at our faces until the men, who could not see what she was doing, called her back to them.

I set up traps all around the village so that most evenings we could hope to have fresh meat. In our explorations of the ruins, we found warm blankets and a sack of barley. I covered over our shelter properly so that it looked like nothing more than a pile of rubbish unless you were close enough to make out the entrance.

And in this way, the days passed, and our world narrowed down to our muddy shelter, our campfire, and the great sky that stretched over us.

All the while my mind turned and turned on the goddess at the supply camp. The way she had looked at me as if I was something terribly out of place.

And with my thoughts of the goddess, my earliest memories kept coming back to me. The woman on the snow-covered beach, her skin as pale as mine, her brilliant red hair. Her huge, dark blue eyes, brimming with tears. Her hand reaching out to me.

Was I taken from her, or did she give me away? Or was she only a dream?

One afternoon, with Moshkhussu's help, I was lucky enough to bring down two fat ducks in a net. I put them over a fire and both of us sat close by the fire to watch their progress, each of us licking our lips.

It was Moshkhussu who smelt or heard him; she gave one short bark of warning.

I stood and saw that there was someone already in the village.

"Stay with me," I said to Moshkhussu.

It was a man, on some kind of mule. The animal was dragging a heavy-loaded sled behind it.

For a moment I thought there were two men walking behind the sled, dark figures, their hoods over their faces, but a moment later it was only the one man and his mount, and no one else on the path.

Moshkhussu crept forward, low to the ground, her hackles raised.

The man wore a blood-red cloak, pulled low over his face. He was coming for us; he had certainly seen us. I caught the gleam of bronze in his beard.

"A fine dog," the man called to me. I could tell, just from those three words, that he was a high-born city man. He sounded just like Gilgamesh.

I walked forward to meet him, my knife in my left hand.

The man lifted his chin at me. He had the eyes of a leopard, but he gave me a perfectly friendly smile. "You can call off your dog," he said. "I will not hurt you."

"I did not set her on you," I said. I did not relax, but I put my knife away.

Moshkhussu's growl deepened, but she sat down next to me and I gave her ears a rub.

The man swung off his animal, keeping his eyes on me.

"I have been smelling those ducks on the breeze." He smiled, nodding.

Was he asking to share them?

The man threw back his cloak from his shoulders, revealing well-muscled, bronze-sheened arms, a sword on each hip, and a set of the same heavy bracelets as the goddess of the orange fire had been wearing.

I made my calculations. "You are welcome to share our ducks," I said.

"I would be honoured," said the man who must surely be a god, and he came to join me on my log. He accepted half a duck and began to eat it with some relish.

"It would be better with salt," he said. "But it is very good nonetheless."

Beneath his blood-red cloak, the man wore a thick tunic in the same colour, heavily embroidered, and leather sandals tied up to the knee. When he had eaten his duck, he pulled a blood-red handkerchief from his robe and carefully cleaned his hands with it.

"I know it is wrong to question a man at his own hearth," he said. "Especially after accepting his hospitality."

"Very wrong," I said.

He turned his leopard eyes to mine. I caught his scent: some sweet soap, very wholesome, very warm. I noticed how clean his fingernails were, for a man on the road.

"Let me speak to you then," he said. "Let me speak to you very openly. And afterwards you can decide if you would like to speak to me in return."

"Very well," I said, trying to sound confident.

Moshkhussu had changed her mind about our hooded guest, and she stretched out her nose to him and sniffed at his robe.

"In the south they call me the Lord of Wisdom," the man said. "Have you heard of me?"

"I know who you are, Lord Enki. There is a temple dedicated to you in Kish."

"Yes, I am Enki. I am one of the twelve Anunnaki. I presume they teach of the Twelve, even in Kish?"

"They teach that it is the Thirteen now."

He smiled. "You are a man of scripture."

"They say in Kish that you are not real gods," I went on. "Not even the new one, Inanna. They say that you are all imposters. That the real Anunnaki are centuries dead. That only their essence still lingers, inside the temple statues."

Enki put out a strong hand to Moshkhussu and scratched her ears. "Do not believe everything you hear in temple."

"I assure you that I do not, my lord."

"The truth is that we Anunnaki are creatures of another realm," he said. "We came down from this realm a long time ago and we made this place our home."

"You came from Heaven. The real ones did, I mean. All that they teach in temple."

He nodded, thoughtful. "For four hundred years, the door between this realm and the realm we call Heaven has been closed. But now a soldier from Heaven has passed through the door and into this world. He brings war and chaos with him."

"I had not heard this."

Enki pulled his hood back from his head. His bronze hair was shorn so short I could see his scalp through it.

"This soldier of Heaven has murdered my brother," he said.

"Do you mean Enlil, the lord of the sky?"

He nodded. "I find myself impossibly sad. Far sadder than I expected to be. We were estranged, enemies really, and yet I am undone by it."

"I am sorry for your loss, my lord."

Moshkhussu crept closer to Enki and put her chin on his left thigh. He gave her head a kiss.

"I have come north to kill this man," Enki said. "To avenge my brother's death. And to put an end to the mischief that this agent of Heaven is sowing here."

"You are not here for the war?"

Again, his leopard eyes full on mine. "No, I am not here for the war. I care no more about humans fighting humans than I would care about a war between two nests of ants. I am here for the real enemy."

"And who is this soldier from Heaven?"

"We don't know his name. But we know he is from a land called Creation, that being the stronghold of the enemies of the Anunnaki."

"I see," I said, although I did not. "When you say 'we', who do you mean by that?'

Enki's eyes flicked to some point behind me. I turned, but there was nothing there.

I turned back to find Enki looking at me full on, unblinking. "The 'we' doesn't matter. The point is, here I am, hunting down a soldier of Creation. Imagine how confused I am, therefore, to find *you* here upon my path."

"I am not sure why that would confuse you, my lord."

He smiled at me, holding my eye. "In the land of Creation, they have a special kind of bodyguard in the palace of the queen. These special bodyguards are very pale-skinned, and they have red hair and very blue eyes." He leaned in a little closer to me. "Does that sound familiar to you?"

I remembered the goddess of orange fire looking down at me.

"My lord, I am not from some other realm. I have never heard of Creation until this very moment."

He stretched out his legs towards the fire. "Better tell me your story then, young stranger, before I am forced to question a host at his own fire."

"I did meet a goddess," I said. "Not far from here, not long ago. A woman with short black hair, spilling orange flames from her bracelets. She also questioned my provenance."

Enki smiled. "That is Ninsun, the Wild Cow of Heaven." His smile turned to a grin. "She was a great warrior, in Heaven. It annoyed her more than you would imagine when we named her the Wild Cow of Heaven. But anyway, she would recognise a soldier of Creation when she saw one."

"She certainly seemed to think me a strange thing to chance on."

"And indeed you are, although I did not actually chance upon you. We sensed you, from a long way off. Sensed you as something very unusual."

"My lord Enki, I am a refugee. That is the whole of it."

"Are you?" He gave me a thoughtful look. "A refugee from what?"

"I was a slave in Kish. I was brought south by the Akkadians as part of the household of Prince Inush, a nephew of King Akka. When the goddess Ninsun attacked us, I fled their supply camp and became a refugee, as you see me now."

"And before that you led a quiet life as a slave in Kish?"

"Yes, but I was a slave in other places also. I do not know where I was born or where my original kin are. Someone once said to me that they had seen people like me in the far north, but I do not remember ever being there. I have one memory that might be of my mother and of a snow-covered beach. I may have been only a babe in arms then. Now that is all of it, my lord. My whole saga. I know of no other realms than this one. I know nothing of Heaven, or this land called Creation that you speak of."

Enki shook his head at the end of this speech. "I am not opposed to believing you. I mean to say, I believe that you may know nothing of where you truly come from. But I can tell you with absolute certainty that you are not from this realm."

"How can you be so sure, my lord?"

"I have my ways," he said, frowning.

I was about to speak, but he broke in on me. "I do find this all concerning. We have been getting wind of you all the way north from Eridu. We could not tell what you were, but we knew something very strange lay ahead and we altered course to see you. And now I find myself face to face with a soldier of Heaven. But one who claims to be only a lost boy."

I gave Moshkhussu the last of the duck and wiped my hands on my trousers. "I'm not claiming anything."

"You are sure you know nothing of this other servant of Creation?"

"Everything you have told me is new to me."

Enki stood, his hands on his sword belt. "What was Ninsun doing, when you saw her?'

"I think she was on her way to Uruk. On her way to her son Gilgamesh."

"Fighting the wrong war," he said. "Well, you will have to come with me now."

"I am not sure that suits me."

"What is your name?" said Enki.

"Marduk."

"Marduk, it suits you to come with me."

I looked once more at his heavy bracelets.

"Why would you want me with you?"

Enki smiled. "Four hundred years, with not one soldier of Heaven anywhere in this realm. And now two, one on the heels of the other. I would like you to stay with me now. You can come willingly, or I can truss you up and put you over the back of my mule."

"Very well, my lord," I said, with as much dignity as I could muster. "Moshkhussu and I will join you."

CHAPTER TWELVE

GILGAMESH

At Uruk

At first light I went back up to the holy palace. In what was once An's dining room, I found the moon goddess and my mother eating soft-boiled duck eggs and mashed peas. They sat in a pool of bright morning sunlight and I saw how young the moon goddess looked now, compared to my mother. But then she had eaten all the *melam* in the world, or so I had been told.

"Your knee is getting worse," my mother said, without looking up from her plate. "You should be off your feet."

"Did you check all of the *mees*?" I sat down at the long dining table, my face set in a grimace as I manoeuvred my leg into position.

My mother wiped her hands upon a cloth. "I do not need to check them, because I am very well acquainted with them. They are mainly *mees* of close combat, for personal use in battle. Nothing heavy, nothing long-range. All of the serious *mees* of war are not here. Enki must have them in Eridu."

"I know he does," the moon goddess said. "He used them against Inanna as she made her way back to Uruk."

I helped myself to an egg, picking it up with my fingers and popping it into my mouth whole, because I knew it would annoy my mother.

"Could the two of you could make your way through the Akkadian army and get to someone with these weapons?" I said.

"I could make my way through the army," my mother said. "I could cause disruption, mayhem even, until the *mees* lost their power. But I could not be sure of getting to some particular person if they simply chose to flee from me."

"What are you thinking of doing?" the moon goddess said to me.

"As my mother has already divined, I was thinking it might go better for us if Akka himself was removed from the field."

"I could perhaps get to him," my mother said, "but as I said, he could flee before me, and then there is the large risk that I might not get back."

"I can ride with you," the moon goddess put in. "I have already been out there once."

My mother ignored her. "The people wait to see what we will do. When they begin to starve, they will no longer wait quietly. They have already begun killing the cats and dogs."

"You are wrong there, mother. They will fight to their last breaths to keep the Akkadians out."

"For a moon or two. Perhaps three. But then Uruk will fall, and the city will be sacked. Everyone inside will be killed or enslaved, the walls pulled down. The city was not prepared for a long siege, and it cannot withstand one."

"I will think of something," I said.

"No trick can get you out of this," my mother said.

I limped back up the steps onto the rampart, my hands shaking from tiredness. I paused at the top of the steps to wait for the pain in my knee to ease.

Harga was sitting in a camp chair at our normal vantage spot, eating his breakfast barley in the Autumn sunshine. "They are still here," he said, stretching one hand out to the army below.

"All right," I said. "I have thought of a trick that Akka will never expect."

"Tell me." He put his bowl and spoon down.

"The trick is, there will be no trick. We will do it the hard way."

"I'm in."

"Harga, you don't know what the hard way is."

"If it involves fighting, I'm in."

"You should hear all the details, before you are in."

"I'm in," he said.

We assembled all the fighting men, women, children, and goddesses in the square outside the walls of the White Temple. Harga helped me up onto the edge of the marble fountain there, so that everyone could hear me speak.

"The plan is simple," I said, lifting my voice. "We will kill all the Akkadians."

All present honoured me with a laugh or a smile.

"I am being serious," I said. "The plan is that we will kill all the Akkadians. One at a time. They are far from their homes. There are only thirty thousand of them. There are many more of us than there are of them. So, we will kill them. It won't be quick or easy. But we can do it if we are clever about it." I waved over a hand at the moon goddess, in her temple finery, and my mother, in leather and armour. "One at a time. Every death a triumph."

My mother leaped up, with marked athleticism, onto the fountain beside me. "I will ride out in the first attack," she said, "if anyone would care to join me."

All present raised a weapon.

I longed to roll my eyes, but instead straightened my spine.

"We can't take everyone," I said. "But there will be a daily ballot. You will all get a fair chance to slaughter the enemy. A small group of us will ride out every day, under the protection of the goddesses' holy weapons, and we will kill some Akkadians and all come home safe. And we will do it the next day and the next. We will wear them down."

I looked to my mother then.

"And we will blight them," she said. She put out a hand to the moon goddess and helped her climb up onto the fountain edge.

All in the crowd pressed their hands together before them

My mother Ninsun, the Wild Cow of Heaven, stretched her hands out to the sky.

"I curse these men of Akkadia," she called out, in her temple voice. "I damn their souls. When we kill them, they will not cross over into the underworld. They will wander the Earth, lost, for all eternity, and in undying agony. I curse them."

The lovely moon goddess lifted her own hands to the sky. "I curse these men of Kish," she said, in a voice I had not heard her use before. "I turn the moon against them. I turn the night upon them. I turn the undead upon their sleeping bodies. They will never again sleep safe."

The chill of all these words spread through the crowd and all present touched their foreheads and their hearts, to keep the bad luck from sticking to them.

"Kill a man, come back safe," I said. "That is the plan. That is how we will vanquish these barbarians, who set themselves up against the gods. One man at a time."

"It's a good plan," Harga said to me quietly, as he helped me down from the fountain. He waited, impassive, as I doubled over with the pain in my knee.

"A good plan," he continued as I stood up again, "but we are still going to die here."

"Encouraging words, Harga," I said. "What would I do without you?"

CHAPTER THIRTEEN

MARDUK

Somewhere south of Uruk

Enki followed the main thoroughfares, such as they were, through the canals and fields. He did not fear meeting people. The people, meanwhile, melted away when they saw the great god coming.

I walked beside him looking up at his hooded face, and then, very often, turning back to look behind us. I had a nagging sense that someone was walking almost on my heels. Moshkhussu, too, kept turning her head and growling. But each time I turned my head, it was only us and the sled his mule was dragging.

"What do you know of this man we seek?" I said.

"He's a ghost," Enki said. "A ghost from our past. I don't yet know much more than that except that my mother let him through into this realm." He looked down at with a frown, as if something had only just occurred to him. "Have you heard anything of Inanna?"

"The goddess?"

"Yes, the goddess. What have you heard of her whereabouts?"

"Nothing at all."

"I heard she was wandering the world with her *sukkal*. But she is a hard one to keep an eye on."

"I've heard about Inanna," I said. "In Kish, I mean. Although they say she is as fake as the others."

"As fake as me, you mean," he said.

As dusk drew in, Enki said: "I could eat something hot."

We roasted a swan that Enki had brought down with one of his magical bracelets, and we ate it with some dried apricots and nuts that he had on his sled.

"May I ask why you are here all alone, my lord?" I said, as I ate my swan leg. "I would have thought that a great god like you would travel everywhere with a retinue."

"Ordinarily, yes. But I've sent the others away from Eridu to safety. My family, I mean, and my men."

"You think your own city is also under threat?"

"Oh certainly," he said. "Perhaps from the Akkadians, perhaps from more serious adversaries. I've sent my people to a place I keep as a secret refuge, for such a day as this one. My *sukkal* is charged with keeping them all safe there. I will deal with this soldier of Creation on my own."

"You must know something about him," I said. "If I am to face him also, you should tell me what you know."

Enki pulled out his handkerchief and began to wipe his hands. "I don't know anything about him, but you know, I do know something about your people. I know that they are impossible to deal with, very dangerous, and unpleasantly independent. That they are slaved to the Anzu, but even the Anzu find them difficult."

"And who are the Anzu?"

"The Anzu are the real enemy. Now enough of your questions, strange boy who may turn out to be liar. It's time we got some sleep."

The next morning, as we rejoined the road, I became more and more certain that two dark figures walked with us, although each time I spun around, there was no one there.

We had not been going long when Enki slowed his mule. He was looking back the way we had come, as if listening to something.

"We need to go off the road now, to the west," he said.

"Why?"

"It's not far," he said. "Keep your eyes about you now."

"Do you sense the soldier from Heaven? Is he here?"

"The goddesses are close."

"The goddesses?"

"Yes, Inanna and her *sukkal*."

"They're here?"

"Yes," he said. "Perhaps I ought to warn you that they will not be pleased to see me."

Moshkhussu, pacing ahead of us, came to an abrupt halt and let out one short bark.

Enki stood up in his stirrups. "Yes, I can see Ninshubar," he said. "Beware the lions. You should put your dog on a lead."

I found myself rooted to the ground.

"Ninshubar?"

Enki looked back at me frowning. "Do you know her?" But then he kicked his mule on.

Moshkhussu turned to me, giving out her low high-pitched moaning noise, which meant, *come on!*

Had Enki said something about lions?

"Yes, I'm coming," I said, to myself, to the dog, to the bullrushes. "I'm coming."

One step and then the next.

CHAPTER FOURTEEN

NINLIL

In Susa

When I awoke, I ate again, and said: "I need more food."

"Whatever you say," said the chief priest, Lamma.

"Afterwards I will go to temple, and you will bring all the sick children to me."

"And the god Utu, my lady?"

"He can stay in his rooms."

The temple in Susa was dedicated to my beloved An, king of the Anunnaki. The ziggurat at the heart of the complex was six storeys high. Quite plain, but everything well done.

The paintings that lined the walls were particularly fine. I looked up in amazement at a portrait of Gilgamesh's parents, Ninsun and Lugalbanda. "You have Ninsun exactly right," I said to Lamma. "Her confidence and certainty."

"She has not visited Susa since long before I was born," the priest said.

"Ninsun was always kind to me." I smiled up at her. "I hadn't realised until now, how much she looks like Gilgamesh."

"We are so glad to have you here, my lady," Lamma said.

A last look at Ninsun's straight black brows.

"I'm ready," I said.

I took my place in front of the altar, beneath the huge wooden statue of An.

"Bring them in then," I said.

The crowd came in, silent. When every seat was full, they sat around the bases of the columns and on every step. The priests began singing, the drums began; the priestesses added in their beautiful voices.

Lamma went into the crowd and brought out the first child.

Until long after dark, the sick children and babies kept coming.

Lamma said: "Surely it is enough now?"

I turned to him. "Why?"

"It is taking so much out of you."

"Just bring me more food," I said. "I don't know when I will be back."

"The word has gone out," he said. "They are coming down from the hills with their sick."

Finally, when I could no longer stand up, and had to sit down on a pew amongst the congregation, Lamma said to me: "It is enough now, goddess. There are no more children to see."

"The adults now," I said. "Let me do what I can for them."

﹏

At the end of it, they carried me out into the streets on a litter.
I was barely able to keep myself upright.

Tens of thousands of people lined the streets. They threw
flowers into the air.

Lamma's daughter, with her new eyes, was passed up to me
to be kissed and to kiss me. Her small soft kisses fell upon me
like blessings.

"I thank you," she said, with tears in her bright eyes.

"No, I must thank you," I whispered to the girl. "I was lost.
But now I am found."

Something had come to me, while I was healing the children.
Something hidden beneath all the other pain.

The memory of my lost baby.

The next day a messenger came to Susa in search of Utu. This
messenger was shown directly to me.

"I was told to bring a message to the god Utu and no other," the
messenger said. Then he looked around at the massed priests, and
the set expression on their faces, and back to me. From a small bag
on his belt, he produced a package bound in hessian.

Lamma read the tablet out to me: "It says: 'It is time.'"

"That's all?"

He nodded.

"Well, there it is," I said. "I knew we would not be here long."

"Do you know where you are going?"

"I do," I said, smiling. "I am going home."

Afterwards, in my chamber, Lamma hovered as I ate my stew.

"Whatever you want to say, say it," I said.

Lamma got down on one knee. "The messenger said..." He tipped his head to one side. "It may not be true."

I knew then that it was something terrible.

"Tell me."

"He says the god Enlil is dead."

I was quiet awhile.

"How did he die?"

"My lady, the messenger said that your divine husband was beheaded. And the head taken."

I nodded. "Was it the Akkadians?"

"The land is in uproar. The Akkadians have reached Ur. But the messenger said that there is talk of a new god in the land. A lord of chaos. An agent from another realm. And this new god, seeking some kind of revenge, was the one who killed Enlil."

"Revenge?"

"That was the messenger's story. I cannot say how much is true."

The table I was sitting at seemed to tip a little, as I sat there holding tight on to it.

"Thank you, Lamma, you can go now."

I lay awake all night. My heart did not beat. No thought went through my head.

I am not sure I was alive.

I did not believe Enlil was in his right mind when he attacked me. Since then, he had always treated me well. He had treated me as a daughter, not a wife.

I had never had more love from anyone, than I had had from Enlil. And now it was too late even to give him my forgiveness.

In the morning I had Utu brought to me. He looked bloated and unwell.

"What do you know of a lord of chaos?" I said.

"What do you mean?"

"Someone has killed my husband."

Utu fiddled with his fat, gold finger rings. "I knew someone was coming from the Great Above."

"Utu, do you know who I am? Do you know who my mother is?"

He lifted both his eyebrows at me. "I think your mother is Tiamat. Why else has she gone to such lengths to get you back? I think you are a princess of Creation."

"Did she send my brother Qingu here?"

"Ninlil, I don't know. Tiamat talked of sending someone. That's all I know. I never spoke to her directly."

"But she sent someone to kill my husband?"

"Ninlil, I only know my part in it. To deliver you unharmed to the Kur."

"Gather your things," I said. "We are leaving for the underworld."

CHAPTER FIFTEEN

GILGAMESH

At Uruk

Harga and I were first to arrive at the elephant gates. My mother had given Harga back his horse and our animals now flashed their teeth at each other very companiably.

"How is the knee?" he said.

I had it strapped up so tightly that I could not move it. Two of my men had forcibly wedged it into its stirrup. They had also taken the precaution of tying me to my saddle.

"My knee is much better, thank you, Harga. Better every day."

"Is that why it took two men to get you onto that horse?"

"You look to your own horse and your own knees."

We were both in our usual fighting outfits: leather jerkins, mesh sleeves, and bronze plates front and back. Full helmets, with face visors. I had taken to using a sword; Harga a spear.

"How many times have we done this?" I said to him.

"It has begun to blur together for me."

My mother and the moon goddess drew up on either side of us, each mounted on a strong mule. Behind them came forty men and women on mules, all heavy with weapons. They all looked calm and relaxed, but I knew, from personal experience, exactly how frightened they were.

"Let us be at it then," my mother said.

Harga and I went out every day, as did the goddesses. Everyone else took their turns according to the ballot, with days off to sleep and heal.

"I'll take the front today," the moon goddess said to my mother. "Let me do it once."

"I'm better at this," my mother said. After a short silence, she added: "You are learning, but I will take the front."

"How is your knee?" the moon goddess said to me.

"Very well. Much improved. They have mixed me a new salve, and it is working miracles upon the wound."

"That's good," she said, giving me her earnest smile.

"I had to break up a fight on the way here," Harga put in.

"Over food?" I said.

"Water." He pulled down his faceplate. "Come on then, let's get this over with."

The familiar grinding of the gates, the fear lurching up in us all, and we were out upon the battlefield. My mother led us, ablaze with orange godlight.

She wheeled left this time; we never knew which way she would ride. The Akkadians began to shift in response, and then our spear of orange fire plunged into their ranks.

First my mother, her bronze sword held high, and then me, swinging a sword, and then Harga, killing all he could with his spear. Behind us came those who had won the day's draw, and at the back, the air around her crackling with white fire, came Ningal, Goddess of the Moon.

It was a frenzy of hacking, cutting, and stabbing, and the screaming of the dying.

A dozen times I was almost pulled from my horse. Someone drew blood on my right shin, before my mother sent a blast of orange flames down upon my attacker.

I hacked, cut, killed, and maimed until it was time to ride back into the city.

That afternoon I limped up to the White Temple, moving not much faster than a tree might.

Lilith and her women boiled up vats of yellow lentils in the outer courtyard of the temple each day. This porridge was passed out, in small clay bowls, to anyone who came hungry. The lentils were almost gone, but the temples still had stores of barley and dried peas.

Lilith broke off from her cooking duties to sit down with me and dress my knee.

"You should be resting," she said.

One of her priestesses brought me a bowl of lentils and a wooden spoon, and I immediately made short work of it.

"I am resting now," I said to Lilith.

She frowned down at my knee. "I'm worried you will lose the leg."

"My mother won't like that, will she?"

"I won't like that."

I put out my bowl for more lentils. "Any word from Inanna and Ninshubar?"

"How would I have heard from them?"

"Priestesses have their ways," I said. "A refugee might know something."

"I've heard nothing."

"And how is morale?" I said, my voice lowered. I looked about at Lilith's women but could not tell what any of them were thinking.

"They are losing hope," Lilith whispered, but then her eyes were caught by something behind me.

I turned to find my mother at the entrance to the courtyard, blank-faced.

"What is it?" I said.

"There's someone at the gates to see us. You should both come."

I thought at first it was an old woman. She was sitting on the bench just inside the elephant gates, dressed in a muddied, green cloak.

There were soldiers gathered around her, as if she might be some kind of threat.

The woman pulled back her hood as we approached, releasing golden curls.

I remembered her crystal blue eyes from the streets of Eridu.

I stood before her, with my mother on one side, and Lilith on the other.

"Nammu," I said. "How did you get past the Akkadians?"

My mother answered for her. "She has a *mee* that makes it hard for the enemy to see her."

"That is useful," I said.

"Tell them your story, Nammu," my mother said. She looked as if she wanted to kick the golden-haired goddess.

Nammu turned her face up to mine, her eyes full of tears. "I did not mean any of this," she said.

The moon goddess arrived at my left elbow. "What is happening?" she said.

"I've let chaos in," Nammu said. "I'm so very sorry."

A short time later, I made my way up onto the ramparts. My good leg, then my bad, agonisingly painful even trussed up so thoroughly. My good leg again. My left hand hard against the wall.

I realised I was still wearing my armour. It was bad for my knee to have so much weight on it.

Finally, the top of the ramparts.

Harga was in his usual chair. He turned to me with something witty in his mouth but swallowed it down when he saw my face.

"Enlil is dead," I said.

CHAPTER SIXTEEN

NINSHUBAR

*Heading north along the
sacred river*

The Egyptian, Khufu, turned out to be a man who could be trusted, so long as you did not mind him stealing your boat from time to time.

We got our boat back and everything that had been in it, and supplies of new food and water as well. The supplies meant we could sail back without ever touching land, although the lions were unhappy for it and had to do their business in the boat.

I had intended to sail straight past Eridu, Enki's city, before heading directly into the river system and then north to Uruk. But as we cut across the gulf of ten thousand islands, a familiar sail appeared in the west and was soon gaining on us.

It was the same skiff we had seen sailing past us when we were camped out on the Euphrates; the same skiff we had gone to war with Enki in.

I released the sail, and let our boat wallow as the boys made their approach. As they also stood to, all sails flapping, the four boat boys all caught sight of Inanna, lying unconscious with her lions beside her.

"Is she alive, my lady?" their captain called over.

"For now," I replied.

"My lady Ninshubar," he said. "We were sent south with a message for you. To say you must return to Uruk at once because the Akkadians were abroad in Sumer. But that was some time ago. We waited here at Eridu for you, thinking that we must have passed you on the river, because you were slow, and we were so fast."

That I made no comment on.

"Since then, refugees have been coming south. My lady, Uruk is surrounded."

"By Akkadians?"

"It is a great siege," he said. "And now boats of Akkadian soldiers are coming down the river and heading across to Ur. Some of them came to Eridu, but they meant only to loot it, not hold it. They say that Lord Enki is heading north towards Uruk."

"Thank you," I said. "For waiting for us and for bringing us this news."

"What should we do now?" the boy said. "We could help you."

I nodded at him as I gathered my thoughts. "We need you to hide. The temple skiff must be kept safe. Will you promise me that? We will need this skiff safe after. That is my order to you, as *sukkal* to the lady of your city."

"Very well, goddess," he said. "We will keep the temple skiff safe." The boys nodded to me, solemn, as they pulled their ropes taut again. They were soon heading out to sea away from us.

I realised that Inanna had her eyes open, watching me. She was sometimes awake for short periods.

I left the sails flapping and went over to give her water and a little dried venison, while she was able to take it.

"Were those the boys from our temple skiff?" she said.

"The boys and the skiff also."

"Tiamat is the most powerful god, in the Great Above," she said, as if we had been speaking of Tiamat only heartbeats before.

"You told me you had had a vision of her, or a dream perhaps."

"I know now that she was whispering to me when I was in the underworld. I think I may have helped her open the gate from Heaven, although I did not mean to."

"Why did she want the gate open?"

"She has someone here. Someone I must go to."

"Drink this water, Inanna."

She took a small sip and laid her head back down on Khufu's camel-felt blanket.

"This person you speak of, is he the dark stranger from your dreams?"

"I think so."

"Did you hear what the boat boys were saying?"

She shook her head.

"Inanna, the Akkadians are running amok in Sumer. I was going to take you north to Uruk, because I thought you would be safe there, but now I am not sure where to take you."

"North to Uruk," she said. "Promise me, Ninshubar. That we will keep going north."

She seemed almost desperate.

"I'll take you north," I said. "I promise."

It had been a tricky business sailing down the Euphrates, but it was harder sailing up it.

I was a sailor now, but I had the current hard against me, and the river was full of new danger. I had to avoid logs and other detritus, sometimes coracles and barges full of refugees, and all too often dead bodies, bloated from their time in the water.

It became cooler, as we tacked slowly north, and I wrapped Inanna in her white fur cloak. "He's close, you know," she said.

"The dark stranger?"

"I am all aswirl, Ninshubar," she said.

"Inanna," I said, since for these few heartbeats I had her. "I think it is too dangerous for us on the river and I think we should finish our journey on foot. I wish we still had those smelly camels."

"I only know we must go north to face him," she said.

"Why must he be faced?"

"I love you, Ninshubar," she said, and was asleep again.

I did not know what the right thing was. It felt foolhardy to go on, but I felt that she would be lost forever, if I did not go on.

She was so light in my arms now, just a little dove, all feathers.

I remembered her swimming off the side of her boat with her fingers widespread and her chin held high. How happy it had made her.

"I love you too, Inanna," I said.

I walked north along the Euphrates with Inanna over my left shoulder and my good flint axe over my right.

"You are alive," she said, in one of the moments when she was awake. I put her down on some grass, so that I could give her food and water while I had the chance.

"I am so happy, Ninshubar," she said, smiling up at me. "Are you happy?"

How could I possibly be happy, in the confusing and upsetting situation I had led us into? With the enemy swarming over the land, and Inanna mostly unconscious? But Inanna seemed only dimly aware of where we were and what we were doing.

"I am very happy, Inanna," I said.

"Are my lions safe?"

"They are right here, and I must say, Inanna, they have behaved very well on this trip."

"I knew you would learn to love them."

"Let us just say that I see their value now."

She was smiling as she went under again.

I no longer stopped to hunt and I would have walked on hungry, and had nothing to feed Inanna, had the lions not brought me their half-chewed offerings.

We travelled along the main embankment that ran beside the sacred river, only dropping away into the bush if we saw people ahead of us.

On the third morning, Inanna had her eyes open, and said: "It would be good to stop and eat."

"All right," I said.

I got us off the main thoroughfare, dropping down a small track into the centre of a sheltering palm grove.

Inanna managed to stay sitting up, with Khufu's blanket round her, as I made us a fire. She seemed more present than she had for a long time.

"Someone's coming," she said abruptly. "I cannot tell who. I don't think it's him."

I snatched up my axe.

"You stay with your mistress," I said to the lions, pointing one firm finger at Inanna.

I bounded up the path and back onto the embankment.

It was Enki, on a mule.

My stomach turned over.

We had beaten him once. Now we must do it again.

I turned to see Inanna creeping up towards me, a hand on each of her lions' heads, their leashes wrapped round her wrists.

"Go and hide," I hissed at her. "It is your grandfather, Enki."

"I must be here." She continued to climb slowly up the bank. Enki was only some ten cords away.

"My girls!" he called.

Inanna leaned over and let the lions of their leashes and they went to him like two streaks of gold. "They do love him," she said, when she saw me frowning.

Enki's mule reared up at the arrival of the lions, but he swung himself off safely, and then he was down on the ground with them. They swarmed over him, rubbing themselves against him.

I lit up my protective shield.

Enki's voice carried along the path to us, so familiar.

"My beautiful girls," he was saying to the lions, putting his teeth on them in play bites. "I have missed you so much."

Behind his mule, on a wooden sled, sat a dark-grey metal chest.

Enki stood and lifted his hands to us. "I'm not here for you two. There is no need to look so warlike.

"Inanna, you should tie the lions up," he added. "There's a boy with a dog behind me and he is very fond of his animal."

"Saffron," Inanna called. "Crocus." She began to fuss over their collars.

Behind Enki, movement. He had someone with him.

For five, six, long heartbeats, I saw who it was, but my mind did not react.

I stood rock-still, my mouth hanging open, my hands heavy beside me.

Then I let my protective shield fall.

"What is it?" said Inanna.

A tall thin figure was coming at us. He had pale skin and hair like the setting of the sun.

He had a brown dog with him on a leash.

Enki turned to the boy and lifted his chin at him. "This is Marduk," he said. "Isn't he a strange one?"

The boy stopped walking when he saw me.

For long moments, we only looked at each other, but then we flew towards each other.

I had forgotten how very blue his eyes were.

"Hello, Shuba," he said to me. He pressed his tears into my neck. "You took your time," he said.

CHAPTER SEVENTEEN

ERESHKIGAL

Heading south from
Nippur

The dark stranger and I walked west towards the setting sun. It was almost dark by the time he let me sit down on a stretch of open grass. He took off his pack and stuffed Enlil's gory head into it.

"Why?" I said.

"You know what he did," he said. "You all know and yet you all protected him. Did he ever deny his crimes?"

"This is what you were sent to do?"

He met my eye and held it. "I was sent to kill Enlil."

I nodded. "The Anzu sent you. They had not forgiven. There was no peace treaty."

He gave a sort of laugh. "The Anzu do not forgive."

"Nammu was a stupid fool."

"A desperate fool. Now stand up and help me find firewood."

I did not stand up. "I am very sad about Enlil. But you and I, we are not enemies."

"Are we not?"

"You should let me go now. I will slow you down. You let me go and we will part as friends."

He shook his head. "You stay with me."

"I will make no attempt to interfere with you, if you simply let me go."

"Ereshkigal, you have been fiddling with the Kur. I need to be sure of getting through all the gates and quickly; and even with the key, I think I will need you there to be sure of it."

"The key?"

"You call it the master *mee*. We call it the key. I need to get the key, then I can return to the Kur. Fetching the key is the second part of my mission."

"The Anzu want the master *mee*."

"Yes, that and Enlil's head."

"Nobody knows where the master *mee* is," I said. "Nammu has been hunting it for many years now."

"Your sister Inanna has it. As I think you well know. We will have to take it from her."

"Why do the Anzu want the master *mee*? Is it their intent to invade this realm?"

"Ereshkigal, they have not shared their plans with me. I am tasked with two jobs. To kill Enlil and secure his head as proof of that, and to fetch the key, which they consider to be rightfully theirs. When I have both things, then I will pass back through to Heaven." He passed me the waterskin. "I will not hurt you," he said. "I need you to be well."

"This is a terrible thing that you agreed to," I said, now that there was no point in being nice to him. "To kill a man you had never met. Why would you agree to it?"

"Enough now, Ereshkigal."

"Are you only a weapon? Are you not a real man?"

"Enough," he said again.

I missed my demons very much as I tried to settle down to sleep that night. Erra had given me his blanket, but it was wet with someone's blood.

I lay thinking about my grandfather Enlil. Was he such a bad man? When I was once very ill, he came to Ur and offered to take me north with him. My father and he fell out over it.

Was Enlil all bad? Now his severed head lay not a handspan from me.

Erra, as he called himself, freely admitted now that he was here on behalf of the Anzu.

Who was he though? He was the enemy. The Lord of War and Chaos. Yet there was still something strange about it all, that my brain could not quite catch at, clever as I was.

Two days later we turned south, following the path of the Euphrates.

I had long ago abandoned my soft shoes and I walked barefoot across the farmland.

"I know that you obey the Anzu," I said to him. "But why do you obey them? Why have you come all this way to kill a man you do not know?"

He turned to me, slow and heavy, his hands upon his weapons belt. "If I could answer you, I would, Ereshkigal."

He walked on.

I walked behind him, mulling over everything I knew about him.

"I see this life on the road suits you," he said, casting a glance back at me. "You walk easier every day. It suits you so well that you have forgotten to complain about it."

"It suits me very badly. I have never felt worse. My feet and my back are in agony."

"And yet I see you walking at a normal speed now, no longer hunching over and crying. And as I said, you do look far more ordinary than you did."

He smiled at me then, his old smile, like the smiles before Nippur, and the beheading of my grandfather.

"What does it mean to look ordinary?" I said, tipping my face up at him.

"Ordinary like a woman. Rather than ordinary like a demon."

He increased his pace, but I pushed on myself to keep level with him. "You look like nothing more than a bear, with that huge beard you are growing. An old bear with a ruined skull."

He laughed. "I cannot deny it."

"I have heard the name Tiamat being whispered of. Is it she who sent you?"

He came to a heavy halt, looking down on me with his mouth pressed tight. "Please Ereshkigal, do not press me."

"I would never press you," I said. But as soon as he had set off again, I said: "Tiamat was the queen of the Anzu, when we fled Heaven. Is Tiamat the name of your mistress? Is it her intention to invade us? Is that her plan?"

He stopped again and turned to me.

How very green his eyes were.

"She wants her key back," he said. "I believe it is the key to many gates. Very, very old, and very, very precious."

"Why do you do Tiamat's bidding?"

"Ereshkigal, please. I have already said too much."

That night we camped in a barley field. He said nothing of hunting and did not light a fire, so we lay down to sleep cold and hungry. He turned his back to me and seemed to be pretending, almost at once, to be asleep.

I kept rearranging my blanket and getting up to stamp the crop down flat beneath me, and then lying again, but there was no sleep in me.

"You know, my grandmother Ninlil said that Enlil was crazed when he raped her," I said to Erra's back. "That someone had done something to Enlil. That's what she said when it first happened."

"Nonsense." He did not sound as if he'd been sleeping.

He turned over to face me.

"That is all nonsense," he said at last. "Lies and nonsense. Excuses."

"I think you have chosen a terrible mistress."

There was then a long silence. We lay and listened to two owls calling to each other.

"I am sorry I said you looked ordinary," Erra said.

"I do not mind looking ordinary."

"All the same, you do not look ordinary."

"How do I look then?"

"You look like a queen," he said. "I did not see it before, when you were dressed in rags, and hunched over and moaning with pain, and with little demons on your shoulders. But I see it now."

"You do not need to be kind to me."

"I am not being kind."

"Tell me about your life on the other side," I said, "so that I can forget about how hungry I am."

He lay quiet awhile and then said: "I was raised in Creation."

"In the citadel of the Anzu?"

He paused. "Yes."

"I know that you are not called Erra."

"I am not Erra."

"Ah, I did not believe that. So, tell me who you really are."

"I cannot, Ereshkigal. If I could, I would speak. But I cannot."

"Why can't you?"

"This is not only about me and my life. Now, sleep."

I felt guilty, that night, for how little I missed my demons as I tried to find sleep. But I liked being with Erra. The thought that I might not have much more time with him, filled me up with terrible sadness.

I thought perhaps he had gone to sleep, but I whispered over to him: "Are you married, on the other side?"

"No."

It was not a "no" that invited further questioning.

I nonetheless pressed on. "Do you have a woman, or many women?"

"No."

"A man?"

"No."

"An animal?"

"Ereshkigal!"

"So, you are not an animal-loving man?"

"Ereshkigal, I am not a loving sort of man."

I thought about all my years alone, except for my demons.

"When you say you are not a loving man, is it because your heart is cold, or because you do not like the act?"

"Enough now, Ereshkigal."

"I was only thinking," I said, "that if you were to insist upon lying with me, then there would be nothing I could do to stop you."

He turned over again in his blanket to face me. "Are you asking me to your bed?"

"I am saying that if you did come to my bed, no one would ever know about it, about how you forced me to do things."

"Ereshkigal, is it normal, in this realm, for an unmarried woman to ask a stranger to lie with her?"

"I am a princess of Heaven. There is no normal for me. I lie with anyone I like."

I saw, against the stars, that he was sitting up. "Can you really bear to come near me, with my head as it is?"

"I do not mind your head."

"How could you not mind it?"

"It's not the part I'm most interested in, I suppose, at this exact moment in time."

There was a long silence between us.

"You can come and get in with me, into my blanket," he said at last. "If you want to."

"If you are insisting, then I will," I said, and got up.

"I am not insisting."

"You told me to come and get into your blanket, and I am."

When I had sat myself down next to him in the dark, he seemed most unsure of himself.

"Should it be like in the rites, like in the temple?" he said.

"I think it can be as you like, when no one else is watching."

I thought for a moment that he was going to refuse to go further, but he said: "I can do what Dumuzi did to you in the rites."

"We can start there," I said. "If you will move over and let me get myself off the barley."

He moved over, and then lay there, apparently waiting for me.

"Will you not take off this armour?" I said.

"I won't do that. But I can undo bits of it."

"Well, let us see if we can manage," I said.

The next day I was very hungry and there was still no food.

"I cannot walk further without food," I said, sitting up from our blanket.

"If I kiss you again, will you stop complaining?" He pulled me back down to him.

"Your scales are scratching at me," I said.

After that I was hungrier.

"I will hunt," he said. "Although it is a terrible waste of time, when I need to find Inanna, and then get back quickly to the Kur."

"Why do you need to be back at the Kur? What is this hurry?"

He prowled off without answering, with his strange black machete.

I lay down awhile, thinking about the feel of him inside me. It was impossible for me to feel any anger towards him, even with my grandfather's head in a sack only half a cord from me.

But he was keeping secrets. And he still intended to leave me and go back to the Great Above.

It was not long before he came back with some sort of fowl, and soon enough it was over a fire.

"I would like to do it again," he said, "while we are together. There will be time enough while the bird cooks."

"If you force me to do it, I will."

"Do you want to do it again or not?"

"I will since you are insisting that I must. But will you take off your armour?"

"I cannot."

"I take my clothes off. Why will you not take yours off?"

"We have managed well enough so far," he said.

That time we did it in full daylight, and he kissed me and kissed me, and was in no hurry to tend to the bird over the fire.

"My time is running out," he said.

"I could help you. If you told me the truth. I am very clever, you know, even though nobody thinks so."

"I know how clever you are, but no one can help me."

He got up and went to fuss with the fire.

I said: "You know, it need not be so ornate, outside of temple. It can be quicker."

He came back over to me.

"Show me," he said.

Afterwards I lay with my head on the inside of his arm, ignoring how uncomfortable the armour was to lie upon, and put one hand out to rest it, very gently, upon one of the great open wounds in his skull.

"Do you remember Heaven?" he said.

"I remember some things, but I was very young when we left."

"In Heaven I don't have the right to a woman."

"Oh?"

"It is just the rule, because of my background."

"Here you have the right to me," I said. "At least while we are alone together and you are forcing me to do it."

I squidged closer to him then, so that I might kiss him on his beautiful mouth.

∞

So, he was a slave.

I was twelve years old when I left Heaven. Old enough to remember the fifth of the Anzu's commandments.

Only the free shall love and bear children.

This man who called himself Erra was not raised as a child of the Anzu. This man, whoever he was, was their slave.

One more small piece in the puzzle that was the dark stranger.

We walked all day along the river, on one of the high banks that they build to stop the floods, with the sun hot on our heads. He walked just ahead of me, but every now and then he would turn to look at me or come back to kiss me.

"They're close," he said.

"Who?"

"Inanna. Others too."

"How can you tell?"

"I have *mees*. Something like *mees*. They let me know."

I stopped walking. "Erra, let us stop this, I beg you. My sister could be dangerous."

"Not as dangerous as I am."

"You do not need the master *mee*. Tell Tiamat that you could not get it. Let her be happy with Enlil's head, as the price paid for the rape of one of her people."

"Come on, keep walking."

"Why not stay here, in this realm? Drink from this river. Breathe this air. Live here. Stop following this path you are on. Stay here with me."

He came and took my hands in his. "Ereshkigal, if it was only about me, I would stop. But the lives of others hang on this. And my time is running out. I cannot stop."

On we walked.

"So, you will go back to Heaven," I said. "With this master *mee*. And Enlil's head."

"Yes." He said it without looking at me.

"And what then? Will you ever come back?"

"I don't know," he said. He walked on ahead of me.

"Because it won't be up to you?" I called after him.

He turned. "Yes. It won't be up to me. I am not the master of my own fate, Ereshkigal."

"Let me help you, Erra."

He kept on walking. "My name is not Erra, Ereshkigal. And no one can help me."

CHAPTER EIGHTEEN

MARDUK

Somewhere south of Uruk

It was my mother Ninshubar, but she was a stranger to me. Her scars were gone and she was dressed up like some high lord. Her arms were wreathed with the same holy weapons that Enki wore, and around her throat was hung an eight-pointed ivory star.

"Hello, Shuba," I said to her. I was smiling but tears and shock welled up in me. "You took your time," I said. The same words I had said to her a very long time before, when I was waiting for her on a path in the old country.

Ninshubar put her warm arms around me and held me to her hard. She smelled just the same, of sea salt and citrus.

"I am here now," she said. She kissed my cheeks and kissed the tears from my eyes. Then she wrapped her arms around me again and for a long while held me close. "I will not let you go again," she said.

"I had lost hope," I said into her neck. "I thought you were dead."

She turned her head to kiss my cheek. "It is a miracle," she said. She stood back from me. "I have something for you! I am going to amaze you."

She took something out of her jerkin and held it out to me, flat on her palm.

My flint knife!

"Where was it?" I said, taking it.

"I finally went back for you," she said. "I found it where you dropped it."

"I have so much to tell you, Shuba," I said.

"And I you, my son." She put her arms around me again.

"What happened to your scars?" I said.

"I took some of the *melam* that the gods have in their blood, but I am still me."

It was only then that we remembered our audience.

An audience of two gods, two lions, one dog, and a grazing mule.

Ninshubar and I took a step back from each other.

"This is Inanna," she said to me. She held out her hand to the goddess.

Inanna was a tiny thing, very thin, with long straight hair and very black eyes. She had the two lions at her heels, and they sat with their fangs bared at Moshkhussu.

"Goddess," I said, nodding to her.

"This is my Potta," Ninshubar said to the goddess. "Oh, I am so happy."

"I would kiss you," Inanna said to me, "but my lions may kill your dog."

Moshkhussu, at my feet, had her eyes on the lions, but declined to honour them with anything more. "Your lions may find my dog hard to kill," I said to Inanna.

"There is no time for this," Enki said, stepping forward.

Inanna froze for a moment. She no longer looked as young and small as she had. "I will decide what there is time for, grandfather."

Enki seemed to shrink into himself. "You do not need to use the *mee* on me. I am here to kill Tiamat's agent. I'm not here for the two of you." He sank down on his knees, breathing heavily.

"Why are you with Enki?" Ninshubar said to me.

"He sought me out," I said, "and then insisted I stay with him." I lifted my hands to the sky. "He insists I am a great oddity."

Enki, on his knees, was still fixed on the small goddess. "Inanna, I'm not here for you. I'm here to kill the Anzu soldier. The flies, Kurgurrah and Galatur, have guided me here. They tell me that the Anzu soldier must die or bad things will happen to this realm."

"I've been dreaming of him," Inanna said.

"He has killed my brother Enlil," said Enki. He was clawing at his neck, as if struggling to breathe. "Now he is coming for that *mee* upon your wrist. When he has the master *mee*, the Anzu will be able to pass through to this world at will. This realm will not be the same after."

Inanna looked around at us all. "The Anzu has strange weapons," she said. "I don't think he is far away." She turned to Ninshubar. "It is the soldier we need to worry about."

"Let's get off this path," Ninshubar said. She gestured down to their small camp in a palm grove. "I think you can release Enki for now."

Enki gasped and fell forward, his lungs heaving. Then he climbed slowly to his feet, frowning at us all. "The Anzu soldier carries superior weapons," Enki said. "But I have some heavy weapons over there on the sled. And perhaps the flies can help us. If we fight together, maybe we can keep the master *mee* from him."

I had a strong feeling then that I was caught up in something that did not concern me. If I had learned one thing, as a slave in Kish, it was never to do more than was necessary.

"Ninshubar," I said, as we all made our way down into the grove. "Is this our fight, do you think?"

She leaned over and kissed my cheek. "Inanna's fights are my fights now."

"Then mine too," I said, although doubtfully.

Ninshubar went through her pack and handed me a flint axe.

"So, Tiamat is the queen of the Anzu, yes?" Ninshubar said to Enki.

"The Anzu are the first family of Heaven," Enki said. "The lords of a land called Creation. Their totem is the lion-headed eagle."

"Oh!" I said. I pulled up my sleeve, to show my tattoo to them all. "I got this in Abydos, in Egypt."

Ninshubar and Enki peered at my tattoo. "That's strange," said Enki. "Why would Tiamat have worshippers in Egypt?"

Inanna was standing apart from us with her lions. "Nergal is very close," she said.

Enki frowned. "Nergal? I know that name."

Inanna was looking up at the path along the embankment. "The stranger's name is Nergal."

"Nergal was the name of Ninlil's baby," Enki said. "The baby that got left behind."

"He's here," Inanna said.

CHAPTER NINETEEN

GILGAMESH

At Uruk

We gathered in the White Temple to decide the fate of Nammu, first lady of the Anunnaki, queen of all the gods of Earth, wife of our beloved An.

And now, betrayer of humanity.

"She has done a deal with the Anzu," my mother said. "With our ancient enemy. And now death and destruction rain down upon us."

Inanna's mother, the moon goddess, stood with her hands tight clenched. "The Anzu soldier tricked her. She did not know he would kill Enlil."

My mother made a scoffing noise. "She handed her son to the enemy. She knew he would be killed. Maybe not here on Earth, but she knew they would kill him."

"For real crimes," the moon goddess said.

I was about to answer that, but my mother was quicker: "Enlil was a good man. Who has lived in honour."

"He was the best of men," I said. "I cannot believe him capable of whatever he was accused of."

"We are not here to try Enlil," my mother said. "We are here to try Nammu for collaborating with our enemies. For opening the gate to Heaven, that we so long ago sealed shut. There is no knowing what the Anzu will do now."

"Enlil took a child," the moon goddess said. "The Anzu have their reasons for hunting him down."

I stepped between the two goddesses, looking from one to the other. "For now, let's lock Nammu up. In the deepest part of the dungeons. Then let us work out what we are going to do next."

My mother stepped back from the moon goddess. "We are besieged, Gilgamesh. Fighting the wrong enemy. I am not sure we can prevent what is going to happen."

"So, who is this man they sent against us?" I said. "This creature of the Anzu?"

"A lord of chaos," my mother said. "Nammu says that is all she truly knows."

At our post on the great ramparts, with the enemy stretched out upon the fields below us, Harga hacked my hair off close to my skull.

I then cut off Harga's curls, letting them fall onto the brick walkway. I had not noticed before how thick his hair was or that amidst the jet black of his curls, there were thin streaks of white.

"You are getting old," I said to him.

"The way this is going, I pray I am lucky enough to get older."

The moon goddess Ningal had refused to chop off her hair in mourning, so we ate our lentils without her that night. It was me, Harga, Lilith and my mother at the table, and we talked all night of Enlil.

"I thought it was only a temple story, of Ninlil being so young, of Enlil snatching her," I said. "I find it impossible that he would do such a thing. I find it impossible to think of him doing anything wrong."

My mother put down her spoon. "I don't know what happened. All I know is that the Anzu benefited from it and the Anunnaki were swept away. All our lands passed to them when we fled. I would not be surprised if they were behind it."

"Do you believe that?" Lilith said.

"I would put nothing past them," my mother said. "Enlil himself believed the master *mee* had been used against him. He says he awoke as if from a dream with Ninlil there and the master *mee* in his hand, and with no idea of what had happened."

She reached a hand out to me and put it on mine. "We did not understand then what the master *mee* could do and that it might have been used against him. Most of us, in the end, came to believe he was innocent. But Nammu could not believe that. And over the years that poisoned us as a family."

"I know he was not a monster," I said. "He was a man incapable of doing anything less than his duty." I found myself unable to see through my tears. "I cannot believe it of him."

Later, on the walls, Harga and I sat together with our shorn scalps cold in the evening air.

"None of them loved him as we did," I said. "My mother mourns because they were family. Lilith mourns because my mother mourns. But they did not love him as we did."

Harga nodded, but said nothing, and a moment later I saw him wipe his eyes on his sleeve. "I did not deserve his love," he said. "He was truly a father to me."

The next morning we went out to kill some Akkadians, as we did every morning. The moon goddess was there as we mounted up, although she kept her cheek turned from us.

We rode out at a different time each day, in order to better surprise the enemy.

That morning I rode out through the gates with Harga on my left and our horses threw up their heads at one another in greeting.

We were close behind my mother, the Wild Cow of Heaven, and now, slayer of Akkadians. She cast one last long glance back at us before she lit up the sky around us with the orange of her godlight, ready to hurl it out upon the enemy.

I remember saying to Harga: "It has the feel of winter in it, this morning air."

I remember him tipping his head to the sky, and me feeling surprised again, because it was so new, to see his skull shorn of its curls. How different he looked; younger and more vulnerable.

I remember the charge beginning and my mother wheeling to the right and plunging into the scattering enemy.

I do not remember the blow that knocked me from my horse.

I think I got onto my feet, in the melee, an axe out in each hand.

I remember my knee giving way.

The jolt of terrible, searing pain.

Going down heavy.

I remember how the sky darkened, as the enemy thronged over me.

I did not see what happened to Harga or the moon goddess.

I did not see my mother trying to get to me, long after our soldiers had fled back into the city.

My mother, Ninsun of the Anunnaki, blazing and fighting. Hacking at the enemy with a dagger when she had no other weapons left to fight with.

Her orange godlight giving out.

How she kicked and punched, lashed, and stabbed, until she was finally overwhelmed.

They say the last word she said was my name.

CHAPTER TWENTY

INANNA

Somewhere south of Uruk

Nergal was almost upon us and all the little fragments fell at last into a seamless whole.

I stood in our small camp in the palm grove, holding on tight to my lions. "It is all about Ninlil," I said to Enki, Ninshubar and the pale-faced Potta.

"How do you mean?" said Ninshubar.

"Ninlil is Tiamat's daughter. Ninlil is the heir to the Great Above. She is a princess of Creation."

I saw now what was about to happen.

I took a great breath in, and I said to Ninshubar: "You must all go."

I grabbed one of her hands and squeezed it with all the violence I could muster.

"Nergal is here," I said. "I must face him alone."

"What nonsense, Inanna," Ninshubar said. "You can barely stand. I'm not leaving you alone with anyone."

"Nergal is Ninlil and Enlil's son," I said. "The baby who was left behind. Terrible things are going to happen here."

They did not flee; they did not heed my words. Instead Ninshubar and Enki leaped into action. Together they unpacked Enki's chest. They took a solid lump of metal out of the box and it abruptly began to unfold itself. A moment later it split into ten dark creatures, of the sort that attacked us on the Barge of Heaven.

The scene seemed to swim about me. I tried to use my master *mee* on the others but could not make it work. What had Tiamat done to me?

"You must all go," I said, almost shouting. "Listen to me. Go."

The Potta was looking at me, open-mouthed, but the others only had eyes for the metal creatures.

"Please," I cried out. "I see it now. You must all go. Please."

A shifting in the air, and two dark figures appeared before me. It was Enki's flies, in their shadowman forms.

"Lady Inanna," said Kurgurrah. "We do not have much time."

"I know what's going to happen," I said.

"Then you know what needs to be done," said Galatur. "We need you to open your mouth and let us in."

"Why?"

Kurgurrah stepped closer. "You already know why, Inanna."

I opened my mouth, and the two dark figures disappeared inside me.

And then all the time that we had, was already gone.

Above us, on the embankment, a man in black appeared, where a moment before there had only been clear sky. He wore a close-fitting black outfit, with a hooded cape over it. He was looking straight at me. The dark stranger.

It was so strange to see him in the world after dreaming of him so often.

I stepped forward towards him, but as I did, his cloak became the surface of a river, and then where he had been standing, was only clear sky again.

At once Enki and Ninshubar spun about, looking for the stranger, but in vain.

I knew where he was, though.

I dropped the lions' leashes and began to run up the embankment and towards the river. I saw the shape of the man in black ahead of me, and then he was gone again.

"I will give you the *mee*," I shouted after him. "Take it from me."

I pulled it from my left wrist and ran with it my right hand. "It is here in my hand," I cried out. "Just take it."

Ninshubar was so much faster than me. She went past me at a sprint. Enki's creatures passed me next, and then Enki, the air around him crackling with blood-red light.

"Accept the *mee*!" I called out. "Please just take it!'

And then, the dark stranger was there again.

A shimmer, a shift, and the Anzu soldier stood before me.

He looked so much like family to me; I had not expected that.

I was about to speak... but could not.

The air all around me was filled with black tendrils.

I could not even move a hand. I could do nothing with my *mee*. I was a fly in amber. I strained my eyes to catch sight of my lions, but to no avail.

"I will just take the *mee*," Nergal said. A deep and gravelly voice; a strange accent.

He put out his hands to take the *mee* from me.

A horrible growling noise and my lions were in the air, leaping at him.

With no discernible effort, and no movement except a quick turn of his head, Nergal sent my lions spinning away from him.

I could not turn my head to see where they had landed.

A moment later, Ninshubar was upon us, smashing her fist into Nergal's face.

I was knocked down; I could see nothing except Nergal's black smoke. Then he had me in his arms, and over a shoulder, and he was running with me towards the river. I still had my *mee* in my right hand, gripped tight. "Just take it," I wanted to say, but I could not make a sound.

On the bank of the river, Nergal threw me down on the grass. I turned my head a fraction and realised that Enki was lying alongside me, motionless.

Nergal was getting something out of his belt when Ninshubar slammed into him for a second time, knocking him to the ground next to me.

At first she was on top of him, headbutting him, biting him, and then they rolled and he was on top. Her face was turned to me when he broke her neck.

I heard it snap.

"Ninshubar," I whispered.

I watched as the light faded from her eyes.

"Ninshubar."

I sat up, and began to crawl to her, but as I did, Nergal put up one hand to me and I was thrown backwards.

I turned my head, just a little, and I could see Ninshubar's left hand, open to the sky.

"Ninshubar," I said.

I was looking into her face, as he kicked her body into the water.

In a heartbeat, in a heartbeat.

    All of the light.

    All of the joy.

    All of the goodness.

    All of it was gone.

PART 4

*"On the wide and silent plain,
dimming the bright daylight,
Inanna turns midday to darkness."*

From "The Hymn to Inanna", by the
Sumerian high priestess Enheduana

CHAPTER ONE

ERESHKIGAL

Heading for the Kur

The dark stranger was covered in blood. I could not be sure whose it was. The whites of his eyes were bright against the crimson and he was breathing hard.

My sister, bruised and bloody, lay before us on the grass.

Erra had cast Inanna's *sukkal* and my grandfather Enki out into the river. The pale boy, the dog, and the lions, were nowhere in sight. There was only my sister, Inanna, lying, very still, in the wild grass at the edge of the water.

I went and kneeled next to her and felt her wrist. I put my face close to her mouth. She was alive.

She had the master *mee* in her open right hand.

Two things warred in my mind for precedence. I wanted the *mee*, but also I did not want Erra to kill my sister. My sister had done me no harm when everything was accounted for. She was only a young girl, and she looked very frail and small, lying there in the grass with bruises and bloody marks up and down her arms. She reminded me of one of my dresser-demons.

"Erra, do not hurt her," I said.

"My name is Nergal," he said, behind me.

I turned to him.

"Nergal?"

Where did I know the name from?

I stood up, putting myself between Nergal and my sister. I slipped the master *mee* into my left sleeve.

"Nergal was the name of Ninlil and Enlil's baby," I said. "I have been trying to remember what they called him. It was Nergal." I went to him and put my hands out to his. "You are Nergal. You are the child they left behind."

"Yes." He looked as if he might weep.

"Enlil was your father," I said. "Oh, Nergal. You killed your own father."

He nodded, taking my hands between his.

Everything made sense now. "Ninlil is no ordinary child of Creation," I said. "She is Tiamat's child. Which makes Tiamat your grandmother. And yet she kept you as a slave and cut wounds into you that would never heal."

He took a deep breath in and then stepped back from me. "I have to get to the underworld."

I looked about us, at all the blood pooled in the grass.

"Nergal, why did you kill the *sukkal*?" I said. "I know you are not a bad man."

He wiped the blood from his eyes. "There are some people you don't need following you through history."

I looked out over the surging river. "Perhaps she will recover."

He shook his head. "She's not an Anunnaki. Whatever she was, she's gone."

"And Enki?"

He shrugged. "Most of his head was gone."

"Him I wish dead," I said. "For his countless crimes against me."

As I spoke, Nergal looked out over the water and I quickly took the master *mee* from my sleeve and slipped it onto my left wrist.

It seemed to shrink a little onto my arm, and pulse.

I paused a moment, letting the feel of it, and the web it connected me to, sink in a little.

I could see where everyone was. A brilliant map of light unfolded in my mind's eye, with all my family placed upon it.

"Ninlil is in the far east," I said. "At the edge of the Zagros mountains."

Nergal nodded.

"So, we are going to meet Ninlil, at the Kur. Your plan is to take your mother with you to the Great Above?"

"We have to cross the Euphrates first," he said. "I can carry you across. Unless you no longer want to walk with me. I will not force you."

"Why is my brother Utu with your mother?" I said. "What is happening?"

He looked from my frown, down to my wrist.

"Give me the *mee*, Ereshkigal."

With great reluctance, I took it off and gave it to him.

"Tiamat has tricked you into a very bad plan," I said.

Nergal took up his bag, lifted me in his arms, and walked us to the edge of the water.

"Ready?" he said.

He jumped into the river with me held tight to him. The water was so cold!

I expected us to go under, but somehow, he twisted around and landed on his back, with me on his front, and then we were surging across the water, me tight in his arms. What would I not do for his armour?

On the far bank he surged out of the water, and set me down on grass, wet but unharmed.

"Do not go back to them, Nergal," I said. "I have not had enough time with you."

He did not answer. Instead he swung his bag over his shoulder and walked on ahead of me towards the underworld.

CHAPTER TWO

INANNA

Heading for the Kur

I stood on the edge of the luminous blue lake.

There were animals all along the shore; all their faces were turned to me.

I put my ankles together and pressed my palms together over my head, just as Ninshubar had taught me, and I dived into the lake.

I plunged into shining blue. I had been frightened before, of the power the lake offered. Now I surged through the electric water and found that I could breathe.

I came to and I was already sitting up, my legs sprawled out before me on the grassy riverbank. I sat alone, beneath a darkening sky.

My master *mee* was gone.

The knowledge of what had happened to Ninshubar was the hard ice where my heart had been.

I looked down at my hands. They glowed blue. I no longer

needed my *mee*. My connection with the blue lake was complete now.

First, I would kill Nergal.

My lions were on the pathway, not far back from the river. They lay as if dead, but they were breathing. I took up a sharp rock and cut my left wrist. I dribbled some of my blood into their mouths, and waited for them to come to, kneeling next to them on the path.

I could see the Potta's body, further along the path. The body of his dog also. In that moment, I felt nothing for either of them. It did not occur to me to help them.

When my lions had staggered onto their feet, I turned and walked to the river. My lions walked either side of me.

I sent out a blast of blue fire and boiled the river in front of me.

As I walked across the muddy riverbed, clouds of steam billowed on all sides.

My lions, very frightened, followed close behind me.

I climbed out on the far side of the river and let the water flow again behind us. And then we walked on across the farmland towards the underworld.

I felt nothing at all. No sadness, no anger. And yet I was weeping so hard that I struggled to breathe between sobs.

The sky grew darker still; storm clouds were gathering. When I turned my tear-soaked face up, lightning forked across the sky.

It began to rain, heavier and heavier, and I stood, as if beneath a waterfall, and let the rainwater drench me.

Lightning streaked again across the blackened sky.

A strange prickling sensation swept over me, from the top of my scalp to the soles of my feet.

I looked down and saw that my arms and feet were covered in

bright points of blue light. Every piece of my skin was covered with them; they were a moving skein upon me.

My tears slowed and I began walking again. I let the blue light trip out from me, and dance towards the horizon.

The truth is I had only played at war. I had been a child, playing with a toy.

Now my true self was forming within me.

I was a pit for the wayward.

A trap for the wicked.

The venom of a snake strike.

I was the raging, rushing flood that leaves nothing behind it.

I was war itself.

Thunder shook the sky and Earth, and lightning lit up the riverplains and the mountains far beyond.

"When Nergal is dead, I will kill Tiamat," I said, as the blue light widened around me.

I flung my face back to the sky and new thunder shook the world. I fell forward onto my hands. The lightning struck down upon the land and back up again into the heavens.

The rain fell on my back, so heavy and hard it hurt my skin, even through my sodden dress.

When I wore the master *mee*, I could sketch out in my mind a crude map of my family. Now, with no *mee* upon my arm, a map of extreme precision was unfolding in my mind's eye; a map of every scrap of *melam* that existed upon the Earth.

I saw all my family, and not just as blurred shapes, but as living, breathing creatures. I saw the girls in the temples of Ur, their veins full of my father's blood. I saw my father, walking, in the low hills of the Zagros mountains. I saw my grandfather Enki, afloat in the sacred river, his heart still beating. I saw my brother Utu, on a mule, riding. Not far ahead of him, on a sedan chair, sat my great-grandmother Ninlil. In the north, I saw An, the king of the gods, lying propped up on a couch, with a servant beside him.

I saw my mother, her hair pulled back from her face, talking to someone. I could not be sure who.

I saw Gilgamesh. He was sat in the mud, badly injured. Had Uruk fallen?

Ahead of me: Nergal, Lord of War and Chaos, and with him my sister Ereshkigal, the Queen of the Night. I saw her reaching out to him. Did she reach out in love?

And then I saw Ninshubar's dead body, floating down the great river.

For a long time, I knelt upon the Earth, and wept.

All the good in the world was gone.

I could no longer tell, as I walked across the Earth, if I was still myself or if I was only the furious storm.

I wore the whirlwind about me, as an ordinary woman might wear a robe.

The storm began to feed my strength. Jolts of pure power lit up my bones and joints. I found myself walking faster; sometimes I ran, a streak of blue, with two streaks of gold fur beside me.

I swam across countless canals and lakes, hard and strong through the water, dragging my lions with me.

The rain fell on me, but it no longer touched my skin. The storm flowed with me and through me.

I was the queen who humbled mountains, leaving them as rubble.

The god who splits mountain ranges.

All would now bend their knee to me.

A thought came to me, a streak of lightning across the darkness of my heart.

I am stronger without the love.

CHAPTER THREE

ERESHKIGAL

Heading for the Kur

For one hundred years, I was in almost constant pain. For a long time, I was lost in the dark.

Now I followed Nergal, Lord of War and Chaos, across the riverlands and I felt no pain. My body was stronger every day.

Yet I was so very sad.

"Do you know how far it is?" I said.

"You've made this journey before."

"A long time ago," I said. "And against my will."

"It's another five days at least," he said. "Unless you hurry up."

But I did not want to hurry.

I had not had enough time with him.

The sky lit up a brilliant blue and then, strangely rapidly, filled up with storm clouds.

Forks of a bizarre blue lightning split the sky from one horizon to the other. Earth-shaking thunder followed a few moments later.

It began to rain, first big fat drops, then a driving deluge.

"Take my cloak," Nergal said. "I don't need it. I only wear it to hide my head."

"I don't mind the rain," I said. I was still wearing Geshtinanna's dress, although it was so covered in mud and blood you would never have guessed it had once been white. With my filthy dress clinging to me, barefoot, and my hair wet to my head, I knew I did not look much like a queen.

I was cold, I suppose, but I found I did not mind that.

What I minded was him going, far too soon.

The sky grew so dark it might have been night-time. It did not seem natural. The rain, instead of easing, grew heavier and heavier.

"Inanna is following us," Nergal said, looking up the blue-flashing sky.

"Is she causing this storm?"

He shrugged. "Tiamat said she would clip Inanna's wings for me. That I need not worry about her. But it seems her wings are now unclipped."

Another great flash of blue lightning lit up the sky above us; the thunder was quicker to follow this time. "She's very angry," he said.

"I expect she's angry that you killed her *sukkal*." I had to raise my voice to be heard over the storm. "But we have her master *mee*. What can she be using to do all this?"

Nergal frowned at me. "She's so full of *melam*. Strange amounts. So much it should have killed her."

"You think her *melam* is helping her do this?"

"Perhaps I ought to have killed her." He paused, frowning up into the rain. "She is pulling down extraordinary power."

"Where from?" I said.

He seemed about to say something interesting; I saw him thinking it over. But then he said: "I'm not sure."

The next day the storm was worse. High winds drove the rain straight into our faces. But we kept on walking.

In the afternoon, we reached a wide canal, the surface of it peppered with the violent splashing of rain drops.

"Take off your armour and wash," I said to him. "I want to lie with you skin to skin."

He had been about to lift me up and carry me over the canal. "There's no time for that."

"Please, Nergal. You stink of death. Please."

"You want to lie with me in this rain?"

"I am telling you I do."

He looked down into the canal and then up at the blue-flashing lightning. "It hurts with it off."

"Show me, Nergal. Show me what you are hiding."

"You cannot want to see it. I do not want you to see it."

"I can already see your head. Do you think that makes me squeamish of you?"

"No," he said. "But then you are famously mad." He sighed out, but then took off his black weapons belt and put it carefully down on the wet grass. I thought then that it would take some great fiddling to remove his armour. But it slid in one piece to his feet and he had only to step out of it.

So, this was him naked. It seemed foolish to blush, after all we had done, but nonetheless my cheeks pricked with blood.

He was covered in some horrible grease, though.

"That grease is foul!" I said. "Get in the water, Nergal, and find some sand to scrub yourself."

He turned to get into the canal, and I saw his back.

Someone had cut the sign of the Anzu, the lion-headed eagle, into the skin of his back. It reached from his powerful shoulders all the way down to the bottom of his spine. The wounds were so deep and fresh that I could see bone and muscle working beneath. It must have been agony to have the rain lashing into it so hard.

Tears sprang to my eyes, but I wiped them quickly away.

"It does not look so bad," I said. "But I can see that it must hurt."

He did not turn, but he nodded, and then he dived into the rain-pocked waters of the canal.

While he was under water, I put my hand to my mouth to stop the upset bursting out of me. By the time he came up and turned to look back at me, I was already smiling warmly at him. "Get scrubbing!" I called.

Afterwards we lay together, with him on top to protect his back at least from some torment. The rain fell through his hair and dropped onto my face.

I could not get enough of him. I could not press him close enough to me and for long enough.

"You are so beautiful," he said.

"Even wet and covered in mud?"

"Beautiful."

I kissed him again.

"How did she do it?" I said. "Your back, I mean."

"They use a special tool," he said, "so that your *melam* cannot help you."

"But why?"

"It's a reminder," he said. "Of who they are and who I am. Of who I belong to."

"It does not have to be so."

He pushed my wet curls back from my face and kissed my mouth. "I admit it, Ereshkigal. I do admit it. I have not had enough time with you."

I knew then that I could not let him leave, even if he never forgave me for it.

Later I watched how the scales slid up his body when he stepped into his armour, only coming to a stop around his neck.

"I am sure I could fix it," I said. "So that it will cover your head."

"You cannot have my armour," he said, pulling his cloak back on. "I see your thoughts moving. It is worth a moon, this suit I stand in."

I pulled my wet dress over my head, and with difficulty, pulled it down to cover me.

"You could give me one small piece of it," I said. "You would not miss one piece. Would the moon shine less brightly with one small piece missing?"

"I need all the pieces, Ereshkigal. I am sorry not to be able to please you in this."

On we walked, through the heaviest rain I had ever known, to the very edge of the sacred riverlands. In the distance, lit up by the blue lightning of the storm, we could see the mountains rising into the sky.

"I will make Tiamat let you go," I said.

He put a hand to my wet cheek. "She will never let me go, Ereshkigal. But this time with you has been everything."

In the howling wind and lashing rain, I began to walk slower.

"Whatever you are plotting, stop plotting it," he said.

"I plot nothing."

"I have the measure of you, Ereshkigal."

"There is nothing to measure."

He took my hand and pulled me on. "You will not like it if your sister catches up with us." He looked at me sideways as we walked. "I have killed one of your grandfathers and attacked the other. Do you not hate me for it?"

"You are the one I care about."

He stopped walking. "Ereshkigal, you do not know me."

I laughed. "You would like to think so."

He put his hands out to me. "I must leave here, very soon. And you cannot come with me. I have said soft words to you, but nonetheless I am going to leave you."

"Walk on," I said. "I am glad you are leaving."

My heart was so full of sadness, as we began the climb up into the high mountains. The rain turned to hail.

I had not been happy in four hundred years. Now this new happiness was slipping so fast through my fingers.

"I know you can walk faster than this," he said, as I crept up a steep and rocky path.

"It is my hip."

"There is nothing wrong with your hip."

"It is ablaze with pain."

"I could carry you."

"That will hurt my back."

He stopped to kiss me, his wet face against mine. "Walk faster."

Neti stood outside his hut, a shepherd's hood pulled up against the rain, although I knew it could not wet him.

"I am compelled to welcome you both," he said, as we made our way past him and into the dry and warm. "And so I do welcome you both," he went on. "And yet I do so unwillingly."

I sat down with relief on my little bed and pulled a blanket around me. "There is no need to sulk, Neti," I said. "I will just have one honey cake, please, gatekeeper. And I believe Nergal will have a whole basket of them."

"Nergal," Neti said. "I have not heard that name before. You called yourself Erra when you were here last."

Nergal sat down at the small wooden table. He looked very large and wet sitting in the little chair. "Where is Ereshkigal's maid servant?"

"If you mean Geshtinanna, she is inside the Kur," Neti said, casting a dark scowl at me.

The gatekeeper then offered his basket of cakes to us.

As I helped myself to two warm cakes, Neti said to Nergal: "Why do you have the master *mee*?"

"We took it from Inanna," I put in. "It was never really hers, you know."

Neti flickered in and out of focus.

"My lady, this man you are with is carrying the head of an Anunnaki, in the bag hanging from his back. It is the head of Enlil, your paternal grandfather."

"I wish he did not have it," I said.

"Madam, this man must be stopped."

"You cannot stop us entering the Kur," Nergal said.

Neti was looking hard at me. "Ereshkigal, you can stop this. I know that you can block the gates if you choose to."

"I do not think I can," I said. "His weapons are better than our weapons."

Neti shook his head. "Do you know Ninlil is on her way here?"

"Of course we know," I said.

"She will be here very soon," said Neti. "And she has quite the retinue with her."

"Oh yes?" I said.

"Your brother Utu is with her, amongst others," he said. "It will be quite the gathering of the Anunnaki."

"And the Anzu too," said Nergal. "My mother is an Anzu. And I am half Anzu."

On the long bridge down to the Dark City, Nergal walked ahead of me, a dark shape against the stars. Every few steps, the bridge would shake and for a moment we would both freeze.

Neti walked just behind me in his blue suit. He was unmoved, physically at least, by the shaking of the walkway. "Inanna is doing this," he called ahead to me. "She is shaking the mountain beneath us."

"I can feel what she is doing, Neti."

"If this man you are with opens the gates to Heaven, the Kur will not survive," Neti said.

"I already know this," I said.

"If he passes through to Heaven with the master *mee*, then the creatures he serves will be free to come here just as they see fit. Who knows what kind of demons may pour through into the Dark City, and then out into the world of light?"

"I know this also."

Nergal turned, careful where he put his feet on the narrow walkway. "Neither of you can stop me," he said.

He kept on walking, down towards the dim glow that was the Dark City.

"If the demons of Heaven come through that gate, they will tear down your temple," Neti said. "They will kill all your pet demons and they will kill you too."

"Neti, everything you know, I already know. It is pointless you speaking to me."

"If it is your intention to go through with him," Neti said, "I do beg you to reconsider. It will only add your certain death to all else that is certain to happen."

"All of this I know," I said.

We followed Nergal through the dark streets to the Black Temple. I had strange and complicated feelings at being back in the Dark City. It felt like home to me. Every statue and turret was beloved to me. Yet how good it had been to be out in the Earthlight!

At the top of the huge steps to the Black Temple, my silver *gallas* stood waiting for me. Beneath their dark hoods, their silver eyes shined brightly. Each tipped its head to me as I made my way up the steps.

Behind the *gallas* stood Dumuzi and his sweet sister, Geshtinanna. Next to them stood Namtar, my fox-eared priest-demon. I at once took Namtar into my arms, squeezing him tight. He smelt so lovely and familiar to me, of candle wax and temple incense.

"My queen, you have returned!" he said, weeping against my chest. "This is the happiest day!"

Geshtinanna came to kneel before me to kiss my hands and then my feet. "Blessed lady, welcome home."

"What's in the bag?" Dumuzi was saying to Nergal. "It smells *bad*."

Namtar, my priest-demon, bowed to me and said: "What are your orders, my queen?"

I looked to Nergal for an answer to that.

"We need to wait here awhile," he said to me. "It will not be long."

"Let us eat, and rest," I said, thinking of my big bed, and taking Nergal into it.

"Very good, my lady," Namtar said, his ears twitching. He leaned closer, and whispered: "What is happening, my queen?"

"Erra's real name is Nergal," I said to them all. "He is Ninlil's lost baby."

"Oh," said Dumuzi. "That is very interesting indeed."

"We can discuss it all at dinner," I said.

So, there were four of us for dinner that night. Me, Dumuzi, Geshtinanna, and the dark stranger whose real name was Nergal. I sat at the head of the table, in an old temple robe, which now seemed a little too big for me. Enki's lovely children sat to my left, both so handsome by candlelight. Nergal sat to my right. He drew his chair closer to mine, so that he could put one hand on my knee as he ate.

It was fish stew for dinner. We did not have many fish in the underworld, and we had not tried eating them before. I had meant this novel stew as a compliment to the company, but the flesh of the fish was rather blacker than I had imagined, and the taste a little sharper.

My guests ate it all though. Their minds, it seemed, were on other things.

Dumuzi and Geshtinanna were very cheerful.

"So Ninlil will soon be here?" Dumuzi said.

"If I let her in," I said.

Nergal took his hand from my lap. "You must let her in, Ereshkigal," he said.

"I don't see why you don't stay," Dumuzi said to Nergal. "Whatever you have promised the Anzu, stay."

"My mother was kidnapped," said Nergal. "Torn from her own mother. I am going to take her home."

Dumuzi shook his head at that. "Tiamat is a monster, by your own account. Why deliver up your mother to a monster? That aside, if you go through the gate with the *mee*, the Anzu will be able to send their armies back through. That is how I understand this. I will die, to pick just one example. Ereshkigal will die. Do you care about that at least? And what of all the peoples of Earth, of this land we have built, do you think they will withstand the Anzu? The honourable thing is to stay."

"You should listen to Dumuzi," I said to Nergal. "Everything he says is true."

Nergal pushed back his chair and stood. "Tiamat has hurt me, yes. She is not perfect. But she did not deserve to lose her daughter as she did. I have said I will bring Ninlil home, and I will."

I put my hand out to him. "Nergal, sit. We will speak of something else."

After dinner, Dumuzi and I were alone just for a moment. "Ereshkigal," he said, very serious. "Let all your fiddling here be put to good. Do not let him leave."

"I never fiddle with anything," I said.

That night, in my soft bed, I held my beloved Nergal in my arms.

"Please stay with me," I said.

"There are people who will die, if I do not return," he said. "People I am responsible for. This is not only about my mother and what she is owed."

"But you are also responsible for me now," I said, and buried my face in his neck.

He stroked my hair but did not answer.

CHAPTER FOUR

GILGAMESH

In the enemy camp, outside Uruk

I sat in the mud, tied to a post, in the centre of the enemy camp. The rain fell and fell. And with the rain fell blows, kicks, stones, jabs, urine and excrement.

The men of Akkadia went this way and that, amidst the busy business of the sacking of a city, but they took the time to try to hurt me each time they passed by.

I saw upon these soldiers' backs and in their hands, the weapons and armour of men I had loved. Gold objects, studded with priceless gems, that belonged in the White Temple. Small children, their faces familiar to me, carried over a shoulder or dragged by their hair.

At night, with beer in their hands, the hard men of Akkadia stood laughing over me and often they recounted the killing of my mother, the Wild Cow of Heaven.

They told me she screamed for mercy when they put their hands on her.

That I did not believe.

They all claimed to have a piece of her and they would show me their relics: a bloodied finger, a scrap of ear.

I remembered my last glimpse of her on the battlefield, her bronze cap pulled low, her straight black brows, her hard eyes fixed on me.

They always said I looked like her. That I was the arrow she sent out through time.

Her face, fixed on me.

And tied to that post, in the Akkadian camp, my lifeblood drained, sometimes slow, sometimes quick, into the muddy earth of the riverplains.

I dreamed of a great monster, vast as a mountain. She was a giant eagle, but with the head and face of a lion.

In her great bird claws she cradled the dead bodies of those I had loved.

My mother. My mentor, Enlil. My lover, Enkidu.

Somewhere a baby was crying and no one was going to comfort it.

CHAPTER FIVE

MARDUK

Heading south down the Euphrates

I came to lying on my back in heavy rain. The droplets fell straight into my mouth.

I ached all over as I sat up.

I had Moshkhussu's leash in my hand, but she was gone.

Everyone had gone. There was no sign of Enki, Ninshubar or Inanna. Nor the dark stranger. The lions were gone too.

I stood up, letting out a groan of pain. As I did so, the sky lit up blue with lightning. Had I ever seen blue lightning before?

I realised I was on the path, on top of the embankment.

Where were they all?

I made my way along the embankment, back towards the palm grove where Inanna and Ninshubar had been camping. I put my hand to my mouth and it came away with fresh blood all over it. I stopped for a moment to vomit.

I looked up: a single vulture, in the black and stormy sky.

I kept on walking along the path.

Not very far along, I found Moshkhussu. She was lying down to the left of the embankment in a patch of battered-down reeds. I scrabbled down to her: she was breathing. I held her to me, listening to her breath, feeling for damage.

Where were they all?

"I will be back in just one moment, my love," I said to Moshkhussu. I laid her down, very gently, and climbed back up the bank.

Where was Ninshubar? There was no one in the palm grove. Only Enki's mule, still tied to its sled. On instinct, I reached out to it and set it free.

I followed the path the other way, back past Moshkhussu, to the great river. To a grassy embankment, muddied with footsteps.

There were pools of blood in the grass. Axe marks, perhaps, in the turf. Someone or something had bled very heavily there.

More blue lightning above and heavy thunder.

I looked out over the river, but all I could see was the heavy brown water, the bull reeds, and the eyes of a hippo, watching me. Where was my mother?

Then at the very edge of the water, something caught my eye. Something bright white, glistening in the rain. It was a star shape, carved in bone, and attached to a thin string of leather. The leather had been neatly cut through. The leather was wet with something, sticky, and red. The back of the ivory star was smeared also with red.

It was Ninshubar's necklace. It had been round her neck when we met.

I did not look again at the congealing blood on the grass. I did not believe that my mother Ninshubar was dead.

I washed the necklace in the river.

I would keep it safe for her.

I found it hard to stir Moshkhussu, although she was breathing, so in the end I picked her up. If I walked slowly, stopping often, I could carry her.

And like that I made my way south, through the torrential rain, following the path of the river.

If Ninshubar had fallen into the river, she would have been swept downstream, so that was where I would go.

I tried to stay close to the edge of the river, or as close as I could, so that I would not miss seeing her, even though there was no good path so close to the water.

I was forced to flounder through marsh and mud and reedlands, Moshkhussu heavy and wet in my arms.

Sometimes my lovely dog would stir and I would put her down, and encourage her to walk herself, but her back legs had no power in them.

I did not believe it.

To have found Ninshubar, to have finally found her, and then so soon after, to have lost her. I did not believe it.

In the evening, it was still raining. On a small spit of sand ahead of me: a body. For a moment my heart leapt, but it was not her.

It was Enki.

Not moving.

I climbed down out of the reeds to stand over him. His head had been caved in. In the mess of his bloodied hair and gashed skull, some pale brain matter glistened silver in the half-light.

Three long crocodiles were lying on the bank just next to him, their ancient eyes on him.

I laid Moshkhussu down against Enki's back, as gentle as I could. And then I sat down next to them, in the dusk and heavy rain.

Where was my mother?

I realised that somehow, one of the crocodiles had come closer. I could smell its dark and heavy breath. I shouted out, and the crocodile slid back from us, but not too far back. Moshkhussu and the god did not stir.

I sat for a while, just trying to think clearly.

After that I kneeled next to the god's head and felt for a pulse in his neck. Yes, he was alive: he was breathing, very shallowly, and although he did not open his eyes, I saw his fingers twitch as I touched his warm throat.

Moshkhussu, lying spine to spine with him, moved her head a little, but did not open her eyes. I listened for her heart but could hardly hear it.

I made no conscious decision. It only came to me that Moshkhussu was dying, and I should let her die in some sort of comfort. The god, too, since he was there.

I sat up over the two of them all night, guarding them. In the morning I carried Moshkhussu up off the sandy beach. Well back from crocodile range, I laid her on a patch of grass. Then I laboriously dragged Enki off the beach to lie alongside her.

There on the grass I made a shelter for them. Just a simple

structure of sticks and reeds, but enough to keep us all dry, and to allow me to build a fire beneath it.

Next I gathered reeds and sticks, but everything was wet, so even with my flint knife, which worked well as a strike-a-light, it took a long time to get the flames going.

As soon as it was done, I remembered that I had not eaten in some time. I felt no hunger, but sitting there, with the fire warming me, I remembered that Moshkhussu had also eaten nothing. She should not die on an empty stomach.

I carefully lifted her chin from my lap and rested it on the grass, and then I went back out into the rain.

First I made sure that Ninshubar's star was safe in the lining of my leather jerkin, and then I fashioned myself something like a spear, from a washed-up stick and my flint knife, so recently returned to me.

While I sat there in the rain, working on the spear, I heard a shout. I looked out onto the river. A huge wooden barge was gliding past, as if magicked up from some dream. It was loaded down with Akkadian soldiers, all looking wet, but very cheerful. We cannot have looked like much to them, one man whittling, another lain down with a dog in a rough shelter, on a grassy bank in some nameless bay. But one of the soldiers came to the edge of the barge, holding on to a rope, and shouted: "Marduk!"

I did not recognise him, but I stood and would have said something. I was too slow though, and heartbeats later the barge was gone into the storm.

I fed Enki and Moshkhussu small pieces of fish, and water scooped up with an old snail shell.

The dog would not take any of it; she would not wake up.

The god did better. At first the food, even mushed up, fell uneaten from his mouth, but I kept chewing it up soft and pushing it into his mouth with a finger, and after a long while, I saw him swallow. Was the cleave in his skull narrowing? In the end, I do not know how long after, he opened his eyes. The whites were entirely bloodshot.

"I cannot stay with you long," I said to him. "I need to follow the river down and find my mother."

He closed his eyes again. "Do you mean Ninshubar?"

"Did you see what happened to her?"

"The soldier killed her."

"Can you sense her? Can you use your *mees* to find her?"

"The flies were guiding me," he said. "Inanna has them now."

"But you have *mees*," I said. "Inanna seemed to sense things with hers."

"Different *mees*."

I found I was crying. "I cannot wake Moshkhussu."

I fetched Enki more water and helped him drink.

"Help me sit up," he said.

I heaved him up and then he turned to face Moshkhussu, sitting himself up. "Give me that stone knife of yours."

"Why?"

"I'm going soft, in my great old age," he said. "Just give me the knife."

I gave him the knife and with one practised movement, he cut into his left wrist, drawing heavy blood. He held his bloody wrist to Moshkhussu's mouth.

"Help me," he said. "The more she gets, the quicker this will be."

"Your blood will heal her?"

"Possibly."

"I didn't know that."

He squeezed at his wrist, to keep the blood flowing. "It's not something we choose to talk about much."

Only a few heartbeats later, I saw Moshkhussu's mouth move and then her tongue appear. She licked at Enki's wrist.

"She will need longer to recover," Enki said. "Sleep here tonight. Do not go rushing off."

That night I woke up in a great panic.

What if Ninshubar was lying close by, desperate for help?

In that moment, I do not think I remembered that Enki was there at all. I roused Moshkhussu and we left Enki there sleeping in the shelter. We did not get far, in the dark and wet, and for a while we lay down. But in the light of day we kept on going, looking out over the brown river at every caught log or bundle of vegetation; at anything which might be Ninshubar.

We slept where we found ourselves when it was too dark to walk.

The next morning, Moshkhussu would not get up. I had thought she was cured, but now she had no strength in her. I gathered her up in my arms once more, huge and heavy as she was.

At some point I lay down in the mud and did not get up. I was only dimly aware of the lashing rain and ground-shaking thunder. I lay with Moshkhussu in my arms and I let us sink, deeper and deeper into the mud.

Sometime after, I do not know when, I was struck by lightning.

A bolt of burning blue fire, blasting through me.

It lit up every fibre of me, a brilliant, luminous blue.

CHAPTER SIX

GILGAMESH

In the enemy camp outside Uruk

The rain turned to hail, and I was still sat out in the mud and my own filth. By then the cold and pain had blurred into one, and I could not tell any more what was real or only nightmare.

"So here he is."

A familiar voice.

I looked up to find a man standing over me in an azure blue coat, his face tilted to one side.

Inush.

Another man emerged from the hail and mist to stand next to him. Older, much thicker set; a long, densely curled beard. The same brilliant velvet, so extraordinary against the mud and squalor of the camp.

King Akka.

"He did not treat me badly," Inush said to his uncle.

He spoke as if I was not there; as if I was not looking up at him from the fouled mud.

"He threatened to torture me, but I was never tortured," Inush said. "He threatened to beat me, but I was never beaten. Roughed up a little on my way down to the prison, but no more than that. I was fed every day and given clean water. He visited me and made sure I had good food and talked kindly to me. I cannot complain of my treatment."

"He raped my sister Hedda," Akka said. "And then he had her murdered."

"I have not forgotten Hedda. But we did take our vengeance. They say he went mad with grief when we killed his friend."

"I didn't rape Hedda," I tried to say, but I do not think they could hear me.

Akka stroked his beard, running his fingers very delicately through the carefully prepared curls. "I cannot fault his courage," he said. "Riding out every day as he did, as if we were the city besieged and he the besieger. There was honour in it, I admit it. He has shown himself a man and a king. That I do own. But what advantage can there be in keeping him alive?"

"There is no advantage to him dead," said Inush. "There are Anunnaki out there still who may need to be bargained with. An and Lugalbanda are both said to dote on him. What is the advantage in killing him?"

I tried to make my mouth form words. I wanted to ask them about Della and my son. About Harga, about Ningal. About Lilith. But I could not get a sound out from my bruised and beaten throat.

"He may already be dying," Akka said. "But very well. Let him come south with us to Ur. Keep him close to you though. The other prisoner, we should send north to Kish." He put a hand onto Inush's shoulder. "Did you find your slave?"

"No," Inush said, still looking down at me. "Missing or dead."

"We will find you another one, just as good."

Inush said nothing to that, his face plain.

Akka, abruptly, laughed. "You could have this one!" he said, pointing down at me. "If he's not too ruined for you!"

Inush smiled at his uncle through the hail, although it was a thin smile, strangely sad.

"Yes, let's see how he cleans up," he said.

"My gods, I cannot wait for a bath," Akka said, turning to look out over the camp.

"There were baths in Uruk, before we sacked it."

"There will be baths in Ur, too," Akka said. "I will bathe with a view of the sea."

He leaned over and kissed his nephew's cheek. "We'll find your slave, Inush. Have heart."

I woke to find a woman, wrapped in a heavy cloak, standing over me.

No, not a woman. Only the shape of men passing.

A woman again, crouching down. Gone again.

"Are you a ghost?" I whispered.

She appeared again and pulled back her hood: it was Ningal, Goddess of the Moon, mother of Inanna. Impossibly clean, impossibly pretty.

"Gilgamesh, do you know what they are they going to do with you?"

"They are taking me to Ur."

"I need to find Lilith," she said. "They are raping and killing the priestesses."

"Go," I said.

"I'll be back for you."

"Go get Lilith."

The moon goddess had already gone.

I could not be sure, later, if I had only dreamed her.

When they came to untie me, I could not stand up, even on the leg that I still thought of as my good leg. They held me upright as they stripped me and sluiced me down with three buckets of cold water. Then they stowed me, in an old blanket, bound hand and foot, in one corner of Inush's tent.

"Keep your eyes on him at all times," Inush said. "He has a habit of slipping away in the dark." He seemed about to dismiss his soldiers when he looked at me again. "Feed him a little soup though, will you? I don't need him dying on my carpet."

They propped me up against a tent pole and I accepted the soup, fed to me by spoon by one of Inush's young soldiers. It did revive me a little.

I then sat and watched as Inush went about his business, at a table and chair set up at the entrance to his tent. It had fallen to him to sort the high-value slaves from the rest and through that afternoon a flow of men and women were brought to the tent, assessed, and sent on. Some were to be sent back to Akkadia, others to Ur, some to the slave traders who had apparently gathered at the edge of the camp. Some were simply sent to their deaths.

Inush made his decisions with two priests of Kish standing with him. He consulted them whenever he was unsure of anything.

Towards dusk, a gang of soldiers brought Lilith in.

She was dressed in orange, my mother's colour. She had bruises upon her arms and neck. Her hair was cropped short of course; cut for Enlil.

Lilith cast a glance about the tent but did not let her eyes rest on me. I could not be sure if she had seen me. Then she held Inush's eye, her chin high.

The leader of the soldiers came forward. "We were thinking to send this one to Ur," he said.

"This is the famous Lilith," Inush said. "You can see she was beautiful once. But why bring her to me? You know what happens to priestesses. I have already ruled on this."

The priests of Kish, in their plain black robes, shifted, uncomfortable.

"My lord, she is a priestess of Ninsun," said the soldier.

"That was not really the goddess Ninsun, who died in the battle," Inush said. "That was a false god. A priestess pretending to be Ninsun. How else did we slaughter her? All of that is settled. So I do not see why you are bringing me this woman."

One of the priests then spoke. "We have killed so many priestesses already. Perhaps now is the time for some leniency if we want to rule this land peaceably."

Inush tapped his fingers on his desk. "It is not unlucky to kill the priestess of a false god. All of that too is already settled, by you yourselves, in agreement with my uncle. There is no bad luck in the killing of the priests and priestesses of Uruk. A hundred of them must be dead already."

The priests both bowed their heads.

But the soldier was still unhappy. "My lord, all we are thinking is, perhaps enough of them have died now. We have seen omens. The blue lightning…" He lifted his face and hands upwards. "Some are saying that we have brought bad luck down on us. Their wish is to avert the bad luck."

Inush stood up. "We have conquered Uruk. We have all the good luck in the world. Do not throw omens at me. Now put this woman with the others, for execution in the morning."

When the slaves had all been sorted, Inush had me taken outside to do my business and then he made them leave me untied. He came over to sit with me on the carpet in my corner, and he shared his food with me.

I found myself shovelling up beans and meat; I was starving. Inush poured me some wine and handed me the cup as if we were friends again. "That's the good stuff," he said. "Taken from your father's cellars."

"My father, who you call a fake. Was my mother's godlight fake?"

"If she was truly a goddess," Inush said, keeping his voice low, "she wouldn't be dead, would she? I'm sorry, Gilgamesh, but it makes no sense for a god to be brought down by ordinary soldiers. I think you've been tricked, just like everyone else."

"I do not think you believe what you are saying," I said.

Close to, Inush had heavy grey shadows beneath his eyes. "It was not our intention that your mother would die on the field. It would have been better for us to have captured her and proved her a false god."

I said nothing.

"I should tell you," he went on, "since I do not think you saw it, that she died gloriously. It was a true warrior's death."

I nodded.

"It was her day to die, Gilgamesh. That is all."

Again, with more strength, I nodded at him. "Where are my wife and baby?"

"Oh," he said, and frowned. "Look, I can't tell you that, but they are safe." He paused, considering. "I have heard though that Enlil is dead. I mean, the man pretending to be Enlil. That he was beheaded, in the ruins of the temple at Nippur."

"I heard the news."

"Is that why your hair is shorn?"

"My dead are piling up," I said.

Inush carefully wiped his mouth and hands on a piece of linen. "Do you believe you will see them again, in the underworld?"

"I don't know what happens to gods when they die."

"Except they were not gods, Gilgamesh," he said. "I see we will not agree on any of this. But all the same, I am sorry for your loss." He stood up from the carpet. "Anyway, we start for Ur at first light."

I breathed in, breathed out.

Slowly, ignoring the pain, I shifted forward onto my knees. I put my hands before me in prayer.

"Inush, I do beg you to save the life of the priestess Lilith. She is the woman who raised me. I love her like a mother. I beg you not to kill her."

Inush shook his head. "That's all done now," he said. He stood up. "This is war, Gilgamesh, not a trip with the ladies to a lake."

Then he called in his boys, to have me bound up and gagged for the night.

CHAPTER SEVEN

NINLIL

Heading for the Kur

I t was no longer only me and Utu upon the road into my future. Now soldiers rode out ahead of us, hunched over in the driving rain, and the priests of Susa followed on donkeys. I was carried upon a soft litter by ten men who had competed for the honour. I had a lapful of nuts and apricots to protect me from my hunger pangs, and a leather rain-shelter over me.

My priest, Lamma, walked next to me, one hand up to hold one of mine. His black robes were wet through from the rain and his face was strangely grey as the storm flashed blue fire across the sky.

"My husband was very good to me, Lamma," I said. "From the day it happened, he only treated me as an honoured daughter. He made it clear I was safe with him, and I slowly learned to believe it. But I could never really love him, because of what happened. I could not forget what he did to me."

"How could you forget?" said Lamma.

"He had to live, all these years, with me holding back myself back from him. But he was innocent."

Lamma was quiet a while, but then said: "My lady, do not be angry with me, but is it possible the *mee* only awakened what was already in your husband? Many men have a beast inside them, however blameless their lives may look to others."

I breathed in deep. "I am very sorry Enlil is gone," I said. "That I am certain of. And in my heart, I fully forgive him for what happened. That I am certain of too."

Behind us, through the blue-flashing storm, came wagons of tents and supplies, and behind the very last wagon came Utu, on his mule, glowering at all around him.

"I did not expect to find religion," Lamma said, still holding my hand. "Not at my age."

I laughed. "Religion came looking for you, and you were already dressed for it."

"Your mother that you tell me of. Tiamat. She has never forgotten you." He was looking at my face very closely.

It was hard to know what to say to him, so I said nothing.

"Should you be going back to her, my lady?" he said. "They speak of her in temple, in the holy of holies. They say Tiamat is a dragon with seven heads."

"I was very young when I was taken from her," I said. "I did love her."

"But my lady, all children love their mothers."

"Lamma, the events of another realm are spilling over into this one. I need to put an end to it all."

"But why not stay here, with the people who worship you? You deserve to be loved."

I smiled at him. "If it was only about me, then perhaps I would," I said. "But I had a son in Heaven. I'm not sure if you know that. I don't know whether he is dead or alive, but it's time I found out." I took another deep breath in. "I should have gone to find him before, but I was not in my right mind."

Lamma kissed my hand. "I hope you find him, my lady. You will be a wonderful mother."

We rode on, through a storm that seemed only to build, into the high Zagros and towards the place where it all began for us, in the very first days, when the Anunnaki first came down from Heaven.

In the evenings, when we stopped to camp, the weather was too wet for fires, but I was happy to eat my food raw.

"I will build a temple for you in Susa," Lamma said. "For you and your husband too. We will not let him be forgotten."

I kissed his hands. "I thank you, Lamma."

The next day our great procession arrived at a small stone hut, set on a boulder-strewn little plateau.

An old man, neatly dressed, emerged from the hut. He bowed to me.

"Hello, Neti," I said.

The rain seemed not to land on him, but rather pass straight through him.

"My lady Ninlil," he said. "It is good to see you full grown and well. You were only a small girl when I saw you last."

I turned to Lamma. "All of you must go now. But I thank you and bless you for bringing me here."

Utu rode up then and dismounted. He gave a nod to Neti.

"My lord Utu," said Neti, bowing to him.

This exchange, and Neti himself, and the small stone cottage; all of this was witnessed, and absorbed, by a great crowd of the people of Susa, standing open-mouthed all around us, drenched to the skin as they were. Some climbed on to boulders, to better take in the scene.

"How can we leave you here?" Lamma said. He held his hands out to Utu, and Neti and the cottage. "What is this place? Where is the gate to the underworld?"

I put my hands to his shoulders and drew the fear from him. "You cannot come further. But I thank all of you for your part in my journey. I bless you all and I bless Susa. Now you must go."

When the good people of Susa had been waved down the mountain, I turned back to Neti.

"Who is inside the Kur?" I said.

Neti seemed about to speak but did not.

"Is something stopping you answering me?" I said.

He flickered out of existence, and reappeared again.

"Is Ereshkigal here?" I said.

"Yes, my lady. And she knows you are here now. She has been expecting you."

"You must tell me everything, Neti. Ereshkigal does not have precedence here."

"There are some things that Ereshkigal wants to tell you herself," he said. He looked over at Utu. "Ereshkigal has given herself precedence. You left her here a long time. But may I ask why you are both here?"

"Utu has kidnapped me," I said to Neti.

"My lady, that is very bad. And yet," he cast a hard eye at Utu, "and yet, my lady, you do not seem much distressed by it."

I looked over at Utu. "It is very bad. But more important than that, I am very hungry. I wonder if, before we make the last climb, whether you might be able to feed me. They tell stories, in temple, of honey cakes."

Neti bowed low. "My lady, it will be my great pleasure to feed you."

I sat upon a small wooden chair in Neti's very neat hut and feasted upon honey cakes, washed down with date wine.

Utu stood at the doorway, wet and shivering violently.

"You might spare me one," he said.

I answered without turning my head. "When your kidnap plot has run its course, you can find yourself something to eat."

Neti leaned down behind the little table and produced a new basket of honey cakes from the cupboard there.

"My lady, I fear that all this coming and going is leading inexorably to another opening of the eighth gate," he said. "The eighth gate is meant only to be opened when the Kur is in the sky. It should not be opened again here. The Kur could collapse; the whole mountain too."

I heard a *rat-tat* noise and looked up.

"It is hail," Neti said. "Hail upon the rooftiles. It is the goddess, Inanna. She is on her way here."

"I would like to meet her," I said. "They say she is strange, like me."

"Oh yes, Madam," he said. "Strange enough, anyway."

"I met her *sukkal*, you know, in Nippur, and I liked her. It feels like a hundred years ago now, but it was not that long ago."

Neti frowned at that but said nothing.

∞

At last we set off for the Kur, first me, and then Neti walking close behind me, impervious to the weather, and finally, Utu. Up the rocky path, my head bent forward in the hail, and down the other side of the crater, to the great, red rock that was the Kur.

When we reached it, I put out one wet hand to the metallic rock. I had a premonition, or something like it; or perhaps the information simply seeped into me.

"Neti," I said. "Who is the man within?"

"Which man?"

"You know which man."

"He has the marks of the Anunnaki on him," Neti said. "That is all I can say."

There was something else, something else that I should know, slipping away from me. "Tell me what there is to know," I said to Neti.

He spread his hands, apologetic. "I am not allowed to say," he said.

"Is it Ereshkigal you serve, or this man?"

"I am not allowed to say."

I ran my hand along the Kur, until, with no noise at all, the first gate opened: a perfect dark circle in the side of the rock.

"Do we not need to leave our clothes and *mees* here?" I said, as I stepped in.

Neti shrugged. "The rules seem to have been abandoned. You can keep your things upon you, my lady."

I watched Utu clamber through the gates behind me.

I said: "You will be punished for your part in this. I don't know how yet. But you will suffer for your cruelty and selfishness. For your betrayal of our family."

"We'll see," he said.

As the seventh gate opened, we were confronted with something unexpected. I expected the gate to open onto a long thin room, with the eighth gate at the end of it. But instead we emerged onto a walkway, with stars above us and a dark abyss below.

"This is new," I said.

Neti walked ahead of us along the high path through the stars. Utu came slowly along behind me.

"If we fell, would we hurt ourselves?" I said.

"I am not interested in testing it," said Utu.

Even high up on the walkway, even before we had reached the strange city that Ereshkigal had created, I felt the presence ahead of me. Yes, the marks of the Anunnaki. But something else. Older traces.

My mind could not understand the traces.

Did I know him?

"My lady, you are not breathing," Neti said to me.

I breathed in the scent of a forest, very incongruous on this strange walkway we found ourselves upon.

"We should hurry," said Neti. "The goddess Inanna is not far behind you."

At the end of the walkway, we walked in small procession through the dark and shifting streets of the city.

Animals, strange and dark, slithered in the shadows.

Ahead, a huge temple, dark against the bright stars of the sky. And at the top of the steps to the temple, a tall man, clad in black.

I was going to breathe in but did not.

A woman appeared next to the man. It was my granddaughter Ereshkigal. She was just the same as ever, her hands upon her hips, her curls rising in a cloud around her head. Behind her stood the two *gallas* that I remembered from our days on the Kur.

The man in black was climbing down the steps. He walked towards me, pulling his hood back from his face. He wore the same armour as my beloved Bizilla, but black where hers was gold.

I knew then both who he was and what he had done.

I took in a huge, shuddering breath.

"Hello, mother," he said.

CHAPTER EIGHT

GILGAMESH

Heading south on the Euphrates

Akka, now king of both Akkadia and Sumer, stood on the foredeck of the Barge of Heaven and looked out upon the great river and the rich green lands beyond.

Even in rain so heavy that two slaves and a heavy leather parasol could not keep the water off him, he radiated a settled happiness.

The rich river lands between the Euphrates and the Tigris were his now, all the way down to the sea. He was the first king of Akkadia to bring Sumer into his empire, and he could very well withstand a little rainwater as he looked over all he had won for himself.

Inush stood beneath his own parasol, a long blue cloak wrapped tight around him.

"You know some fool tried to burn this ship?" Akka said to him.

"It was lucky you were there to stop it!" Inush replied.

The two men laughed together at the thought of such a prize as the Barge of Heaven being rendered up as charcoal.

I was tied to the middle mast, in the gangway between the rowers. My hands were trussed behind me, my ankles tied in front of me. A gag was bound tight around my mouth. I had been wet and cold so long that I no longer had the strength to shiver.

Inush glanced round once at me; he knew I was in earshot.

He turned back to his uncle. "There'll be heavy flooding, if it goes on like this," he said. "It's very early, for rain like this."

"It's lucky we're already afloat," said Akka, all happy complacency. "But they tell me Ur is built upon so many ancient cities that it stands high above any flood. We are wise to be going south right now."

We were on the main branch of the Euphrates by then, with four barges following behind us, and behind them, a handful of the giant coracles the Akkadians use to move goods and cattle.

The men of Akkadia grunted with every pull on the oars of the Barge of Heaven, and above us all, the blackened skies sparked with vivid blue lightning.

My mind went to Lilith, her hands bound, bruises on her arms and throat. Della and my tiny son. I had no idea where they were.

And where was little Ninlil? Where were Inanna and Ninshubar? Were they still far away, hunting their lost boy? Or had they been swept away by this tide of war and chaos?

I thought of Harga. Did he make it back behind the walls on the day my mother died?

"Are you awake, Gilgamesh?"

It was Inush.

He had abandoned his parasol and was already wet. He sat down close beside me and stretched his riding boots out before him. He cast one look about the ship; Akka was nowhere in sight. Then he leaned over and loosened my gag.

"On the second day of the siege," Inush said, leaning in close to me, "your mother rode into our camp and set fire to our boats." He lifted his eyebrows to me. "In the melee, someone close to me was lost. A tall man with very pale skin and red hair. And very blue eyes. Did you ever see him? Did your mother take him to Uruk?"

I gathered my thoughts. "Did he have a tattoo on his arm, of an eagle with a lion's head?"

Inush's face lit up. "Yes. That's him."

I shook my head. "He came in to give me water when I was a hostage at Kish. A long time ago. But I have not seen him since. I'm sorry Inush, but that's the truth of it."

He nodded. "Thank you, Gilgamesh." He paused, looked around, and then leaned in so close I could feel his breath on my ear. He said: "He won't hurt them. Your wife and child. You need not worry about that."

"Thank you, that's kind," I said. I turned my head to him and looked him full in the face. "Did they kill Lilith?"

"She escaped," he said, holding my eye. "I promise you. She has not been caught."

"Really?"

"Yes. So stop casting your dark looks at me. As far as I know, she's alive."

I gave Inush my good smile, my full-strength grin. Then I sank my teeth into his nose and bit down hard.

He pulled away from me, screaming.

There was blood everywhere.

I spat out his nose.

"That's for my mother," I said.

Inush was still screaming; his face was a gory mess. There was blood all over the deck. He slipped and fell.

A laugh burst out of me, as I watched the blood spill from the hole in his face.

It was the kind of wound that would never really heal well.

Men came to drag Inush away from me; more came to jump on me. It took several blows to my face, before they could wipe the grin from it.

CHAPTER NINE

NINLIL

In the underworld

I had last seen my baby in the realm we call Heaven, or sometimes the Great Above.

What did I remember of him?

Only the smell of him, perhaps. And the love I felt.

I knew him at once, although he was a large and powerful man now. He had Enlil's eyes.

I put out my hand to him and as I touched his chest, I was overwhelmed by the swirling pain he had within him; the yawning agony in his head and across his back.

"You came here for me," I said.

He closed his scale-covered arms around me. "I came here to rescue you."

In that moment, I did not feel much in need of rescue, but I did not quibble with him. "It should have been me that came back for you. I see that now."

My son stood back to look at me, his hands on my shoulders. We were the same height.

"I am so pleased to find you well and strong, mother."

"What has happened to your back and scalp?" I said.

He shook his head and did not answer.

"Did Tiamat do this to you?"

"Mother, it is only a reminder. That disobedience is always punished. You know how she is."

"I'm not sure I do know," I said.

He took my hands in his and we stood a while, our heads bowed together. I was for those moments, perfectly happy.

"Was it Tiamat who took you from me?" I said.

"I'm told so. Kidnapped from my cradle."

I remembered to look about me. Ereshkigal was standing with her hands on her hips, frowning at us. The silver *gallas* stood without emotion behind her. My kidnapper Utu leaned against the outer wall of the temple, looking angry. A host of strange demons, like animals but in no form that I recognised, watched us with bright eyes from the steps down to the city. And in the bright-lit doorway of the temple stood two of Enki's handsome half-god children, whose names I could not recall.

I looked up at the edifice that I found myself standing beneath. A huge building where before there had only been one small room, with the eighth gate in it.

"Did you do this?" I said to Ereshkigal.

She gave a sort of shrug. She was looking at her brother Utu.

"Why are you here?" she said to him. "What has this to do with you?"

"This concerns all of us," said Utu.

I listened to their words, but all I could think of was the pain inside Nergal, flowing to me through his hand.

I realised that despite everything pressing down on us, I needed to heal my son and I needed to do it at once.

"I need somewhere quiet," I said to Ereshkigal. "To be with my son."

"We should go on," Nergal said. "Before the goddess Inanna comes. She is very, very angry with me."

"Please, Nergal," I said to him. "It will only take a few moments."

In the small tablet room behind Ereshkigal's throne, I sat and put my hands upon my son. My warm sea poured into him. I crept down his spine and pieced together the skin that had for so long been flayed open. I pieced together his skull and made the scalp whole. I wheedled out and destroyed the poison that had stopped him healing. There was so much more pain in him, but that would have to do for now.

At the end I put my head on his shoulder and for a while I let the sea flow between us.

"I came to get you," he said, frowning, anxious. "To take you home. But I see you so well here. I am told you loved your kidnapper." He paused, turning his eyes from mine for a moment, before going on. "And what if Tiamat is angry with you when she gets you back? What if she cuts you open as she cut me open? All my life she has been desperate to get you back. But what if it is only to hurt you? Ereshkigal believes it is madness for me to go back."

I smiled at him. "Ereshkigal is looking very well."

He did not blush, but he flattened his mouth and again, looked away from me for a moment. "We also need to consider that Bizilla and many others will pay for my failure if I do not bring you back. But then there is also a very high chance that Inanna will kill me, and perhaps you too, if we do not pass through the eighth gate before she gets here. I killed her *sukkal*. It was in battle, but I regret it now." He put his forehead on my shoulder. "Mother, I do not know what to do."

I kissed his hair. "My son, we are going home today, just as you planned. It's the right thing. I need to face up to my past. I need to face my mother." I kissed him again. "Let us rise up into the Great Above together, my beautiful, long-lost son."

CHAPTER TEN

MARDUK

On the banks of the Euphrates

Enki was there when I woke up. It was still raining, but the thunder and lightning had passed. I was lying naked in the mud.

Moshkhussu lay with her head in Enki's lap. He was feeding her small pieces of meat.

"What are you doing?" I said.

"I'm looking after you," Enki said. "It is unlike me, I do grant you. You have a sort of appeal to you that I have not yet learned to resist."

I sat and looked down at myself. "Do you know where my clothes are?"

"All your clothes have been burned to a cinder," he said. "This beach was hit by lightning last night. And yet you and the dog are well and all your scars have gone. Interesting, isn't it?"

"My scars?"

"You had marks all over your back. They are gone. Your tattoo has also gone."

I peered down at my left shoulder; my tattoo had indeed gone, leaving no trace.

"You were struck by the strange blue lightning, and you seem better for it," said Enki. "Very, very strange."

He handed me my flint and Ninshubar's bone star. The pendant was charred and the leather was gone, but it was whole.

"But then this wasn't ordinary lightning," he said. "I think Inanna has gone after Nergal. And she is drawing on the Earth itself for power. Something none of us have ever been able to do, although I have heard such things are possible."

"I must go after Ninshubar."

"Soon," said Enki. "I'm not sure you are quite yourself yet. I think you should sleep."

I was going to protest, but I think I must have passed out.

I dreamed that I was sitting cross-legged next to Ninshubar. Our bare knees were almost touching, mine so pale, hers so dark. Her eight-pointed star was bright around her neck; the leather was new. We were outside a hut built from reeds, with a small fire blazing before us.

I woke up with a great start, joy flooding through me. "She's alive," I said, the words bursting out of me.

I realised I was lying with my head on Enki's lap. I smiled up at him. "She's alive."

"You do not know that."

Moshkhussu stuck her face into mine. "You are well!" I said to her.

I sat up, kissing and rubbing at Moshkhussu. I felt good; strong. My aches and pains had gone.

"I need clothes," I said to Enki. "I must go quickly."

"It seems very unlikely you will find her."

"My lord, I saw her in my dream. I saw her bare knee, next to mine. I saw her star at her throat. She was warm, she was breathing. It was a vision."

"It was just a dream."

"You are wrong, Enki. She has the *melam* in her. She has survived. It was not a dream, it was prophecy. Now get up. We must get moving. We must find her."

He stayed where he was, sitting on the grass. "Marduk, the *melam* offers protection and healing. But it is not perfect and she was not born with it in her veins. She may very easily be dead."

"If so we will find her body and revive her."

"She is probably in the belly of a crocodile by now. Or chopped up for relics by some busy villagers. I cannot see us finding her."

"Enki, I am going and I will find her. Come or don't come. I am grateful for what you have done so far. I must ask you for one more thing though. Will you give me your cloak? I need to fashion myself some clothing."

I took his heavy cloak and transformed it as best I could into a robe, with a rope of knotted reeds tied around at the waist. With clumsy fingers, I fashioned string from a thread pulled from the cloak, and that I used to tie Ninshubar's star around my neck, and my knife around my arm. Then I made myself a spear.

"You do seem better," Enki said.

"I'm strong now," I said. "Strong and clear in what I need to do."

"So it seems."

"I am going to see her again, Enki. Do come with me. I feel I owe you. We will be safer together."

"Is that so, child of Creation?"

I turned to look at him. "How can I be a child of Creation, when I was born here?"

"*If* you were born here," he said. "We only know you were young here. All the people of your kind are birthed by Tiamat."

We stood and looked at each other a while, he with his fine clothes and his ancient weapons. Me with a home-made wooden spear, and barefoot, and with an outfit fashioned from a cloak, and my dog of war sat at my ankles.

"I think the lightning has woken you up," he said. "Which is very interesting. But we owe each other nothing. There is no reason to stay together."

"Ninshubar survives," I said. "Come find her with me. Together we will be a small army. We will have more options. We can help you get to your refuge."

"You are a very difficult person to resist," he said.

"I am always being told that." I gave him my good smile. "And you may improve my chances. This is your country. You may have information I will need."

"Well, that is honest." He smiled back at me.

"But also you will be safer with me. I feel it."

He sighed. "All right, I will stay with you, for now at least," he said. "While I work out what is best."

We walked for half a day and reached a narrow canal. There were the remains of a reed-sculpted bridge on either side of the waterway, but the stretch that spanned the canal seemed long gone.

Moshkhussu stopped when she reached the water, looking back at us. We would have to swim and not for the first time that day.

I came to a stop, my bare feet pale against the mud. I looked down and then out across the water. It was far too far to jump.

But then, on an impulse, I did jump.

I leaped. I flew, with a feeling of great ease and grace, through the air.

I landed light and strong on the other side of the canal. I turned back to grin at Enki and Moshkhussu. She threw herself into the canal and doggedly made her way across to me.

"Did you see that?" I called out to Enki. "Did you see how I jumped?"

"Now that is very interesting indeed," he said.

CHAPTER ELEVEN

ERESHKIGAL

In the underworld

I sat upon my blackthorn throne, wishing it had cushions on it. For the first time in a long time, my back was aching.

"I could get you a fur blanket," said Namtar, looking up anxiously at me.

I was too focused on my brother to answer him.

"One hundred years I have been here, and you have never been to see me!" I said to Utu.

"You could have left and come to see me," said Utu. He stood sullen at the bottom of the steps to my throne.

"But why now? What are you doing with Ninlil?"

"I've been promised *melam*," he said, looking down at his gold rings.

"I had *melam*. I could have given you mine if you had asked for it."

He laughed. "I will take it from you now, sister, if you are offering."

I shrugged. "I gave it to our sister Inanna," I said. "When she came to visit." There was no need to go into the details of that.

Utu flattened his mouth for a moment. "If there is anyone in the world without a need for *melam*, it is Inanna."

"This is all beside the point," I said. "You have kidnapped Ninlil. Turned against your family."

Utu bowed his head and came up smiling. "Sister, do you lecture me on family loyalty, when you have taken an Anzu as a lover?"

"Better a lover than a kidnap victim!"

He was shaking his head. "We can argue about this another time, sister. Now I just want the *melam* I was promised for bringing Ninlil here and I will go."

Namtar was coughing at my elbow. "My queen, look how pretty it all looks."

Oh, and it was very pretty! Namtar had assembled a small congregation.

In the front, Dumuzi and Geshtinanna, both so handsome by candlelight. Behind them, Neti, the gatekeeper, in his blue suit, looking stern. Then arranged all about, to make the scene complete, a host of my most lovely demons.

I returned to frowning at Utu. "Go and sit down," I said.

"What can Nergal and Ninlil still be doing?" Dumuzi called out, as Utu made his way into the pews.

"She has her hands on him," I said. Which I did not like. But if she was able to heal his wounds, as Utu said she might be, of course I was happy about that.

"And we are just going to say goodbye and let them go off?" Dumuzi said.

Namtar turned on him, unexpectedly cross. "This is the goodbye ceremony," he said. "As has been explained."

The dust of the dead fell heavier and heavier.

"If I could stop them I would," I said.

At last the two of them emerged: the goddess Ninlil, the Anzu who had always been amongst us, and her son Nergal, child of both the Anzu and the Anunnaki.

My grandmother Ninlil was so fine now. When I had last seen her in Nippur, she had been an awkward little bird, fallen from its nest. Now she was as tall as Nergal, straight-backed and broad-faced. Her eyes were no longer too big for her head. I saw in her now the same strength I saw in her son.

She might have been his sister, not his mother.

The two of them looked about at the pews and all the faces turned to them.

Nergal approached the steps to my throne. His bag, with its ghastly cargo, was already over his shoulder.

"Ereshkigal, we are going now. May I speak to you in private?"

"No," I said, blinking back tears. "This is the goodbye ceremony."

Ninlil approached, her smile very kind.

"I am glad to see you looking so well, Ereshkigal," she said. Even her voice had changed: softer now, all grown up.

"I am quite unwell," I said to her. "My hip and my back are a great trial to me."

Namtar appeared beside her, tipping his fox-ears low. "My queen, your brother asks to come forward."

"Oh, very well," I said, scowling at Utu.

Utu stood up from his pew and came closer, looking around him with distaste at my demons.

"It's Nergal I need to talk to," he said.

"Speak to him then," I said.

He frowned at that, but said: "Nergal, I brought her. I have done my part. Now for your part."

Nergal paused a moment, but then said to his mother: "Did he treat you well?"

"I suppose so," Ninlil said. "He wasn't interested in hurting me."

"Then I will keep Tiamat's promise to you," Nergal said to Utu.

He went into his belt and produced a small black sphere.

Utu took it from Nergal as if it was of no real significance to him. Then with no further declarations, and no goodbye for me, his sister, he walked back out into the Dark City.

We all watched him go in silence.

"I was so nice to him when he was little," I said at last. "But he grew up horrid."

"He is a servant of the Anzu," Nergal said. "Just as I am. I cannot stand in judgment on him."

"Well I can," I said.

"I'm going now," Nergal said to me.

"Go then. We have already said our goodbyes."

I looked down at my lap.

He came up the steps to me and lifted my chin with his fingers. He kissed me, firm, upon the mouth, and then the forehead.

"Goodbye, Ereshkigal."

He turned to go without speaking again, one hand on his Ninlil's back. They walked out through the great doors, into the Dark City, without turning to look back at me.

For some few strained minutes, we all kept our places, although I did dab my tears away on my skirt. Then a demon darted in from the outside. "They are upon the road," she said.

Neti leaped up from his pew, as did Dumuzi and Geshtinanna. They came to join Namtar at the steps to my throne. The five of us were all very grim.

"Is it done?" said Dumuzi.

"Yes," Neti said. "The eighth gate is locked. I doubt the old gods themselves could get it open now."

"How did you do it?" said Geshtinanna.

"We have corrupted the master *mee*," said Neti. "It will not open the gate."

"It was me who thought of it," I said. "It was me who worked out how to break it. Although I only had it on my wrist a moment."

"It was very, very clever of you, my queen," said Namtar.

"They must never know we have stopped them," I said. "It must seem like an accident. As if the master *mee* is simply not working. Or as if the Kur has stepped in to protect itself. We must all be utterly astonished when they return."

"Madam," said Neti, "you have a long track record of deceit and misdirection. If I was them, I would instantly suspect you."

"They will struggle to prove it," I said.

Geshtinanna, looking worried, said: "Won't they simply force you to undo it?"

"He loves me," I said. "And she is all goodness. Let us see how it all plays out."

"And the other gates?" said Dumuzi.

"All locked," said Neti.

"They will need to be double locked, against Inanna."

"Dumuzi, they are locked and she does not have her master *mee* to open them again," I said. "We are all tucked in here. No one can get in and no one can get out. We are all safe and snug."

We all looked about us, at the dust falling in the temple of darkness, and the bright faces of the demons, and then Geshtinanna came up the steps to kiss both my hands.

"All hail the Queen of the Underworld," she said.

"Nergal's going to be very angry," said Dumuzi.

"But he will be here, safe, with me," I said. "That is all that matters."

My throne shook beneath me.

"If indeed we can keep Inanna out," said Neti.

I gripped the arms of my throne. "Do not fail me, gatekeeper. This time my sister cannot be allowed in."

CHAPTER TWELVE

NINLIL

In the underworld

I walked with my son, Nergal, along the road to Heaven. The dust of the dead fell so heavily upon us, it might have been snow.

The road was paved with slabs of black stone. All around us, beneath Ereshkigal's starscape, lay dark and empty fields.

My feet grew heavier and heavier.

There was still one thing I needed to do before returning home.

"I think there is something you want to tell me," I said to my son.

We stopped to look at each other.

"I did not know if you knew," he said.

"I was told my husband was killed by an agent of Creation."

He took a great breath in. "Mother, I have been told you loved Enlil. But I didn't know that when I was sent to kill him. And I still don't understand how you could have loved him, after what he did."

"I know."

I sat down on a rock beside the road, and Nergal sat down next to me.

He said: "Did Tiamat lie to me, about what Enlil did to you?"

"Not exactly. But do you know my brother Qingu?"

"Of course."

"Do you think him a good man?"

He was quiet a moment. "Do you blame Qingu, for what happened with Enlil?"

I nodded and took his hands in mine. "I think so. And what I am certain of is that Enlil would have been a good father to you. You would have loved him if you had known him. And he would have loved you so much."

Nergal took his hands from me, and wiped tears from his face.

"I am not trying to hurt you, by telling you," I said. "We must be honest with each other. Now give me your bag."

"Why?"

"Just give me the bag."

He opened the bag up, watching my face, and passed it to me. I looked inside.

Those beloved features, now so bloated, grey, rotting. The terrible stench of a dead animal.

I had to overcome deep revulsion, but I did it anyway. I reached out and lifted the severed head up in my hands. The astonishing weight of it. The flesh so cold and clammy.

I lifted it to my mouth and took a bite out of the scalp. Skin, hair, and bone altogether. I forced the mouthful down.

"It is not so bad," I said.

Nergal's mouth had fallen open. "Mother, what are you doing?"

"Do not stop me," I said.

I ate my husband's head, even as I gagged on it. I crunched down the bones and slurped up what was left of his brain.

Nergal moved to kneel before me, watching, pale.

"Tiamat wanted the head," he said.

"She will get his head. But it will be inside me."

When I had finished, I licked the rotting flesh from my lips, and then licked my fingers, lest I lose any trace of him.

"Let us go on then," I said. "I am ready now to see my mother again."

CHAPTER THIRTEEN

GILGAMESH

Heading south to the city of Ur

On the deck of the Barge of Heaven, the Akkadian officers convened with their king to discuss the manner of my death. At first all present were keen to kill me then and there and throw my body out into the Euphrates. The king, however, had another idea.

"If we kill him now, no one will ever believe it," King Akka said. "We should do it in Ur. We can make a big show of it, and when we have done killing him, we will let the body of the Lion of Uruk rot upon those famous walls. The people should see his corpse decay. Then they will believe it."

So I lay upon the bloodied deck of the Barge of Heaven, front down, trussed like a pig, and battered from head to foot. I lay with my bloodied right cheek pressed to the damp wood of the deck and found that I could see out through the railings, across the rain-pressed river.

League upon league, I lay and bled, and looked out over the waters of the holy river, and the wet green lands along the bank.

I was past pain by then, past grief. I simply lay and looked out on my beloved Sumer and thought: *No man can escape life's end.*

We stopped for a while at a busy dock on the east bank of the Euphrates. I watched the to and fro of vessels out on the river, and listened to the comings and goings of the Akkadians upon the Barge.

It was Larsa; we were in Larsa. Not yet in Ur, then.

The sun came out and I watched the mist burn off the river. For a moment, I thought I saw a sailing boat, one square sail up, in the centre of the river. There was a woman sat at the stern, with her dark hood turned to me. Then the boat was gone, as if burned off with the mist.

I heard steps, and a voice close-by. Akka. Speaking to me.

"The people are saying it was some devil creature that killed Enlil."

I was gagged, and my neck was roped to my hands; I could not turn my head to look at him.

"Ungag him," Akka said.

When the gag had been wrenched out of my mouth, I still could not turn to look at him, but I said: "You mean the false god Enlil."

"What?"

"Do you admit it was Enlil who died?"

"Just tell me what you know of the creature who killed him," Akka said.

"They say he's from another realm," I said.

"An Anunnaki?"

"An Anzu. A different family. And they're on their way to Earth, by the way. Did your spies also tell you that?"

"You claim new gods are coming?"

I smiled to myself. "They are your true enemy. Not the good people of Sumer."

"I'll treat the good people of Sumer well enough," Akka said, "once we've dug out the poison in your temples and palaces. And these stories of new gods, of so-called Anzu, I don't believe it. It is only desperate nonsense. The old lies aren't working, so now you try new ones."

As they gagged me again, he still had words to spit at me. "How very easy it has been, Gilgamesh, to clear away your family. Four hundred years, they were here, and then only the word of us coming had them running for the mountains."

CHAPTER FOURTEEN

INANNA

Entering the underworld

I walked now with a sheen of blue fire dancing about me. The flames kept the rain off me.

My lions were still with me, but they kept their distance, one eye always turned to me.

On the third night, I slept lying down upon open rock, with a view out over the storm-racked plains below.

I no longer dreamed. All that was over now. The weakness and confusion were gone.

When I woke, I said to the mountains: "Today is the day I will kill him."

At dusk I reached the familiar hut, smoke seeping from its chimney.

Neti at once appeared, walking backwards in front of me. He was wearing his shepherd's outfit.

"Inanna, no," he said.

He had his palm up to me, to stop me.

I put up one blazing hand of blue fire in reply and Neti disappeared.

Over the hill I went and down into the crater, driving the rain and wind before me.

I turned when I reached the bottom of the slope.

Saffron and Crocus had stopped following me. They were crouched down together on the rim of the crater. They no longer wanted to follow me.

"Go then," I said, and I walked on to the Kur, dry and warm inside my bubble of blue fire.

The dark red rock of the Kur was slippery with rain. I put my face close to it.

"I can see you," I whispered. "My flies know what you are."

Neti reappeared, now dressed in the neat blue suit that he wore inside the Kur. The rain fell straight through him.

"Inanna, the gates are locked against you."

I smiled.

I put out one hand to him and scorched him with raw power.

Neti was gone.

Then I pulled down all the energy I could and blasted it all at the Kur. Thunder rang out; the ground shook.

A moment later, the door to the Kur sprang open.

"Open all the gates," I said.

A pause, and the second gate sprang open, and the third, and fourth, and fifth, and sixth. I stepped into the Kur and I looked down a corridor of doors; all stood open, blue light flickering. At the very end, I could see the seventh gate, that led down to the Dark City.

A glimpse, ahead, of a dark figure. Flickering, gone.

"I see you, Neti," I called out. "And I know now what you are!"

I walked from gate to gate, stepping over into each new space with strong and confident steps.

"I know who you are loyal to, Neti," I called. "I know who you wait for."

At that Neti materialised, almost solid looking, in front of the seventh gate. He looked so old and grey, in that moment, he might have been pressed from ash.

"Child of darkness," he said, his voice very faint. "You must not go any further."

"I must and I will," I said, smiling.

"My task is to protect the gates between the realms, come what may, for all the time that will come."

I smiled at him. "Your tasks do not concern me."

"Inanna, they concern us all."

"And yet you will let me by."

"The eighth gate will open if you go any further," he said. "Ereshkigal will not let you kill him. All this I have already seen."

I struck him with my brilliant blue lightning, and watched him fall, as heavy dust, to the metal floor.

The seventh gate swung slowly open.

Out gushed the sweet forest air of the underworld. I turned once, and looked back down the line of gates, at the glimpse of the world of light beyond. And then I stepped, with one firm foot, into the world beneath.

I let my fires gutter for a while, as I made my way out onto the long and narrow walkway that led down to the Dark City.

I had only been walking a short time when I saw someone ahead of me on the walkway. He was walking towards me.

The man began to walk slower; he had seen me, even in the dim starlight. But of course he could not see my smile.

A heavy-set man. A god. It was my brother Utu.

"Who goes there?" he called out.

The man had done nothing at all for me when I was murdered by Ereshkigal's monsters. Now he conspired with the enemy; the whole pattern of it was obvious to me.

With one sweep of a hand, I sent out a blast of fire so fierce and strong that Utu was swept off the walkway.

He screamed, long and hard, as he fell into the starry abyss. For a few moments I could see his round face as he fell, pale yellow against the deep.

As I made my way onwards to the Dark City, a small note of pleasure bubbled up inside me. Soon enough though it had disappeared, in the numb sea of my rage.

CHAPTER FIFTEEN

ERESHKIGAL

In the underworld

We were sat at dinner, all looking very fine, when the table shook so violently that our wine glasses tipped over.

Neti appeared in the doorway.

"The defences did not hold," he said.

I stood, gripping the table, overwhelmed for a moment with panic.

"My sister?"

"Inanna is already inside the Kur," he said.

Dumuzi and Geshtinanna stood up, and Namtar came forward from his post beside the door.

"She is going to kill Nergal," I said to them all.

"Can you be sure?" said Dumuzi.

"I am absolutely sure," I said. "We must stop her." I turned to Namtar. "Summon all the demons. Gather them up outside the temple."

"We can help you," Dumuzi put in.

"Anything we can do, we will do," said Geshtinanna.

I shook my head. "You two should hide."

Neti took a step towards me. "Madam, I am not sure you can stop her."

The dust fell heavier and heavier.

"I will not let her touch him," I said.

I walked to my bedchamber, my mind whirring. Neti walked with me, and my silent *gallas* followed on behind.

"Where is Nergal?" I said.

"Almost at the eighth gate."

"And Inanna?"

"On the walkway. She has just pushed your brother Utu to his death."

Pain shot up my spine. "Perhaps we need only delay her," I said.

Neti shook his head. "Only if you open the eighth gate, Madam. Which you are not going to do."

I said nothing to that.

He watched impassive as I took off my long temple gown and put on a simple linen shift. I had the idea that I did not want anything tripping me.

I saw that Namtar was at the door.

"Where did you hide my secret things?" I said.

He went over to my bed, crouched down, and lifted a flagstone beside it. Beneath the stone, laid out on velvet, were my most precious found-things and amongst them, four ancient *mees* that I had long ago discovered hidden in the Kur. They had never wanted to work for me before, but I knew there was hidden power in them.

If they still refused to work, I had my *gallas*. And I had my precious demons. We would have to do.

The floor beneath me moved; I almost fell, and ended up sitting on my bed, with plaster falling all around me.

I stood and picked up my candle. "I will not let Nergal die."

Neti looked blank at that.

"He will not die today," I said. "Those are my orders to you, Neti. Do you understand me?"

"I do understand you, yes. But you are making a terrible decision."

I walked through the twisting corridors, my candle held high. The dust of the dead fell so heavily that at times I could not see five steps ahead of me. Neti walked silent behind me, his hands neat behind his back, and behind him came my silver monsters, leaving deep footprints in the dust.

In the temple, my dressers were waiting for me, all holding up sticks and other small weapons.

I shook my head at them. "You little ones stay in here. I do not want you hurt."

The chief amongst them came forward, her tiny ears twitching. "We are all coming," she said. "We will all lay down our lives for you, if that is what it takes."

I wiped away a tear. "Follow me then."

Outside, Namtar stood at the top of the steps to the temple. Down below, in the dark square, the shadows roiled with demons. Some were no wider than my hand. Others were the size of buildings, and they seethed huge and black against the sky.

I went to the top of the steps, with my *gallas* close behind me, and I called out to all my beloveds.

"My sister is coming," I said. "We must not let her pass."

Below me, the darkness heaved and shivered.

Namtar, at my elbow, said: "We will not let her pass, my queen."

I said to him, very quiet: "I know I am selfish, to risk us all for just one man."

He put his hand out to me and took my hand and lifted it to his soft mouth. "You are the one we follow into battle. We follow you full-hearted. Unquestioning."

"Thank you, Namtar," I said.

And then we stood there, in the light thrown out from the temple doors, to wait for my sister and her fury.

CHAPTER SIXTEEN

GILGAMESH

At Ur, city of the moon gods

I do not remember our arrival at Ur.

I came to myself again in darkness; wet bricks beneath me. I tried to move, but every piece of me was in pain.

An old man's voice, close to me. "Who are you?" He prodded me in my back. "You. Who are you?"

When I did not answer, he prodded at me again. "Who is this?"

Another voice, a younger man, a little further away. "Does it matter?"

It made me smile, even in my pain, to hear their accents. The same lilt as Inanna and her mother.

"I think it does matter who he is, my lord," the older man said. "If they have put him in here with us, it is to execute him in the morning. Which means he will die alongside you. I would like to know who will be dying alongside you. It ought to only be family and servants."

The younger man laughed. "Beloved uncle, I am not sure there are precedents for the correct way to murder a king."

I pushed myself, very slowly, onto my back. "King of what?" I said.

After a short silence, the younger man said: "I am the King of Ur."

"Were you too slow?" I said.

"I don't follow."

"Were you too slow to open the gates?"

"Ah yes, I took a night to think it over. And so my wives and daughters are sold as slaves, and they have been killing the royal men in batches. We are the last of the royal family to be executed."

I breathed in, breathed out. "I am Gilgamesh."

"The famous Gilgamesh?" the king said.

"For what that is worth."

The old man clapped his hands together in the blackness. "Then you are family to us. The blood of the Anunnaki runs deep in the city of Ur. All the kings here can claim Nanna, the moon god, as their father."

He sounded quite cheerful, for a man about to die.

"And we are fellow kings," the king said.

"I am no longer king of anything," I said. "And anyway, I was never crowned."

I could not see the King of Ur, but I could tell he was sitting on the floor, just as I was. It made me smile when he said: "I will come north for the ceremony, when you do get crowned."

"Well, you would both be most welcome," I said. "For now though, where is the god Nanna?"

"He left us when we heard that Uruk had fallen," said the king.

"Gone in the night," said the old man.

"Ah," I said. "So, how do they do it here, the executions?"

"They fling you from the top of the Moon Tower," said the king. "It is seven storeys high."

I nodded to myself in the dark. "You know, my family, for all their faults, have never found the need for this sort of thing."

"True enough," said the king. "I did not mean to disparage Nanna. He has kept Ur safe since time out of mind. And yet it seems a distant dream now, those days so recent, when the city was going on just as it always had."

We were all quiet a while in the darkness.

"It's about now that I like to get rescued," I said.

"Have you escaped prison before?" said the king.

"More than once. I have a man called Harga, who is clever at this sort of thing." I nodded to myself. "I'm not sure he survived the fall of Uruk."

"He sounds like a good man," said the king.

"I will agree with you when he opens that door and lets us out."

But Harga did not come.

I awoke in dim light to find that the door to the cell was open. Akkadian soldiers bustled in, in force.

Two men picked me up, taking an arm each. They grimaced at the smell of me. My legs would not take my weight, so they dragged me out into the antechamber beyond. There, by the light from one small, barred window, they strapped me into my bronze breast plate, copper-plated skirts and lion helmet.

"You have forgotten my sword," I said, giving them my smile. "And my axes."

The men did not smile back at me.

When they had finished with me, they propped me up on a brick bench that ran along the wall beneath the window. I looked down at my useless legs; my left knee was hugely swollen and black with bruising.

Along to my left was the king. He was a handsome man, dark-skinned and black-eyed, with a long, curled beard. He looked very regal in the white satin robes and crescent-shaped crown they had dressed him in. His uncle had been put into the white robes of a priest of Ur. He gave me a kind smile when he saw me looking.

The soldiers left and for a short while it was just the three of us in that small, plain antechamber. The two royal men came to stand next to me, peering out of the window.

"What can you see?" I said, craning my head around. I could only make out squares of dark-grey sky above.

"There are crowds waiting," said the king. "It's still raining."

"I was hoping for news of a flat roof," I said. "Something we could easily climb out onto."

The uncle turned to me. "It is a four-storey drop and there are Akkadians in the street below us."

The king said: "They are bringing round a horse, to the front of the barracks. One of those Asian animals."

I must say, they held themselves well, these two men about to meet their deaths.

I said: "Is it black, the animal? It might be mine."

"Black and very beautiful," said the king, standing on his toes to see better.

"I did not know he survived," I said. "I fell from him in battle."

I looked again at the king and realised that he reminded me of Inanna.

"I meant to ask you," I said, "do you know the goddess Inanna?"

The king gave me his careful smile. "Only since the day of her birth," he said. "We rang the bells from sunrise to sunset on the day that she was born. The miracle Anunnaki."

"She was best friends with one of my nieces," the uncle said.

"Where is the goddess now?" the king asked.

"I have no idea at all," I said. "I wish I did. I would have liked to see her again."

The uncle raised his eyebrows. "It is said that you spurned her."

"That is not true."

"It's what her father told us."

I tried to keep my answer light. "It is not much of a defence, but I was already married when I met her."

They both laughed at that.

And then all of us grew sombre, as we waited for the soldiers to return.

They were obliged to drag me bodily down four flights of stairs to get me out of there, my feet trailing. Out in the street, in the rain that fell like a waterfall upon us, they heaved me onto my quivering horse.

They had to strap me to the saddle to stop me falling.

This awkward scene was watched over by scores of very wet Akkadian soldiers, as well as by the King of Ur and his uncle. The two royal men had had their hands bound neatly behind them, and it seemed they would be walking on their own feet to their deaths.

"It will be good to see Ur," I said, smiling down at them through the rain. "I was carried in unconscious, so I have not yet seen this famous Moon Tower of yours that Inanna is so boastful of."

"It is only a shame that it's raining for you," the king said. "The city is at its best in sunshine."

The soldiers were finished with me; it was time to go.

We three royal men nodded at each other.

"I wish you safe passage to the other side," I said.

"The same to you, Lord Gilgamesh," the king said, his wet face tipped up to me. "I will pour you a glass of wine tonight, in the halls of the Dark City."

"Until then," I said, with one last nod to them.

As we emerged from our side street into a wide avenue, the townsfolk were pressed tight together along the pavements. All dipped their heads as their king walked by. He turned this way and that as he walked, looking everyone he could in the eye.

The uncle came next in our procession, looking straight ahead of him. Behind came a cluster of Akkadians, on mules, and then me on my horse, with the rain running off my helmet and straight down my back. Behind me came another score of soldiers, all bristling with knives, and spears, and battle axes.

I wondered if I would really see the king and his uncle that night. I remembered Enlil sidestepping my questions when I asked him if I would see Enkidu again in the underworld. I remembered the hero of the Great Flood, on the far side of the world, warning me never to believe the stories of the Anunnaki.

I found I could not bear it, if the stories were not true.

In the crowd, a baby cried out, pressed close to its mother's chest. My heart lurched, for my own son, who I did not know at all and now never would.

The Moon Tower was like a tall, thin ziggurat, each level of it smaller than the one beneath.

"What a thing," I said to myself, my head tipped back into the rain as I stared up at it.

The tower stood in a ring of fine temples, each surrounded by palm trees and small lakes. Beyond stood the great walls of Ur, five cords thick and a hundred cords high. The tops of these walls were lined with dark shapes. It took me a while to understand that the shapes were dead bodies, tied up to stakes.

Beneath the tower, under a large, leather rain shelter, stood King Akka. He was separated from the people of Ur by one full banner of his army, drawn up in battle order.

Akka showed no sign of even knowing me as my horse drew level with the front line of his men. I could see no sign of Inush, but perhaps he was watching from some window.

They took the King of Ur up first. He was led into the small door at the foot of the tower and then after long minutes, he emerged above us. With Akkadians on either side of him, he stepped up onto the low wall that ran around the top floor of the tower. Rain fell straight into my mouth, as I strained to see what was happening.

A blur of white; a scream from the crowd.

The horrible impact.

And then the King of Ur lay before us. One of his feet seemed to quiver, but no noise escaped him.

Akka watched the king die with no expression on his face.

"The uncle next," he said. He did not turn his head to look at me.

As the uncle came tumbling down from the sky, one of the soldiers holding my horse turned to the others and said: "We ought to start untying him."

I was about to say something very witty, about there being no need to hurry, but a strong and heavy tiredness had come upon me. As the men unstrapped me, and dragged me off my beautiful

horse, I thought: *These are the last people who will ever touch me,
at least while I am alive to feel it.*

They would probably dine out on my death every night for the
rest of their lives.

I put one hand out to the horse to feel his rolling muscle and
thin coat one last time. I almost asked the men about what would
become of him, but it seemed a thing too small to ask, when two
men who had ruled this city lay dead just a cable or two from us.

"It would be easier if you put your arms over our shoulders,"
one of the soldiers said.

"Do I care to make it easy for you?" I said. But I did it all the
same.

And so with my arms around two soldiers, I was dragged out
of the rain and into the dark, incense-filled room at the base of
the ziggurat.

Men were coming down from the roof, having finished their
work with the uncle.

"You want help with him?" one said.

"We can do it," said one of the men I was leaning on.

The stairs were dark, narrow, and steep, however. They could
not get me up there, arranged as we were. After some discussion,
they carried me up, one in front with his arms under my armpits,
and the other below, with my feet. The two other soldiers in our
party took their turn every flight or so.

Time and time again, in the gloomy half-light, and with all
of us wet and slipping, they bashed my head on the brick wall or
smashed my spine into the steps.

I had by then entered a curious state. I felt my pain, but I felt
very distant from it.

I was thinking over all the things I was about to leave undone.
My son would never know me, and that was a terrible shame.

I would never again put my arms around my father, the hero Lugalbanda.

I would have liked to live as King of Uruk. To truly rule there, in a time of peace. To build up those great walls again, that my father had built. I would have liked to have left a real legacy, earnest as that was.

I thought about Inanna, the black-eyed goddess. I had said I would take her swimming. I should have taken her swimming. I should have spent more time with her. I thought how good it would be to lie in bed together and talk about all that happened since last we met.

I thought about Enkidu, and how very alive he had been, and how little time we had had. His eyes, like sea water over white sand.

And then they were carrying me through a narrow oak door, and we were out in the rain again.

We were on the terrace at the top of the Moon Tower. I caught a glimpse, beyond the city walls, of white-flecked open sea.

They set my feet to the ground, close to the low wall that ran around the roof terrace, and I caught a glimpse of the huge, dark crowds below in the streets.

Drums began to beat in the crowd below.

"He won't be able to get up onto the wall," one of the soldiers said. "We'll have to throw him over."

There were two men holding me up; for a moment, as they shifted their holds, my weight was on my feet, and my legs could not take it. I went down over backwards, the two soldiers falling with me.

Both scrabbled to their feet again, swearing.

For a short while I lay on my back, looking straight up into the rain, my mouth open for the sweet taste of it.

A moment later, I realised that the rain had stopped.

It was falling all around us, but it was not falling on me.

Instead, Harga was there, an axe in each hand. He made short and bloody work of the soldiers.

Then Harga and Ningal, the moon goddess, were both crouching over me; Harga frowning, Ningal, her dark curls tied back, a picture of concern.

I laughed. "You have Nammu's weapon. Can it hide us all?"

"I hope so," said Ningal. "It hid us when we entered the city."

"She can't keep it going long," said Harga. "So, you need to get up."

"That's wonderful advice, Harga. But neither of my legs is working."

"Well, nonetheless, we need you to get up and walk," he said.

"This is an odd place to be rescuing me from," I said, still flat on my back. "Why not grab me when I was still on the horse? Then you could have just led me off."

"Gilgamesh, we have travelled the length of Sumer to rescue you," Harga said, looking very angry indeed. "We have been hiding up here all night, in order to make sure of your escape. We have watched Ningal's friends die and done nothing, because we could not save the two of them and also save you. Why not make your complaints about all this when we are safely back in our boat?"

"I can help you carry him," Ningal said to him.

"Oh, for all the stars," I said. "I will get up. Just give your arm, Harga."

"Hurry then," he said. "Ningal, you keep the shield up."

I dug within myself, took a deep breath in, and with Harga pulling me, I sat up. Then I pushed and pulled myself upright, holding on tight to Harga. The trick was to pretend that the pain was fake; that I was doing no harm at all to my legs by standing on them.

"Stay conscious," he said. "You cannot pass out."

The dark and windy staircase down.

My left knee might only have been made of jelly. I looked down and saw that a piece of bone had pierced the flesh.

The agonising, obliterating pain had become a sort of blur.

Ningal's face, turned back to us every few steps.

Two flights down and we heard the unmistakable sound of men running up the stairs towards us. Ningal veered left through a doorway, and then turned back to us, with one finger pressed to her lips.

We were in a small room, lined with wooden shelves and open boxes of clay tablets. We had the strange experience then of watching the men of Akkadia charging up the stairs, as we stood silent and invisible to them, just a few steps inside the room. When they had gone up past us, Ningal darted down the stairs, with me lumbering and wincing behind, and Harga struggling with the weight of me.

In the entrance hall to the Moon Temple, more soldiers appeared. "What is happening?" one said.

They could not see us.

We stood still for a moment, just to the left of them. It took every piece of strength I had not to cry out or collapse.

"Is this Anunnaki nonsense?' one of the soldiers said.

The doorway behind him was empty. Ningal led us quickly round him and out into the rain and the crowds. Had anyone been looking very closely, they would have seen a small patch of ground where no rain fell. But everyone was looking up at the roof of the tower, or at King Akka, standing with his hands on his hips. On the roof, soldiers were massing, and looking back down at the crowd.

Ningal stopped for a moment, looking at the bodies of the king and his uncle, her face creased with upset. Then we were threading our way through the crowd, Harga by then carrying almost the whole weight of me.

My nose began to bleed; the blood pouring down my front.

"I have you," Harga said to me. "It is not far now."

CHAPTER SEVENTEEN

INANNA

In the underworld

I walked through the Dark City. With each step I took, the ground shook.

I looked up at the twisted faces of the statues that lined the way, and wondered who they were meant to be.

Ahead lay the fabulous shape of my sister's palace and the Black Temple, throwing up twisting towers against the starscape.

A long time before, I had walked these streets and been very frightened.

I was no longer scared.

In the streets ahead of me: dark movement.

Ereshkigal's demons were sweeping towards me, and my sister was walking out ahead of them with the *gallas* on either side of her.

She looked strangely strong and sure of herself, as she approached me; she was no longer the slumped creature that I remembered. She had *mees* on her wrists; *mees* I did not recognise.

I stopped walking and began to draw energy into me.

"Inanna," my sister called out. "Stop there and we will not hurt you."

A moment, a pause, then out it all came.

Blue lightning surged upwards out of me, forking out across the starscape.

For a few heartbeats, the Dark City looked like any other city, bleached ordinary by my blue light.

Then my blades of light cut down into the demon army, and my sister's monsters began to boil and scream.

Ereshkigal spun around, and then came at me, her hands outstretched to me. How strange to see her features brightly lit.

"Inanna, I beg you to stop," she said. "These demons have done you no harm."

That made me laugh. "Ereshkigal, they tore off my flesh, and ripped out my throat, and then they hung me dead on a hook!" I laughed again. "Your lies are very silly."

"Oh," said Ereshkigal, sagging a little. "I had forgotten about that. But that was not their fault. They were only doing as I asked."

"Should I kill you instead?"

"No, Inanna. There is no need to harm anyone."

"If your demons get in my way, they will die."

"No," she said, imploring. She took a step towards me. "Please, Inanna, stand down."

"If they move aside, I will hurt no more of them. It is Nergal I have come to slaughter. That is the vengeance at hand. Does that make you happy?"

I saw at once that it did not.

"No," she said. "Please. No. I have shut the eighth gate against him, although he does not know it yet. He will be trapped here forever. He will bother the realm of light no more. Inanna, he will do no more harm."

"I am going to kill him before he gets to the gate."

"Please, Inanna."

I realised she was trying to make her *mees* work.

With one twist of my hand, I threw Ereshkigal hard to the ground and raked her with blue flames, and then I walked on past her as she writhed and screamed.

I let the fire stream out ahead of me towards her demons. I made for myself a wall of burning blue, and I walked onwards behind it.

The demons began exploding into dust before me.

Ereshkigal, her head and hair badly burned, was staggering along behind me. "Inanna, if you do not stop this, I will have to open the gate."

I sent another blast of fire at her, sweeping her from the road.

Then I burned up the last of her demons in my flames. I boiled them alive, in the true-blue light.

When the carnage was done, I swept on through the city. Past the Black Temple, and along the stone-slabbed road to the eighth gate. Far ahead of me, high up on a dark hillside, a square of gold began to come to life.

Ereshkigal was opening the gate.

I began to run. When I reached the hill, I propelled myself upwards, bounding from one rock to another, my light bursting over the hillside.

The ground beneath me began shaking violently. Rocks began rolling down towards me, some monstrously large. The gate began to throw out shards of rainbow light.

I kept climbing, fast and strong inside my blue fire.

Ninlil and Nergal were standing hand in hand on the small stone platform beneath the gate. They were watching me, then turning back to the gate, then turning back to me again.

My step-grandmother Ninlil, who I had never met before, was a tall, strong creature, not the tiny waif of the temple stories. She put out her hands to me as I stepped up onto the stone platform.

We stood only a few steps apart, the two of them dark against the blazing gold of the gate behind them.

"Inanna," she said. "I'm Ninlil."

Nergal's hands were moving to his belt. Black swirls of godlight began pouring towards me.

I found I could simply wave them away.

I threw a blast of fire at Nergal, sweeping him, screaming, off the platform, and down onto the rocks to the right of me. His weapons were something amazing, compared only with Anunnaki weapons. But they were nothing compared to the power I now had.

Ninlil fell to her knees in front of me, her hands held up before her.

"Inanna, I am your grandmother, Ninlil. That man is my son. I know he has killed someone you love, but he has also killed someone I love and I forgive him. Please do not hurt him. He has done things only because he has had to. Just let us go. In moments we will be gone."

Nergal was climbing back up to the platform on my right-hand side. The square gate was growing brighter and brighter. The platform, meanwhile, had begun to shake so hard it seemed about to become unmoored.

"Please, Inanna," Ninlil said. Her face was gold now with the light from the gate. "Please listen to me."

"Your story doesn't matter to me," I said to her, as Nergal reached her side.

Then I blasted the both of them with my fire, setting their clothes and skin alight.

Behind them both, the gate now stood fully open, a neat square of light and fire.

I thought I had done enough to kill them both, but as my blue fire cleared, Nergal was still there, alive. He was dragging Ninlil backwards through the gate.

I ran forward to grab them, but as I reached out for them, my hands touched the light that came bursting out of the gate.

Something hard and cold closed around my right wrist.

"No," I said.

In the swirling, gold light, I saw dark feathers.

And then I was falling.

CHAPTER EIGHTEEN

MARDUK

Outside Eridu, Enki's home city

The city of Eridu stood at the entrance to the Euphrates, one shoulder to the great river, another to the unending sea.

Enki and I sat together, beneath the inadequate shelter of a palm, to consider our next steps.

"There's a slave market here," Enki said. "And also a market for holy relics. Bits of the ark from the time of the Great Flood, that sort of thing. If anyone knows anything of Ninshubar or anything of her has been found, we will find out here."

"I'll go in," I said. "I'm not known here. You keep Moshkhussu with you while I am gone."

"You are the strangest-looking person I have ever seen. You will certainly attract the wrong kind of attention. I will go in. I have these *mees* to protect me, although they are not the best *mees* I have ever had. This is my city. Built with these two hands. You wait here with the dog."

"I do not fear a fight," I said.

"No doubt that's true. But your people can be killed, let me assure you of it. Better we keep you in the background until you have worked out the edges of your strength."

He was back before dusk. The rain had not abated, and he came back with his robes plastered to his skin.

"And?" I said.

"No sign of Ninshubar."

He sat down with his back to our palm, in what dry there was, and accepted Moshkhussu's heartfelt greeting.

"If you could see what they have done to my beautiful palace," he said. "To all the irreplaceable treasures."

"Akkadians?"

He spread out his hands to the sky. "The city is lawless. Akkadians, yes, but also pirates. Vagabonds. Gang lords."

"And no Ninshubar?"

"No one has heard anything of her. I even went to the temple she used to loiter in. She has not been seen there."

I thought for a while. "What about Ur? Is that not just on the other side of the river?"

He shook his head. "The river is leagues and leagues wide here. It's a long way to Ur. And the weather is terrible."

"Could she have ended up there?"

"It's in Akkadian hands. Solidly in their hands. If she's there, we will not retrieve her."

"I will go on to Ur. If she's not there, I will think of what next. But it makes no sense to search here and not in Ur."

After some long moments, he said: "I can find us a boat. But after Ur, you must start listening to me. We should go to my refuge."

"Where is this refuge?"

"Hidden in the marshes. Impossible to find unless you already know where it is."

"We will find Ninshubar, then we will go to your refuge. Now let's go."

"Let's set off for Ur in the morning."

"We should go now."

"Your people are all truly impossible," Enki said. "That is their reputation. It is coming back to me now. That they are unreasonable and extremely difficult to control. Designed to make good decisions in faraway battles, but this is the price of that independence. This terrible character that you all have."

"I would like to hear more about my people," I said. "We can talk about it when you fetch us our boat."

We put out into the gulf at dusk, still in heavy rain. The wind was whipping up white horses as far as the eye could see.

It was a small boat, with one set of oars. I set myself to row, while Enki, as wet as any man could ever be, sat the back of the boat.

As we made our way slowly out into the river mouth, the evening rain gave way to a heavy fog that sat low on the sea.

"It's hard to know where I am headed, facing the rear of the boat as I am, and in this fog," I said.

Enki shrugged, unhelpful. "We will be two days crossing the river in these conditions," he said. "And I have no powers for seeing through fog."

The fog only thickened as night approached, and I was not at all sure if I was heading towards Ur.

"At least it has stopped raining," I said. "Everything is improving."

It was then that a shout rang out behind us.

I spun around to see another boat coming fast at us out of the fog.

"Mind out!" someone shouted.

A strangely familiar voice.

Moshkhussu gave a wild growl and in the boat that was about to collide with us, two dogs, black shapes in the mist, started up with a terrible howling.

"Those are my son's dogs," said Enki, peering hard ahead.

The oncoming boat had two boys sitting in the stern, one large, one small. Two women and a fighting man sat in the middle of the boat, all three holding oars. At the prow, there was a man in a bronze chest plate sitting on the deck. He had his legs stretched out in front of him.

A laugh burst out of me.

It was the Lion of Uruk.

He looked leaner and harder than when I had last seen him. He was even bloodier and more battered. All the boy in him had gone. But it was him.

"Gilgamesh!" I called out.

"Marduk!" he shouted back. "Terrible slave boy! What are you doing here?"

"I did tell you I would escape!"

And the two of us smiled at each other, as we caught on to each other's boats.

CHAPTER NINETEEN

INANNA

Lost

I stood barefoot on soft green grass. Amnut, my childhood friend, was kneeling in front of me, her face almost to the ground.

"It is the hairiest caterpillar I have ever seen," she said, turning her beautiful smile up to me.

I looked around me. All I could see, league upon league, was unending green grass and the soft blue sky.

"Inanna?"

"Yes?" I looked back down at Amnut.

"Inanna, look at this."

I had the strangest feeling that I did not know why I was standing there. That something was wrong. That I had forgotten something important.

But what?

I kneeled next to Amnut and put my head close to hers, to look at the caterpillar. She smelled just as she always did, of the lavender oil her mother sprinkled on her clothes.

She held out her hand to me, with the green caterpillar wriggling in her palm.

"It is very hairy indeed," I said.

"Come on," Amnut said. "They will be looking for us. Time to get back."

"Yes," I said, standing up. I was wearing the plain linen dress that I always wore on insect hunts. Amnut was wearing a black, close-fitting body suit that I did not recognise. It seemed to have tiny black scales all over it and it clung to her neck and wrists.

I saw, on a distant hill, a tall, dark-skinned figure. A woman with an axe in one hand and a spear in the other, and over her shoulder, a bow and quiver of arrows. I was going to call out to her. Although she was so distant, I thought she said: "Inanna."

But I must have imagined it because a moment later she was no longer there.

"Come on then," Amnut said. She was right in front of me, and she put out her hand to me.

I looked around again, but there was no sign of the woman with the bow. And then I looked down at Amnut's smooth brown hand. A strange kind of fear rose in me, that the thing I had forgotten was a terrible thing, and that I must remember, or so many awful things would happen.

I looked again for the woman with the bow.

But here was only the grass and the sky.

Yes, there was no one else here, only me and Amnut, and here before me, Amnut's small, warm hand.

I noticed that her eyes were blue.

Were Amnut's eyes always blue?

"Come, Inanna," she said. "Come, my friend. It is time you went back home."

And so I put my hand out to her.

END OF BOOK TWO OF THE SUMERIANS

A NOTE FROM THE AUTHOR

This work of fiction is set in the world's first civilisation, Ancient Sumer, which lies beneath what is now modern Iraq. The novel draws on the surviving myths from Sumer and the Akkadian civilisation that came after it.

Should you be interested in unpicking which parts of this story are based on the archaeological record from Mesopotamia (as the region is generally known), which are drawn from ancient myths, and which are purely my invention, I hope these notes will help somewhat.

Gilgamesh's storyline

The best-known piece of literature about Gilgamesh is of course the *Epic of Gilgamesh*. I covered most of the events in that epic in the novel *Inanna*, the first book in this series.

This novel draws on the partial myth called "The Envoys of Akka" and also the fact that Gilgamesh was perhaps, in real life, a king of Uruk in about 3,000 BC.

Ninsun, Gilgamesh's mother, is a character in the *Epic of Gilgamesh* but only a bit-part one.

Lilith is a character from the myth "Inanna and the Huluppu Tree", which I covered, in my own fashion, in book one of this series. Her relationship with Ninsun is an invention.

Ninlil's storyline

There is an ancient myth known as "Enlil and Ninlil". You can dress it up any way you like – call it a creation myth, call it only symbolic – but it reads at least to my mind as an account of the abduction and rape of a young girl.

The archaeological record shows that Enlil and Ninlil seem to have gone on to be a very popular husband and wife divine pairing in the temples of Ancient Mesopotamia.

From those two elements – the horrifying beginning, their apparently successful marriage in the sacred texts – I came up with my version of the myth and made it a central thread running through this trilogy.

The killing of Enlil at the hands of Nergal is my own invention, inspired by the idea that Nergal (who is often described as Enlil and Ninlil's son) might have been conceived during Enlil's attack upon Ninlil.

Ninlil's consumption of Enlil's rotting head and her strange ability to grow are pure fiction.

Inanna's storyline

This book opens with what is one of the central, surviving Inanna myths: the story of her visiting Enki in order to rob him of his *mees*.

For the record I have only really changed two key bits of the myth to suit my story. Firstly, as in the first book in this series, the *mees* in my story are ancient weapons, brought down from Heaven by the gods. In the original myths, the *mees* are a curious mixture of the palpable (the shepherd's hut, rebel lands, etc.) and the abstract (righteousness, wisdom, etc.) that together represent, I suppose, what it is to be a human living in ancient Sumer under the rule of the Sumerian gods. The *mees* were somehow also physical objects, but how they took physical form is unclear.

Secondly, in the original, Inanna tricks Enki into giving her the *mees* by getting him drunk. There is a lot of drinking in my version, but I've obviously introduced the use of the "master *mee*" in order for her to trick him out of his collection of *mees*.

The rest of Inanna's story in this book is not drawn from any particular myths but is inspired by her title (Queen of Heaven and Earth) and also the hymns or poems written about her, particularly those exploring her more warlike aspects.

I was inspired by Sophus Helle's beautiful new translation of the work of Enheduana, by the way, for the scene in which Inanna walks to the underworld with a storm spilling out of her.

Ninshubar's death in this book, by the way, is my invention.

Ereshkigal's storyline

In ancient Mesopotamian mythology, Nergal is a god of war, pestilence, scorched earth, plague, chaos... someone to be avoided, you might think. But it seems he did have a good side, because Inanna's sister Ereshkigal, queen of the underworld, fell madly in love with him.

Her love for him is recorded in a key Mesopotamian myth known as "Ereshkigal and Nergal". In it, Nergal comes down to the underworld and ends up passionately involved with Ereshkigal. When he then leaves the underworld, Ereshkigal is devastated.

She simply has not had enough time with him, and she is so upset and angry that she threatens to raise all the dead if she does not see him again.

As for Nergal, he is also sometimes known as Erra, and he is said (by some) to be the basis for the Greek Heracles. He is also said to be a son of Enlil and Ninlil, and is recorded as a co-regent of the underworld, alongside Ereshkigal.

Tiamat

The goddess Tiamat, she "who bore them all", is the star of the hugely important Mesopotamian myth known as the *Epic of Creation*. I won't say too much about her here, as she is only glimpsed in the darkness in this book. But she is very much a central figure in Mesopotamian stories about how they and their gods came to be.

(She is not Ninlil's mother in the myths, by the way.)

The Anzu appears in the *Epic of Anzu* but also in other Mesopotamian myths. It is a creature that is half lion and half eagle, and sometimes it is a scary monster, and sometimes a big bird that needs caring for. My use of it as the family name for Tiamat and as the totemic image of her clan is an invention on my part.

Marduk's storyline

Marduk became *the* top-tier god in ancient Mesopotamia as the millennia passed. He is the central hero in the aforementioned *Epic of Creation*, or at least in the Babylonian version of the story.

In the myths, he is a son of Enki. Hence me putting the two of them together in this book, although in my story Marduk is not actually Enki's biological son.

Further reading

My copy of *Myths from Mesopotamia*, by Stephanie Dalley, was much thumbed, highlighted and scribbled upon during the writing of this book.

As mentioned, I also found *Enheduana*, by Sophus Helle, delightful and helpful.

If you haven't yet read *Inanna, Queen of Heaven and Earth*, by Diane Wolkstein and Samuel Noah Kramer, I do recommend it. It's the book that helped me work out how to make Inanna's stories into one epic tale.

ACKNOWLEDGEMENTS

Thank you so much to my early readers: Jon Absalom, Jack Absalom, Aldo Absalom, Chloë Wilson, Sapphire Medeema, Blue Medeema, Buzz Medeema, Clementine Wolodarsky, Esther Addley, Jo Emerson, Katharine Braddick, Sarah Boseley, Catherine de Lange, Ed Smith, Susie Mullen, Bethan Ackerley, and Martin Worthington. Particular thanks to Ed for some incredibly thoughtful and helpful last-minute suggestions.

Reading a book in its fledgling stages is a massive chore and a huge favour, and I am very grateful to you all.

All errors, anachronisms, misinterpretations, and general howlers are very much my own.

Thank you to my brother-in-law, the cartographer Tim Absalom, for the map of Sumer.

Thank you very much indeed to Daniel Carpenter from Titan Books, who commissioned the Sumerians series and edited both this book and *Inanna*, the first in the run. Also thank you to his colleagues Olivia Cooke, Charlotte Kelly, Katharine Carroll and Paul Gill at Titan.

Thank you to my literary agent Ian Drury, and his colleagues Gaia Banks and Lauren Coleman at Sheil Land Associates.

And finally, thank you to all my family and friends for their amazing support through all these years in the boggy marshes of Sumer.

ABOUT THE AUTHOR

EMILY H. WILSON is a full-time writer based in Dorset, in the south of England. *Gilgamesh* is her second novel. Emily was previously a journalist, working as a reporter at the *Mirror* and *Daily Mail*, a senior editor at the *Guardian* and, most recently, as editor-in-chief of *New Scientist* magazine. You can follow her on X (formerly known as Twitter) @emilyhwilson or on Instagram @emilyhwilson1, and you can find her website at www.emilyhwilson.com.

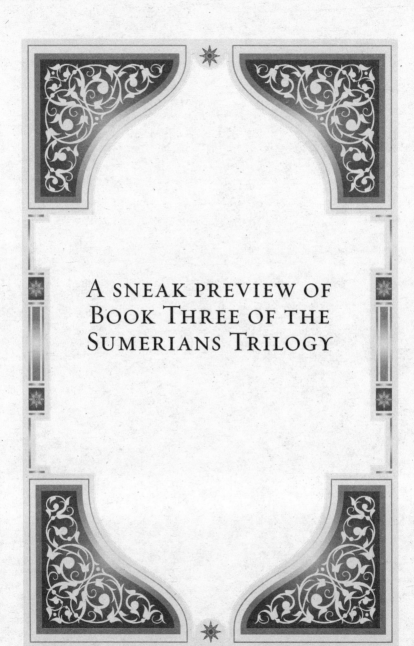

A sneak preview of
Book Three of the
Sumerians Trilogy

CHAPTER ONE
HARGA

They say there are days in the deep marshes, in high summer, when the frogs boil alive in the shallowest stretches of water. I had never believed it.

Now I believed it.

My comrades and I had disguised ourselves as marshmen for our canoe journey through the sweltering reedbeds. My black robes and turban were soaked through with sweat and the air was so humid that I could get no relief from it. I did not know how longer I could bear it without boiling up from the inside, like some giant frog.

Meanwhile clouds of insects swarmed at my mouth and cheeks, the inside of my nostrils, the wets of my eyes, and my ankles and wrists. They also landed in greedy flocks on my sweaty back, pricking at my flesh through the damp cloth.

Every muscle in me strained to flap the insects away. To throw myself out of the canoe into the murky water. But one short pebble shot behind us came a canoe of eight hawk-faced marshmen, our colleagues for the day. With the hard eyes of these men on me, I was obliged to sit in perfect stillness as the sun beat down and the insects mounted fresh attacks.

We had gone out in two boats to do the thing that needed to be done.

One ancient wooden canoe for us, scimitar-thin and long, the wood blackened by time and wear. Another just the same for the black-robed marshmen.

In these low but elegant vessels, and in absolute silence, we slid through the endless wilderness of reeds and small open waterways, with the frogs calling out to us in shattering unison.

I glanced back at the marshmen and all eight of them turned their black eyes to me.

All so deadly serious. But then everything is deadly serious to a marshman. Even when they drink and dance, or tie up a sandal, you would think their lives depended on it.

I turned back to the reed beds ahead of us; reeds that might at any moment reveal a hut or a fisherman sat out on the water in his boat, or indeed a boatful of enemy soldiers.

My two boys were stood at the front of our canoe, poling us along with reasonable dexterity. They passed well as locals in their borrowed robes and seemed most at home in the stinking water world we were travelling through. They pushed on their long wooden poles, pointed out crocodiles to each other, and flashed each other smiles, quite as if neither had noticed the heat or the insects.

These two boys had come to me in the usual way.

I found them hanging around in the main square at Uruk. They weren't pretty and they weren't polite, and they were starving.

Both were missing teeth and fingers. They were boys who weren't going to make it. So I added them to my crew and soon enough they had a bit of flesh on them, although nothing was ever going to make them pretty.

When Uruk fell, there was not much time to be worrying over my gang of boys. But I kept these two close to me, them being the newest of my crew and the least likely to survive if cast out on the wind. The short boy we had named Tallboy, and the tall boy we had named Shortboy. Such were the heights of what passed for humour in the barracks at Uruk, before the Akkadians set fire to the place.

As for the boy in the back of our canoe, he did not come to me in the usual way.

Indeed, he was not the usual sort of boy.

I turned and cast a brief glance at Marduk.

He was a tall young man and very unusual to look at.

His skin was so pale and so translucent you could see his veins through it. His hair was unnaturally red; his lips so berry-pink they might have been painted on. His eyes were a deep blue, strangely dark against his skin.

For this mission through the marshes, he had daubed his pale face with marsh mud, and he sat now with his muddy chin resting on the head of one of the three dogs he travelled everywhere with. One was an Akkadian dog of war and the others were high-bred court dogs with black coats and razor-sharp ears.

I had told him not to bring the dogs, but Marduk was an impossible person to deal with. He was Ninshubar's boy, though, so there was no question of refusing to deal with him.

Sensing my eyes on him, Marduk cast me a luminous smile, his teeth so very white against the dark pink of his lips.

At that moment a flamingo lifted off to our left and the two black dogs began barking.

Oh, the shocking hullabaloo of it, the dogs writhing around, and birds lifting off everywhere all around us!

Any chance of secrecy was gone.

My cheeks burned with the humiliation of it; that this appalling breach of discipline should be witnessed by the close-faced occupants of the boat behind!

"Control them," I hissed at Marduk.

The dogs quickly stopped with their frothing about and barking, but only to stand with their front paws up on the edge of the canoe, tipping us over to the left as they stretched out their snouts after the now-distant flamingo.

"Marduk, you are going to get us all killed," I said. "Keep them quiet or I will put them over into the water."

We travelled on in grim silence, while the shame of what had happened slowly seeped through my bones.

At last Marduk whispered: "I am sorry, Harga."

I rolled my shoulders but did not answer.

"Have you ever had a dog of your own?" he said.

I didn't answer that either, but took a smooth pebble from the leather pouch at my waist and begun rolling it around between my fingers.

In fact I did once have a dog. A good dog, clever and alert, always thinking how to help me. But that was when I was very young and had not yet learned the true cost of happiness.

Oh, the memory of that good dog, and how he trusted me.

Marduk put a cool hand on my right shoulder. "What is it, Harga?"

I rolled my shoulders again and he took his hand from me.

"I thought you said something," Marduk said. "You made a noise."

"You just keep a look out," I said. "And keep those dogs quiet. Perhaps there is some deaf old man here, many leagues distant, who has not yet heard us coming."

"Smoke!" said Shortboy. He pointed at the reeds to the left of us. "I can see a hut."

The two boys pushed us over to the left and straight into the reeds.

"Knives out, lads," I said, as the front of the boat pushed up against solid land. "Keep your ears open. I want every single one of them dead. Man, woman, goat. Everything here dies today."

Tallboy gave me his gap-mouthed grin. "Everyone dead, sir," he said.

The canoe full of marshman came swarming up beside us. I made eye contact with the leader of the marshmen, and he twitched his eyebrows at me, almost imperceptibly, by way of agreement. This was definitely the place, then.

I took out two more pebbles from the leather pouch on my hip.

The boy Marduk stood up behind me and with a bronze axe in each hand, leaped out onto the island with super-human lift and poise.

The three dogs leaped out after him onto the muddy bank.

I pulled my sling shot from my belt and made the secret signs on my chest.

"May the gods of Sumer look kindly on us," I said.

ARCH-CONSPIRATOR

By Veronica Roth

Outside the last city on Earth, the planet is a
wasteland. Without the Archive, where the genes
of the dead are stored, humanity will end.

Antigone's parents – Oedipus and Jocasta – are
dead. Passing into the Archive should be cause for
celebration, but with her militant uncle Kreon
rising to claim her father's vacant throne,
all Antigone feels is rage.

When he welcomes her and her siblings into his
mansion, Antigone sees it for what it really is: a
gilded cage, where she is a captive as well as a guest.

But her uncle will soon learn that no cage
is unbreakable. And neither is he.

For more fantastic fiction, author events,
exclusive excerpts, competitions, limited editions and more

VISIT OUR WEBSITE
titanbooks.com

LIKE US ON FACEBOOK
facebook.com/titanbooks

FOLLOW US ON TWITTER AND INSTAGRAM
@TitanBooks

EMAIL US
readerfeedback@titanemail.com